Camp Cryptid
Book Two

SHIFTING
Hearts

B.L. BROWN

GOOD INTENT PRESS

Cover Art by The Caprica

Map Illustration by Lindsey Staton

1st edition 2025

ISBN 979-8-9900634-6-4 (ebook)

ISBN 979-8-9900634-7-1 (print)

The real pack is the family you made along the way.

This one is for the parents and caregivers.
You're doing great.

Content Warnings

While the tone of the *Camp Cryptid* books is lighter in spirit than that of my other series, *Witch of the Demesne* and *Witches of C.R.O.W.*, the characters in these pages live in a fictionalized world much like our own. As such, there are references to and instances involving the following topics and potential triggers. Please take care of yourselves.

XO — B.L. Brown

Internalized and vocalized racism, biases both conscious and unconscious, discussion of pregnancy and childbirth, on-page sexual acts (WILDLY consensual), mild profanity, controlling/manipulative parent

A Note on Names

When I set out to explore the wolven culture and community found in *Camp Cryptid*, I started with the word "wolven" and dug into its etymological roots in Middle English ("wulven" and "wilven"), Old English ("wylfen"), and Proto-West Germanic ("wulfin"). These roots pointed me towards a Viking-esque culture, with their focus on family and strength in numbers, central meeting spaces, and an Alpha who functions like a Jarl. As I dug into Norse mythology, Sköll and Hati, the sons of the wolf Fenrir, particularly stood out as the sort of Gods the wolven and werewolves would worship, while allowing a distinction between their two very distinct species.

While the inhumans of Otherworld worship many gods, each species has their main god to whom they appeal. The wolven pray to (or curse) Sköll, who chases the sun, while the werewolves appeal to Hati, who chases the moon.

All this in mind, traditional wolven names are Nordic in origin.

<u>Pronunciation Guide</u>
Aksel — AX-el
Elias — Eh-LIE-as
Gitta — GEE-tah
Lennart — LEN-art
Jan — Yan
Jarl — Yarl
Jens — Yens
Jörgun — YORE-gun
Nils — NEE-ls
Skölläng — SH-coal-ayng
Sköllburg — SH-coal-burg
Sölldal — SH-coal-dahl
Solfrid — SOL-frid
Svana — Sif-ANA
Ygrid — EE-grid

Elkwater Music Camp

Elkwater, WV

— · —

The Last Night of Camp, 1987

"Is this okay?"

"Of course, it's okay." Jess straddled his hips, gripping his shoulders to take most of her weight. Soft grass cradled her knees, and large hands rested lightly on her thighs, fingers trembling with nerves. "We're adults, why wouldn't it be okay?"

"I don't know." He swallowed, eyes wide in the lantern light. Beyond their place in the grass, the waterfall burbled pleasingly down the quartz rockface, and the yellow glow of a fat, late summer moon danced across the surface of the hidden lake. "We don't have to."

"I want to." She eased lower, biting her lower lip at the press and stretch. She wanted this. She knew she wanted it, even if she was scared. It was natural to be nervous. This was a big step. It was life-changing, and clearly, Aksel felt the same, or he wouldn't have reverted to his shy, hesitant self.

The sweet wolven boy she trusted. The boy she—

"Jess," he breathed, attention fixed on his lap where their bodies met. She held her breath and dropped lower, watching the emotion play over his sweet, open face—lips parted on a pant, eyes dripping molten amber—stopping when the pain made her gasp. Her body tensed, and Aksel ripped his eyes to hers.

"I don't want to hurt you." He tightened his hold on her thighs, pressing against Jess to lift her away.

She clamped her knees tight. "I don't think we can avoid it," she said, silencing his argument with a soft kiss. "But it's worth it, Aksel. I want to."

Slowly, he nodded and slid his hands to her waist, bracing Jess rather than guiding. She eased lower, arms trembling from holding as much of her weight as she could, and buried her face in the crook of his neck. It hurt, but the pain was manageable. And if everything she had read in magazines at the grocery store and learned from other counselors in the camp was true, it wouldn't hurt for long.

"I think—" Her voice hitched on a sharp gasp. "I think we should do it all in one go."

"Jess—"

"On three." She scraped her teeth along his neck in the way she knew he liked, and a low rumble built in his chest. "One."

"Gods, Jess."

"Two."

Aksel adjusted his grip, and the thickness between her thighs seemed to pulse. His hips twitched, his body tight with restraint, so Jess said, "Three," and lightly bit down on the crook of his neck.

She dropped onto Aksel as he jerked and entered her in a thrust. Her eyes flew wide, the burn and the pain flaring high only to be erased by an overwhelming rush of pleasure.

"Aksel," she panted, scrabbling her hands at his shoulders and arms. Good lord, she could feel him *everywhere*. "Oh, God, this—this is—"

"G-Gods." He eased her up, rocking his hips and guiding her down until there were no words. Only their gasps and mingled pants rising above the gentle rush of the waterfall.

1

AKSEL

"EARTH TO HARALSON."

Mac's clipboard smacked the pole beside his shoulder, jolting Aksel upright and fully awake. His wolf rushed to the forefront, raising his hackles and sharpening his teeth. He scanned the parking lot and the trees, assessing the camp for any threats, and found only his boss grinning widely at him.

Like him, Mac wore her deep green Elkwater Music Camp polo, tucked into cargo-pocketed hiking pants. A walkie-talkie hung from her belt beside a ring of keys, and her short reddish-brown hair was hidden beneath a camp baseball cap. A full head shorter, Mac had to angle her face up to meet his eyes under the brim. "Hey man, late night?"

Aksel shook his arms out, forcing his wolf back down. Drop-off day always had him on high alert, the sheer number of strange faces and new scents keeping his wolf prowling just beneath the skin.

He'd mentioned it to Mac once, years ago, but when she suggested he skip the check-ins and glad-handing, he declined. Better to be bombarded by all the noise and new faces now, rather than lose control of his wolf in front of a class of teenage strangers.

Still, the avalanche of foreign smells was a lot to manage.

"No." He tugged on the collar of his polo, settling into his body. "Why?"

"Hm." She dropped a shoulder against the post that had previously held him upright. Not that he was dozing off in the middle of arrivals, more like zoning out to dampen the chaos. But the sun was baking, the air was humid, and he *might* have been up too late the night before. "Crick said she saw you at Meander's." Mac named the locals' favorite restaurant in Elkins, the nearest town to the camp. "With a cute brunette."

Aksel's face warmed. He coughed into a fist, raising an eyebrow at Mac. "And?"

"*And*, I thought that was interesting since Ramble saw you on a date in Buckhannon on Friday. With a blonde."

"Lots of blondes around here," he answered. "Maybe she's a friend."

"Sure. A friend." Mac hit him with a hard look, then turned her bright smile on an approaching family. "Hi! Welcome to Elkwater. Can I help you get situated?"

"Hi, yes, please." The mother jostled a toddler from one arm to the other, using her tail to slide a shy teenager forward.

Purple-tinted, scaled hands clutched a black instrument case to their chest, and in the one brief look they gave Aksel before staring at the ground, he caught a glimpse of acid-green eyes with slitted pupils. Naga. "We're supposed to check in at the Orchestra Hall, and Anassa"—she sent a fond but annoyed look to the teen—"left the camp map printout at home. In Point Pleasant."

"Not a problem." Mac pulled a map from her clipboard and a pen from behind her ear, circling a building in the middle of the camp and drawing a line from where they stood at the entrance to the cabins. "Check in with Sanoya as you pass through, tall, wispy, moon-eyed. She should be at the assignments table with our assistant director. They'll point out where you can drop your bags." A sweep of her pen drew a shortcut over a small bridge, through a breezeway between buildings, right up to the orchestra hall. "And Rolf'll get you settled in the Orchestra Hall."

"Rolf." The mother repeated. Her eyes slid toward Aksel. "Is he wolven?"

"Rübezahl," Aksel said, "and a skilled harpist. Bring him a turnip, and you'll be his favorite camper." He winked at the teen, winning a small smile and flick of their tongue before they slithered off with their mother and younger sibling. His answering grin fell away as he looked at Mac.

"So." She smirked, eyes twinkling, and nudged him with an elbow. "Two dates in one week? That's a lot for you."

"Yeah." He shoved his hands in the pockets of his shorts. "Maybe."

Mac angled her head, reading his posture and, in the way she always could, reading him. "Pack pressure?"

"Doesn't cover half of it."

She swept her clipboard in the air, fanning away his grumble. "Tell them to lay off."

"It's not that easy." Aksel dropped his head back, squinting at the sun. "Our numbers are small enough as it is."

So few of them had fallen through. In the Otherworld, as inhumans had taken to calling it, the wolven of Aksel's homeland numbered in the hundreds of thousands. Who knew how many roamed the borders of other kingdoms and domains? But here...

Twenty-four Sköllburg wolven had been on that patrol, and they were all that fell through from a pack of over one hundred. When the shock of the fall had settled, the Sköllburg Alpha, Lennart, met with the leaders of other displaced packs, whose numbers were just as small. Together, they determined that unless certain measures were taken, the wolven of this world were going extinct.

"Someone has to keep the pack healthy."

"And that someone has to be you?" She waved her clipboard again as if she could erase what was firmly Aksel's reality. A waft of humid air danced over his face, scented with dust, pine, and the mingled odors of a hundred sweaty adolescents. He wrinkled his nose and rubbed it with the back of his hand.

"Who else is there?"

"Gitta," she named his foster sister, and Aksel barked a laugh. "Or someone who is even *remotely* interested in a relationship?"

"It's not that I'm not interested."

"Aks, I've known you since 1989, and in that time, I have never seen you date, much less glance at any human or inhuman, male, female, or otherwise." She rolled her eyes like an annoyed sister. "And they want to force you on some other wolven to, what, replant the family tree? It's not right."

"It's what the pack needs."

"But does it *have* to be you?" Mac countered. Aksel stared at her. Hard. He didn't like relying on his wilder side to win arguments, but sometimes, a good, hard Alpha Stare was what it took. "Fine." She relented and waved her clipboard at him a third time.

Sweat and dust tickled his nose, but this time, there was something else mixed among the scents. He sniffed, the tickle in his nose growing and reaching for a memory he could not grasp.

Without warning, his wolf lurched to full alertness.

Aksel whipped his head to the parking lot, scanning the crowds, the kids, the cars. His nostrils flared, and he closed his eyes, inhaling deeply to fill his lungs.

What was that?

"You alright?"

Instead of answering, he tipped his head back, taking small, testing sniffs and flicking his tongue out to taste the air.

"Yo, Haralson, what's up?" The alarm in Mac's voice brought his attention back to her. Hazel eyes wide, the faint stink of fear rose from her person.

"Shit, sorry, Mac." Aksel adjusted his ballcap, forcing his shoulders to relax and mentally beating the wolf back with a stick. "Nothing, just a scent."

"Should we …" She glanced around at the busy camp, and Aksel could have smacked himself. Only a year ago, a werewolf had harassed Avery, the assistant director, and her girlfriend, Cricket. Of course, Mac would be afraid; it was the first day of camp, and here he was catching phantom scents on a breeze and reacting as if the grounds were under threat.

"It's nothing," he assured her. "I promise. I just thought I smelled—"

"Hey, Mac." Avery came rushing by, her frizzy red hair escaping her hair tie. She grabbed Mac's arm and dragged her toward the canteen. "Cooky's been radioing you for ten minutes; there's a kobold infestation in the pantry."

"Ah, crap. Again?" She shoved her clipboard at Aksel, shouting, "You're in charge, check the list!" as she ran off. Their scents lingered, wafting away on a hot summer breeze, leaving Aksel alone with a memory he could not place.

2

JESS

THIRTEEN YEARS HAD PASSED since she last walked the main road of Elkwater Music Camp. Thirteen years since she'd heard the creak of the mattress coils in a rickety bunk.

Thirteen years gone in a snap.

Jessica blinked at the ceiling, swallowing a lump in her throat.

"Mom, seriously, do *not* start crying again." Kendra snapped her blanket in the air and let it settle over her mattress, carefully adjusting the corners until it lay flat and straight.

"I'm sorry, honey. I can't help it." Jessica sniffled and gave her daughter a watery smile. "You're all so big and grown. This is the first summer we're spending apart, I'm allowed to be a little weepy."

"You're staying at an apartment in Elkins." Kendra cocked a hip and crossed her arms. "You'll see us again on Saturday."

"A whole week." She nodded sagely. "Practically a lifetime."

Kendra narrowed her eyes, staring hard at her mother for a moment before her lips pressed together in a suppressed smile. "You are so weird."

She dug into the duffel bag perched on a chair and pulled out a well-loved stuffed wolf. Hesitantly, she glanced at the other bunks. Of the six, three were occupied, and two had odd lumps tucked under the blankets beside the pillows. Without a word, Kendra did the same, safely hiding her stuffy out of sight before unpacking her clothes into a drawer beneath the bed.

"Are you done yet?" Jan's head popped up in the window beside Jessica. He drummed his hands on the sill, looking from Jessica to his sister and back. "Jarl and Jens wanna go off-leash. Can we go?"

"No." Jessica stood and shooed her son from the window, leaning out to yell at his brothers. "They have a scheduled time for that!"

Jarl and Jens, already half undressed, howled in frustration. "C'mon, Mom!"

"After dinner, with the rest of the shifters," she said. "You don't know these woods, and beyond giving me a heart attack, once I leave, the counselors are liable if you go missing or get hurt."

"All the reason for us to go now," Jarl replied, "while you're still here."

"Don't piss her off, dude," Jens muttered behind a hand, wary eyes on Jessica. "Or she'll never leave."

Jessica fought back a smile as the trio skulked and tugged their shirts back on. The three had sprouted in the last year, and Kendra was not far behind. Soon, her children would tower over her, but for now, they were all knobby knees and lanky arms. Still, for all the gangliness of youth, Jessica saw hints of their father in the broadness of the boys' shoulders and the amber color of their eyes. But only hints. Kendra took the most after him, with her lighter skin and wavy brown hair, while the boys favored Jessica and her father.

"I'm ready." Kendra kicked the drawer shut and tugged on an oversized hoodie. The image on the front was faded, a mere ghost of what it had been thirteen years ago, and the elastic in the cuffs at the wrists had long since stretched out. Something panged in Jessica's chest at the sight of the hoodie and the worn, barely visible Elkwater Music Camp logo.

She had cherished the sweatshirt, wearing it throughout her pregnancy and to cuddle her babies to sleep. Even as an infant, Kendra had been drawn to the garment. Whenever she fussed or cried, Jessica put on the hoodie, and Kendra would nuzzle against the cotton, snuggling in as close as she could.

The hoodie had disappeared from Jessica's closet three years earlier, and she decided against saying anything when her daughter began wearing it in the heat of summer. Lord knew she had retreated to the soft comfort and the memories in the cloth enough times over the years.

Instead, Jessica made a few calls, got a brochure, and began her campaign.

It was not easy to win over her parents. Her mother wanted the kids to go to summer sessions at the University of Charleston, a prestigious music camp geared toward orchestral programs and Division I or Big 12 collegiate bands, but Jessica had argued for Elkwater.

"I want to do this for them," she had said one night over dishes. "They struggle at Sacred Heart, I want them to know what it's like to be with—"

"Monsters," her mother, Irene, snapped. She set her wine glass down hard on the marble countertop. In the living room, Jessica's father rattled the newspaper he had been hiding behind.

"Other inhumans," Jessica corrected. "People who will understand them."

"*We* understand them, and that is enough. They will go to the program at Charleston; I'll have your father wire the money to—"

"I want to go."

Kendra surprised them both. She was always quieter than her brothers, slinking along the edges of rooms, ever watchful and as painfully shy as she was eager to please. But it was not her habit of sneaking up on people that had surprised Jessica. It was that her unassuming daughter had spoken out against Irene.

"Mom always said she learned more about the oboe in her first summer there than from any of the tutors you hired."

"Kendra!" Irene balked, but Kendra kept on.

"And I saw the flyers; it's the same instructor. *And* they have a harpist from the Vienna Philharmonic teaching orchestra this year."

"Dr. Engelstadt just hired three Elkwater graduates into the Charleston Symphony," Jessica's father, David, added from behind his newspaper. "And the Payne girl works there. Didn't she get accepted to Carnegie Mellon?"

"See?" Jessica extended an arm to her father and rounded her eyes in a pleading look at her mother.

"Good Lord, it's a mutiny." Irene finished her glass of pinot grigio and grabbed the bottle.

Kendra stepped beside her grandmother and dropped her head on her shoulder. "Please, Grandma?"

And how could Irene argue with that?

"Mom!" Jarl barreled into the room, hauling Jessica back into the present. "Jens says I have to sleep on the floor because there's only two beds to a bunk."

"And Jan won't let me have the top bunk," Jens whined from the door.

"You idiots don't even have a bunk assignment yet," Kendra scoffed.

"She's right," Jessica added, then told her daughter, "Don't call them idiots."

"Sorry, Mom. I will." She hung her head and moped to the door, muttering, "When they stop acting like idiots."

<hr>

"And keep an eye on your sister." Jessica fluffed a pillow and tossed it onto the lower bunk.

"What?" Jan balked, his voice cracking. Jens barked a laugh, and Jarl's tail wagged from under the bed. "Kendra's never been in trouble a day in her *life*. Why do we need to keep an eye on her?"

"Because she's a scaredy-cat," Jens chortled.

"Because she's *shy*." Jessica lightly swatted her son's arm. "This is a big step for her."

"Wasn't this her idea?" Jan asked, and Jarl barked, literally, in agreement. His snout poked out from under the bed, followed by two paws, his head, and shoulders. The bedframe wobbled as he wormed his way out, and Jens yelped in fright, gripping the top bunk's bed rail.

"Yes," Jessica said. She grabbed Jarl's scruff and hauled him the rest of the way out. He hopped to his paws and broke into a full-body shake, before leaning against her legs. She idly scratched behind his ears. "Which means you have your sister to thank for a summer in the woods with other inhumans, and not wearing your Sunday best while playing Mozart's 'Requiem' until you hear it in your sleep."

"She has a point, bro," Jarl said around a mouthful of teeth. He slunk half-shifted into the closet, and Jens tossed a shirt after him.

"Well, if Jarl agrees." Jan rolled his eyes, but a small smile flitted across his face. "We'll watch out for her, Mom."

"Thank you, baby." She pulled him into a side hug, dropping a kiss on Jan's cheek. Though he feigned disgust, he leaned into her embrace as he always had. Only a few seconds older than his brothers, Jan had always been the sweetest of her babies, and the fiercest defender of their little pack.

Her friend Svana, a wolven with the Skölläng pack in Charleston, once mused that he might be an Alpha. Jessica disagreed. A protector, Jan may be, but from her limited understanding, he was too easy going and mischievous, too ready to follow another's lead. So they had taken the conversation to Svana's husband, the Skölläng Alpha, Jörgun, who had laughed himself out of the room.

"Don't know why she can't keep an eye on us." Jarl, haphazardly dressed in basketball shorts and a t-shirt, flopped on the bottom bunk. He rolled onto his belly and grabbed two corners of the fitted sheet, attempting to tuck them both at once. "She's in the drum major track. They'll all be up in the tower while we sweat our balls off in the field."

"Language." Jessica swatted one of his hands away, helping him fit the sheet.

"Just saying." Jarl flipped around and started tucking the third corner while Jessica managed the fourth. "She'll have better eyes on us than we have on her."

"Good." Jessica smiled at her boys, disasters that they were. "She'll be able to call me when you three get into trouble."

An electronic bell rang outside the cabin, and all three boys perked up, sniffing the air. Tongues lolled from their mouths, and they sighed as one. "Dinner."

In a flurry of arms and legs, they squeezed out of the cabin. Jessica followed, hesitating on the cabin's porch as they ran down the stairs, turning to wave and yell, "Bye, Mom!" before joining the crowd of campers.

A few cabins down, she spied Kendra among a group of human and inhuman girls. She smiled and sent her a shy wave that panged something in Jessica's chest. Rubbing her breastbone with a knuckle, she headed toward the parking lot.

This would be good for them. Good for her. Her babies would get a chance to get to know their inhuman sides without their mother or grandparents hovering. A chance to learn about their culture and the lessons she couldn't teach them by herself. From musicians and counselors, from kids their age who had not been sheltered away and forced into a mold they could never fit.

And maybe, if she were lucky, they would get to learn from other wolven as well.

3

—·—

AKSEL

AKSEL PICKED THE LABEL on his bottle, tearing a soggy piece off and rolling it between his fingers to create a little ball. He flicked it away and began to work on a new section of the label.

"—three months' salary in July alone," his date, Beth, said. She was rambling about something. A job? Why would she be talking about her job? They were co-workers during the year—Beth taught drama at Elkins High School, where Aksel taught band and orchestra. Why would she be talking about work at the start of the summer?

"A new plot this year, thank Sköll." Beth rolled her eyes and smiled into her glass. "I'm cast as the ingénue."

Aksel glanced at her, forcing a smile.

What in the hells is she talking about?

It wasn't that he was purposefully not paying attention. Gods knew he had tried to at the start of their date. But he'd been distracted all day, ever since that scent kicked up at the camp and dragged him into a long-lost memory. He could not grasp it and had not been able to snuff it out. Through move-in, the first dinner, and the following staff meeting, Aksel had been zoning out, his head fogged by the haunting scent of soft florals and a hint of something rich and earthy.

What *was* it?

"I'm thinking of taking a cruise over winter break," Beth said. "The Bahamas, or Bermuda. Somewhere warm."

"Yeah." Aksel rolled another beer-label ball.

"I'll probably have to book an interior cabin. It's cheaper than an ocean view. Unless I have someone with me to split the cost." Her shoe bumped against his leg, nudging his calf and then his knee. When it trailed low again, Aksel realized she was intentionally sliding her foot up and down his leg.

He blinked into the present, looking up from his beer bottle to stare blankly at Beth.

Thick, golden-blonde hair pulled into a ponytail, a soft, feathered fringe dusting her brows. Even in the dimly lit interior of The Porchlight, he could tell she wore just enough makeup to make her eyes look huge. Innocent. Her lipstick was a subtle shade to draw attention to a mouth he supposed was inviting.

Aksel supposed a lot of things. An attraction to Beth was not one of them.

She darted her tongue out, wetting her lower lip before pulling it between her teeth and ducking her head to peer at him from under her lashes.

"I'll probably book in the fall," she said in a low voice. "A few months from now, there's time to think about it."

"Uh..."

"Enough time to get to know each other." She swept her leg up his calf again. "Properly."

Aksel jolted upright, his elbow bumping the table's edge. His bottle toppled, and he fumbled at it, grasping the neck and hastily pulling it to his mouth. Beth's foot fell away. She frowned, dropping back against the vinyl booth with a huff.

Even disappointed and borderline pouting, she was magazine model beautiful. It was just that Aksel didn't care.

Her looks, smile, and flirtatious body language glossed over Aksel like water on a duck's back. Like with Sandra the night before and Violet last week. Beautiful women, stunning wolven. Inhumans any red-blooded male or female, as his foster sister liked to tease, would drool over.

Except Aksel.

"Why don't I make this easy for you." Beth grabbed her purse, pulled out a few dollars, and set them on the table. "Thanks for the nice night, Aksel."

She rose and slid out of the booth, standing at his shoulder and contemplating him with a cock of her head. The ponytail bounced over her shoulder, and she trailed her finger over his bicep in a last-ditch effort for the sake of both of their packs.

Nothing.

With a nod, more to herself than to him, Beth left.

He sat in the booth for a long moment, staring at the space she had filled and trying to grab hold of anything other than relief.

"Wow, that was painful." A tall, limber female dropped into Beth's empty seat. She shook her head, braids dancing. "Someone should tell her it's polite to run over roadkill a second time."

"What?" Aksel squinted at his foster sister, not liking the wide, shit-eating grin she wore.

Gitta winked. "You know, to make sure it's dead."

Finally, something other than relief rose in Aksel's chest. He squirmed in the booth, embarrassment warring with the desire to crawl beneath the table and hide. "Hells, Gitta, how much of that did you see?"

"Enough." She shook her head, her smile turning incredulous. "Trust me, *enough*. That's what, the third one this week?"

"Second," he muttered. "Violet was technically last week."

"Right, missed the cutoff by a day. How dare I." She swept up the bills Beth left behind and slipped them into her pocket. Aksel opened his mouth, and she waved him off, raising two fingers high to catch the bartender's attention.

With all the parents in town dropping off their kids at the various camps around Elkins, The Porchlight was busier than usual. Aksel had been lucky to find a booth for himself and Beth, and as the bartender's gleaming red eyes flicked toward Gitta, he realized luck had little to do with it.

"The pack knows you're trying," Gitta said, drumming her fingers on the table.

"Does the pack know I'm failing?"

Gitta didn't say anything.

Aksel scrubbed a hand over his face, dropping his head back against the booth. "I don't know what's wrong with me. Beth is beautiful."

"I'll say."

"And she was flirting with me," he continued. "I think."

"You think?"

"She did this thing," he explained.

Gitta barely hid her smirk. She leaned forward, propping her elbows on the table. "What, like piss on you?"

"Gods, no. That's disgusting."

"Says the male on the meat market."

Aksel snarled, hating that she had a point. Marking territory was a *thing* with wolven, but not, Sköll be damned, by pissing on each other. Unless, he supposed, someone was into that sort of thing. It would certainly get the point and the scent across. There were rumors of panther shifters in the Southeast, and anyone with a housecat knew they had a habit of spraying. So maybe, but ... No. No way.

Most shifters, especially wolven, opted to physically mark their mate in a more easily distinguishable way: with a bite. As for the scent, from everything Aksel had been told as an adolescent wolven, the melding of scents was far less painful and far more permanent.

The steel toe of Gitta's boot pressed against his calf. She sent him another grin and bruisingly dragged it up his leg. "Was it like this?"

"Yes." He hissed and pulled his leg away. "But not like she was trying to break my shin. New moon, Gitta, what is wrong with you?"

"Me?" She stole his beer and swallowed the rest of it. "What's wrong with you? That *was* flirting, you numbskull."

"I—" He narrowed his eyes in thought. "I think she was trying to invite me on a cruise."

"What?"

"With her."

Gitta gave a disbelieving snort and devolved into cackles while Aksel replayed what he had caught of the one-sided conversation. A cruise. The Bahamas?

New moon, he should have been paying attention. He should be taking all of this more seriously. The pack was strung out enough as it was; without new alliances and new blood, they'd die out. It was hard enough to carve a life in this new world without an existential threat lingering over his head.

Aksel had done well enough. With perfect pitch and an ear for music, he'd excelled in the placement programs his foster pack had set up for him and had been lucky to be fostered by Gitta's family in the first place.

The Sköllburgs had been close with Aksel's family in the Otherworld. It was only natural that he fostered with them when he entered his adolescence, learning to hunt and stalk from an Alpha. A privilege.

And then they fell.

So many years on, he barely remembered the actual fall, only flashes of the night. Running on Gitta's heels, her fluffy tail bristled in moonlight. Lennart's howl shattering the silence of the stalk, the call to the hunt.

He'd been running, a scent teasing his nose, and then—nothing. No earth, no sky, no moon or stars.

His body had shifted, and when he hit the ground again, stones and twigs pierced his young skin. Gitta cried somewhere nearby, whimpering for her parents and Aksel. He remembered crawling to her, curling his larger, softer body around her, and hiding them both in the undergrowth. Her mother, Ygrid, had found them sometime near dawn, wrapping them in what he now knew were stolen bedsheets. She led them to what remained of their pack, stranded and alone in a new, unmagical world.

So few had fallen through, and most of them were already mated. Gitta and Aksel were two of the few young wolven on the run that night. Now, they were two of the few that remained unmated; all eyes were on them to grow the pack, form alliances, and bolster their numbers.

Or leave.

Aksel wasn't cut out for the lone wolf lifestyle. He knew that well enough from an adolescence lived on the fringes. Fostered into the Sköllburg pack, cut off from their world and his own family.

No, despite what Lennart thought about him, Aksel was pack. He wanted the camaraderie and the companionship. The safety in knowing the pack had his back, no matter what, because he had theirs. And with each failed attempt at finding a mate, he let them down.

"Two beers." Dusty, the bartender, sidled beside their table, wings tucked in close against his back as he set down two bottles. His antennae twitched in a wave at Gitta, and he smiled at Aksel, red eyes gleaming. "Bad date?"

"The date was fine." He grabbed a bottle and pointed it across the table. "Current company leaves something to be desired."

"Ah, shut up." Gitta took up her beer and raised it in a toast to Dusty. "Cheers, man."

Dusty mimed his cheers and turned his attention to Aksel. "It is hilarious how bad you are at dating."

"Seriously." Gitta took a big swig.

"I mean," he continued, "I've seen Beth leave with the first man to tell her she's pretty."

"You try that line on her yet?" Gitta asked.

Dusty's eyes glowed a deeper red. "No."

She laughed, mirth dying away as she glanced at Aksel and took in his stooped shoulders. Were he shifted, his ears would have been pressed flat against his head. "Hey, Aks, don't worry about it. Dad knows you're trying. He's got your back with the pack, alright?"

"It's not alright, Gitta." He spun the beer in his hands. "I don't know what's wrong with me. Ygrid and your dad have set me up with some of the most beautiful females in a hundred-mile radius. A wolven any man or inhuman would shit their brains over—no offense, Dusty."

"None taken." He shrugged and sent Aksel an easy smile while tugging on the collar of his Iron Maiden muscle tank. He glanced at the bar, antennae twitching as the front door opened. "If I could shit brains, I would do so for Beth."

Gitta curled her lip in a snarl. "Dude, gross."

Dusty grinned, winking at her before spinning around with a shake of his wings and slipping behind the bar.

"And you"—she kicked him under the table—"stop putting so much pressure on yourself. Everyone knows you're trying. Hells, half of us are here tonight."

Aksel straightened, alarm raising the short human hairs on the back of his neck. He scanned the crowd in The Porchlight and, sure enough, close to a dozen of his pack sisters and brothers and a few of the elders filled the bar. Not unusual for a waning night in Elkins, but had they all seen how colossally he'd tanked his date?

Heat rose in his cheeks, and Aksel buried his face in his hands. "Ugh, I owe your dad so much."

"Hey, whoa. None of that." Gitta's beer bottle clinked against the table, and she gently gripped his forearm. "You haven't had nearly enough to drink to be this weepy. What's going on?"

"Nothing," he muttered into his palms. She squeezed his arm, and Aksel straightened, tucking his hands beneath his legs. "It's nothing."

"Bullshit." Gitta nudged his beer closer, waiting.

"I'm just in my head."

"No shit, Sherlock. Come on. Spill it."

Aksel took a breath, holding it briefly before shaking his head on the exhale. He rubbed his nose, trying to dislodge a faint tickle that had lodged itself in his sinuses. "It sounds nuts."

"I'm a whelp-free lesbian wolven in a dying pack that sent *you* out as our last great hope. Try me."

"Well, when you put it that way." He scanned the bar again before leaning over the table and lowering his voice. "I caught a scent earlier."

"A ... scent."

"At the camp," he explained, rounding his eyes and giving her a *look*. "Only briefly, there were a lot of people around, and it was probably a lotion or a shampoo, but I could swear that—"

"A scent," Gitta paced out, "or a *scent*." At Aksel's silence, she straightened, a slow grin stretching across her face. Pearly white teeth shone back at him, interest glinting in her amber eyes. "Oh, my Gods."

"It's probably nothing."

"But what if it isn't?" Her grin widened. "Don't tell me you're still hung up on her."

"I'm not," he said.

"It's been thirteen years, Aks."

"I know!" he shouted, then hunched and whispered, "I know."

"And you're still this messed up about, maybe, potentially catching her scent?"

"I told you it was nuts." He grabbed his beer and drank.

"Let's think about this." Gitta settled in, always ready to problem-solve. "Maybe she has kids at the camp. What's the youngest group, ten? Eleven?"

"Eleven, mostly."

"There, see?" She rubbed her hands together. "Maybe it was her, and she's got a kid attending their first summer. A lot of people do that. Elkwater's a magical place."

"Are you implying she got pregnant in college?" Aksel's voice was too loud, even to his ears. An unfamiliar heat rushed over his body, his vision narrowing to a tight point on his pack sister.

He was half-risen when Gitta put her hands up in surrender, pressing them against the air. "Easy, Aks."

A few wolven glanced over, and at least one of the elders wore a curious half-smile. Aksel ran a tongue over his teeth, startled by the sharp prick of shifted canines. He rubbed his nose and sat heavily in the booth.

"I'm only saying, you two hooked up thirteen years ago. People move on; hells, you were just on a date."

"Because the pack—"

Gitta waved her hand. "Yeah, yeah, the *pack*. You also didn't stay in touch."

"Not my fault," Aksel grumbled. "I wrote her."

"And did she ever respond?" she countered. Aksel let his glare speak for him. She shrugged breezily. "Just sayin'."

Aksel sniffed and rubbed his nose again. The tickle had increased to an outright annoyance, and if he didn't sneeze soon, he would lose his mind. "I think I've had enough for one night."

He pushed his beer toward Gitta and rose. She clinked the bottle against hers, happily humming and yelping when Aksel threw himself back into the booth. Every hair on his body raised in alarm, his ears half shifting without warning and pricking forward. Gitta stilled, eyes intent on him. "Aks?"

He swallowed, working his jaw and willing his teeth to shift back before speaking. "She's here."

"Who's here?"

It took every bit of his willpower to turn his face toward Gitta and say, "*Jess.*"

"What?" Gitta popped onto her knees, peering over the back of the booth. "Where?"

"At the bar."

"There's no one at the bar." She looked again, then amended her statement. "I mean, no one we don't know."

"What?" He swung around the table, kneeling next to Gitta with his fingers gripping the booth back, eyes barely rising above the vinyl. "She was just there." He pointed to the far corner, beside the bartop jukebox, at the only empty seat in The Porchlight.

No Jess. No ghost from his past. Just a barely drunk beer and a pile of cash.

4

—·—

JESS

THIRTEEN YEARS LATER, THE exterior of The Porchlight was just as she remembered, with the same weathered clapboard and blinking OPEN sign in the tinted window. The posters on the walls were different; the curb had been repaired, and the posts repainted. But otherwise, it was the same, just as all of Elkins was the same.

It made her angry.

Nothing changed here; time had stood still while Jessica lived a lifetime.

Four lifetimes.

She exhaled, letting out as much of the anger as she could, and smoothed the front of her capris before stepping onto the curb. Another quick breath, and she shoved open the door. Dave Matthews Band blasted over the lively chatter of humans and inhumans, and the clack of pool balls. Jessica ducked her head as she entered. It felt illicit, somehow, to be back here as an adult.

She hadn't spent much time in bars and didn't drink beyond the occasional glass of wine on a Saturday night with her parents. Between the kids, school, and work, there was never enough time. Forget drinks with friends, birthday parties, or bachelorette parties. She had missed all of that when her babies were small, and the next thing she knew, they were teenagers, and she was in her thirties with a hard-won bachelor's degree and eight years of experience as a junior accountant at her father's orthodontics practice.

The urge to turn tail and leave was overwhelming. It was too loud, too dark, too crowded. Though there was no record scratch and no heads whipped her way when she entered, Jessica did not miss how each person sniffed as she walked by. Nor did she miss the cocked heads and narrowed-eyes following her to the bar.

How often had she seen her boys do just that?

Wolven, she thought. It settled her nerves. Wolven, she knew. God bless, wolven, she could *handle*, and that knowledge gave her enough confidence to order.

"A beer," she told the bartender, a rangy mothman in an Iron Maiden tank top.

"I assumed," he answered.

Jessica met his gleaming red eyes.

He waited, and after a long moment, chuckled, his antennae twitching. "Alright, miss ma'am, I give. What sort of beer would you like?"

Jess gave him a carefully cultivated non-nonsense mom look, and he smiled. Or, at least, she assumed it was a smile. His eyes narrowed at the edges, and the thin lines that made up his mouth curved upwards.

"Had you pegged for a tourist come to see the freaks," he said. "But you didn't flinch."

"Why would I flinch?"

"Most of 'em do." He shrugged and grabbed a glass, eyeing Jessica before turning to the wall of taps and choosing one. "I take you for a light lager lady, and if I'm wrong," he set the glass before her, "it's on me."

"I—thank you." She took the beer and glanced around, trying to decide where to go. The Porchlight was crowded, and every booth and stool at the bar was full. The man beside her saw Jessica looking and hopped out of his seat. His nostrils flared in a move she recognized as wolven, and he gestured at the stool.

"Please."

"I couldn't."

"I was just leaving," he assured her. He set a twenty on the counter and adjusted his baseball cap, nodding at the bartender before shouldering through the crowd.

Jessica took his seat, wedged in the corner near the jukebox. The stool wobbled and spun, and she set her beer down, taking in the crowd. Most of them were tall and athletic-looking. Some were lean, others bulky with the muscular builds and statures she associated with wolven.

In them, she saw suggestions of Jan, Jarl, and Jens' eventual size. Their paws were still comically large when they shifted, and they were all elbows and knees in their human form, taller than Jessica by inches, but their shoulders were developing a solid sturdiness, and the other day she caught the trace of muscle in Jarl's arms.

She searched the crowd for anyone resembling Kendra. Short, soft around the edges. While Kendra was built like her mother and grandmother, her hair and eyes, as well as her pale complexion, were all her father's.

A group of wolven at a pool table parted, allowing the player to aim and shoot, and Jessica froze.

There, across the bar, standing beside a booth with his eyes wide and fixed on her, was Aksel.

"Oh, Lord." She grabbed her beer and jumped off the stool, darting around the bar to wedge herself in a corner by the bathrooms. Her hands trembled, spilling beer over the edge of her glass, and her pulse pounded hard enough that she felt it in her temples.

This was a terrible idea. What was the thinking, showing up over a decade later with *kids* and enrolling them in his camp?

It was nuts. Absolutely nuts, and she knew it was nuts when she did it, but she didn't know what else to do!

Svana and every other inhuman she had ever spoken to had urged her to let her kids connect with their nature. With their kind.

"For their sakes," they had said. "Try to get in touch."

Let them know their culture. Let them know where they come from.

So she had formed the Charleston Inhuman Outreach with Svana and enrolled her babies in integrated sports leagues and summer programs. Doing her best with her limited means. It wasn't until Svana recommended a summer at Elkwater— "You loved it there!"—and Kendra stole the hoodie that she even considered bringing them here, and *this* was exactly why.

Jessica knew Aksel worked at the band camp. She knew he would be one of their instructors. Had known there was a chance they might run into each other, either in town or at one of the various parent events held at the camp. But in a bar, with no warning?

No, thank you.

She had only come in here to avoid sitting alone in her rented apartment, not to face her past on her first night in town.

Slinking around the corner, Jessica set her beer on the counter, pulling a five-dollar bill from her purse and hoping it covered her tab. With a last glance at the crowd, she darted back into the shadows and slipped out the rear door.

It was a short walk to her summer rental, a top-floor apartment recently vacated by the construction crew that had performed the renovations on Elkwater, and not nearly long enough to calm her nerves. Thankfully, the first floor remained dark—the owner's daughter and her girlfriend not yet home.

The rental agent had assured Jessica that while they were young, they wouldn't be a nuisance.

"They spend a few nights a week at the camp during the summer, and the girlfriend sometimes leads overnight backpacking trips. Grew up around Green Bank, I think."

"And the other neighbors?" Jessica had asked, gesturing to the door beside hers.

"A teacher at the high school," the agent answered. "And the top unit next to yours is empty."

Noise wasn't a worry, not really. Her days would be spent dialing into the internet to work ... once she got to a Circuit City to buy an Ethernet cable long enough to reach the modem box downstairs.

That had been the major selling point of the apartment: internet access. Any closer to the camp and she hit the radio-free zone, so Elkins and the only wired household in town, it was. What the agent had failed to mention, however, was that the apartment was BYOC.

Bring Your Own Cable.

Luckily, Jessica had some spreadsheets saved locally. She closed the door behind her, mounting the stairs and anticipating losing herself in work and numbers to get Aksel's face out of her mind.

He looked the same, but not. Same soft cheeks and warm eyes. His rich, brown hair was longer than she remembered, and he wore it swept back from his face, with a close-trimmed beard defining his jaw.

She'd only caught a glimpse of him, but a glimpse was all it took to send Jessica right back to that last night. To have her recalling the soft, surprised little "o" those kissable lips had made when she and he …

"Nope." She hauled her brick of a laptop out of a bag and turned it on, curling her lip as she drove the little red nub to direct the cursor.

An Ethernet cable and a mouse, she thought. *And a keyboard.*

Lord, she hoped they had a Circuit City out here. There was no way she could close the books on time with this little laptop nipple.

The monthly reconciliation she had been working on loaded, every cell on the spreadsheet filled with a string of numbers, some red, some black. Stimulating stuff. Jessica got to work, her attention continually straying to Aksel at the bar. The last night of camp. Numbers blurring and columns bleeding together.

The slamming of a door rattled the windows, jolting her upright. A muscle pinched in her lower back, and Jessica squinted at the oven clock.

10:30PM.

"Figures," she muttered, closing her laptop and standing to stretch. "First night alone in thirteen years, and I fall asleep *working*." Another glance at the clock had Jessica rubbing a hand over her face and heading to the bedroom.

5

— · —

AKSEL

"WE'LL START WITH THE eight-to-five, and for those of you sticking with us for the summer, you'll be moved up into the advanced class where we work on six-to-fives." Aksel strolled between his campers, seated criss-cross-applesauce in the grass, taking notes. It was a good class; he could tell that immediately. The intro drum major kids were usually a good group, polite, kind, and attentive, which meant two things: his favorite camper was in this class, as was his most challenging.

"Who can tell me what eight-to-five means?" He spun and addressed the campers. Hands shot up, and he smiled, nodding to the pale batboy in the third row. "Yes, Hank?"

"Eight steps between the five-yard lines," he whistled through thin lips and sharp teeth.

"Excellent. And how many inches is that per step?"

Hank adjusted his wide-brimmed hat, sending Aksel a vacant stare.

"Anyone?" he prompted the group.

"Twenty-two point five," a voice called from the last row. Aksel followed the sound, unable to locate the speaker. At a subtle point from a juvenile sasquatch, he leaned to the side and spotted the gnome hidden by the sasquatch's bulk. "Or impossible if you're my size."

"How do you account for that?" another camper asked.

"Twice as many steps," another answered, and the campers giggled.

Aksel scanned the group and found the culprit, wondering which they might be: his favorite or most challenging.

The source of the voice was a human girl, tan with a mass of wild brown waves beginning to frizz in the humidity. Her legs were tucked into an oversized WVU hoodie, and she hugged her knees to her chest, the tips of white tennis shoes poking out from beneath the hem.

"Let me ask you this," Aksel countered. "How does a drum major keep time?"

Silence. The campers looked to one another, trading shrugs.

"It's tough up in the tower." Aksel strolled the aisle, raising his voice over the roll of drums from the campers practicing across the field. "Instruments get in the way; taller musicians block the shorter. A well-trained band never misses their mark, but they're relying on you to keep time. So, is it in your head? What if there's a distraction or you sneeze? How do you get back on time?"

More silence, and then—

"The center snare," the same girl answered. Aksel assessed her, and she hugged her knees tighter, tucking her chin until he thought the sweatshirt might swallow her altogether.

"Exactly," he confirmed. "Nice work."

She jerked her face up and, for a flash, less than an instant, familiarity struck. He blinked, shaking the vision away. But for a moment, she almost looked like—

"The band can see you, and you lead the band." He pressed forward, pacing the aisle and distracting himself in the lesson. "You're not just a 'human metronome'; you're a field conductor in constant communication with your team on their podiums to keep everyone on time. And you do so by keeping an eye on the center snare's feet."

"But that doesn't answer the question," another student, a young satyr with horned nubs just peeking through his hair, said.

"Doesn't it?" Aksel replied. When no one spoke, he smiled. "You make the shortest member of the drumline your center snare."

They ended the morning session atop one of the newly built podiums on the western edge of the field. Aksel pointed out the parts of the camp they could see—the canteen, the roofline of the cafeteria, and the newly built crescent roof over the amphitheater.

"Use your surroundings to direct your band." He extended an arm to the southeast. "See Bald Knob, just there?" A chorus of heads nodded, and he swung his arm in a line to the north. "And Barton Knob there." More nods. "I like to keep everyone grouped between those two points. That way, if anyone struggles to keep formation on a diagonal, I can easily spot it."

"And what, yell at them to keep up?" the girl in the WVU hoodie asked. Aksel glanced over, and her eyes rounded. She clapped her hands over her mouth as though the words had slipped free without thought.

He tucked the corner of his mouth, deciding her snark wasn't intentional. "I marched with the first naga at OSU. The lead drum major made us take an inhuman anatomy class, learning all about naga, letieche, and lamia so we could recognize the bunch and coil of muscle to keep time. And when that failed—"

Aksel glanced back at the campers, each hanging on his every word. Pride thrilled through him. To have the attention of a pack, listening and learning from *him*, a wolven foster, was something he might not have ever earned in the other world. Something he certainly wouldn't have in this one, but at camp? At the high school?

Aksel was their leader. Not the out-of-place foster, not the wolven who couldn't keep a date long enough to spare the pack he had.

Here, he was the Alpha. Sure, it was a pack of hormonal preteens, but they would grow up with his lessons and his words rattling around in their skulls. They would carry his advice onto the fields of whatever colleges they attended. Or they wouldn't, but he would still be up there, teaching them long after they left Elkwater behind.

"—when that failed, we rearranged the positions." He pointed to the field, drawing their attention to the intermediate marchers in formation. "Shortest on the inside, in two lines down the middle."

"That's a gnome!" The gnome hopped up and down, gripping the top rail to watch the field.

"A gnomish center snare, pivot rotations, and diagonal formations," Aksel confirmed. "And naga and sasquatch in the cross-sections. Makes it easier for our shorter marchers to crab or roll-step if they can't manage an eight-to-five. On the inside, they—"

"Have less distance to cover," WVU said. Her eyes danced over the marchers, and she gave an approving nod. Only then did the rest of the campers smile and nod as well. Aksel took that in, realizing that this girl would be neither his favorite student nor his most challenging.

She was going to be both.

The lunch bell rang, and the campers rushed off the podium before Aksel could properly dismiss them, spilling onto the stairs and bolting across the field. WVU lingered at the stair rail as Aksel descended.

"Better hurry," he said. "You don't want to be at the tail-end of the buffet."

"I'm waiting for my brothers." She jerked her chin at the field where the marching band dispersed. "They won't want to eat with me, but we're supposed to check in with each other a couple of times a day."

"You must be close."

She shrugged and tugged the cuffs on her hoodie. He had just about decided that was all he'd get from the girl when she replied, "My mom asked them to look out for me."

"Isn't that what big brothers are for?"

She shoved her hands into the front pocket and kicked a grass knob. "They're only older by three minutes."

Alright.

Aksel pinched his lips between his teeth, deciding it was better to remain silent than further poke the bear, as it were.

"Here they are," she said, stepping away. He assumed it was to avoid being seen with a teacher, something Aksel had long ago gotten used to, but then three wolven adolescents ran up, dropping mouthfuls of clothes at her feet before yipping excitedly and nipping her heels. They nudged her along, jumping over each other and tumbling in the grass as she picked up their shirts and shoes.

For her part, WVU tried not to smile, but Aksel got a glimpse of one before she yelled, "Jarl! Jan! Stop! Ugh, Jens, don't tear my hoodie." She swatted one of the wolven's ears. He let go of her sleeve, butting her in the hip with his head instead, and the three of them buffered her along to the dining hall.

Aksel walked a fair distance behind them, taking off his hat to run a hand through his hair. Tipping his head back, he sniffed, then inhaled as a breeze drifted towards him, freezing as he caught that same curious scent.

His eyes flew wide, and he jerked his face to where the girl and wolven trotted over a bridge, an unfamiliar feeling brewing in his belly.

"Everything alright?" Sanoya, the camp's life sciences teacher, drifted beside him, her wide eyes hidden behind even wider sunglasses. She twirled a lock of white-blonde hair in her fingers, scanning Aksel's face.

"Yeah," Aksel sighed. "Just being haunted by a ghost."

She cocked her head, dusty purple lips pursed. "That is impossible. None of the ghosts came through."

"A figurative ghost, Sanoya." Aksel refitted his cap and faced her. "I keep catching a scent."

"Oh?"

"Yesterday at drop-off, last night in front of my apartment, and just now."

"Interesting." She gazed down the path, where the three tails of the wolven pups disappeared around a building. The girl followed, hesitating and glancing over her shoulder before scurrying after her brothers.

"Well," Sanoya said with all the effort of a shrug, "you've always had a good nose."

6

— · —

Jess

Jessica threw her car into park, taking a moment to sit before climbing the stairs and, *finally*, starting her work day after losing eight hours tackling electronics stores across half the state.

She had started at a mom-and-pop-style general store in Elkins, where they directed her to Buckhannon. The owner of the handyman store there had directed her to Bridgeport, where she finally found a mouse and a keyboard, but the pimple-faced Circuit City employee had stared blankly at her when she asked if they had an Ethernet cable longer than six feet. So she headed further north to Morgantown, where she finally found a cable long enough, she hoped, to reach the modem box on the side of the townhome.

A day lost to driving and popping in and out of stores, and she still had the monthly close to tackle.

The sun was low on the hills when she drove back through Buckhannon, and full dark had set in when she reached her apartment in Elkins. Letting out a long, centering breath, Jessica grabbed her purse and purchases, dropped her bags on the stoop, and went to examine the modem box affixed to the rear of the house.

Locked.

"Shit."

Of course, it was locked. This was one of the few wired households in Elkins. Most people had to drive to the library or the internet cafe in Buckhannon to get online. Leaving your modem box unlocked was asking for the neighbors to leech.

Jessica eyed the townhome, judging the distance from her bathroom window to the modem box, and fought back a groan. If she were lucky, the cable would reach.

She flicked the lock. "I'm going to be working on the toilet at this rate."

After leaving a note for the landlord's daughter and her girlfriend requesting the key, Jessica tossed her laptop bag and purse in the passenger seat of her car and drove back to Buckhannon. The young man working at the counter startled when she walked into the internet cafe, glancing at the clock on the wall with a frown.

"We close in forty-five minutes."

"That's alright." She patted her laptop bag. "I just need to plug in for a few minutes and download some files."

He showed her to an empty desk, running Jessica quickly through how to connect and pay. She thanked him, drumming her fingers on the desk as her laptop powered on and the modem connected. After the usual series of screeches and whistles, the landing page for her email loaded.

A message from her mother waited at the top, with the subject line, "Hello."

It was brief, thankfully, demanding an update on the camp and the kids, criticizing Jessica's choice to live in Elkins for the summer, and giving a little bit of "your father" talk, followed by a diatribe on how Jessica's choices looked for his practice, the church, the community.

She had long ago grown numb to her mother's special brand of criticism. It had been almost nonstop from the moment Jessica told her she was pregnant to the morning she and the kids hopped on I-79 and headed north,

"How does this make *me* look?"

Jessica wished she could say she was numb to it after thirteen years, hell, after a lifetime, but it still hurt, especially where her children were involved. Kendra, Jan, Jarl, and Jens had done nothing to deserve Irene's spite, and for the most part, their grandmother kept it from their very keen ears. She was supportive in her way, and that had to count for something.

If they showed an interest in a sport or hobby, Irene was the first to suggest they sign up, with her checkbook ready in hand. She was in the front row at every recital, constantly showering her grandbabies with clothes, toys, and games. Tickets to the symphony and trips to the zoo. The biggest Christmas trees, the largest Thanskgivings. They did not want for anything Irene could supply, and in turn, Irene saved all of her spite for the daughter she could not mold into a picture-perfect reflection of herself.

After taking leave from school in her first semester at WVU, Jessica needed her parents' help. Throughout her pregnancy and her babies' infancy and toddler years, the pursuit of her bachelor's degree, and efforts to carve out an identity from the fog of early, unplanned motherhood, Irene and David had been crucial to her survival.

Supportive, in their way, until Jessica dared to reach.

She kept her response short at first: drop-off went well, and Kendra had been assigned to her old cabin. The boys bunked together; the camp was exactly as she remembered, yet not at all. Then, she wrote about how she wanted to cry and scream and rage while wandering through Elkins, where nothing had changed. Wrote about seeing Aksel across the bar and running away because she was too scared to be near him. Too afraid to tell him the truth of where she'd been and what had happened.

And then she deleted it all and started over.

> *Mom,*
>
> *Elkwater is just as I remember; I'm sure the kids were tired of me saying that over and over. Kendra is in my old cabin. She couldn't wait for her old mom to leave so she could meet*

her bunkmates. And the boys were just as excited as we knew they would be. Jan opted for the orchestra track in the second half of the summer. I'm sure he'll come home as a maestro!

We miss you both!

Love,

Jessica

She sent the reply, clicking quickly to the next email. From Svana, the subject line was a series of exclamation points that had Jessica's pulse rising.

Jess—

The vote was unanimous! You officially have the full support of the Charleston Inhuman Outreach to pursue partnership opportunities with Elkwater Music Camp. I've gone ahead and scheduled a meeting for you with the director, Mackenzie Murray (who I think you know?), for Thursday afternoon. I know that's fast, but the foundation we're trying to partner with seemed excited about this opportunity, and it sounds like the rest of the board wants to move fast.

I know you're already starting to panic, but don't, okay? All you need to do is run Murray through who we are. Tell her your story, fill in the parts she might not know. Remind her that you went to Elkwater, and you know their mission

> *better than anyone. Think of what this will mean for inhu-*
> *man kids across the state.*
>
> *You've got this, Babcock!!*
> *-Svana*

Jessica exhaled, shaking out her hands and re-reading the email. This was it, this was everything she had worked toward for thirteen years: a way to connect humans and inhumans across the state, and beyond.

Before meeting Svana, she hadn't even known there were inhumans in Charleston. It was only through her mother's connections that they had even learned about Elkwater Music Camp, and Jessica still couldn't believe Irene had agreed to let her attend. But somehow she had, stating it was their duty as "daughters of West Virginia" to be welcoming and kind to their "new inhuman neighbors."

Those two summers had changed the course of her life, introducing Jessica to a new, rich world and setting her on a course that led to now and this dream: to bring humans and inhumans together, beyond Elkwater Music Camp.

And it all started with Svana and the Charleston Inhuman Outreach.

While Irene dismissively called it Jessica's "little charity," the Outreach was so much more than that. She had grown up with privileges other kids in Charleston did not have, and her children had been extended those same privileges. This was her way to give back and help create a brighter future for inhuman kids who might not otherwise have the same opportunities as her kids.

Through the years, she and Svana had assembled a group of humans and inhumans, representing as much of the changing face of the world as they could. A handful of naga nesting in Kanawha State Forest, wolven from Svana's pack, the Skölläng, a few sasquatch from Coal Fork, and a group of gnomes displaced by nearby mountaintop mining operations.

In getting to know the families who had fallen from the Otherworld to earth, it was easy to see how fortunate Jessica was to have been born a Babcock, and the advantages the wolven had in looking human outside of their shift. From the moment she became aware of it, she had thrown herself into bridging the gap between humans and inhumans.

After all, as the human mother of three wolven pups, wasn't she something of a bridge herself?

Forming a partnership with Elkwater was going to be work. A lot of work. Conference calls with the Outreach and potential donors. Frequent drives to the camp. Her kids would hate seeing her there so often, but the opportunity to foster better connections between humans and inhumans ... Lord, what a worthwhile endeavor.

Invigorated, she logged into her worksite, grabbed the files she needed to work for the night, and drove back to Elkins with a foreign energy buzzing through her. So much of the last thirteen years had been about survival, and now, with the kids enrolled at Elkwater and her dreams within reach, Jessica almost felt like she could breathe.

Anticipation for her meeting with Mackenzie Murray fueled her through her accounting work. Hunched over her laptop at the kitchen counter, she idly spun the tiny metal disc covering a quarter-sized hole in the wall beside her laptop, losing herself in debits and credits, and deliberating expense requests until the numbers blurred. At 10:30 PM on the nose, the slamming of a door beneath her feet rattled the windows in the panes. She sent a mean look to the hardwood floor beneath her feet and took the return of her downstairs neighbor as her cue to go to bed.

⚜

Muffled rock music and the aroma of freshly brewed coffee crept from behind the door. Jessica knocked again, louder this time, and a moment later, the door swung open. A faun stared back at her, coppery eyes intent on Jessica beneath a head of wild blonde curls.

"Hello," she said, her smile revealing a slight slit in her upper lip and large, blocky teeth.

"Hi, I'm sorry to come by so early. I was just wondering if you saw my note?"

The faun stared blankly at her. "Note?"

"I left it on the door." Jessica pointed to where she'd hung the note, the space now empty. The faun followed the gesture, and her brows raised.

"Ah, the neighbor might have grabbed it," she explained. "He sometimes grabs the mail for us and brings in packages since we're not home every night. Want me to check?"

"No, that's alright." It was barely six o'clock, and Jessica had only knocked on their door because she heard the music when she headed out for a morning walk. "I just need to borrow the key for the modem box."

"That I can help with." The faun pushed the door open wider. "I'm Cricket, Avery's girlfriend. It's Jessica, right? From upstairs? Want a coffee? Tea?"

"I—yes. Sure." She followed Cricket inside, letting the door close gently behind her. "Coffee, please."

"You got it." She grabbed a mug from an overstuffed cupboard, filling it to the brim while keeping up a pleasant chatter. "Avery's a coffee girl. I can't stand it. Too much caffeine makes me all jittery. Oh, but peach tea? *Sweetened* peach tea? Oak and ivy, now that's a drink worth leaving the woods for. But I'm an early riser, always have been. Avery likes to sleep, so I always get a pot brewing for her." Cricket paused and squinted at the coffee pot. "Though I'm still figuring out the measurements. Always make too much."

She handed the mug to Jessica, who took it in both hands, careful not to spill any. It was hot, black as midnight, and likely strong enough to have Jessica wide awake for days. She took a polite sip, scrunching her face into a thankful smile to keep from wincing.

"Thank you," she forced out. Cricket beamed and began digging through a kitchen drawer. Jessica snuck to the sink, subtly pouring half the coffee down the drain. "Mind if I grab some milk?"

"Not at all." Cricket waved at the refrigerator, intent on the junk drawer.

"How long have you lived in Elkins?" Jessica asked.

"Not even a year," she answered, slamming the drawer and opening a cupboard stuffed with what looked like office supplies. "Avery's mom bought the house at the end of last summer. It was already separated into apartments—we lived in your unit upstairs until they finished renovating this one." She closed the cupboard, pinched her lips, pushing them up to her nose, and frowned at the apartment. "Where the hells is that key?"

"What's going on?" A young woman with wild red hair padded into the living space. Dressed in cut-off jean shorts and an Elkwater Music Camp polo, the deep green set off sky blue eyes, and Cricket visibly melted at the sight of who Jessica assumed was her girlfriend, Avery.

"Upstairs Jessica needs the key for the modem box." Cricket hooked her thumb at Jessica, who lifted her mug in greeting.

"For internet access."

"Oh!" Avery perked up. "Right, hold on." She spun to face a desk, digging through the drawers while Cricket scoured the bookshelf. An alarm beeped somewhere, and Jessica glanced at the clock. Six thirty.

"Do you need to get going?"

"Hm?" Cricket checked her watch. "Oh. Crap. Aves, we need to get to camp. I'm leading a hike in, like, forty minutes."

"The key?" Jessica asked, hopeful.

"I'm so sorry." Avery rushed into the kitchen, filling a mug with coffee right to the brim. She knocked it back, swallowing the contents and setting the mug down with a loud clack. "We'll look again tonight, promise."

"That's alright." Though, as the sore muscles in her neck and back reminded her, it was not. "You two get going. I'll head to the library. Or Buckhannon."

"You can work out of here," Cricket offered. She jerked her head to the desk. "Just unplug Avery's computer. The internet logon is in the top drawer."

"I couldn't ..."

"We insist." Avery grabbed a backpack from the sofa, heading for the door. "We should be back around seven or eight. Although"—her attention strayed to the door—"the neighbor has a key for the box. We could ask him to—"

"I really don't want to be a problem," Jessica said, backing out of the apartment.

"Please, use whatever you need. Our spare key is in the flower pot; help yourself to coffee, food, whatever. It's the least I can do for losing the key." A faint blush colored her cheeks, and Jessica did not miss the adoring look Cricket sent her.

"C'mon, Aves." She ushered her girlfriend out the door. "Jessica can figure it out."

"Thank you!" she called after them. They both waved before hopping in a blue Subaru Forester, sharing a quick kiss before Avery put the car into reverse and tore out of the lot.

7

— . —

AKSEL

By the third time he wandered their aisle, Aksel had to admit he was being weird. Not intentionally, but no counselor or teacher focused this much of their attention or energy on one row, much less one table of campers.

Yet here he was, strolling the aisle behind the wolven triplet's table as they lobbed bits of food at each other, much to the entertainment of the humans and inhumans around them. At least they kept misbehaving, which gave him a reason to linger beyond, maybe, possibly catching that odd scent again.

Stop being weird.

He slowed behind their table, berating himself into turning around, when Jan—or was it Jarl?—scooped a sauce-covered meatball from his plate, closing one eye and aiming his spoon at his target across the table.

"No throwing food," Aksel barked, putting a little wolven growl in the words and immediately regretting it. Jan/Jarl yelped, and the meatball arced through the air. A hand popped up at the last second, and marinara sauce splattered Aksel's shirt as the girl from his class, Kendra, he had learned, plucked the meatball out of the air.

"Nice catch," he managed.

"Sorry." Kendra's cheeks flushed a deep red, and she whirled around, putting her back to him. Her scent wafted to Aksel's nose, rising above the garlic, onion, and herbs, and he froze.

It was faint. So faint, but it was there—the maddening scent that had been teasing him. Almost, but not quite. It wasn't an exact match, but it held all the bright, summery notes. The crispness of a river and earthy loam. A scent like fuchsia and forest green.

A scent he knew.

An awkward quiet filled the table, and though he knew he'd overstayed his tenuous welcome as a teacher, Aksel couldn't move. He was rooted in place, looming over the kids and making them nervous.

A strange sensation washed over him, a tingling in his fingers and itching at the base of his spine. His heart fluttered wildly in his chest, and the triplets exchanged wary glances.

"Mr. Haralson?" one of them, the one with the tight curls and fade, Jens, asked. Beside him, his brother's nostrils flared, catching the scent of an oncoming shift.

Over-sharp canines pierced Aksel's tongue, and the familiar prickle of his ears elongating and sprouting fur began in his lobes.

Shit.

He needed to leave. Needed to get out of the cafeteria before he shifted. What in Sköll's name was happening? Aksel couldn't remember the last time he'd lost control like this. He had to have been, what, eighteen? But it had come on so fast, and if he didn't move, if he didn't run and stretch his legs, he was going to—

"Cooky needs you." Mac grabbed his arm, wheeling Aksel around and forcing him into the kitchen. She guided him to the prep table, shoving him onto the edge. "Breath, buddy."

And he did. Mac was the camp director. His boss before she was his friend. She was the Alpha here, not him. Mac. Not Aksel.

He exhaled all of his pent-up, unshifted energy in a rush and sagged forward, gripping the table's edge to keep from puddling to the floor.

Mac waited, feet a shoulder's width apart, arms crossed. "You want to tell me what that was about?"

Without looking, he knew she was frowning. He could hear the concern in her voice behind the stern tone. Could smell that every fiber of her was intent on him. A human didn't become the director of Camp Cryptid without being able to read the signs of her campers and employees, and there was no human more attuned to inhumans than Mac.

Hells, the woman had spent a summer baiting a faun out of the woods, of course, she'd know how to recognize an impending shift.

"I'm sorry." He blinked, bringing the room into focus. "I—"

"A quarter of those kids have never seen a shift, and you just started wolfing out in front of them all. Did you even hear yourself?"

Aksel whipped his face up, finally catching the anger she was trying to tamp down. "What?"

"You were *growling*."

"Mac, I swear, I have no idea what happened. That's never happened to me before."

Her eyes trailed his face, reading Aksel in a manner that always had him wondering if she were fully human. There were Seers in the other world, descended from the fair folk, but Mac was born and raised in Charleston. She had been thirteen when the inhumans fell through and vividly remembered the news reports from the day. As she told it, the news broke, and she grabbed a backpack with her six essentials and set off monster hunting.

Whatever Mac was looking for in his face, she found it. Her shoulders relaxed, and her stance eased. "Walk me through it."

"I caught a scent. And I—"

"A scent?" Mac's eyebrows crawled to her hairline. "Aksel, we're in the cafeteria; find a better excuse."

"You don't understand."

"Try me."

Aksel pulled off his baseball cap and tossed it on the table, running both hands through his hair and tousling the strands in the human equivalent of a dog shaking away its stress.

"I caught it at drop-off," he started. "And it's been teasing me for days."

"How can a scent tease you?"

"Easily," Cooky interjected. "I caught one a while back, lingerin' near the walk-in." His whiskers twitched at the fridge, and three of his tails flipped burgers on the grill. "Followed it through the galley to the head. Took days before I finally figgered it out. Drove me plum crazy."

"Cooky." Mac closed her eyes and pinched the bridge of her nose. "That was black mold; we had to renovate the entire kitchen."

"Worked out tho, didn't it?"

"Sure fine, but it was *mold*, Cooky. It was detrimental to your health, not teasing you."

"Tomato, tomato," he replied, pronouncing the word the same both times.

Mac rolled her eyes and brought her attention back to Aksel. "So, why did you wolf out?"

"I don't know," he repeated. "It came on so fast; I think I need to talk to Len."

"About a smell."

Aksel pushed from the table and paced the kitchen. Mac let him, keeping her distance to let the caged wolf work it out. If he could pinpoint the source of that scent, if he could identify it, that should be enough to scratch the itch and let him put the whole thing to bed.

"It started at drop-off," he said aloud, "but I caught it at The Porchlight, and at my apartment."

"Your apartment?" Mac fully tensed at that. "Do you think it's—" Her gaze darted to the kitchen door and the cafeteria beyond.

Aksel followed her look and stopped, standing at his full height. "It's not that," he assured her. "The odds of another werewolf targeting Avery are slim to none. They'd have to get past the sentries in the pack first, and even if they managed that, they've got me."

Mac flicked her eyes to him, body taut as a wire.

"It's not the werewolves," he said again, "but I think it might be wolven."

At that, she exhaled. Wolven were known and friendly, compared to last summer's werewolf problem. "Oh well, just that, then."

"I think it's the triplets," he said, finally voicing the thought out loud.

"Jan, Jarl, and ... shit." Mac scratched her head. "What was the third one?"

"Jens."

"God, what a mouthful."

"They're old wolven names, very traditional," he explained. "But I can't figure out why those kids would carry that scent, much less why it would be at a bar."

"A scent you can't place," Mac clarified.

Aksel nodded. "It's like an old memory."

"Could they be from your home pack?" she asked. It was a good idea, one Aksel hadn't considered, and he gave it a moment of thought, dismissing it just as quickly.

"No, it's on the girl, too. Kendra, with the big hoodies. The triplets are wolven, but that girl is all human, and the scent is too ingrained to have been picked up from a foster situation."

"Mm, not a foster." Mac shook her head. "They're quadruplets, not triplets."

Aksel went stock still, Mac's words ringing in his ears. "Come again?"

"Same birthday and everything; you can check their file if you don't believe me. Those four kids were born on the same day to the same mother."

"H-how?" Aksel gaped at her, the world rocking unsteadily beneath his feet. "She's not wolven."

"Then you probably scared the hell out of her, Aksel."

"But ... *how*."

"Hell if I know, man." Mac threw her hands up and spun for the door. "Ask their mom. I'm meeting with her later this week. But until then, you need to get a hold of yourself and whatever this half-shifting nonsense is."

"Why?"

She twisted at the waist and narrowed her eyes at him. "Do I *really* need to clarify the why?"

"No, not that. Why are you meeting with their mom?"

"Oh." Mac waved her hand in the air. "Some new partnership we're chasing with an outreach group in Charleston. It's a great opportunity, but it means more eyes are on us now than ever. I can't have any of the weekly kids going home on Saturday and telling their parents about teachers who can't control their shifting. Got it?"

Mac hit him with her Camp Director stare until Aksel slumped against the counter.

"Sorry, Mac. I'll—"

"Hang out back here, cool off. Your next class is, what, Field Formations at three?" Aksel nodded, and Mac sighed. "Go for a run if you need to. I'll tell the kids ... something. Clarify that you're wolven, and not a werewolf."

With that parting blow, Mac left. He knew she hadn't intended her last words as an insult. Still, after last summer, the camp had to launch a whole educational campaign clarifying the differences between werewolves and wolven.

In Aksel's mind, the differences were obvious. For starters, they weren't even the same species. A werewolf was beholden to the moon and, though some were born, could also be made with a bite. Wolven, on the other hand, were able to slip from one skin to another, shifting from human to wolf and back in the span of a few heartbeats. They were in tune with their wolves, which was a magic all its own. But for human parents reading the newspapers and hearing the story from their kids, he understood how the lines could blur.

Mac was right; all eyes were on them. With the expansion of the grounds, the nonsense with that werewolf, and the faun moving into the woods around the camp, they needed this summer to run smoothly. Everyone, from the most seasoned employee to the newest counselor, needed to be committed to the Elkwater cause.

And they were. That was the magic of this place.

Elkwater got into your bones. It tickled your nose like a scent you couldn't escape, and new moon, hadn't Aksel tried.

He had sworn off the camp following his first summer in college. After a week hunting high and low for Jess, he'd finally had to admit to himself that she wasn't coming. That she had broken yet another promise.

It didn't stop him from waiting at the arch at the start of the next week, searching every arriving face for hers.

Or the week after.

Or the next fourteen. Waiting at the arch. Sitting in his shifted form in the grass and, finally, hiding under the porch of the director's cabin.

Sixteen weeks of watching and waiting like a lovesick puppy for a woman who never came. And here he was, twelve years later, working every summer at Elkwater and waiting, though for *what* Aksel no longer knew.

8

JESS

MUSIC FROM A SMALL dance studio followed Jess down the road, away from the bustling main street of Elkins. Leftovers in hand, she slowed her walk, enjoying the warm night and the chirping of crickets harmonizing with the faint strains of Britney Spears. It felt good to stretch her legs and enjoy the fresh air after a day spent playing catch-up.

The internet was reliable as promised, and Jessica lost herself in monthly accruals and credit reconciliations, only looking up from her laptop when her stomach cramped and grumbled. So, in a rare treat, she took herself to dinner, carefully avoiding The Porchlight as she walked to and from the Italian restaurant she had noticed downtown.

Now, as she came alongside the townhouse, Jessica eyed the modem box, again judging the distance from her bathroom window. Maybe it was the optimism of the day and the week ahead—functional internet, getting ahead of her monthly close tasks, the meeting with the camp director—or maybe it was the glass of wine she had indulged in over dinner, but if she squinted and cocked her head, she thought the cable she bought in Morgantown might be long enough.

Pleased, she swung her leftovers bag as she walked around the front of the building, stopping short at the sight of a massive wolf at the door. As silently as possible, Jessica retreated around the side of the building, pressing her back against the wall and holding her breath. When the wolf did not come rushing after her, she peered around the corner.

Massive paws stepped lightly on the porch, a long fuzzy snout sniffing Cricket and Avery's door. The door knob. Nearly twice the size of the wolves at the zoo, it rose onto hind legs, paws braced against the frame, and sniffed a path around the top of the door.

Then, it traipsed off the porch and sat facing the building, cocking its head like it was studying the door leading to Jessica's rental.

She pressed a hand to her mouth, studying the wolf, no, the wolven. Only wolven were this *large*, and even in the low light, the markings on its fur struck her as familiar. It had been thirteen years since she'd seen them, but she had read and studied and asked enough wolven to know that their markings were hereditary.

Her boys wore that same crest of woody brown on their shoulders, and their tails bore the same snow white tuft at their tips.

She pressed against the wall, scrunching her eyes closed as her heart thundered. This was always a possibility, nearly a certainty. Elkins was small, and she'd already seen him at the bar. It was only a matter of time before he caught her scent.

Would he even remember it after all this time?

They used to make it a game. Jessica would hide, and he would seek her in the camp, often finding her beneath the bleachers, in the woods, or in an empty practice room. She had thought it romantic, then, how he could pick her out of a crowd with his eyes closed. Now, it made her feel sick.

If he saw her, they would talk and he would ask her what had happened and why she hadn't come back to the camp as they had agreed. And she would ask him where the hell he had been. She would demand to know why he stopped writing, why he left her alone to raise their—

A wind kicked up, and Jessica held her breath. It teased her cheek, dragging her hair away from the building and the wolf.

Downwind.

Jessica exhaled, sagging against the clapboard, ears straining for any sound. He had to leave eventually. Or maybe he wouldn't. Maybe she'd have to sleep out here, curled up with her leftovers.

Minutes passed, and a door slammed, rattling the windows in their panes. Jessica glanced at her watch and stifled a smile. Ten-thirty, on the nose. She peered around the building—no wolf, no gleaming eyes in the woods. A lamp flicked on in the downstairs apartment, casting a triangle of light across the yard to the driveway, reflecting off Jessica's windshield.

The neighbor came home, she thought. *Must have scared him off.* She tiptoed along the side of the building and unlocked her door, easing it shut and creeping up the stairs as quietly as she could.

Only when she lay in her bed, staring at the ceiling, did she realize there were no headlights to announce her neighbor's approach. No crunch of gravel as they walked up to the apartment. That the only car in the driveway was hers.

⁂

"Just shove it under the door when you're done." Cricket dropped the key in Jessica's hand. "Or give it to the neighbor if he's around. We're at the camp tonight, so won't be home 'til tomorrow."

"Oh, alright." She waved at the faun, who smiled and scampered across the lawn, hopping into Avery's Forester. The little car was barely out of sight before she ran up the stairs, grabbed the cable, and plugged it into her laptop on the kitchen counter.

Stretching it along the wall, she fed it through the crack between the open bathroom door and the frame, stringing it across the back of the sink.

Too short.

"Noo," she groaned and glanced out the window, back into the apartment. Then got to work moving the couch and shoving an end table into a corner, not caring if the cable was more of a clothesline as it stretched across the apartment, through the crack between the door and frame, across the back of the sink, to the toilet.

So she moved the end table by the bathroom door, set her laptop on the surface, and pulled it through the crack in the door, running it along the back of the sink, across the toilet, and out the window ... where it dangled uselessly halfway down the wall.

"Fuck!" Jessica clapped her hands over her mouth, listening as hard as she could. It was barely seven in the morning, and while Cricket and Avery left around six-thirty each day, she never heard the downstairs neighbor until closer to eight.

Nothing.

Jessica exhaled, taking a moment to calm and center herself. The cable wasn't long enough to connect her laptop to the modem and router, unless she was resigned to working in the bathroom. She eyed the toilet and contemplated the cushions on the couch and kitchen chairs. It could work, and it was only a few hours a day.

Dial in, check her email, save her reports locally, and then move to a more comfortable place to do her actual work, such as the kitchen counter where the funny little disc hung on the wall.

It wasn't the worst plan, and Jessica wasn't above admitting that she was desperate for this to work, for reasons beyond wanting to avoid a drive back to Morgantown.

"Okay." She puffed her cheeks on an exhale. "One more try."

Laptop: on the back of the toilet. Cable: dangling out the window. Jessica: running down the stairs with the key.

Sweating and panting, she unlocked the modem box, revealing the router, modem, and several cables that fed into a hole in the wall. She stretched onto her tiptoes, fingertips brushing the end of the Ethernet cable. Grabbing it, she pulled it towards the router, and it stopped three inches shy.

"Come *on*." Jessica tugged again. And again, gaining half an inch. "What is your problem?"

There was some slack, so she tugged again, this time catching the faint groan of bending metal. Releasing the cable, she backed up, eyeing the neighbor's window and the Ethernet cable tangled in an antenna barely visible over the eave.

She considered that and scanned the side of the house. The windowsill looked about six feet off the ground, thanks to Victorian architecture and the cellar below. If she stood on the sill and rose on her tiptoes ...

Without giving too much thought to it, Jessica hauled a metal trash can under the window and climbed up. The can wobbled as she raised a foot to the windowsill. The angle was awkward, and the sill higher than she'd assumed, forcing her to jump to bring her other foot up. Metal clanged and rattled, and the can toppled over, rolling across the lawn as Jessica grabbed the roofline.

"Of course." She dropped her head, taking a steadying breath before reassessing the eaves and antenna. "Finish the job." She toed along the windowsill. "Figure the rest out later."

Which was basically how she'd lived her life up until this point.

Get pregnant? Finish the job and figure the rest out later.

Have three pups and a baby girl? Raise the babies and figure the rest out later.

Bachelor's degree? Same. Managing the books as a junior accountant in her dad's practice? Take a wild guess.

Jessica had managed every pit and windfall that had come her way; she could handle this.

What was being stranded on a windowsill to a woman who had become wildly adept at improvisation over the years?

She eased along the edge, rising onto her tiptoes to grab the Ethernet cable. And then she gave it a good, hard tug, and another, to untangle it from the antenna. Metal groaned, threatening to snap, and with a loud *twang*, the cable released.

"Yes!" Jessica eased back along the windowsill, cable in hand, and, when she was directly over the modem box, she dropped it. The plastic end clacked against the waterproof cabinet, and she pumped her fist. "Success."

Glancing again at the ground, Jessica called on vague memories of fire safety training and the best way to escape the second floor of a burning building. She began to lower herself, and the window slid open.

"Can I help you?"

The low, rumbly voice made her freeze, her heart skipping about five beats.

"Um..."

"Um?" the downstairs neighbor asked.

Jessica shut her eyes tight enough that bright colors exploded behind her lids. It couldn't be. It was a coincidence. A cousin. Another man—male. She was tired and confused, and now she was nervous on top of everything else. An uneasy dizziness made her head swim, and her arms began to shake. "Sorry, I'm just ... the trashcans."

"Trashcans?" The voice rose in pitch, sounding strained.

"They fell over," she explained. "I can't get down."

"Do you need help?"

"No, I just–if you could put the trashcan back under the window, I can manage it."

A long, quiet moment followed, and the neighbor sighed, his heavy exhale teasing Jessica's shins. "Hold on a second."

Minutes passed before his front door slammed, rattling the glass in the window pane. Footsteps crunched over gravel, stopping beneath Jessica. She closed her eyes, focusing on breathing and holding onto the roofline.

"Doing alright?"

"I'm stuck on the side of a Victorian. Do I look like I'm doing alright?"

That earned a chuckle, and the sound did something funny to her belly. Lord, this couldn't be happening. Just let her get off this dumb windowsill so she could die of embarrassment in peace.

His footsteps disappeared behind the building and stayed gone. Jessica risked opening her eyes, scanning the empty yard, and straining to hear any sound from her neighbor.

Nothing.

She swallowed the nervous lump in her throat, too bewildered that he'd left her there to be mad, and glanced down.

Good lord, had the ground gotten *further* away?

Her belly swooped, and she tore her face to the sky, eyes clenched shut. "Bad idea."

"Alright?" he called over the rattle of metal from somewhere behind the house.

"You get one more stupid question," Jessica yelled back. She tucked her chin, breathing in slowly and counting on the exhale to take her mind off the slick sweat coating her palms and the butterflies in her belly, flinching when metal slammed against the wall. "Oh, Lord."

"Can you reach the ladder?"

Jessica opened one eye, spying the topmost rung of the aluminum ladder he'd dropped beside the window. She reached for it, her legs quaked, and she immediately slapped her hand against the roofline, gripping tight.

What the hell was wrong with her? Heights hadn't bothered her for *years*, and this was only six feet! She should be able to lower herself down. Instead, her arms felt like jelly, and her legs were apparently made of rubber bands. She was hot and cold at the same time, and the more he talked, the more she was convinced this whole experience was an actual nightmare.

"I can't," she whimpered.

"One step at a time," he said, his voice gentle and low. "Just ease over. I'll keep the ladder steady." When she didn't move, he grunted. "Don't you trust me?"

"I don't *know* you," Jessica retorted. She regretted the words the moment they were out. Offending the only person offering to help her get down was hardly a smart move.

That was it. No other reason.

He cleared his throat, lightly jostling the ladder. "Do you want to get down or not?"

"Yes."

"Then what's the hold-up?" He drummed his fingers on a rung.

"I'm apparently afraid of heights." Jessica tightened her grip, pulling herself closer to the window. "Even small ones."

"It's no taller than me."

"That's not helping."

He snorted. "Well, we've got to get you down somehow." The ladder creaked as he climbed up. "I'm going to grab your leg and steady you. Is that okay?"

Jessica nodded, biting her tongue. A broad, warm palm wrapped around her ankle, and goosebumps rushed up the limb, her skin singing from the contact.

It had been years since anyone other than her kids touched her. Too long, if this is how her body responded to a man bracing her bare ankle, how *scandalous*.

"Inch over," he instructed.

She did, focusing on the warmth of his hand and the placement of her feet. Her fingers ached from gripping the roofline, and sweat broke out along her back. The ladder groaned, and the press of his palm shifted, sliding up her leg to brace her knee. Jessica almost cursed herself for wearing capris instead of a skirt, and stilled as the inanity of that thought struck home.

"Is it alright if I grab you?"

At that, her heart did a gold medal-worthy flip. She nodded, eyes again cinched tight.

"Jess?"

"Yeah," she rasped, unable to fill her lungs. What was *happening* to her? "Yes."

He let go of her leg, and in the absence of his touch, it clicked.

He called her *Jess*.

Her eyes flew open. She whipped her head to the side. "Wait, how did you—" And froze.

There he was.

Aksel Haralson, thirteen years older and better for it, gazing at her with the same intensity as he had all those summers ago. An edge of worry tugged the corners of his mouth—a mouth that was just as plush and kissable as it had been in their youth.

"Oh. Lord." Shock seized her. She released the roofline, tipping back with her heart rushing into her throat. Aksel caught her; of course, he caught her, slinging Jessica over his shoulder in a fireman's carry and rushing down the ladder.

He set her down, hands firmly on her waist, as Jessica regained her balance. His eyes, warm eyes like liquid amber, scanned her face. "Are you alright?"

"Are you?" she asked.

"I—" Aksel straightened, blinked once, and kissed her. It was like stepping into an old coat, his mouth fitting over hers like it was tailor-made. She gripped his shoulders, pulling him in and parting her lips.

At the testing press of his tongue, at the slightest taste of him like an ingredient she'd been missing for years, Jessica broke through the surface of the haze that had settled over her at his presence. She broke free from the kiss, pushed herself away, and smacked him.

9

— · —

AKSEL

WHAT THE HELLS WAS that.

Thirteen years. Thirteen *years,* and he kisses her the moment he sees her? *WHAT.* Who does that?

Aksel, apparently. And what did Jess do? Ran off, and rightfully so. But not before slapping him and, honestly? He deserved it. Who went around randomly kissing women in distress? Much less their *ex-girlfriend* from summer camp?

He had tried to keep it together, but new moon, he'd been falling apart from the moment he saw her in the window. What the hells was she thinking, climbing the side of the house? And then he had to go and open the window, getting a nose-full of *her.* Obviously, he'd asked if she needed help. He couldn't leave her stranded there, but did he have to go and grab her leg? Her waist?

The minute, the instant Aksel touched her, it was like he'd caught fire. His heart had damn near stopped when she tipped back, and it pounded out of control as he grabbed her and

81

rushed her to the ground. The need to protect, to ensure she was safe, the need *to have* had been overwhelming. It was still overwhelming.

Where was that desire with Beth, Sandra, or any of the wolven he'd tried to date? Gone. Absent. Nonexistent. Yet he took one look at Jess, and thirteen years of pent-up sexual desire came roaring to the forefront.

Even now, pacing the yard in front of her closed and locked door, Aksel fought the urge to shift and barrel it down, caught between desire and the maddening need to take, protect, claim.

What the hells is happening to me?

She ran off. Of course, she ran off, wriggling out of his arms, slapping him with all the force she could muster, and then she ran to her apartment and slammed the door. The deadbolt thudding into place had been a punch to the heart, the scent of her panic and fright overwhelming, even in his human form.

At least now he knew he wasn't crazy. That tease in the air haunting him for the last few days; it had been *her*. Jessica.

Jess.

Her, but not her, different in a way he couldn't place, and Jess, all the same, marking Avery and Cricket's apartment and the door to the rental unit upstairs. Her scent at the camp. On the kids.

Those kids.

Aksel stopped his pacing and shook from shoulders to toes.

They were *her* kids. The underlying scent was nearly identical. Jess and not-Jess.

A growl built in his throat, his gums prickling as his teeth descended, the wolf clawing to the surface, rabid at the thought of another mating *his* Jess.

Aksel clenched his fists, taking deep breaths to calm himself and stop the shift. He needed to gain control. First at the camp, and now at her door? He was no better than a pup, letting his emotions and hormones get the best of him. Little by little, the wolf eased away, though the threat of his other nature simmered uneasily beneath the surface. When he felt he had himself leashed enough to speak, Aksel knocked on the door.

Nothing.

He listened, catching the low murmur of a voice on the other side.

"Jess?"

The murmuring stopped.

"Go away," her muffled voice came through the door.

"I want to apologize. I don't know what came over me." Which was true, but would she believe him? "Please, Jess, I'm sorry. I know it's been forever, and that's hardly a way to say hello after thirteen—"

The door flew open, and a red-eyed, furious Jess glared at him, her tan cheeks darkened by an angry flush. "Hardly a way to say 'hello'? You never even said *goodbye.*"

"I—what?"

"I wrote you." Her voice broke. She pressed the back of her hand to her mouth, wide, watery eyes glaring at him. "Letter after letter after letter, and you never—"

"Well, you never showed up."

Jess straightened, her face falling utterly still. "Excuse me?"

"At the expo game," he said. "Against WVU." Gods, why was he still talking? It was dumb, he knew it was dumb, but now that she was here, right in front of him and laying the blame at his feet, he couldn't stop. "I went, where were you? I waited for you at the student center, just like we agreed in letter after letter, and you never showed up."

The color bled from her cheeks, and Jess pressed a hand to her stomach. "That's what you're mad about?" Her voice was small, weak, and Aksel hated it. He wanted her laughing and smiling. Not ... broken. "You're upset because I never showed up to that stupid expo game after I—and you—the moment I knew, I tried to call you. I *wrote* you, and you never wrote back."

The door slammed, rattling the windows, and Jess's feet pounded up the stairs.

Aksel stood there for a moment, running those last words through his mind. She wrote him? When? And the moment she knew *what?*

They had promised to meet at the game. Aksel had waited for hours, and she never showed. The letters stopped, and thirteen years had passed.

"Ugh." He sat heavily on the stoop and scrubbed his hands over his face. "Why the fuck did you *kiss her*."

"Kiss who?" Gitta called out. Aksel burst to his feet, halfway down the stairs before he realized he was snarling. She backed up, raising her palms. Though it was early, barely eight, Gitta was fully clothed in jeans, a white V-neck, and Doc Martens. Her eyeliner was smudged, and there was a scent entwined with hers, like crisp air at altitude in the pines. "Whoa, dude, put your teeth away."

He stopped short, shaking his head and clenching his jaw, muttering an apology around a mouthful of fangs.

"Ooo-kaaaay." Gitta raised both her brows and waved her pointed finger at him. "What is this all about?"

"Jess."

"This again?"

"She's upstairs." He hooked a thumb at her door, growling at Gitta when she leaned around him and sniffed.

"Yo." She snapped in his face and held his eye. "Hackles down, Aks. I just came by to drop off your car, not circle your neighbor."

"Sorry," he muttered, then shook off his wolf and tried again. "Sorry— wait, what were you doing at the camp?"

"Almaden called last night." She named the camp nurse with a small smile. "And Mac's been calling you since dawn."

"Why?" He checked his watch. "I don't have any classes until ten."

"Dunno." Gitta shrugged and strode around him, climbing the steps and nearing Jess's door. "Came to get me when you didn't answer."

"I never heard the phone ring. Just Jess messing with the … modem box." He dropped his head back with a groan. "I bet she unplugged my phone."

"Well, from Mac, through me, to you: if you're going to run off all feral, at least answer your phone." She tossed him his keys and faced Jess's door again, glancing back at Aksel with an eyebrow cocked in question. When he didn't growl, or rather, when he mentally beat his wolf into submission and suppressed the rising growl, she stepped closer and sniffed.

"Huh." She sniffed again and leaned back, scanning the front of the building and landing on Avery and Cricket's door. "It's there too."

"Yeah."

"Smells just like at the bar." Gitta scratched her cheek, eyes narrowed in thought. "And familiar. What *is* that? It's in the camp, too."

"She has kids," Aksel blurted, winning a genuine look of surprise from Gitta.

"Oh."

Not trusting himself to talk with a straight face, he stalked around the townhouse. Gitta followed, hovering behind him as he fiddled with the modem box. The phone line Jess had been messing with dangled beside the box. He followed it up to her window, which was cracked open a few inches, then back down again to the jacks. "Triplets. Or quadruplets, but I can't figure out how."

"Well, when a human and another human love each other very much—"

"They're wolven."

Gitta's jaw clacked shut.

"At least, the boys are." A quick look at the map inside the door told him which jack was hers, and he plugged it in before fiddling with the rest of the cables. Most of them fed into a pipe embedded in the wall, pulled through to their destination with a long, snaking tool one of the renovation crew had rigged together. Cricket liked to drink her cousin's home-distilled acorn whisky and pull it out to challenge Aksel to jousting tournaments. "The girl is human."

"Oh," Gitta repeated. "Well."

Tugging on the cables feeding into the pipe, Aksel felt for the tag identifying his phone line and followed it to the appropriate jack. Sure enough, it had been pulled slightly free.

He pressed it back into place, and the phone in his apartment immediately began to ring.

"Better get that," Gitta advised. He shot her a look before stalking inside and grabbing his phone from the cradle.

"Yeah?"

"You coming in to work today?" Mac asked. Aksel winced at the bite in her words.

"I was planning to."

"Are you under control?"

"His ex-girlfriend has kids at the camp this summer," Gitta damn near hollered into the phone. Aksel glared at her, curling his lip to show her a sharp canine, and she grinned, winking at him.

"I see," Mac said. "Is this related to the cafeteria incident?"

"I..." Aksel sighed and rolled his eyes skyward. How to explain what this was when he didn't even understand it himself? "I think so? I don't know."

"Can't have you around the kids, bud," Mac said. "Take the morning, get yourself together, alright?"

"I've got formations at ten."

"And you beat all that knowledge into my head when you were my drum major at Ohio State," she replied. "I can cover your morning class, but I have a meeting with an outreach rep this afternoon. Think you can handle advanced orchestra, or do I need to reschedule?"

"No!" he said, too quickly. Too loud. Gitta grimaced and pressed her hand palm-side-down in the air in a gesture for him to tone it down. "Don't reschedule," he said in a more normal voice. "I'll be there."

He had to be there because if he had to sit in his apartment beneath Jess all day he was going to go feral.

"Alright, see you then."

Mac hung up, and Aksel gripped the phone, eyes unfocused.

"Sooo." Gitta took the phone from his hand and hung it up. "What happened in the cafeteria?"

"I caught her scent on the kids and started wolfing out," he replied in a monotone.

"Oh. Shit. We need to get you to Dad."

"No." Aksel snapped into focus; attention leveled on his foster sister. "Lennart doesn't need to know."

"Come on, man. Wolfing out in front of the kids? Without warning? It's not like you to lose control like that, and when have you *ever* lost it over a smell?"

"It's nothing. A girl I once knew is living upstairs, and her kids are my campers. Not a big deal, I just need a second to sit with it."

"Aksel—"

"I'm fine, Gitta." He wide-stepped around her, pulling his shirt over his head. "Let's just ... let's go for a run. Sweat it out on the ridge."

"Don't you think we should—"

Aksel shifted abruptly, nipping at her ankles and darting out the door. She would follow. Gitta always followed. It was instinctual. As much a part of her as her hair and nails. Daughter of the Alpha, Gitta was firmly pack.

A moment later, his ears pricked at the sound of her footfalls behind him. Together, they eased into a steady, speedy pace, cutting across yards and sprinting over a fishing bridge crossing the Tygart Valley River. He led her down a deer path and through Glendale Park, aiming for the trails winding up Rich Mountain.

The run gave him the space and silence he needed, allowing Aksel to think.

So Jess was in town, so what? Thousands of people came to town throughout the summer; it was only a matter of time before she returned to Elkins with a family.

And why shouldn't she have a family? Thirteen years was plenty of time to meet someone else, have a relationship and sex, and get married. Maybe there was a wolven back home ... where was it? Charleston. That was it, Charleston. Maybe there was a wolven pup she'd already known, and Aksel was a bit of fun for the summer. A way to blow off steam and feed hormones.

The thought made him sick, and even as his mind rejected the idea, Aksel pressed into his run, bounding over a creek.

Gitta yipped, landing next to him in a tumble of paws and fur, and Aksel playfully snapped his teeth at her before bunching low. In a powerful push, he launched off a boulder onto the drudge above, outrunning his foster sister and his worries all at once.

10

— · —

JESS

MIDDAY SUN BEAT DOWN on the dirt and gravel lot, raising heat snakes and choking the air with soup-thick humidity. Muted brass and the dull rapport of a drumline traveled from the field, lending a nostalgic, dreamlike quality to the camp.

Jessica adjusted her sunglasses, squinting at the Elkwater sign. Her nerves hadn't settled since that morning, and driving to the camp only made them worse. Aksel had left around noon, that much she knew. The slamming of his door rattled her windows, and while she hated to admit it, Jessica watched him walk to his car, which had appeared at some point, in his camp polo and drive off.

An hour later, she'd done the same.

He was here, and Jessica was here. Why was she nervous? She had been invited as a member of the Charleston Human-Inhuman community and representative of the outreach program. Their poster mom for years until she worked her way into the role of Outreach Coordinator.

She had every right to be here.

Shaking off her nerves, Jessica started across the mostly empty parking lot. Two dozen or so cars with college stickers clustered near the main entrance, counselors, instructors, and employees, she assumed. Jessica had parked away from them, at the far end of the lot. It felt appropriate. She didn't belong here. Not really.

The Director's Cabin sat at the far end of the parking lot, a two-story log cabin-style structure with a green tin awning over the wrap-around porch. Two rocking chairs angled to face each other flanked a small end table, and a well-used boot scraper had been bolted just beside the door.

Jessica knocked and straightened her blouse, smoothing the wrinkles from her dress pants. The door opened a moment later, and a faun with a halo of chestnut brown curls wilder than Jessica's smiled at her. Unlike Cricket, who was whip thin and held a gangly youthfulness, this faun was thicker around the middle and hips, with soft arms and a sweet face.

"You must be Mrs. Babcock," the faun greeted, extending a long-fingered hand. "I am Ramble, Mac's spouse."

"Hi." Jessica took their hand, silently thanking Svana for her crash course in inhuman adoptions of human pronouns and terms. Where Cricket had been referred to and introduced as Avery's girlfriend, Ramble introduced themself as a spouse, rather than a husband or a wife, meaning they preferred to be referred to as they/them. "It's nice to meet you, and please, call me Jessica. I'm not married, and Mrs. Babcock is my mother."

"You got it." Ramble winked and held the door open wider. Just like Cricket, their smile revealed a split in their upper lip, and blocky, flat teeth. "Come on in, one of our instructors had a bit of an issue, and Mac is covering his class. She should be here shortly."

"Nothing terrible, I hope." Jessica stepped inside, immediately struck by the homey, woodsy environment. Although it was summer, the interior of the cabin still held the faint scent of woodsmoke and pine. A woven rug filled the entry hall, and woodland scenes decorated the walls. Jessica recognized a few of the landscapes—a professional photograph of the Blue Ridge Parkway in fall, Snowshoe blanketed in the white quilt of winter, and a thirty-foot cascade of water down the quartz face of a rock wall.

Her cheeks heated, and she looked away.

"Oh, no," Ramble answered. "He just had to attend to some, um, inhuman things."

She did not miss the question in Ramble's glance, and Jessica put on what she hoped was an easy smile. "I know how that is. The school is constantly calling me about one of my boys shifting in P.E. Each of them swears it was an accident, but, well, you work here and I went here." She shrugged and shook her head. "You know how it is when they hit puberty."

Ramble stared at her, lips parted and ears twitching beneath their curls. Jessica pulled her lips between her teeth, afraid she had misstepped, and then they bleated a laugh.

"I forgot! Yours are the wolven boys, yes? And your daughter is ... Kendra?"

"Yeah." Jessica nodded weakly, her stomach sinking. It typically was not a good thing when an adult knew her children's names only a few days into school. Or camp.

"Oh, you look worried." Ramble lightly touched her elbow. "Do not be, they are fitting right in. We are excited they are staying for the summer. It is nice when we get a batch of kids who stay for longer than a few days. I know Mac loves getting to know them better. I like to think she has instilled that level of care in all of us." They smiled and gestured to an open door just off the entry hall. "Have a seat, I will radio for Mac. Would you like a coffee? Tea?"

"A water?" Jessica asked, stepping into a well-used office. Papers cluttered the desk and filled one of the two chairs facing it, and the walls were covered in framed photographs spanning multiple decades. "Please."

"Of course."

Ramble tapped a photograph hanging beside the door and left Jessica alone with Elkwater's past. She set her bag on the one empty chair and approached the photograph, taking in the girl the faun had tapped.

She vaguely remembered Mackenzie Murray as a teen.

As "daughters of West Virginia," they had both been dragged to boring brunches and high teas hosted by their mothers. Two years younger than Jessica, her thick hair was cropped short and swept back from her face in the picture on the wall, but Jessica's attention strayed to the counselor sitting beside her with a tambourine in hand. Young, fresh-faced, and bright-eyed, the braids her mother had let her wear that summer were pulled back with a scrunchie, and her eyes were on the counselor sitting across the fire.

Sweet-faced, soft around the edges, and grinning right back at her.

An itch built behind her eyes, and Jessica spun away, following the years through the other photographs on the wall. The camp grew—there was a groundbreaking ceremony for the concert hall, a picture of college-aged humans and inhumans with shovels clearing a trail—and so did the subjects. Mackenzie reappeared, gripping a clipboard and wearing a staff polo. And again, on the amphitheater stage, playing her saxophone while campers and a younger Ramble beamed at her from the front row.

Jessica glanced at the desk and the one photograph there—Ramble again, wearing a flower crown and a cream-colored bodice and breeches, and Mackenzie "Mac" Murray in a fitted, pale blue tuxedo and bowtie. They held hands, smiling adoringly at each other beneath an oak tree in full spring bloom.

The intimacy in their shared look came across through the photograph, and Jessica pulled her eyes to the pictures on the wall, fighting off a prickle of tears as she immediately landed on a photo of a marching band. Boys and girls, naga, wolven, gnomes, and sasquatch clustered around their instructor.

He must have been twenty, maybe twenty-two, standing tall with a sturdy broadness just revealing itself from the softness of youth. Jessica glanced back at the campfire photo, at herself, so innocent and happy in that final summer, and then back to Aksel and his band. Aksel with a conductor's wand in the orchestra room. Aksel grinning at someone off-camera as he polished a trombone. Aksel with a cluster of students on a field podium.

Once she began picking him out of the pictures, she couldn't stop. He gained height and muscle; his arms thickened, a beard appeared at a campfire, and vanished in a candid taken in the cafeteria.

She rubbed a knuckle against her breastbone, an unfamiliar tightness seizing her throat as she watched the boy she knew grow into a man. Broad shoulders and muscles beneath a delicious padding. A sturdiness that made her belly flip. Good lord, she'd felt that sturdiness just this morning. The strength in his arms, the ease with which he had carried her down the ladder. How broadly he had filled her door. All that brawn, all that size, and he'd kissed her like—

"Jessica, hi!" The door crashed lightly against the wall, and Mac rushed in. She set a glass of water down on the edge of the desk closest to the guest chairs. "Sorry I'm late; someone always needs me around here."

"No—" Jessica cleared her throat, pinching the front of her fully buttoned blouse in an attempt to will the flush away. *Get it together, woman.* "No problem, I was just looking at the wall."

"Great, isn't it?" Mac smiled and hurried behind the desk, pulling off her baseball cap and tousling her hair—the same thick mop, though more grown out on the sides than in the campfire picture. She eased into her rolling chair with a quiet groan, then stopped herself and shot Jessica a guilty look. "Please, sit. I know I need to."

She did, crossing one leg over the other and forcing herself to sit up straight. "It sounds like it's been a busy day; we can reschedule if you need to."

"Oh, no." Mac waved her off. "Just the normal fun of running a summer camp, you remember how it is. Don't get me wrong, it's nice to get back out there, but also reminds me that I should leave teen instruction to the professionals."

"Aren't you the camp director?"

"Yes, exactly." A broad grin wrinkled her cheek. "I know better than to stray out of my lane. Mostly because my spouse yells at me whenever I do." The radio on Mac's belt chirped, and she unclipped it, twisting the knob and dropping it on the desk. "Speaking of, better stay focused. That thing will start squawking as soon as the session bell rings." Easing back in her chair, Mac's demeanor shifted from the easy-going camp director to a businesswoman in a blink. "You're here to talk about a partnership with" —she glanced at a notepad on her desk—"the Charleston Inhuman Outreach, right?"

"Right." Jessica uncrossed her legs and sat forward in her chair. "We're a newer organization, and we have only been formally organized for about six years, but we began our efforts about twelve years ago." Once she started speaking, sharing the history of the Outreach, and letting her passion seep into the words, the last of her nerves vanished. Mac nodded, easing forward in her chair until her elbows rested on the edge of the desk, her hazel eye wide and attentive.

Jessica told her of the efforts they had made in the Charleston area, the fundraisers and after school programs, the integrated city programs the Outreach had spearheaded, and closed with, "I know we're a younger group, but the more inhumans have made themselves known to the broader world, the more I think we need to heighten our efforts and build a broader community."

"And why here?" Mac asked.

Jessica straightened, surprised by the question. Was there an angle to this? An ulterior motive? Mac had just renovated the camp; perhaps she was only interested in programs that could offer more from a partnership. Clout or exposure. All the Charleston Inhuman Outreach program could offer was a footprint in the state capitol.

Svana's email floated into her mind, and the advice she had given: *You went to Elkwater, and you know their mission better than anyone. Think of what this will mean for inhuman kids across the state.*

"Because it's Elkwater." She pointed to the photograph of the campfire. Mac twisted around, staring at the photograph. "*The* Camp Cryptid. Where else is there?"

A small smile softened Mac's face. "You mailed that picture out a week after camp ended."

"You kept it."

Mac swiveled around, her smile turning mischievous. "Did you know you're the reason we teach life sciences?"

Jessica's stomach plummeted, the blood rushing from her cheeks in a fell swoop. A long, tension-fraught moment passed before Mac widened her eyes and slapped her hand over her mouth.

"Oh, my God, I am so sorry," she finally said.

"No need." Jessica pressed her hand to a flaming cheek, gripping her knee in an attempt to stay calm. "But I suppose that means you understand why Elkwater."

"I do, yeah." Mac lowered her hands and turned the wedding portrait to face Jessica. "I really, really do." She grabbed a notepad and a pen and pulled her chair closer to the desk. "What sort of a partnership did you have in mind?"

11

AKSEL

THREE WOLVEN PUPS BARRELED into the breezeway, tripping over each other's tails and tumbling in the dirt to avoid colliding with Aksel. He hopped out of the way, pressing as flat as his bulk would allow against the wall of the orchestra building to give them room to pass by. One of them, Jens, he thought, yipped his thanks, trotting after his brothers. Kendra rounded the corner a second later, hugging three backpacks to her chest and wearing an expression of long-standing annoyance.

"Need help with those?" He gestured to the armload.

Kendra stared at him, her gaze fierce and back straight. She tightened her arms around the backpacks. "No."

"O-kay."

"Where were you?"

Aksel cocked his head, taken aback by the challenge in her tone. "One more time?"

"Earlier, during field lessons." Kendra rolled her shoulders, unable to hide a tiny wince of discomfort from holding all

100

those bags. "Director Murray ran our class. And you weren't at lunch."

At that, he narrowed his eyes. Kendra narrowed hers and held his gaze.

Interesting.

"I had something I needed to do," Aksel said. At the end of the breezeway, the trio toppled out onto the grass, wrestling and nipping each other's tails and legs. One of them yelped, and Kendra whirled around, all of that intent focus switching to her brothers on a dime.

"Jarl, Jens, Jan," she barked their names. All three froze, ears pricked toward their sister. She stormed over and tossed a bag at each of them.

"Cut it out and get changed."

As one, they lowered their heads and slunk over, taking up the bags in their mouths and trotting away.

"Impressive." Aksel followed her out of the breezeway. Kendra glared at him over her shoulder.

Her hair was twisted into two thick braids today, and for once, she had foregone the oversized sweatshirt, opting for gym shorts and an Elkwater t-shirt with the sleeves cuffed. Aksel was struck by how much she resembled her mother. It wasn't just her height; it was in the sweep of her brow and the cut of her jaw. But there was someone else there. An intensity that Jessica did not possess, and a glow in her eyes that was pure wolven.

"They know to listen to me," she replied. Her gaze drifted past Aksel, and she backstepped. "Mom?"

Mom? Aksel twisted around, backstepping just as Kendra had. Mom.

Jess.

Fifteen feet away and approaching too quickly for him to duck into the breezeway and hide. She had changed since that morning, swapping stretchy capris that were far too tight for him to maintain any focus for a pair of pressed and pleated dress pants and a silk blouse the color of a sunset. Her hair was styled rather than held back by a headband, framing her face in soft, thick curls that had his wolven self clawing for the surface.

"—kept you so long." Mac's voice came into earshot. "Most visitors here on business aren't as interested in the day-to-day of the camp."

"More into numbers?" Jess asked.

"Exactly." Mac nodded. "They want to talk about runways and revenue cycles and investment opportunities. It's nice to show someone around who actually wants to talk about the camp."

Jess smiled, her attention straying from Mac to the path ahead, where Aksel and Kendra stood like deer in headlights. Her face lit up in a smile that punched him directly in the heart. "Hey, honey!"

"H-hey," he replied softly. Jess scrunched her nose at him and cocked her head.

"Oh, my God, not you," Kendra muttered as she walked by. "Hey, Mom." She awkwardly hugged Jess, who smiled knowingly. It was weird enough being a teenager at summer camp for the first time. Aksel assumed the girl was boiling with embarrassment from her mom being here as well.

But then Kendra waved her hand at him. "That's Mr. Haralson, my drum major instructor. He's alright, I guess."

He had barely gotten over the surprise in that statement when Jess smiled. At him this time. "Alright, huh?"

"Yeah." Kendra squirmed out of her mother's hug. "I thought you weren't picking us up until Saturday?"

"I'm not, sweetheart. Just drove down for a meeting with Director Murray." She smiled at Mac, who waved. "Elkwater is interested in working with the Outreach."

Kendra perked up, looking between Mac and her mom. "That's cool."

"I think so."

"Does that mean we can come back next year?"

Jess hid her surprise well, but Aksel caught it all the same. It was in how her smile became closed-lipped, and her brows rose. A mother trying to hide how pleased she was. "That sounds like a—"

"Director—*shit*. I mean, Mac!" Avery hollered as she ran up to them, red hair frizzing behind her. "Oh, God. Campers. Crap. I mean, shoot."

"Jessica." Mac extended an arm to Avery. "This is our Assistant Director, Avery Payne. Avery, this is Jessica Babcock with the Charleston Inhuman Outreach."

"Oh. *Oh.* Hi, yeah, she lives upstairs. Our moms are friends." She grabbed Jess's hand in both of hers, shook it wildly, and let go. "Mac, I'm so sorry. I have to drive down to Flatwoods. I should be back by lights out, but if I'm not, does that throw off our ratio?"

Aksel did a quick mental tally of campers to counselors and staff, coming to the same conclusion Mac had, judging by her sigh. It threw off the ratio of students to adults by one.

"This about your brother?" Mac asked.

Avery nodded, and Aksel walked over, a fierce need to protect driving his step.

The previous summer, Avery and her girlfriend had been targeted by a werewolf, and the incident led to the disturbing revelation that Avery's father, a prominent lobbyist named Nathan Payne, had been forging his daughter's signature to buy up the land around Green Bank. The sales had been brokered by a third-party investment firm out of Atlanta, staffed by werewolves. While no one knew why Lunar Asset Management wanted to involve itself, Aksel knew that werewolves seldom gave their prey up easily.

Avery's reaction to the events and learning the truth about her father was to throw herself into her relationship with Cricket and become deeply involved with the inhuman community in

Elkins. Aksel did not know too many details, only that Avery's mom's family owned the construction company in Pittsburgh that renovated the camp. As a part of that, the Payne family had bought the townhouse where Aksel now lived to serve as a site office.

With it had come the quiet request from Ramble over drinks at The Porchlight, asking Aksel if he would be interested in moving in next door.

"Just to keep an ear on them," they had said.

The decision to move from his tiny studio apartment near the high school to a spacious two-bedroom in downtown Elkins at a steep discount had been a no-brainer. Still, despite the economy of it all, Avery and Cricket were part of Elkwater. Part of what Aksel thought of as his pack. He would have paid the full rate to make sure they were safe from any werewolves still skulking around.

"I need to go bail him out," Avery explained. "*Again.*" At Jess's startled look, she whirled to face her. "He's decided to start protesting mountain-top mining and keeps forgetting what 'No Trespassing' means. I swear, it's nothing awful. Just stupid."

"I get it." Jess nodded.

"Can't you let him stew in the cell for a night?" asked Mac. "It might be good for him."

"That's what I said!" Avery threw her hands up. "But my *mom* disagrees and—"

"She pays your rent," Mac finished with a sigh. "And Cricket's leading the overnight?" Avery nodded. Mac frowned. "It throws us, but I can figure it out. Maybe Almaden can stay for the night. Drive safe and call me when you're back, alright?"

"I can stay," Aksel offered. "Just need to borrow the camp phone and make a call."

Mac exhaled, her shoulders dropping about six inches. "Oh, thank God. You don't mind?"

"Not at all," he assured her. "Lennart knows Elkwater is pack." Though he'd still be pissed that Aksel was canceling an arranged date.

Not that he wanted to go on it anyway.

"Awesome, thanks, man." She gripped his elbow, then whirled on Avery. "Alright, come on. Let's figure out who can cover your evening duties, and I'll print out directions.

"Thank you so much, Mac. I'm so sorry he keeps doing this."

She waved her off and faced Jess. "Thank you so much for today, Jessica." They shook hands, Mac gripping her wrist in a move that Aksel knew she reserved for the people she valued. He raised his eyebrows, glancing between them. "It's not often I get to show someone around who understands what we're doing here. I hope we lived up to your memory of Elkwater."

"More than," Jess assured her. "Sorry to have taken up so much of your day."

"Not at all. I—" The electronic dinner bell cut her off. A frown flickered across Mac's face, and she let go of Jess's hand to rub her temple. "Of course. Dinner."

Jess glanced at Aksel, who explained, "We need to keep a specific ratio of adults to children, and we're one short."

"I thought you were staying?" Was that relief he heard in her voice? Or plain curiosity?

"I am, but Mac has to go do Director Things and Avery's heading out."

"Oh." Jess glanced from Aksel to Avery to Mac. "Do they have to be an employee?"

"...no?" Mac answered.

"Then, I suppose"—Jess glanced at her daughter, who had removed herself from the adults and studied her shoes in a pretense at not listening—"I could stay, until you're freed up again."

"I can't ask that of you," Mac said, though her tone and relieved expression said anything but.

"We'll consider it part of the tour." Jess winked. "You're helping me get a real feel for the camp and how we can be better partners."

"Oh, you're good," Avery said. "My mom would love you."

Jess beamed at her, then called to her daughter, "It won't be too weird if your mom stays for dinner?"

"No," Kendra glumly replied. "But don't expect me to sit with you."

Jess picked at her food, answering his weak probes into her day with as few words as possible. The friendliness she'd shown Mac and Avery frosted as they stood in the buffet line and vanished altogether when they sat at a table in the corner of the cafeteria.

Still, he managed to learn that she'd come to the camp that day as part of an "outreach," and when he'd asked what kept her for half the day, she answered, "Advanced orchestra."

It wasn't until he asked if she still played the oboe, that Jess looked up, and it hit him all at once. Her dilated pupils, the parting of her lips, and a new layer to her scent. Their gazes locked, and a heat built in his belly, thrumming in his veins. He gripped the edge of the bench, hand out of sight and unable to look away.

Ah, Sköll, what is this?

Again, the prickling in his ears and the itch of a shift under his skin, his wolf running so close beneath the surface that he feared even a singular friendly word from Jess would have him sprouting ears and a tail.

She squirmed, and her eyes dropped to Aksel's mouth. He fought the urge to lick his lips, swallowing the growl threatening in his throat. The moment stretched, the awkward tension over hot dogs and mac and cheese ready to snap, and she blinked.

It burst, releasing Aksel from the hold of whatever *that* was, and allowing him to blurt, "I'm sorry."

"What?" Jess sat back, gripping her fork.

"For this morning. Again." He shook his head slowly. "That was out of line, it was inappropriate, Jess. I don't know what came over me, but that doesn't excuse it. I'm sorry."

"It's okay."

"It's not okay," he said, too loudly. The counselors at the next table glanced over, and Aksel hunched into himself, lowering his voice. "It's not okay," he repeated in a whisper. "I haven't seen you in thirteen years. You have kids, and I—" He palmed his face and groaned before saying again, "I'm sorry."

"Aksel." Jess reached across the table, lightly placing her fingers on his arm. Tiny fireworks exploded beneath his skin, lighting up his arm and setting off an odd thrumming in his veins. He clenched his teeth and jerked his arm away, hating the hurt that flashed across her face.

Jess curled her hand into a fist and pulled it into her lap. "I'm sorry."

They stared at each other for a long, heavy moment, Aksel's heart thudding in his chest from that brief touch.

"We can't both keep saying sorry," he finally said.

"Right." Jess nodded. "Yes." A sly grin curled the side of her mouth. "Sorry."

An answering smile bloomed on his face, and Aksel chuckled. Jess joined him with a quiet laugh, almost shy, and a lovely blush darkened her cheeks. Finally, she broke away, returning to her plate, only this time she speared her dinner with the fork and took a hearty bite.

He allowed himself to watch her, to look at her, noting how age had sharpened her cheekbones and drawn lines at her mouth and eyes. She looked tired, he thought, but happy. More comfortable in her skin even now, at the awkwardness of this dinner.

"It's good to see you." He dropped his gaze to his plate, just in case his words sucked all that loveliness away. "I was overwhelmed, I think, when I realized it was you."

"Me too." Jess went still for a breath, then speared her dinner again. "I mean, it's good to see you, too. Sorry."

Aksel whipped his head up, ready to tease her, but the stricken look on Jess's face stopped him.

"Shit." She dropped her head. "Sorry, I'm a mess. This whole summer, I just—"

"The kids?"

She eyed him warily, and Aksel waited. How often had he seen mothers trying to hide their tears at drop-off? Or fathers issuing stern reminders and directives in a last-minute effort to protect their children before leaving them with strangers?

Finally, Jess exhaled and sagged her shoulders, relief easing the strain as she recognized that he understood. "This is the longest we've ever been away from each other," she admitted. "They've had the random sleepover, but never all at once. Lord, look at me."

I am. New moon, I am.

"I couldn't even make it a week before I weaseled myself into dinner in the same cafeteria as them." She swept a hand across her face, and dropped her eyes to her plate, meticulously poking bits of hot dog and macaroni with a focus that told Aksel she was trying hard not to look at him. "And I've planned a whole day of activities for the one night I have them before I drop them back off. A hike to the observation tower, tubing the river, the murder train. They'll probably just complain the whole time and ask to stay at the apartment eating junk food."

He hated it. He wanted those eyes on him, that mouth smiling at him. It was an overwhelming need to have her look at him, talk to him, engage with him, and that had him saying, "It must have been hard."

She went still but did not look up, which allowed him the chance to wince. Of course, it was hard. They were just kids the last time he saw her. Horny eighteen-year-olds with a half-assed plan to see each other again that deflated as easily as a Baked Alaska.

Wait. Do those deflate or melt?

New moon, it was hard to think straight with Jess right in front of him.

"What must have been hard?" she asked without looking up.

"Raising kids. They're what—" He racked his brain. They had campers from 6th grade up to Seniors. "Eleven?"

That earned him a look, but not the one he wanted. He had hoped talking about her kids would earn him some goodwill or grant an opening. Instead, she looked wary and somewhat frightened, like a caged, cornered animal. New moon, he was an asshole, forcing his ex—was she ever even his girlfriend?—to sit and talk to him.

"Twelve." She cleared her throat, gaze drifting over his head. "Thirteen at the end of October."

"Right." That was ... distressing and absolutely math he had no interest in doing right now. He could barely think straight with her looking so, so ... what was that look? Expectant? Annoyed? Whatever it was, he could not think straight, much less consider human-wolven gestational periods and backwards math. He licked his lips, grasping at the first thing to pop into his head. "Have dinner with me."

That brought her attention back to him.

"Aren't we doing that?"

"Not here," he scrambled. "Somewhere quiet and–and—"

"Alone?" Jess circled her fork at the cafeteria, and the noise of Elkwater came rushing back in. Lively chatter and laughter, the scraping of benches across the linoleum, and the clatter of trays and cups. "I would like that."

"Really?" He sat up straighter.

"Of course." She sent him a shy smile. "It will be nice to catch up with the fa—a friend."

Friend.

That word hit him like a punch to the gut.

Friend.

Of course, she'd see him as a friend. What else could he be? They were just kids, and now she was grown. A mother. A woman. *Gods, is she a woman.*

"Aksel?" Jess lightly touched the back of his hand, jerking him from his thoughts.

"Yes!" he said, willing himself not to jerk away. "I mean, yeah, sure."

"Daydreamer." She shook her head with a fond smile. *Daydreamer.* No one had called him that since her, and hearing it again did something funny to his insides. He braced for the itch of a change. For his wolf to rage and snap, but beyond his belly warming, a sense of calm rushed over him. A rightness. How often had she called him that whenever he zoned out with Jess cuddled by his side, content to exist in the moment without any deeper thought than her. Here. Now. "That hasn't changed, at least."

Jess's gaze flitted over him, this time with a hint of appraisal. At that, his wolf rustled and preened, sitting him up taller.

"Tomorrow?" he asked.

"I'd love to." Jess gathered her tray and stood, leaving him with, "I look forward to it, Aksel."

He left the cafeteria feeling inordinately proud, whistling as he walked toward the Director's Cabin to use the phone. Lennart would understand a last-minute cancellation, and Beth was reasonable. New moon, *she'd* been the one to call Aksel's pack and suggest a second date, which was far more decency than he deserved. He owed it to the pack to at least try, but she would understand how important the camp was, and if she didn't, he could point out how her dedication to performing on the murder train was admirable. The cast must feel like a pack to her. She would understand Aksel's commitment to Elkwater.

"Hello?" Lennart answered on the second ring. A TV in the background blared the evening news.

"Hey, Len, it's Aksel."

"Hey bud, you callin' from the camp?"

"I am." He ran a hand through his hair, exhaling in a way he hoped sounded disappointed. "Hey, I was wondering if you could do me a favor. I'm stuck at Elkwater for the night and have to cancel on Beth, but I don't have her number with me."

"Ah, tough luck, Aksel. You going to be stuck up there tomorrow, too?"

"I—no." He smiled to himself, thinking of what the next night held. Jess, alone. With him. "I should be able to get away tomorrow."

"Then you're all good," said Lennart. "Pup called earlier say-ing she was stuck on the murder train tonight, but she didn't have your number, so she phoned us. Left you a message on your machine, but I guess you haven't heard it yet."

"No." He cradled his forehead in his hand, massaging his temples. "No, I hadn't." This was alright, it was fine. He was getting home eventually tonight. He could call Beth in the morning and feign sickness or another camp emergency.

That was it. A camp emergency. He'd bring her number and call from Mac's office. Easy.

"Hey, thanks for handling that, Len."

"No problem, pup. Good luck with the kiddos."

He left Mac's cabin and wandered the grounds, stopping to holler at the counselors and older campers under the bleachers, keeping a fair distance behind them as they scurried back to their cabins. Guilt dogged his step, and he shoved it aside, focusing instead on Jess and tomorrow night. What kind of food did she like? He'd smelled Italian wafting from her window earlier in the week, which ruled out the bistro. Maybe she'd want some-thing more local. More Elkins.

Like me.

He shook his head, wafting away the ridiculous thought. Still, this dinner with Jess was important. *She* was important, not just because of their history, but because for the first time since he could remember, Aksel felt something when she was around. Desire and interest, where with Beth or Sandra, he was simply ... there. That had to mean something, right?

"What were you doing with my mom?" Kendra demanded from a cabin.

Aksel stopped, shoulders hitching as if he'd been caught doing something wrong. Slowly, he faced the preteen on the porch. "Catching up," he answered truthfully. "Your mom and I are old friends." Aksel gestured at the camp behind him. "We were campers and then counselors together."

"Hm." She pushed off the porch rail and descended the steps. "She never talks about you."

Ouch.

"Why would she?" he countered. "We knew each other before you were born."

Kendra lifted her chin, appraising him like an Alpha appraises an unruly pup. "She rarely ever talked about this place. I found pictures in Gran's photo album and shoved in a box in Mom's closet." She shrugged and doled out her next line like it was a treat. "And a sticker on her old oboe case."

Aksel smiled. "I gave her that sticker."

"I peeled it off."

"Ah." He put his hands in his pockets, attempting to remain calm. Aksel was used to teenage sass, but this was different. It was testing and personal in a way he couldn't define.

"I'm just saying." She sized him up with a look and climbed the stairs, throwing one last barb over her shoulder before disappearing within the cabin. "If she never talks about you, you probably weren't that good of friends."

12

—·—

JESS

JESSICA PRESSED HER HAND against the tile, balancing on the lip of the tub as she rose on tiptoes to check her outfit in the mirror. She had not planned on going out to dinner with anyone other than her children when she packed and, three outfits later, she did not feel any more confident in this outfit than she had in any of the previous ones.

The sundress was too low-cut for a friendly dinner, and the dress pants and blouse combination was too businesslike. At least the tunic top covered her rear, and the wide belt gave her the semblance of a waist without drawing too much attention to her thighs.

Sighing, she hopped down and stepped into close-toed wedge heels. Her feet would be killing her by the end of the night, but the added height gave Jessica a little confidence boost. She might have the body of a mother of four who did her best, but she'd always been proud of her legs, short as they may be.

Checking her makeup in the mirror, Jessica fluffed her hair and forced a smile. "I guess this is as good as it gets," she told her reflection and flicked off the bathroom light.

A glance at the clock in the kitchen had her frowning.

Half past five.

Aksel would be home any minute. He'd called her from the camp, confirming their dinner and telling her he'd be home by five-thirty.

"I'd like to shower before dinner, if that's alright?"

"Of course," she had said. That was only reasonable.

"And then ... would you like to walk together?"

And she'd said "No."

Why the hell had she said no? He was her neighbor; it only made sense, but she'd spoken before she could consider it, and now she was stuck waiting out the clock in her apartment until Aksel got home.

It would only be *more* awkward if she left right as he pulled up, and Jessica had already made this whole scenario, hell, the whole summer, awkward enough.

Showing up out of nowhere, enrolling her kids in his camp, renting, albeit unknowingly, the apartment upstairs, giving him a faceful of crotch when she got stuck in his window. All of that before she dropped the real bomb.

"Hi, those kids? Yours, by the way. Thought you should know."

"Ugh." She grabbed a glass and filled it with water to keep her hands busy. Her fingers trembled with nerves, and her belly wasn't any better. This was a disaster from beginning to end, and all Jessica could do was ride it out.

Aksel's apartment door slammed shut, rattling the windows. The glass clattered in the sink as she grabbed her purse, rushing down the stairs as fast as she dared in her wedges, and quietly opening her door. Muffled music played from his apartment, and his curtains were drawn, allowing Jessica to tiptoe unseen across the yard.

It felt like that last night of camp all over again, sneaking out of her cabin and stepping over the creaky floorboard to avoid waking up her counselor, who had slept all summer in a hammock on the porch. Only now, she was a grown woman sneaking out to go on a date—was this even a date?—with the unknowing father of her children.

"What the hell am I doing?" Jessica glanced back at the townhouse, and before she convinced herself to run up the stairs and feign illness, she scurried toward downtown Elkins.

⁂

Condensation dripped down her glass, leaving small puddles on the table. Jessica drew idle circles in the moisture, gazing out the window and watching life in Elkins pass by.

The mothman bartender from The Porchlight swept the sidewalk in front of the bar, and a cluster of wolven waved and greeted him as they walked inside. A female-presenting naga and a man pushing a stroller stopped to cross the road, giving Jessica a glimpse at the serpentine toddler enjoying a cup of puffs.

"Can I get you anything while you wait?" Jessica's waiter, a juvenile sasquatch already too big for his Meander's shirt, stepped beside her table.

"Oh, no." She straightened, awkwardly drying her fingers on her thigh. "Not yet. My friend should be here soon."

"You got it." He smiled and pointed to her glass, turning to leave. "I'll get you a coaster for that. Oh, hey, Aksel."

"Hey, Whit, how's it going?" Aksel's voice rose over the din of the restaurant, coming near.

"Good, good," Whit replied. "Can't complain." He hooked a thumb at Jessica and grinned, brown whiskers bristling. "Neither can you, yeah?"

"Can't say that I can." Aksel stepped into view, eyes flicking to Jessica. A wide smile broke across his face, and she just about stopped breathing. "Can I get a beer?"

"You got it." Whit shot finger guns at him and spun away, leaving Jessica alone with Aksel.

He'd trimmed his stubble, cleaned up the neckline, and swept his hair back, styling it with gel so the rich brown ends curled against the collar of his button-down. The three-quarter roll of his sleeves put powerful forearms on display, and the shirt was fitted to his broad shoulders, clinging just tight enough around the cushion of his belly. Jessica pressed her knees together, dying for him to turn around because, judging by the cut of his jeans, the view promised to be spectacular.

Aksel was handsome. Jessica knew this. As a counselor, he'd been the most attractive person she'd ever seen. It was what had led to her and him and the last night of camp. But as a man? Good God, she'd be lucky to get out of this friendly dinner alive.

"You look beautiful," he said, sliding into the booth. His voice was a low rumble shooting straight to her chest, whirring around Jessica's ribcage and trickling into her belly.

"So do you," she replied, breathless. The realization of what she'd said struck, and she threw out her hands, nearly toppling her glass. "Handsome, I mean." She grabbed her sweet tea, gripping it tight to hold onto something solid. "You look handsome."

He grinned, a canine tooth dimpling his lower lip. "I can be beautiful."

"Of course you can. Why couldn't you be beautiful?" Please, someone put her out of her misery. "My sons are beautiful when they aren't filthy or wrestling with each other. Or talking. Why wouldn't you be beautiful?"

Aksel cocked his head, the move so dog-like, so Jan, Jarl, and Jens, that it shut her up, even as the urge to tell him danced on the tip of her tongue.

It shouldn't be so hard. Three words, and it would be out. Over and done with.

You're their father.

She could say them, and this date/not-date/awkward dinner would be over before anyone could read too much into anything.

They're yours. You have four amazing children who I love more than anything on this earth, and I want you to know that they're yours, and they're wonderful, and I wouldn't take any of it back.

"Your kids," Aksel started, pausing when Jessica tensed. He sat back, elbows set on the table's edge with his forearms bracketing the menu he pretended to read. "They're loving Elkwater."

"Are they?" It came out breathier than she would have preferred.

"Yeah." His eyes darted to hers, then back to the menu. "We can always tell. Not that many kids don't like Elkwater, but the ones who love it ... they fit in. Like it's where they were always meant to be."

"That's wonderful." How Jessica managed that around the lump in her throat was a mystery for the ages.

"You sound surprised."

"They hadn't mentioned it." She shrugged and scanned her menu, the words blurring together.

"Ah. Kendra used the camp phone this morning; I assumed she was calling you."

"Probably her Gran," Jessica explained. "Or Gran called her. They've always been, well, close isn't the word I would use, exactly, but my mom sees a lot of herself in Kendra, I think."

"Do they look alike?" Aksel no longer pretended to scan the menu, his gaze now sharp and intent on her. But instead of feeling uncomfortable under that direct gaze, Jessica felt heard. Felt listened to in a way she hadn't in thirteen years.

"No. Well—yes. I suppose. I don't know if you remember, but I'm bi-racial." She let that hang there, pleased when he nodded and waited for her to continue. "My mom is white." His brows twitched, but he stayed silent and—oh, God, it was all going to come out now, wasn't it? "She has a good heart and good intentions, but she put a lot of pressure on me. 'Everyone is watching.' That's what she always said."

"I remember."

Of course, he did. Jessica told him everything that summer. How Irene took her to have her hair chemically straightened and put her in ballet and orchestra, Girl Scouts, and cotillion. How all she wanted to do was hike and canoe and stay at Elkwater forever, making the camp her home in a way Charleston had never been.

She had told him that she'd gotten into OSU, but her mom refused, saying, "You are a daughter of West Virginia. Your ancestors were Wheeling Delegates. No daughter of these hills is attending college in *Ohio*."

Instead, Jessica went to WVU, as her mother had decreed, and four weeks later, she deferred her coursework indefinitely, running back home with her proverbial tail between her legs and four babies in her belly.

"When my babies were born—" She swallowed or tried to, but her tongue was suddenly as dry as parchment. She grabbed her sweet tea, downing the glass in a handful of swallows right as Whit slid into view, setting a beer down for Aksel.

"Would you like a refill?" he asked Jessica.

"Yes," she gasped. "A Zima, please."

"And a plate of Irish nachos to start," Aksel added

"As you wish." Whit gave them a cute little bow and disappeared again.

Aksel sipped his beer and set it down. He opened his mouth, and Jessica jumped the gun.

"The boys were born first. Three squirming little pups, all glossy coats and pink noses." The words tumbled out, rolling faster and faster like a boulder down a hill. Maybe, if he heard this story, he would put it together himself and spare Jessica the effort. It was a foolish thought, but at that moment, she felt every inch a fool.

"The nurses didn't know what to do, so they rubbed their backs and noses. The room was so quiet, just the little grunts of my babies. Then my mother yelled, and one of the nurses snapped out of it.

"'Give them to their mama,' she said, and then all three of them were on my chest. Three wet little pillbugs in my arms." She paused and sniffed, pressing a knuckle under her eye. Aksel sat rapt, staring at her with his lips parted and nostrils flared as if he could inhale her words. "I can still hear the little sounds they made."

"Rooting," Aksel whispered.

"I'm sorry?"

Aksel shook his head, a twitch to jar himself back to the present. "Rooting for, um … milk." He squirmed endearingly in his seat, cheeks pinkening beneath his stubble. "Healthy pups do that when they're born. They smell their mom and root for her. It's a good sign." He cleared his throat. "Breeding."

"A sign of good breeding?"

"Something like that." An odd expression came over his face, and the sweet blush darkened. For a brief moment, Jessica thought he looked angry, but then it vanished, and he laced his fingers together, waiting for her to continue.

"They had been on me for less than a minute when the next contraction hit. The nurses freaked out, and I almost dropped Jens." Jessica closed her eyes, briefly allowing herself to relive that moment. The pain had come out of nowhere, a vice around her abdomen, every muscle shrieking. "Less than a push later, there was my baby girl. Kendra."

She opened her eyes to find Aksel still staring at her, his face open, eyes wide. "Did she root?"

"She wailed." Jessica smiled at the memory. Her babies, their first breaths, and the sound of Kendra raging into the world. That day had been full of so much pain and so much hope. Jessica had held her babies, all of them, and felt a piece of her expand in a way she never thought possible. "Ten fingers, ten toes, and lungs to make Celine Dion jealous. My baby girl wailed, and the world stopped to marvel at her." And then the rest of the memory crept in, replacing the warmth with an unwelcome cold. "She's never shifted; I don't even know if she can. My mom was right there with me, standing by my head. Still as a post when the boys were born, but when she saw Kendra, she sagged against the bed and said, 'Thank God.'"

"Jess." Aksel went white as a sheet and reached across the table.

The move made her eyes burn, and she took his hand, relishing in the zing of his touch and the warmth and strength of his fingers pressing against her palm.

She needed to keep going. Needed to get this all out, and if, at the end, he heard what she wasn't saying, then maybe it was for the best this happened now. Better that he knew and had the chance to tell Jessica to take her kids out of the camp. Better that she had the chance to erase herself from his life before the summer wore on.

"She loves my boys in her way," Jessica pressed on. "Loves them as well as she can, but my mom—she faced a lot when she married my dad. Then they had me, and it got worse with her family. I think she acts the way she does out of a desire to protect us from the same scrutiny she faced, and she tried to raise me the way she was raised, as a 'daughter of West Virginia,' whatever that means. But I'll never fit into some of those spaces, and that's fine."

"No."

"It's *fine*." Jessica shot him a look that had Aksel's throat bobbing. "But when she saw Kendra, when my girl stayed a girl, I think my mom thought of her as being made in her image. Another chance." She blinked away the tears in her eyes, voice cracking as she kept going. "Another daughter." A bitter laugh escaped her, and Jessica met Aksel's eyes, ready to lay it all out for him to see.

His face was a mask, stoic and strong, but not in a way that kept her out. No. His fingers shook against her hand, the muscles in his arms flexed. His expression, his posture, might be a mask, but it was a mask keeping him *in*.

"It's funny," she said, holding his intense gaze. "Kendra and I, we both take after our fathers."

Aksel sucked in a tight breath, his fingers twitching against her palm. His tongue darted out, wetting his lips. "Jess—"

"What the hells is this?" A blonde woman stormed up to their table, clutching the strap of her knock-off Coach bag and angling her body toward Aksel.

"Shit, Beth." Aksel ripped his hand away, sweeping it through his hair.

"I thought you had plans tonight," Beth snarled, a low rumble building in her throat.

"I do." Aksel gestured at Jessica and sat up straight, rolling his shoulders back.

"With her?" Bright blue eyes swept from Jessica's hair to her clothes, giving Jessica a chance to do the same.

She was gorgeous; Jessica could admit that much. Thick, honey-blonde hair held back with a clip, full lips, and a tanned and toned body that had likely never been within fifteen feet of a diaper or a breast pump.

"Yes," Aksel answered plainly.

Beth huffed and stomped her foot. "She's *human*."

"And?"

"*And* we were supposed to be having a date tonight." Beth crossed her arms, waiting. Aksel did not respond. He'd gone preternaturally still, his attention fixed on Beth in a way that gave Jessica goosebumps. "You. Me. *Wolven*. And you canceled to take out some human?"

"I did," he said in a tone Jessica recognized. She used it on the kids when they argued or fought. It was a Parent Voice, or, considering Aksel, his Teacher Voice. The voice you used with a child stepped out of line.

Beth must have heard it as well. She bristled, the hairs at the back of her neck visibly raising. "Did you consider what the packs might think?"

"Honestly, Beth, you and the packs never crossed my mind."

Beth's mouth dropped open with a tiny grunt before she recovered herself and glared at Jessica. "I have to make a call."

That said, she stormed off in a cloud of Clinique Happy.

Aksel sagged forward, dropping his head into his hands and grumbling quietly. Jessica sat there, at a loss for what to say, and Whit chose that moment to pop by with her Zima and a broad grin.

"Y'all ready to order?"

13

AKSEL

JESS SEAMLESSLY NAVIGATED THE rest of their awkward dinner, casually directing the conversation toward trivial subjects like movies, their jobs, and band camp gossip. Aksel took it as a good sign when she suggested a walk, letting her lead the way up and down the main street and side roads until she stopped and faced him.

"That woman—"

"Can I buy you a drink?"

Jess raised her eyebrows. But she didn't say no, so he pointed over her shoulder at The Porchlight. "Is that wise?"

"When have you ever known me to be wise?" he answered with a wolfish grin, pleased when Jessica's eyes twinkled in response, and she headed for the door.

It might be a terrible idea to risk being seen with her again, but the longer Aksel walked beside Jess in broad view of the entire town of Elkins, the less he cared.

Yes, Beth could cause him a world of trouble, but a switch had flipped in his brain when she looked at Jess with such disgust. His wolf had roared forward, barely held in check by Aksel's tight grip on a mental leash.

Beth had to have heard how close he came to quite literally tearing out her throat. There was a reason their packs had set them up on a date. It was the same reason Aksel had gone out with Sandra and the wolven before her. Kim? Or was it Violet?

Beth also should have known better than to challenge Aksel in the heart of Elkins. She might teach at the same high school and work the murder train, but Beth's pack, the Skölldal, lived over the ridge in Buckhannon. Elkins and the Monongahela belonged to the Sköllburg.

Just as The Porchlight was a Sköllburg bar.

What looked to be most of Aksel's pack crowded the interior, along with a decent showing of Elkins residents, both human and inhuman. Dusty glanced at the door as they walked in, raising a hand in greeting and flicking an antenna at the far end of the bar where Nils and Inge, a wolven couple from his pack, promptly vacated two seats.

They smiled at Jessica, and Nils winked at Aksel as they carried their drinks into the crowd. He grabbed the back of a stool and angled it for Jess, who nodded her thanks and climbed up. Her wedges dangled above the floor, and she idly kicked her feet in a way that made a happy little rumble build in his throat.

Maybe a drink wasn't the best idea. He'd almost lost control with Beth, and every minute he spent with Jess poked at his restraint, especially when she was so damn *cute* kicking her feet like that.

"What can I get you?" Dusty asked as he approached, setting a full glass of beer down for Aksel. "Not a lager gal, that much I know."

"Oh, Lord, I am so sorry." Jess's cheeks darkened. She gripped the bar's edge and leaned forward. "It wasn't the beer's fault."

"Of course, it wasn't." Dusty's eyes gleamed brighter, and he pointed at Aksel. "It was the big guy, wasn't it?"

Jess sat up ramrod straight, darting a look at Aksel. "I—"

"A Zima," Aksel snarled.

"Too easy, man." Dusty's antenna twitched, eyes flickering with laughter as he ducked to grab Jess's drink from the fridge. He popped the cap off and set it down on a coaster. "Be good, kids." And walked to the other end of the bar.

Aksel sipped his beer, still standing beside Jess's stool, while she picked at the label on her drink. Halfheartedly, she raised the bottle and clinked it against his glass.

"Cheers." Jess sent him a slight smile and took a sip.

"I've been on a lot of dates," Aksel replied. At her widened eyes, he amended, "It wasn't my idea."

"Okaaay."

"The pack needs it."

Jess lowered her bottle and sent Aksel a look that loudly cried 'bullshit.' "The pack needs you to date blonde women?"

"Blonde wolven," he corrected. "And brunette. One of them was a redhead." He took a bracing sip. "And two of them had black hair." At her silence, he added, "The pack needs new blood."

Jess set her bottle down and swiveled to face him. One arm on the bar, she draped the other across the backrest. "Are you a pack of vampire wolven?"

At the tiny, sly smile the joke pulled onto her face, Aksel's shoulders relaxed. He settled on his stool, legs bracketing her knees.

He'd always loved how she teased instead of demanded, gently prodding Aksel, knowing if she eased his nerves and left herself open, he would walk right through that waiting door.

"The packs are thinning," Aksel said in a low voice. "There aren't enough of us to keep the bloodlines healthy, so Lennart started playing matchmaker."

"Lennart. Your foster father?" Jess asked.

He nodded and continued. "It started as a way to build alliances. Our packs were larger in the other world. Most wolven never left the territory they were born in unless they were young Alphas searching for a mate. It's part of what eventually led to packs fostering wolven from other territories."

"But there are less of you here," Jess filled in the rest. "So you're forming alliances with other packs and trying to avoid having a bunch of inbred wolven running around Appalachia."

"Something like that." Aksel chuckled, scooting forward on his stool. He shouldn't be talking about this. It was pack business, a problem for the wolven to face and fix. But this was *Jess*. He'd never kept anything from her. New moon, years later, and that easy trust was still there.

"One of the wolven at the Outreach mentioned something similar," she said.

"Outreach?"

"The Charleston Inhuman Outreach." She dropped her gaze to the bar, lowering her voice. "I wanted my kids to know where they came from."

Aksel cocked his head, ears pricking to hear what Jess wasn't saying: she had sought out other inhumans for her kids to be around, which meant their father wasn't in the picture. A not-so-quiet part of him thrilled at the knowledge there wasn't an adult wolven to contend with. But another part of him, the part he tried to downplay in his pack, raged at the idea some wolven asshole had left Jess alone at her most vulnerable.

"It's part of why I was at the camp," she continued. "We're forming a partnership with Elkwater to help more inhumans in the Charleston area get in contact with their community." Jess paused, considering a thought. "You know, I should get Svana—my friend, in Charleston—in touch with Lennart. Maybe she knows an unmated wolven or two."

"Maybe." Aksel sipped his beer. Neither he nor his wolf liked the idea of Jess playing matchmaker. Unless she was the intended match.

At that thought, coming from as far out of left field as possible, Aksel chugged half his beer. Jess sent him a look, and he blurted, "I think they hoped I'd mate Gitta."

"Gitta." She narrowed her eyes, nose scrunching. "Your foster sister, right?"

"Yes. Wow, great memory."

"Thank you." Jess looked up at him with a small, bashful smile. "Why don't you marr—*mate* Gitta?"

"Easy." The wolven in question dropped her arm across Aksel's shoulders, extending her hand to Jess. "I'm very, *very* gay."

"Hi, Very, Very Gay." Jess took her hand without missing a beat, the bashful smile widening into a friendly grin. "I'm Jess."

"With the *dad* jokes!" Gitta laughed. "I like her already." She shook Jess's hand, nostrils flaring as she caught her scent. Though it was typical for a wolven to commit the scent of a new acquaintance to memory, most wolven didn't lean in and take a second sniff.

But Gitta did. The smile on her face hardened. She darted a look at Aksel, brows furrowing slightly.

"It's great to finally meet you." She released Jess's hand, raised her arm, and snapped. "Dusty, pay up!"

"Is it her?" Dusty called from the middle of the bar. Gitta answered with two thumbs up, and his antennae shot straight. He dropped his head back on a groan and ruffled his wings. "Ah, man."

"Aks thought he saw you the other night," Gitta explained to Jess with a sly grin. "I believed him; Dusty didn't."

"And Dusty now owes her three drinks." The mothman in question slid a freshly poured beer across the bar to Gitta's waiting hand.

"I'm gonna cash 'em all in tonight." She tapped her glass against Aksel's, eyes twinkling as she sipped.

"Wait 'til closing, and I'll join you." Dusty set his elbows on the bar. "Putting a face to the name after all these years is cause for celebration."

Jess cast a wary look at Aksel, and he covered his face with his hands. "Still got that trench out back, Dusty?"

"Yeah, why?"

"Grab a shovel, I'm gonna go lie in it."

Gitta barked a laugh and patted him on the back. "Alright, I think that's enough torture for one night." She smiled again at Jess. "It's great to meet you. See you around?"

"Yeah. Yes!" Jess sat up, putting on a weak smile. "I'm here all summer."

"Great." Gitta waved her beer between them. "You kids behave."

"I'll take that as my cue." Dusty pushed away from the bar, tapping Jess's elbow. "For what it's worth, Aksel didn't sell you short." The red gleam in one eye blinked out in a wink. "It's a nice face."

He sauntered away, wings tucked and stride cocky. Aksel sipped his drink, but not even the cold beer could cool the flush in his cheeks.

"Did they take you in after the fall?" Jess asked after a few silent moments.

"Before." He forced himself to look at her, and simply meeting her gaze was enough to erase the embarrassment. She'd leaned closer. Close enough that her scent teased his nose, begging Aksel to erase the distance and nuzzle against her neck. Instead, he cleared his throat and, through the grace of the Gods, managed to hold her eye. "It's a tradition, of sorts. When a pup is identified as an Alpha, they foster with a different pack to keep tensions low." He dropped his gaze to her mouth, and the question poised on her lips. "Two Alphas in a pack is a risk. I'm sure you've seen with your sons how rash adolescent wolven can be."

"Rash is an understatement," she replied with a wry smile.

"A young Alpha is dangerous. They feel"—he scratched his throat and tugged on his collar as the old sensation came clawing back. The constant itch under his skin. The feeling of his human form being too tight—"leashed. Restrained. It can result in a challenge to the pack Alpha, and those don't tend to end well."

Especially when the new Alpha happens to be the son of the old one.

"That's why I was with the Sköllburgs when we fell, and why Lennart, our Alpha, is so keen for me to mate."

"Do you want to?" she asked it calmly. Quietly. But there was an edge to the question, as though Jess had her preferences in how he answered.

"I don't know," he said to the space between them, smaller now, her scent stronger. "I guess?"

"You guess?" She tipped her head to the side, leaving it at a perfect angle, should Aksel decide to remove those inches and feel those soft lips against his again. "That's not a reason to mate someone."

"I know," he sighed. "I want to do right by the pack, and if I mate, there's the chance I could start a pack of my own, but I—" He dropped his arm low, freezing when his fingers brushed the outside of Jess's leg. She blinked, her tongue darted out to wet her lips, and when she did not move away, Aksel lay his hand flat against her knee. "I don't feel anything for those wolven. No interest, no attraction. Nothing." Taking a chance, he slid his hand up her thigh, watching her face. Jess's eyes darkened, and her scent shifted, becoming heavier and more intoxicating. "I've only ever felt desire for—"

"*Aksel.*"

14

— · —

Jess

Anger exploded across the bar, setting off every inborn, very human instinct in Jessica to run. *Hide.* Her heart lurched into her throat, and her body betrayed her, falling still as prey does when there is nowhere left to run.

She was not alone.

Every wolven went still, their conversations ceasing as all eyes shot to the large figure filling the door. A white shirt stretched thin over muscled arms and broad shoulders, and the pointed tips of extended canines were visible beneath his curled upper lips. The neon light from the beer signs on the walls painted his dark skin in blues, yellows, and purples, and a thick mass of locs was pulled back from his face, giving the chiseled bone structure a ferocious mien.

Oh, Lord.

His narrow-eyed glare found her, and a tremble built in her arms as she recognized the sheer power now focused solely on her.

An Alpha.

Svana's mate, Jörgun, was an Alpha, the only one Jess had ever spent any time around. A kind man and soft-spoken, his command was undeniable. When he entered a room, the walls themselves fell silent. He could afford to speak quietly because when he opened his mouth, even the trees listened. It was a subtle command. A vibrance of authority that set Jess at ease whenever they shared the same space. When Jörgun was present, Jörgun was in charge. There was nothing for anyone else to do but obey.

This Alpha's presence was different. Electric. This was a wolven who led with a bark as fierce as his bite. Though the room did not fear him, they respected him differently than the Charleston wolven respected Jörgun.

But Jessica was not pack, and his presence gave her nothing but fear.

A tiny, pitiful whimper squeaked past her lips. Aksel's hand on her leg gripped tight, pulling her attention back to him.

Eyes narrowed and lips pressed firm, his nostrils flared, and whatever he caught in her scent or the room set off a low growl. It rumbled in his chest, rising in strength and volume as the hand on her knee tightened further.

"Haralson," the Alpha barked. "Outside. Now."

Aksel sat taller, eyes narrowing and never breaking away from hers. He ran his tongue over his teeth, and in that move, his words came rushing back to mind.

If I mate, there's the chance I could start a pack of my own. Two Alphas in a pack is a risk.

"Breathe," Jessica whispered. Svana had walked her through this, warning her that the boys would test her leadership, especially if one of them proved to be an Alpha. It was her job, as their mother, not to assume that role but to guide them. To teach them how to manage these situations and walk back from a challenge they weren't prepared to win.

One look at the wolven in the door was enough to erase all doubts that he was weak. But Aksel was large and strong. He had thrown Jessica over his shoulder like she weighed less than a pillow, and his focus on her, the deep, threatening growl, spoke to the possessiveness an Alpha felt towards their—

No. Not me.

Regardless, while Jessica didn't know everything about wolven, she knew enough to recognize that if Aksel were to challenge, things would get messy and fast.

"Take a breath, Aksel."

Jessica was no one. An ex-girlfriend from a forgotten past, and Aksel was an Alpha without a pack of his own.

She placed her hand over his, curling her fingers under his palm. "Not here."

Aksel's expression remained hard and focused, but little by little, the growl quieted, lessening to a quiet vibration she felt more than heard.

"Now, whelp," the Alpha shouted again. Aksel closed his eyes, exhaling briefly, and then shot from the stool.

He strode across the bar, shoulders back and head held high, muscles straining against the sleeves of his button-down, and stepped right up to the head of the Sköllburg pack. Impossibly, the tension in The Porchlight thickened. Dusty had cut the televisions and stereo at some point, and no sound could be heard as every soul present held their breath.

There was a scuffle from somewhere to Jessica's right, and a dark shape darted from the crowd. Gitta swatted the back of Aksel's head with a hand and skirted away as he spun with a snarl.

"Tuck your tail, bro," she admonished, whirling toward who Jessica now knew to be her father. "Take it outside."

Both male wolven faced her, postures at the offensive, and Gitta pointed across the bar.

At Jessica.

"Out," she snapped, "side."

Aksel followed her arm, meeting Jessica's eyes, and his shoulders sagged, the fight fleeing his body. He cast her a long, apologetic glance before shouldering past Gitta and her father, disappearing outside.

The bar slowly returned to life once Gitta and the Alpha followed Aksel out, everyone speaking in low, hushed tones as an argument raged outside. Only when an abrupt silence fell did the pack within the bar return to full volume. No one left, and while they weren't outright staring at Jessica, they certainly cast her suspicious looks. After a few awkward minutes of attempting to melt into the floor, Dusty swooped in and offered to walk her home.

"Oh, no, thank you." She pulled a ten-dollar bill from her wallet. "I don't want to be a bother."

"Aksel's got a running tab. " He waved her money away and offered his arm. "And the pack will keep an eye on things until I get back. Besides, the big guy would never forgive me if I let you wander off without an escort."

"It's only three blocks," she argued, ignoring his arm and heading for the door.

"Three blocks in Elkins," Dusty said, following closely, "which is patrolled by the Sköllburgs, and Aksel is a Sköllburg." He held the door for her, lowering his voice to add, "But he's not the big guy I'm talking about."

At that, Jess paused on the sidewalk. "Why would the Sköllburg Alpha care if I had an escort home?"

"Because you're with Aksel."

"I'm his friend."

"That's what I said." Dusty's eyes flickered in what Jessica interpreted as the mothman frantically looking anywhere but at her.

"Hm." She adjusted her purse strap and continued walking, with Dusty right beside her.

"Lennart's a good wolven," he said after a moment, "and he takes care of Elkins and the people in his territory. *All* of the people. You live here, even if it's only for the summer. He'll care if anything happens to you."

"He has a funny way of showing it." There was more acid in the words than she intended, but her heart had barely stopped hammering since the bar, and the implication that Lennart Sköllburg knew who she was didn't help.

"Yeah, he must be having an off night." Dusty shrugged. "Sorry you had to see that. Things are a little tense in the pack right now."

"Aksel said as much." She turned them onto her street, disappointed to see the lights were still off in Aksel's apartment. "Are their numbers really stretched so thin that the pack is arranging matings?"

"More like marriages." Dusty's wings shot out, and his shoulders twitched. "You can't force a mating, but you don't need to be mated to mate if you get what I'm saying."

"Right." She nodded, deciding she'd rather not follow that train of thought when she knew the truth of it well enough. "So this is purely a eugenics thing."

"Eugenics." Dusty sounded out the word, flicking out a long, tubular tongue as if he were tasting the consonants. "That the racist perfect breeding thing?"

"It is." Jessica mounted the steps to the front porch, mollified when Dusty stayed on the front walk.

"We learned about that in high school. Along with segregation and the Civil Rights movement, and *that's* what I don't get about humans."

"Civil Rights?"

"No." Dusty scratched his cheek, red eyes flickering as he thought. "More like how humans spent all this time putting other people down, with eugenics and slavery, fighting whole wars over the right to be or not be dicks to people, only to turn around as an entire species and start shitting on us instead."

Alright, so that is *not* where she thought this conversation was going.

Jessica let her keys dangle in the lock and waited for Dusty to keep talking. It was the best trick in her arsenal when faced with such comments. Be silent and wait for them to talk themselves into a hole. Or, when necessary, slip out a "What an odd thing to say" and leave.

Dusty, unlike most humans she knew, caught on quickly. "Not everyone, of course," he blustered. "There's good humans, I mean. Like Mac at the camp. And Avery, she's a sweet girl. And—and you."

"How do you know I'm a 'good human'?"

"You're with Aksel," he said. Jessica raised her eyebrows at the slip. "I mean, friends with Aksel. And you have those kids."

"Those kids," she repeated, keeping her voice as cool and level as possible.

"No, I mean, shit." The mothman spun in a circle, wings ruffling. "I just meant to say that for someone not from here, you're one of the good ones."

At that, she went still, a cold calm rushing down her limbs. Jessica was no stranger to those words. She had heard them all her life from relatives and inhumans alike. Didn't make them hurt any less, and somehow, coming from one of Aksel's friends, they hurt more.

She'd been a fool to come back here. To think she could gain anything from returning to Elkins and Elkwater or seeing Aksel again. It was stupid and selfish, and in a way, Dusty was doing her a favor by reminding Jessica that she didn't belong.

A cold determination cemented itself among her bones. She'd been a fool, yes, but the summer was just getting started. No more distractions. No more fake dates with the unknowing father of her children. This summer was for her kids, not her, and it was time she recognized that. Aksel was a distraction. *She* was a distraction. Letting him put his hand on her knee, leaning close and angling her neck the way she'd seen Svana entice her husband. What had she been thinking?

He had responsibilities to his pack, and she had responsibilities to the Outreach and her kids. She needed to focus on work and forming a partnership with Elkwater. Dusty's roundabout reminder was the push she needed to remember that.

"Thank you for escorting me home," she paced out coolly, turning the knob and tearing her keys from the lock.

"Shit, Jess, I'm sorry."

"It's Jessica," she replied and shut the door in his face, storming up the stairs and straight to the bathroom.

Her entire body sang with energy and frustration, all from the fight she had overheard and Dusty's asinine comments. It had been a long time since she had faced this sort of scrutiny from the inhumans in Charleston. There, she was a known entity. The single mother of the wolven, working her fingers to the bone alongside Svana and the other members of the Outreach, determined to help inhumans find a place and a home.

Here she was nobody.

Settling on the toilet, Jessica tore open her laptop. Sleep would be a long time coming, so she might as well put this energy to good use.

She anxiously drummed her fingers on the counter as the machine booted, bouncing her knee as she waited for the dial-up to connect.

Her email loaded, and Jessica couldn't click fast enough on the unread message from Svana:

Subj: New sponsorship opportunity - Mountaineers Daughters

Jess -

Exciting news! We we've been talking with a member of the Mountaineers Daughters, a philanthropic foundation

---

based out of Charleston (the old money kind, so you know they're always looking for a pet project. I want us to be that pet project). They heard about the partnership with Elkwater and expressed a sizable amount of intere$t.

We sent over the baseline comms we have, and they asked for a full proposal by the 15th. If their board agrees, they want to send members up to tour the camp at the end of July.

I scheduled a meeting for you with a grant writer at WV Wesleyan on Wednesday; they owe me a favor from back when we fell. Ask them <u>anything</u>, and they'll help you frame the proposal.

Reach out to Murray at the camp and rope her in; she'll be a fabulous asset when it comes to wooing old money.

This is happening!!

Keep up the amazing work, Momma.

Svana

She read the email a second time, a third, and let out a long sigh of relief. This was the distraction she needed. A way to focus her energy and make a difference. Jessica unplugged her laptop and rushed to the kitchen table, where stacks of reference books and email printouts were waiting. Grabbing the nearest book, she opened it to the page she had marked and fired up the word processor on her laptop, immediately getting to work.

15

AKSEL

"WHY ARE YOU WASTING time with that woman?" Lennart shouted.

Aksel clenched his fists, closing his eyes and calling Jess's voice back to mind.

Take a breath.

And exhaled. The calm in her words, the peace on her face. Oh, he heard the worry and saw the tension in her body, but Jess had held it all in, keeping it together so he wouldn't fall apart.

How had she known?

Gods, why *wouldn't* she know? She'd raised three wolven and made friends in the community. She was smart and cunning in such a quiet, lovely way that the urge to rush back into the bar and sweep her into his arms was overwhelming.

Did she know what an anchor she had just been? How her quiet, steady presence had kept him from going for Lennart's throat?

"New moon, Dad, give him a second." Gitta's boots stomped out after her father, stopping at the low growl he sent her way.

"Stay out of this, pup," he snarled. "This is between me and the boy and that *woman*."

"Her name"—Aksel whipped around—"is Jessica."

"I don't care what her name is. You have a responsibility to the pack, whelp. To your own kind." Lennart's long legs ate up the sidewalk, and he stopped nose-to-nose with Aksel. Though they were of a size, broad-shouldered, and muscled, Lennart was every inch the Alpha. Rock hard, where Aksel's build held a soft, comfortable padding. His chiseled features might as well have been hewn from stone, and he shared his daughter's fierce, burning brown eyes. "This little stunt you pulled tonight almost single-handedly destroyed an alliance I have been building since we fell through to this Godsforsaken earth. I had to talk Lindberg down from—"

"Is this about Beth?" he blurted. Lindberg Skölldal was the Alpha of the Skölldal Pack, and Beth's uncle.

"Of course, this is about Beth!" Spit dashed against Aksel's cheek. His lip curled back, canines elongating as a growl of challenge built in his throat.

"Whoa, Dad." Gitta attempted to wedge herself between them. "Aksel, put 'em away."

It wasn't the first time she'd had to walk them both down from a challenge, and Aksel prayed one day it would be the last. He loved his foster father and respected the hell out of him, but there were times when he wanted nothing more than to snap his teeth and lay the challenge everyone knew was coming. The camp was a reprieve, as was teaching, giving Aksel a semblance of pack leadership and the command his wolf wanted, but his position as a packless Alpha chafed, the leash tightening year after year.

"You brushed off the niece of an Alpha to gallivant around town with a human woman," Lennart snarled.

"Dad, stop." Gitta slapped her hand against the center of her father's chest.

"You brought her in front of the pack," he continued. "What sort of a message does that send?"

"That we live here," Aksel barked back. "That she's my friend." Gitta shot him a look, her head cocked, and lips pursed in a thoughtful frown. "That I'm not a slave to the Sköllburgs to be paraded around for breeding."

"*YO!*" Gitta snapped her teeth at Aksel, forcing him back half a step, then turned on her father. "Lower your voices or take this elsewhere." She jerked her head at the street and the audience of humans and inhumans that had stopped to watch their fight.

Lennart's ears twitched, the tips sharpening, and he cleared his throat.

"Bickle Knob," he told Aksel and Gitta, turning away as he pulled off his shirt. "Now."

He disappeared down the narrow alley beside the bar, and almost immediately, a massive, pitch-black wolf darted across the street and disappeared into the shadows heading east.

Aksel followed, stashing his clothes in one of the waterproof crates the pack kept around their territory. He caught Lennart's scent the instant he shifted and tore off after his Alpha. Elkins passed in a blur, and the tap and scrape of his claws over asphalt and concrete gave way to the near-silent padding of paws over the undergrowth.

At a sharp yip to his right, he glanced back, spotting Gitta running half a length behind him. She nipped the leg of another wolven, forcing them off the deer trail, and barked a warning at another. This argument was not for the pack's ears, a lesson both Gitta and Aksel knew well. The Alpha and his family were to appear strong. Unified in all things. Lennart had broken his rule in confronting Aksel in The Porchlight, but Aksel had done just as poorly arguing with him in the street. This was between an Alpha and his foster.

The last thing anywolven needed was for this to be seen as a challenge.

Five miles to the east of Elkins, the Bickle Knob observation tower rose above the Monongahela. On a clear day, the tower's view shed provided an unobstructed 360-degree view of the Tygart River Valley and the rolling hills of the Monongahela

National Forest. On a dark night like tonight, it offered privacy away from inhuman ears.

A rickety wooden structure, the pack used it frequently to store a cache of clothes and rest during their surveillance runs. It hadn't taken Lennart long to join a search and rescue crew after the fall, and many of the pack had followed his lead.

The human SAR Team, for their part, had recognized the benefit of having a pack of wolven running in their operations and had quickly accepted the Sköllburg pack as family. Lennart had all but taken over by the time Aksel and Gitta graduated from high school, and now, whenever a hiker or pack of Girl Scouts went missing, Aksel worked with the rest of the wolven to run the rescue efforts.

Lennart was already shifted and clothed in a pair of grey sweats by the time Aksel and Gitta ran up, and he'd barely pulled on a pair of basketball shorts when the Alpha tore into him.

"We took you in." Lennart marched up close, invading Aksel's space in a show of dominance. "We raised you as our own. You owe this pack—"

"I owe you nothing!" Aksel roared back. "You did what was required of you as an Alpha, and I am grateful, Len. To you, Ygrid, and Gitta. Honestly. But I don't owe you anything."

Somewhere behind him, Gitta gasped, and Lennart went still, nostrils flaring and muscles bunching. Aksel braced himself for the attack. He'd spoken too freely, letting his wolf run his mouth and *new moon*; now that he'd given in to the shift, there was no holding back.

"None of us expected to get stuck here, but we did, and you kept me. Raised me. Made me into the wolven I am today, and I am *grateful,* Len, but I'm not your pet to be knotted, mated, and bred."

"No one is asking you to knot the bitch."

"Whoa, dad, what the fuck." Gitta rushed up in a sportsbra and men's boxers, ignoring her father's warning growl. "That is absolutely *not* how we talk about women."

"Beth's a wolf, just as he is, and they owe it to their kind—"

"I'm more than my balls," Aksel bellowed. His voice bounced off the trees, echoing across the hilltop, and all three wolven froze, ears pricked for any answering sound.

Instead, there was silence.

Lennart broke first, shaking his head and running a hand through his unbound locs. "No one is asking you to knot Beth," he said carefully, "but the packs need new blood."

Gods, how could he explain? Beyond the pressure, beyond feeling like a hunk of meat set out on display, the thought of sleeping with any of the wolven he'd been presented sent Aksel headlong into a panicky spiral. On each of those dates, he'd felt cornered and caged, retreating into an apathetic, dissociative state just to get through the night. The thought of actually sleeping with any of the females, with *anyone,* turned his stomach.

There was only one person he'd ever felt drawn to in that way, and for the sake of the packs, she was off-limits.

"Does it have to be me?" Aksel whined in a low voice.

"Who else is there?" Though Lennart did not look at his daughter, the implication was there. "The survival of our pack depends on this, Aksel. We need new blood."

"And we'll find it," he said. "But does it have to be now? What's the rush? The packs are stable; no one is threatening your territory." As soon as he voiced it out loud, clarity struck Aksel like a bolt of lightning. "Is it ... is it me?"

Lennart pressed his lips together. Beside him, Gitta tipped her head back, studying the observation tower and the view shed at the top.

"I don't want the pack," Aksel stated, stepping forward as he did. "I've never challenged you. I directed all of that energy at the camp and my job. *They're* my pack, Len. I don't want yours."

Lennart shook his head again and sighed. "You're a good leader, Aksel. Those kids respect you; everyone can see it. Half that camp would follow you to the end of the world, human and inhuman alike."

"Len—"

"You might view Elkwater and the high school as your territory, but it's not the solution. An Alpha needs a pack of his own. Wolven to run and howl with, to secure a territory. Sooner or later, you'll feel the call. Mating with Beth or Sandra, any of them, is only the first step to ensuring you aren't a threat to the packs that fell with us."

"A half step," Aksel muttered, putting his back to Lennart and taking a moment to center himself.

Take a breath, Aksel.

Jess's voice, again, soothing his wolf from miles away.

Everything Lennart said made sense. He *was* an Alpha without a pack, and he felt the strain of that every day. But if Aksel were going to mate and father pups, if he were going to force himself into a situation like *marriage*, he had hoped it would be with someone who didn't make him want to run for the hills.

"I think what Aksel means to say is that he'd hoped for a true mating." Gitta kept her voice level and set her hand on Lennart's arm. "Like what you and Mom have."

"Even in the wealth of the other world, Ygrid and I were lucky to find each other." His shoulders sagged under her touch.

"And Inge and Nils?" Gitta named a mated pair in their pack. Only a few years older than she and Aksel, with a litter of pups nearing school age. "They're true mates. Shouldn't we want that for ourselves?"

"In this dead world?" Lennart scoffed. "Good luck."

Gitta crossed her arms, scowling at her father. He was right; they both knew it, but it didn't hurt any less. In the other world, they would have had a chance to roam and mingle with wolven, seeking out a true mate if they desired. Here, their choices were more than limited, and the odds of finding that person were practically non-existent.

"Hard to mate when you're not interested," Aksel grumbled.

"Then find it within yourself to be interested," Lennart replied, "or you will learn firsthand how hard it is to find a new pack."

Aksel flinched back, and Gitta slapped her hands over her mouth.

Being cast out and forced to roam as a lone wolf was a punishment. In the Otherworld, an Alpha could survive and thrive, forming a pack and carving out a territory of their own, but here, with their decimated numbers and narrow strip of mountains, it was a death sentence.

"Dad, you wouldn't."

"Wouldn't I?" He glowered down at his daughter. "Every day that Aksel defies me, he challenges my authority in the pack. You both swear he doesn't want my position, yet he paraded that woman around Elkins and into The Porchlight. In front of my pack." He hit Aksel with another warning snarl. "I can't force my daughter to go against her nature any more than I can condone the further loss of wolven blood in this Gods forsaken world. It all hinges on you. Date. Mate. Breed."

"Len—"

"It is your *duty* as my foster and an Alpha to see that the wolven continue to thrive. When I return from the SAR training in

Roanoke, I expect you to have every intention of mating with Beth, and forgetting that human woman."

That said, he stalked for the woods, shedding clothes and shifting as he hit the shadows.

Gitta and Aksel stood in silence, though she began pacing a ways away, no doubt working through the emotions of her father's words. Lennart wouldn't force a mating on her, but the defeat in that proclamation, the disappointment, no doubt weighed as heavily on Gitta as it did on him.

While she skulked and licked her wounds, Aksel raged. Lennart might be out of line in demanding Aksel to date and mate, but breeding? He would be lying to himself if he tried to claim that did not hold any allure, and Lennart's demand spoke to a quiet part of Aksel that he rarely acknowledged. How could he breed if he couldn't form a connection, romantic or otherwise, with anyone?

He'd long ago tucked that dream away, and the resurgence of those desires, when he felt none for any wolven he'd ever met, only confused him further.

Because, *yes*, he wanted to breed.

He wanted pups and a family like Lennart, Ygrid, and Gitta had. He wanted a pack of his own, and in his inability to form any sort of connection with someone who could help him achieve this, Aksel had made Elkwater his pack. Mac and Ramble, Sanoya and her Hidebehind, even Avery and Cricket. They were sisters to him, the Hidebehind a distant cousin no one ever saw. And his students, the ones who lingered in the band room at lunch and came running to him with broad grins and college acceptance letters in hand, those were his kids. They were all he needed, and he had been satisfied until Lennart started up with this breeding talk.

He had been *fine* until—

"Are you going to tell him?" Gitta interrupted his thoughts. Arms crossed, she watched him closely, eyes narrowed and gleaming in the moonlight.

"Tell him what?"

"That you mated her."

"*What?*" The hairs along his neck and shoulders prickled, shock almost forcing a shift then and there. "Who?"

"Jess." Gitta strode over and sniffed him. "Sköll, does she even know?"

"Gitta, I have no idea what you're talking about." He backed away, heart racing as panic set in. Mated? *Jess?* When would he have even managed that?

"Fine, play stupid." She threw her hands up, annoyance twisting her face into a scowl. "But if you haven't mated her, you've at least marked her. She *reeks* of you, and you reek of Alpha male possession whenever someone so much as mentions her name."

"I'm not playing stupid, Gitta. We had dinner and a drink; you saw how that ended." He threw his arm at the woods, and they both glanced in the direction Lennart had stalked.

"I know what I smelled, Aksel." She raised her voice, fists clenched at her sides. "Half the pack smelled it, too. Why do you think Dad is so pissed?"

"Because I won't whore myself out for the pack," he hollered back. Because he would not do as he was told, because he could not. Something was wrong with him. He was broken in some vital way, had been for as long as he could remember, and now it was going to blow up everything in his life, including the friendship he was trying to build with Jess.

Take a breath, Aksel.

Gods, her voice was so clear, as if she were right beside him. He swept a hand at his ear as if scratching an itch. Gitta cocked her head, hands on her hips, waiting for an explanation. But there was none.

"I didn't mate her," he said.

"Fine." Her face darkened, her teeth revealed by a snarl. "Lie to me, too. But whatever you did, you only have a month to figure it out." She stormed off in the opposite direction.

"I'm not lying," he called after her.

"Whatever." Gitta raised her arm, middle finger extended, before dropping forward as she shifted and darted into the night.

16

— · —

Jess

Despite loving her children more than anything else on God's green earth, Sunday afternoon could not have come quicker. A storm rolled in early Saturday morning, making pick up at the camp a muddy nightmare and canceling the hike she had planned. Then, high winds picked up in the afternoon, blowing down trees throughout the Tygart River Valley and halting service on the murder mystery dinner train until the tracks were cleared.

Which left Jessica holed up in a two-bedroom apartment with four surly pre-teens, a limited selection of VHS tapes, and hasty groceries gathered during a very soggy run to the nearest store.

Far from what she had hoped the first family night of their summer vacation would be. The kids leapt from the car when she dropped them off at camp the next day, the boys only running back to hug her goodbye when Kendra snapped at them to do so.

She lingered in the parking lot for an awkward length of time before driving back to Elkins and, with nothing better to do, she got to work.

The monthly close for her dad's practice had been buttoned up. Still, there was payroll to run and expenses to reimburse, patient billing to reconcile against insurance coverage, and invoices to draft for the senior accountant's approval. When Jessica wasn't hunkered over the toilet with her bulky laptop balanced on the tank, she focused on the Outreach and the new proposal, driving the length and width of Randolph County and into neighboring counties to visit libraries. Her meeting with the grant writer at West Virginia Wesleyan College had been fruitful, and she left there with an armload of books and reference materials to add to her ever-growing pile on the kitchen table.

It was hard, exhausting work, and Jessica collapsed into bed each night with a satisfied smile. The partnership was barely in its infancy, and her proposals to the Board and the new foundation still needed work, but she was doing it. Jessica Babcock: single mother, junior accountant, and Outreach Coordinator.

It kept her busy and focused, which was a blessing because when she wasn't working, or driving from library to library, her mind wandered to the previous Friday. To Aksel, and whatever that had been at the end.

Who was she kidding? She knew what it was: an Alpha calling a pack member back into line. She had seen Jörgun do the same on a few rare occasions, raising his voice in warning when another wolven tested him. One harsh word, peace resumed, and the pack carried on.

The incident on Friday had been different, and the argument in front of The Porchlight was still on her mind.

Why are you wasting time with that woman?

A better question might have been, why was Jessica wasting any time on Aksel? It was silly, she knew it was silly, and yet she'd still agreed to go to dinner with him, gleefully skirting around the real issue and naively hoping he would get it.

Hope was fickle and dangerous. Jessica knew that, yet still she'd hoped Aksel would somehow pick up on what she wasn't saying. But to what end? What did she want? Closure?

Liar, her brain not-so-helpfully added.

"Shut up." Jessica adjusted her grip on the steering wheel, glaring at the one stoplight between Elkins and Elkwater. She was already late for pickup, and thinking about Aksel while stuck at a red light behind a slow-moving logging truck was doing a number on her patience.

Thinking about him wouldn't do her any good. When had it ever? Aksel only led to disappointment and heartbreak, no matter how badly she wished otherwise. It had become a mantra over the last week.

Aksel is heartbreak.

During her drives, and on the few nights she'd lain awake in bed, pretending she wasn't listening for the slamming of his door or the rattle of the windows announcing his return.

Aksel is heartbreak. Aksel is pack, and the pack had expectations of him.

To mate and breed.

As it had all week, her heart fluttered and sped, an uncomfortable heat building in her chest. She drummed her fingers on the wheel, taking long, steady breaths. It was hormones. Perimenopause. *Something* that had her body flashing hot and rage boiling at the thought of Aksel mating and breeding anyone.

Anyone else.

"Come on, change already," she told the red light. Not that it would help. She was still stuck behind a truck going negative twenty-five miles per hour, leaving her alone with her thoughts for longer than necessary.

Thoughts like recalling the weight of his hand on her leg, and the heat of him walking beside her. The warmth in his gaze as she unburdened herself to a male she hadn't seen in thirteen years. The growing desire she couldn't have because he was needed for *breeding*.

Her stomach twisted, revolting at the thought of Aksel touching anyone but her. The heat in her chest flashed to her limbs, and the light turned green. Jessica pinched her lips together, eyes watering as the truck crept through the intersection. The moment the shoulder was available, she yanked on the steering wheel and pulled over, shoving the door open to empty her stomach onto the asphalt.

Digging in the door well for a tissue, Jessica blew her nose and stared at the ground, panting as the nausea dispersed.

What the hell was that? A panic attack?

Jessica didn't get panic attacks. She was calm and collected. She had to be for her kids and her work, and now she was throwing up over some boy who couldn't even write her back?

"Get a grip." She swept a knuckle under her eye and checked the clock on the dashboard. Fifteen after. "Shit."

***

Empty.

No bags, no boys. The cabin was empty, and Jessica was late.

She had let her kids down on the first day of their longest weekend together.

With the Fourth of July on a Sunday, camp drop-off was delayed until Monday, meaning she had two whole days with her babies, and she was *late*.

After the failure of the previous weekend, she'd been determined to start this one off on the right foot. Good weather, fun plans. Just her and her kids, and she hadn't been able to show up on time.

"Fuck." She sank onto the edge of a bunk, covering her face with her hands. In the grand scheme of things, this wasn't a big deal. She knew that. Still, every time she was not there for her children, it felt like she had let them down. Like she had failed as a mother, and even though she knew she had not, it was a guilt that came with the job.

"Are you alright?" A soft voice floated through the door.

Jessica raised her head, stilling at the sight of a willowy, ethereal inhuman lingering on the threshold. In an Elkwater polo and denim cutoffs, her eyes were hidden behind a pair of large, round sunglasses, and moon-pale, waist-length hair floated on an absent breeze.

"I'm fine." She sniffed and rubbed her nose with the back of her hand.

"You don't look fine." The woman floated into the room, head cocked as she took in Jessica. "You look upset. And before you argue, I spend my days with pre-teens and teenagers, so I am fairly good at determining what an upset human looks like by now."

Despite how crummy she felt, Jessica laughed. "Fine, overwhelmed then." The woman nodded, accepting the correction. "I'm late for pick up, and I guess I let it get to me."

"You are the mother of the wolven?" she asked.

"I am." Jessica straightened, gripping the edge of the mattress. "Jan, Jarl, and Jens are mine. How did you know?"

"And Kendra," the woman hummed. "I believe I have you to thank for my job."

"Excuse me?" Jessica rose, unsure if she should be startled or offended.

"Jan, Jarl, Jens, and Kendra Babcock," the woman recited. "Mother: Jessica Babcock. Father—" She paused and looked at Jessica, who was too stunned to speak. "None listed. Jessica Babcock attended Elkwater Music Camp from 1985 to 1986 and then returned as a counselor for the summer of 1987. *I* assumed the role of Life Sciences Instructor in the summer of 1988 to educate our campers on Human/Inhuman biology and anatomy. So, I believe I have you to thank for my job."

Jessica clenched her teeth. How infamous *was* she around here? Better question, if she was so infamous, how was Aksel so oblivious? "I guess."

"Thank you." The woman leaned in close, bringing with her a midnight chill. "I like it here very much. It has been nice to have stability in this world and influence over those of us who fell."

"You're welcome?" She rose and skirted around the inhuman, who spun slowly to face Jessica as she sidestepped for the door. Smiling, with her hands behind her back.

"You will find the remaining campers at the amphitheater," she said.

"Thank you," Jessica squeaked as she headed down the stairs.

"No, no," the woman called after her. "Thank you."

A dozen kids littered the amphitheater benches, chatting, toying with their instruments, or watching the wolven tussle at the foot of the stage. Cricket and Avery huddled beside a copse of trees along the edge of the amphitheater, the redhead arguing with a young man with her same blazing hair. On the stage, Mac watched the argument play out, and beside her, his arms crossed and eyes narrowed, Aksel scanned the crowd of campers.

Jessica halted, her breath catching at the sight of him. A week had passed since he'd stormed out of The Porchlight. A week without hearing the windows rattle as he returned home, and here he was in his Elkwater polo, stealing the breath out of her lungs. The deep green brought out a hint of auburn in his close-cropped beard, and the sleeves hugged his biceps in a way that had Jessica wanting to do the same.

"Good Lord, get ahold of yourself," she muttered and charged down the aisle, making it two steps before his attention snapped to her. Not angry, not surprised, but steady and focused. He adjusted his weight from foot to foot, arms dropping, and the movement caught Mac's attention. She glanced at Aksel, then followed the direction of his gaze.

"Hey, Jess!" She waved and hopped off the stage, meeting her halfway up the aisle with a big smile. "Great to see you again."

"Sorry I'm late," Jessica said, holding her hand out.

"Not a problem." She ignored her hand and gathered her into a quick hug. "We've got a bunch of parents stuck in traffic." She fluttered her fingers at the campers strewn about the benches and Jessica's kids. "Avery's brother says there's some protest on Route 33 slowing everybody down."

"Protest?"

"Mountaintop mining," Mac explained. "Kid got tangled up with some hippies and keeps landing himself in jail for their eco-stunts. The only reason Michael isn't strapping himself to a road sign right now is because Avery bailed him out of a county jail last week, and we've been babysitting him at the camp."

"That's what that was about?" Jessica looked again at the faun and two redheads arguing by the trees. Where Avery appeared every inch an assistant camp director in cargo shorts, an Elkwater polo, and her hair pulled into a messy bun, her brother wore the pressed khakis and white button-down uniform of a prep school golfer.

"Wild how some people react to things." Mac shook her head and tutted. "Anyways"— she clapped her hands, smiling at Jessica—"I owe you an apology; it's been a crazy week. *Yes*, I would love to help you with the proposal for that foundation, and the last of the renovations to the faun settlement should be finished by the time they come to tour the camp. We can even show them the residence cabins we're building."

"Oh, Mac, there's no need to apo—"

"No running!" Aksel yelled from the stage. The snap of authority in his voice whipped her face around in time to see Jens barreling up the aisle in a blur of fur. She braced herself, bending her knees and centering her weight, and he skidded to a halt inches shy of crashing into her. Tongue lolling, Jens barked a cheerful "hello", slinking forward to nuzzle her hand. Jessica scratched him behind the ears, and Jan and Jarl bowled them over, burying her in a pile of puppy.

Laughing, she wriggled onto her knees, cuffing one pup behind the ear and wrapping her arms around another. Jens yelped as she twisted and brought them both to the ground. He bounded away, tail fwapping Jessica in the face.

Lord, she'd missed this. These moments used to be a daily occurrence when her boys were young. Now that they were approaching thirteen, they'd gained a self-awareness, keeping a careful distance. Jessica couldn't remember the last time they'd gone puppy in public like this, and it eased some of the day's frustration.

"Knock it off." Kendra stalked toward them. Jens lightly nipped her toes and bounded out of her reach. Jarl did the same, teasing his sister and colliding with Jessica, knocking her back into a bench. She hissed at the flash of pain, and a deep, forceful bark sounded from the stage. Jessica sat up, barely registering that all three of her sons had stilled and sat, attentive on the figure powering up the aisle.

Aksel charged past Kendra, who watched him with a stoic, narrow-eyed gaze, and stopped at Jessica's feet, hand outstretched.

"Are you alright?"

"I'm fine." She started to rise, and a low, warning growl rumbled in Aksel's chest, freezing Jessica in an awkward side plank.

She arched an eyebrow, intending to lead with an "Excuse me?" when the look of utter shock on his face stole the words.

Hand still extended, his eyes rounded, the pupils broad and dark, and his lips parted in a tiny, surprised "o", as if that warning growl had surprised him as well.

"Are *you* alright?"

He blinked, shaking away whatever *that* had been with a canine shiver, and dropped to one knee. "Can I help you up?"

"One of us will have to answer a question first." Jessica put her hand in his, the muscles in her arm twitching at the static shock of his touch. And just like that, all the frustration and the quiet annoyance she'd been living with for a week vanished.

Poof. Up in smoke.

Aksel gently grabbed her elbow with his free hand and helped her up, not letting go until she was steady. Even then, he did not move, gazing at her with a mystified expression.

"Hello," Jessica said.

His mouth curved in a smile, eyes warming.

"Hey, Jess." The low rumble of his voice shot straight to her belly. It drew her in, closing the distance between them, and that precious smile deepened, crinkling his cheeks. "How was your week?"

A whine from the boys spared her. She pulled her hand away, and Aksel clicked his tongue. At the sound, all three pups broke into action, circling their mom before fussing on Mac.

She laughed and pulled a bag from her pocket. "Sit."

They did.

"Shake." Mac held a hand out to Jens, who dropped his paw into her palm. "Good boy." She tossed him a bit of jerky from the bag and turned to Jarl. "High five."

"Oh, my God, did you teach my children *tricks?*" Jessica laughed.

"Gotta appeal to their nature." Mac winked at her and tossed a bit of jerky to Jan. He jumped in the air, jaws snapping around the treat. "Come on, guys, let's get your bags and give your mom a minute."

She led them from the amphitheater, collecting Kendra along the way.

"I am so embarrassed." Jessica covered her face with her hands, her cheeks blazing hot. "Have they been holy terrors all week?"

"Not at all," Aksel answered. "They're excited to see their mom. It's a good thing." He brushed her arm with his fingers, and Jessica pulled her hands away from her eyes to peer at him. "Shows what a great job you've done raising them."

"I—" Hot embarrassment sizzled into an altogether different sensation. Jessica hadn't come here for his approval, but it was important all the same. He liked them, his kids, and approved of how she'd raised them.

The words danced on the tip of her tongue.

They're yours.

I hope you're proud of them.

And she swallowed them down, looking away from Aksel to find Kendra watching them from the last bench with a frown.

"Can we go?" she asked.

"Of course." Jessica leapt at the excuse to flee, hurrying down the aisle with burning cheeks. "Let's get this weekend started."

⁂

"Alright," she parked the car and twisted to face her boys in the backseat. "What are we thinking for dinner? Pizza? Tacos?"

"Burgers!" Jens and Jarl shouted.

"We had burgers last night," Kendra whined from her seat in the front.

"Red meat! Red meat! Red meat!" the boys chanted.

"Looks like we're outvoted, kiddo." Jessica turned off the car and stepped out, nearly bowled over by Jarl and Jens bolting for the apartment. Jan plucked the keys from her hand with an, "I got it" and sauntered to the door.

Kendra dropped into the rocking chair on the porch, pulled a book out of her hoodie pocket, and settled in.

"You want to come inside?" Jessica asked. "Tell me about your week?"

"I'm good," she answered, face hidden in the pages. Jessica sighed, knowing better than to pester her daughter, and trudged upstairs where the opening strains of the MASH theme song played from the television.

"Thirty minutes." She announced, dropping her purse on the kitchen counter and pulling open a drawer full of menus. "Then we're heading out."

"Moooom."

"Don't 'Mom' me." She flipped open a Meander's menu, scanned the items, and set it aside. *Too soon.* "Since the weather's nice, I thought we could walk downtown before dinner. See Elkins on a Friday night."

"We saw Elkins," Jarl whined. "All four blocks and the one stoplight."

"But you didn't see the train depot," Jessica sang. The menu for a Venezuelan restaurant caught her eye. She flipped it over, her stomach rumbling at the picture of pulled beef, plantains, and black beans.

"When are we getting tacos?" Jens dropped his head back on the couch, blinking upside down at her.

"I thought we were getting burgers."

"No one wanted burgers," he said. "We all want tacos."

"Alright, alright." She shoved the drawer closed with her hip. "Go get washed up; we're hunting for tacos."

⚜

The boys led the way, stopping at store fronts to joke about the window displays or comment on the people or whatever else they saw inside worth mentioning.

"Take a left." Jessica pointed down the street toward the Venezuelan restaurant, and the they started into the crosswalk. While it wasn't exactly tacos, she figured their chants of "red meat" would be appeased with slow-cooked beef and pork.

"Jess?" A female voice called from a block away. "That you?"

Jessica squinted down the road, taking a second to place the woman. "Gitta?"

"Yeah, hi!" Gitta jogged forward, running easily in Doc Martens and torn jeans. A buffalo plaid flannel was knotted at her waist, her heather gray crop top showing off toned, tattooed arms, a trim waist, and pierced belly button. She pulled her mirror-coated aviators off and set them atop her head, sliding the arms between braids worn in two low tails. "How's it going?"

"Good." Jessica backstepped, surprised by the wolven woman's friendly approach. She'd heard the argument in the parking lot, and it wasn't a stretch to assume she wasn't a favorite human of the Sköllburg pack. "We were just heading to Las Arepas for dinner."

"You're not going to the park?"

"Park?" Jens whirled around, ears pricked. He spotted Gitta, nostrils flaring as he caught her scent, and punched Jarl in the arm, who grabbed Jan, and the three of them sniffed the air before trotting to Jessica's side.

"Who is this?" Kendra asked in a low, somewhat menacing voice. She stepped beside and slightly before Jessica and her brothers, adopting a defensive and wildly out-of-character stance.

"Kendra—"

"Gitta Sköllburg." The wolven female cut her off, dropping her eyes to linger near Jessica's knees. "Aksel's foster sister."

"Hm." Kendra sniffed and turned around, pulling the book out of her pocket and resuming her reading.

"I'm so sorry," Jessica apologized. "My daughter seems to have forgotten her manners."

Gitta lifted her gaze, eyes dancing over the boys, the back of Kendra's head, then back to Jessica. Her nostrils flared slightly, eyes widening in surprise as they had in the bar last Friday. "Not a problem," she said, her voice light and easy in a way that rang false. "Not a problem at all."

"So what about this park?" Jarl asked, dancing from foot to foot.

"Oh, right." Gitta smiled at him. "It's First Night."

"It's the second of July," Kendra muttered.

"Yeah, but it's *also* First Night," Gitta said, "which is kind of a big deal around here."

"How so?" With all the research Jessica had done looking for activities and tourist attractions in the area, she hadn't seen any mention of a "First Night."

"Elkins tradition," Gitta explained. "On the second of July, the town hosts a movie night, and everyone gathers on the lawn at Glendale Park. There are food trucks, a farmer's market, a midnight howl. They even hire a photographer; you all could get a family photo! Oh, and Elias, one of our pack, hauls out his smoker." She gestured at the road behind her, and the string of people and inhumans heading toward the city park with blankets, chairs, and coolers. "He's a competition pitmaster, owns a BBQ joint east on Route 33. Every year he stays up all night smoking brisket and chicken for First Night."

Had Gitta been shifted, Jessica was certain her tail would be wagging.

"Mom, can we go?" Jens bounced on his toes, hands clasped together, and puppy dog eyes on full display. "*Please?*"

"We don't have any blankets," she said weakly.

"The pack always brings extra," Gitta said. "And chairs, drinks, you name it."

The pack.

Jessica swallowed, scrambling for a polite deferral. If this was a pack event, all the more reason for her not to be there. Not only because of the argument and the very loud opinions Gitta's father held, but because Aksel would be there. She couldn't insert herself into his life any more than she already had. And what if that woman from the restaurant was there?

"If it helps," Gitta said in a low voice, "my dad is out of town for search and rescue training."

"Mom, please?" Jan grabbed her hand, tugging Jessica down the sidewalk. "A midnight howl!"

"And brisket!" Jens added.

"What movie?" she asked. Maybe it would be R-rated or one of the creepy animated films her children hated. The ones with the dinosaurs and the dead dogs.

Gitta tapped her chin, feigning deep thought. "I think tonight is *Robin Hood: Men in Tights*."

"What!" Kendra slammed her book shut, and Jessica inwardly cursed. Of course, it would be her daughter's favorite movie. "Mom, we *have* to go. Come on."

"Alright, alright!" She put up her hands and let herself be dragged along, putting on a brave smile as she asked Gitta, "Where is this park?"

17

AKSEL

JUST AS IN THE camp, he smelled her before he saw her. The unique blend of floral perfume and the mouth-watering honeyed shea butter she rubbed into her skin. It danced over the crowd, teasing Aksel's nose before it became an outright tickle.

He had hoped she would find her way to the park. First Night was a big draw for locals, with food and drink vendors, face painters, and balloon animals for the kids. Humans and inhumans drove in from miles around to celebrate in Elkins, not only because of the American holiday but for what else it represented.

The anniversary of the fall.

It wasn't widely advertised, but every inhuman in the park knew why they gathered: for community and each other. It was a secret piece of togetherness that had evolved over the years, pulling them together into a family, if only for one night, before the packs ran back to their territories and the faun trickled back into the woods.

Yet for all the people crowding the park, all the scents distracting his nose, he caught hers immediately.

The world fell away as he hunted for Jess; sounds muting until the conversation he had been in became a quiet drone.

He spotted Gitta chatting with somebody, and as the crowd shuffled, she was revealed. Still dressed in the cuffed jeans and boatneck t-shirt she had worn at the camp, Jess smiled at whatever Gitta said, as oblivious to the naga slithering backward as he was to her. They collided, his far larger and stronger body nearly knocking her down. Gitta grabbed Jess's arm, shouting a friendly "Look out, pal."

He waved his apology, slitted yellow eyes flitting over Jessica before he turned away.

Something hot and prickly built in Aksel's chest, and a sticky sweat broke out over his back. There were too many humans and inhumans jostling Jess as she worked through the crowd. She was so small, so fragile. Any one of the sasquatch could crush her as easily as Aksel could crush the beer can in his hand. The urge to charge through the crowd and gather her close rose within him, and aluminum popped under his fingers.

"Hey man, you good?" the wolven beside him, Karl, asked.

"Hm?" Aksel snapped back into himself, tearing his eyes off Jess and back to the group.

"I know that look." Nils smiled and shook his finger at Aksel. "That right there is a wolven with intent."

"What is that supposed to mean?"

"Hey, yeah." Karl grinned and punched Nils in the arm. "You made that same face any time Inge looked at me before you two were finally kno—"

"Alright, I'm out." Aksel shoved his half-drunk beer into Karl's hand and shouldered between them.

"Tell me it's Beth!" Nils yelled after him. "I've got twenty bucks on her!"

Aksel flipped him a middle finger without looking back, and their laughter followed him through the crowd. He forced a smile onto his face, hoping it passed for genuine, and made his way to Jess.

Gitta spotted him first, and her bug-eyed, pinch-lipped expression from held-back laughter told him he'd failed.

He scowled at her, which made Gitta laugh outright. "Hey, Aks!" she called out. "Look who came out for First Night."

"Hey, Jess." He raised his hand, waving it side to side.

"Hello." She smiled shyly at him, eyes darting to his hand, which Aksel still held up like he was waiting for a high-five.

He dropped his arm, shoving both hands into his pockets and rocking back on his heels. "It's, uh, good to see you."

"New moon," Gitta muttered, rolling her eyes. "I caught them headed to Las Arepas and had to make sure they didn't miss out."

"Great call. Their food is good, but nothing beats Elias's brisket." Aksel shuffled his feet, unsure where to look, when all he wanted to do was stare at Jess. A lovely flush had darkened her cheeks, and her distracting scent was ten times stronger now that he was close. "Do you have a place to sit?"

"With us, numbnuts." Gitta lightly pinched his shoulder as she slid by. "I'll take the kids and get them settled." She hooked a thumb over her shoulder at the preteens behind her. "Then we'll see about grabbing the photographer for a family photo."

She said this directly to Aksel, but he was too distracted by Jess's kids to wonder why.

How could he not have noticed them standing *right there?* It was like the moment he saw Jess, nothing else mattered, and thus, vanished from sight.

"Hey, Mr. Haralson," Jens greeted as he walked by.

"Don't do anything I wouldn't do," Jarl advised.

"And if you do, ew, that's our mom, you freak," Jan added.

They followed Gitta through the crowd, with Kendra walking a few steps behind like a string of ducklings. Or pups learning the hierarchy of a pack, which, now that he considered it, they were.

As if she heard his thoughts, Kendra glanced back. She pointed two fingers at her eyes, then swiveled her wrist to point them at Aksel before turning around and disappearing into the crowd.

"I swear, that girl," Jess muttered. She pinched the bridge of her nose. "You'd think I never taught her manners."

"She's protective of you," he said. "That's a good thing."

"I guess." Her brow wrinkled, and Jess rose onto the balls of her feet, searching for her kids in the crowd.

"They'll be fine, Jess." Aksel placed his hand against her lower back.

"I'm not worried about them." She lowered to the ground and jerked her chin in the direction they had walked with Gitta. "I'm worried about everyone else."

Aksel barked a laugh. "Gitta and the pack will keep them out of trouble."

Jess lowered her gaze, landing it at the base of his throat.

"I always wanted them to have a pack," she said in a low voice, near a whisper, but he heard it all the same. It was full of sorrow and wanting, the wishes a mother held for her children, and he had no doubt Jessica would move the moon and stars to make those wishes come true.

Absently, he swept his thumb in an arc along her spine, giving Jess the support and silence to gather herself and her thoughts. She leaned into the touch, flitting her gaze up to his. Rich, chocolate-brown eyes peered at him beneath thick lashes, and Aksel fell.

No, falling wasn't quite right. It was more like a swan dive, head first, with a broad smile on his face, into the same waters he swam thirteen summers before. Anything she asked of him, sit, stay, beg, he would do in front of every human and inhuman in the park.

It was in the sorrow of her words, the heartache, and the want of so much good for her kids. In the wistful expression she wore as she searched for her children and Gitta. In the heat of her body burning his palm, and the intoxicating scent he had caught through the crowd.

Gods, Gitta was right, wasn't she? And Nils and Karl. He'd marked her, or his wolf had clocked some intent to mate her and failed to fill Aksel in, but now that he was here, with her, he had to admit it was true.

He wanted her, had always wanted her, more than he'd wanted anything or anyone else in this world. In *any* world. And she was right here, if only he could make his mouth move.

It might have been a blessing that he could not manage the words.

I always wanted them to have a pack, she had said, and only one reply formed in Aksel's mind, burning unspoken on his tongue:

They have one.

"Good evening!" The parks and recreation director, Pat, a large sasquatch-like inhuman with glowing orange eyes, greeted the crowd. A hush fell across the lawn as people found their seats, settling in for the movie. "Welcome to the Fifteenth Annual First Night!"

Applause broke out, howls and whoops and hisses from the inhumans among them. Pat pressed his hand in the air, quieting everyone down.

"We have a special treat for everyone, courtesy of the Green Bank Library. First Night proudly presents Mel Brooks's *Robin Hood: Men in Tights!*"

"*TIGHT* tights," a pair of voices sang out from the front of the lawn. Aksel clocked Avery's red hair gleaming in the sunset and Cricket giggling beside her.

Taking a risk, Aksel took Jess's hand, swallowing a happy whine when she curled her fingers against his. "Come on, let's go grab a seat."

※━━━ ━━━※

"You mean you changed it *to* 'Latrine'?" Cricket asked Jarl.

"Yeah," he grinned, putting on a terrible Cockney accent. "Used to be—"

"Language!" Jess hollered from the end of the walk. A chorus of groans answered her, and Cricket rubbed her knuckles against Jarl's head.

"Next time, buddy," she said in a stage whisper. "When the old folks aren't around. I won't tell." She winked and hopped onto the porch, where Avery unlocked the door. "You kids be good!"

"We will," the boys sang back. Cricket crossed her arms and sent them a disapproving look.

"Not you." Avery jogged her chin at Jess and Aksel, lingering on the front walk. "*Them.*"

"You can never trust old people. They get up to all sorts of 'old people stuff.'" Cricket made air quotes with her fingers and then gagged. "Like puzzles and laughing at the jokes in *Reader's Digest.*"

"Ewwww," the boys said, earning a parting laugh from the girls as they disappeared into their apartment.

"Like she would even know what old people get up to," Aksel said. "Fool of a faun lived in the woods until last summer."

"Says the grown wolf who slept at a summer camp all last week," Jess slipped out under her breath, sending him a sly look. "Alright, bedtime, boys." She tossed the keys to Jens, who wasted no time opening the front door. They charged up the stairs, leaving the door wide open behind them. Kendra lingered, aiming for the rocking chair on the porch, and Jess cleared her throat. "You too, young lady."

"But Mom—"

"It's past midnight. Everyone got to howl; now it's time for bed."

"Ugh." She rolled her eyes, stifling a yawn as she trudged inside, closing the door quietly behind her.

Jess lingered by the door, head cocked. No doubt listening for her daughter's footsteps to clear the stairs.

"She's up," Aksel said, flicking his fingers at the door. "And one of them is digging around the fridge."

"Jan, probably." Jess wrapped her arms around herself and sat on the top step. "He's about a half inch shorter than his brothers, but the way that kid ate today, I'm sure he'll catch up by morning."

"They're going to be tall." It was obvious and an obviously dumb thing to say. Already, the boys were taller than their mother, and most wolven males managed to hit six and a half feet. New moon, Lennart was close to seven feet tall, and Gitta looked most of their pack in the eye.

Jess angled her face toward him, staring at Aksel for a beat. "Yeah, they are."

He wandered to the stairs, torn between wanting to sit beside her and give her distance, if that was even what she wanted.

Though he'd leaned away when the photographer took their photo, she sat beside him during the movie, their shoulders brushing and fingers tangling out of sight. But somehow, this was different in a way Aksel had no idea how to navigate. Every internal inch of him wanted to gather Jess close and give in to the urges that had nearly driven him mad throughout the night.

He wanted to nuzzle her throat and inhale her scent. Wanted to grab her and hold her close, never letting go, and he no more understood those desires than he understood where they had come from.

Thirteen years was a long time to go without any sort of attraction to anybody, human, inhuman, or otherwise, and the sudden rush of need and desire was enough to drive him feral.

"That's a good thing," he said.

"You say that a lot," she said, scooching to the side and patting the top step.

Aksel was no fool. He sat beside her, perhaps a hair too close, and told himself it was to keep her warm with his body heat.

Warm on an eighty-degree night at the start of July.

Sköll, he was an idiot.

"Aksel?" Jess nudged his arm with her shoulder.

"Sorry." He laced his fingers together between his knees. "Sometimes I don't know what to say."

"What?" She laughed, tucking her hair behind her ear and angling herself to face him. "No, you daydreamer, I asked how long you've lived here."

"In Elkins?"

"In the townhome." Jess fluttered her fingers at the house. "The rental agent made it sound like it hadn't been on the market that long."

"It wasn't," he answered with a sigh. He didn't want to keep anything from Jess, but what had happened last summer had shaken the entire community. Lennart still wasn't sure how far-reaching the effects of the werewolves would be, and the threat of them encroaching on pack territory had partially driven his campaign for Aksel to mate. "There was an issue last summer, and when the construction crew moved out, I assumed the lease to keep an eye on Cricket and Avery."

"Does this have to do with Avery's brother?" Jess asked carefully, as though she did not wish to overstep but wanted to know the details. He could not fault her for that; she had every right to know, not just as a tenant but as a mother whose children stayed here on the weekends and at the camp where Cricket and Avery worked during the week.

"No, um." Aksel pinched the back of his neck, shooting her a sidelong glance. "With a werewolf."

"A ... a werewolf." Jess sat straight, staring at him. "Those are real?"

He nodded. "Fell through when we did, though they tend to keep further south. We're not entirely sure why, but a pack of them fixated on Green Bank, using their asset management firm to buy up the land and squeeze the faun out. One of them chased Cricket over the ridge, then targeted Avery."

He shook his head, opening and closing his hands between his knees.

"They're good girls. Responsible, if a little ridiculous. They take care of each other, but everyone feels better knowing they aren't living here alone."

"Everyone?" Jess cocked her head.

"I ... they're pack." He shrugged. One word explained it well enough, and Jess would understand.

Avery was part of Elkwater. She was family. Pack. *His* pack. And when Cricket came along, haunting the camp and living in Mac's cabin, she also became part of his pack. It was just as he'd explained to Lennart: he was no threat to the leader of the Sköllburg because he had a pack of his own. In no world would

Aksel be comfortable with two of his pack living by themselves, especially after they'd been threatened by scumbag werewolves and Avery's piece of shit dad.

"An Alpha protects his pack," Jess whispered, crossing her arms over her front and angling her body away from him. Not a large amount, but enough for Aksel to panic at the minuscule distance she put between them.

Something he had said, some facet of him had just pushed her away, and in that panic, his mind grabbed onto the one thing he could think of to draw her back in.

"The boys don't have a pack."

Jess bit her lips, her eyes rounding as she edged further away. *Shit.*

Aksel clenched his hands together, knuckles grinding. His wolf snapped and bit, barking at Aksel to grab her, hold her, tell her it was alright. "It's tough to be a wolven without a pack, Jess."

"I know."

Her whispered admission sounded so defeated that it snapped something in his mind. The urge to protect and care overwritten by a ferocious need to hurt; to punish the wolven who had gifted her with those pups and left them without the guidance they deserved from a sire and a pack; whatever *asshole* had left Jess to raise them and navigate motherhood alone. It was a confusing mix of protectiveness and rage, giving voice to a thought he felt guilty for having.

"Where is their father?"

A sheen of tears filmed over her eyes, reflecting bright in the moonlight. Her lower lip quivered. She opened her mouth to answer, then closed it and leaned away, pushing against her knees to rise, and Aksel couldn't have that.

Jess belonged next to him. It was as obvious as the moon in the sky. She belonged with Aksel, not crying over some mutt who left her alone. A tug beneath his rib cage surged him forward, an unfamiliar heat blooming in his chest. He wrapped his arms around Jess, holding her close. She gasped, her fingers knotting in the front of his shirt, and buried her face on a sob, clinging to him as her shoulders shook.

"Jess—"

"Please," she sniffled. "Don't ask me that right now, it's been such a nice night. I can't—"

Her words cut off on a hiccup, and Aksel tightened his arms around her. She felt so small, so precious against his bulk. He cupped the back of her head, holding Jess as she cried. Her warmth bled into his palm, across his front, speeding the beat of his heart.

"You did the right thing, bringing them here." *Bringing them home.* The thought rang clear across his mind, stark and true. "That couldn't have been an easy thing to do. Uprooting your kids, trusting them to other people ..." Her sniffling slowed, and Jess turned her head, pressing her cheek against his heart as she listened. "New moon, I can't imagine how hard this has been, but you did the right thing. They can be ours"—she stiffened and let out a tiny choked sound that had him rushing through the rest of his thought—"Elkwater's and the pack's for the summer. We can teach them what it is to be wolven if you like."

"I do," she rasped and raised her head. Tears streamed down her cheeks, breaking Aksel's heart further. "Aksel, I need to tell—"

"Can I?" he asked, cupping her cheeks for fear she would pull away. Jess's eyes widened, and her lips parted enticingly. She held his gaze, held her breath. "Please?"

Jess curled her fingers in his shirt, barely dipping her chin in a nod before she hauled Aksel forward.

This time, her lips were soft and welcoming, the kiss an invitation he was all too happy to accept. A lingering press, a peck that became a nibble. Jess caught his lower lip in her teeth, and the heat in his chest exploded outward, consuming Aksel like a wildfire.

He slid a hand to the base of her neck, driving the other down her arm to her hip and dragging her into his lap. The angle allowed her more control over their position, raising her above Aksel. Jess took full advantage, detangling her hands from his shirt to drive them into his hair, nails gently scraping his scalp.

A shiver ran down his spine, gathering in his belly as a deep, satisfied rumble. He nipped her lip in return, darting his tongue out in a silent request for entry. She sighed into him, lips parting and tongue meeting his. At the taste of her, the wet heat of her mouth, and her weight in his lap, Aksel was ruined.

Who was he kidding? He'd already been ruined by this woman, holding a torch for the love he'd lost at eighteen, and here she was. In his lap, sweeping her tongue against his. The tips of her fingers scorched lines down his throat, nails dragging at the front of his shirt before she pressed her palms to the swell of his stomach.

A deep, muffled groan rose in her throat, and Jess wriggled in his lap, adjusting to straddle his legs and deepen the kiss. She felt like fire in his hands, all heat and passion, warming Aksel from the inside out. Her body molded to his, soft breasts pressed against his chest. Plush thighs dimpling in his grip.

The satisfied rumble grew to an outright growl. He cupped her rear, hoisting Jess away from his groin so she wouldn't feel the feral need she had instilled in him.

How long.

How long since he'd felt this mad? This wild? Gods, if she so much as rolled her hips, he'd come in his pants, and what would she think then?

That he was still the same teenage wolven she'd bed and fled so long ago.

Not that the reality was much different. Jess had been his last, his only, and here she was—stroking her hands up his body, humming in his mouth, her sweet scent surrounding him as her every delicious curve pressed against hi—

A window slammed shut, and Jess pulled away on a pant, thighs tensing as she held herself over him. She pressed her palms flat against his chest, eyes wild and wide. Her chest rose and fell steeply, moonlight shimmering on skin glistening in a dewy sweat, enticing enough to lick. "Aksel, I—"

Lights flickered on and off in Avery and Cricket's apartment, drawing Jess's attention away. She stared at their window, huffed a tiny laugh, and made to crawl off his lap. When he did not—could not—let go of her waist, Jess set her hands over his, gently pulling them away.

"The kids ..." She slid off his lap and brushed her hands down her thighs as she rose.

"Right," he rasped, taking a deep lungful of air to come down from the high. "Of course." He tugged the front of his pants, remaining seated as he twisted to face her and hide the first erection he'd had in close to two decades.

Jess's eyes dropped, and she bit her lip, swaying toward him before shaking her head and darting for her door. She opened it silently, lingering on the threshold and turning at the last moment to whisper in her soft, sweet voice, "Good night."

18

_._

JESS

JESSICA STARED AT THE ceiling, fighting the urge to check the time. She'd only be disappointed that half the night had passed while she tried not to think about that kiss on the stairs and how *right* it felt.

Aksel's hands on her waist, her thighs. His tongue testing her lips before sweeping in.

She owed Avery and Cricket a thank you for slamming that window. Otherwise, things would have escalated to somewhere Jessica knew she wanted to go, as well as she knew she had no business going.

What had she been thinking?

Who was she kidding—she knew what she'd been thinking.

She'd been thinking, "Dear lord, I can't answer these questions right now," and "Oh, my God, he smells so good," and "His arms are so strong," and "Safe."

Jessica rolled over, curling her hands under her cheek and watching her daughter sleep. With her face slack in rest and absent the serious expression she wore day after day, Kendra looked younger than her twelve years. The book she had been reading lay open on her stomach, the pages wrinkled and bent. Jessica gently tucked the bookmark between the pages, scanning the front cover before placing it on the bedside table.

Then, she returned to staring at the ceiling, attempting to ignore how her body sang from Aksel's hands. Her heart still pounded in her chest, her blood heated from the memory of that kiss.

The growl he'd tried to hide when she caught his lip in her teeth.

She could hear it now, could still feel it reverberating against her chest, rumbling down, down, down ...

Jessica pressed her knees together, cinching her eyes closed. Her entire body was hot and fevered, her lips tingling as if that kiss had been mere moments ago instead of hours.

When was the last time a man had had *this* effect on her?

Thirteen years ago.

The thought had her slipping from the bed, tiptoeing across the room, and quietly closing the door behind her. Bluish moonlight filled the apartment, lighting the way to the bathroom. She closed that door as well, turning on the faucet and running cold water over the inside of her wrists.

"This is ridiculous." Jessica shoved the window wider open, enjoying the caress of a faint, humid breeze against her cheeks before she sat on the bathtub's edge, head in her hands.

When that didn't help, she lay in the bathtub, hoping the cold, hard acrylic would cool her skin. Calling on all the old tricks she had learned raising four children, Jessica closed her eyes, took long, slow breaths, and listened.

The apartment was silent. No creaking floorboards or rattling pipes. Sheer silence, allowing Jessica's mind to wander in the safety of a silent night.

Of course, it wandered to Aksel and his broad chest. The way his button-down clung to broad shoulders, the rolled cuffs revealing strong forearms dusted in dark hair. The sturdiness of him, all thick muscles beneath a comforting softness. How it felt being held against him, hearing that big, booming heart.

How close she came to telling him.

They could be ours.

God, if only he knew. He had to know. How could he not know? Kendra looked just like him, and the boys were shifted half the time. They were almost thirteen; he had to have done that math. Was he playing a game?

As soon as she thought it, she rejected it.

Aksel did not play games. He was open and earnest and kind and—he'd never written her back. He could have written her, but he didn't, yet he'd kissed her back.

Forget kissing her back. He had kissed her *first*. That had to mean something.

Yes—that you're horny and lonely, and he's the first man, human or inhuman, to pay you any attention in thirteen years.

And good *God*, could he kiss. She fell back into the memory as easily as closing her eyes, breaths deepening, skin heating. Jessica had never done drugs, but she imagined this was what it felt like—her limbs heavy, her movements slow and languid. A weight filled her chest, her breasts aching for touch.

So she did, skating her fingers over their curve and gasping at the zing of pleasure. She grasped her breast, pinching the nipple and biting her lips to keep from crying out as a new, foreign sensation coiled in her lower stomach. A dull throbbing and an ache so long gone she'd forgotten the feeling.

Glancing at the door, locked, Jessica took her nipple between two fingers, pinching as she slid her other hand beneath the waistband of her pajamas and stroked over her panties. Another zing had her eyes flying wide, her fingers tugging cotton aside to feel flesh against fevered flesh.

Damp met her touch, silken and slick. Following the urge growing in her belly, Jessica circled the crest of her sex, whimpering as stars burst in the corners of her eyes.

At that first brush, it was as if a switch had flipped in her mind, urging her to plunge a finger between her lips. She cried out silently as pleasure blinded her senses. It was good, so good and so new, and not enough at all. A second finger joined. A third. A delicious ache building in her groin as she stretched and filled herself as best she could.

It wasn't enough. God *damn* it, it wasn't enough to satisfy, and she didn't know how to get there; she didn't know half of what was happening other than she needed more.

More stretch, more thickness, more weight.

Pressing her free hand atop the other, Jessica ground against her palm, seeking the friction to achieve the release she so desperately needed. It was there with every crook and stroke of her fingers, with the pressure against her clit and the need rising inside of her until she thought she might burst.

She bit her lips hard enough for tears to bloom in her eyes. Right as she began to accept her failure, just as she began to accept that she needed more than she could give herself with the limited tools at her disposal, a deep, masculine groan crawled through the window.

The sound arched her back further, granting Jessica the angle she needed. She whipped her head to the side as sheer pleasure rocketed through her body. Hips bucking, teeth scraping her lips to keep from crying out. A high, tight mewl escaped, the pleasure burning thoroughly through her and, deep within her chest, so deep she could have ignored it if she wanted to, a sense of pleased approval thrummed like the faintest strum of a tightly wound string.

A chord struck in perfect tune.

"Stop complaining, this is fun." Jessica reached across the table and flicked Jarl's wrist.

"Yeah, for normal-sized people," he grumbled back. Jessica had to hand that one to him. The bench seat, where all three of her sons were crammed together, was an artifact from another time. Three of her could have fit comfortably on the narrow seat, but her sons, with their gangly limbs, were packed in tight with their legs reaching across the floor to butt against her feet.

Listening to them gripe about seating was not what she'd had in mind for her night with the kids, but here they were: crammed together in a booth on a train bumping down what felt like an ancient rail line.

She could have driven them to Clarksburg for a movie, or to the library to pick one out, but no. Jessica wanted something fun to do as a family that didn't involve being on the floor above Aksel with his soft lips and strong arms.

This summer was about her kids. *Not* about pursuing the fantasy of a love affair with their absent father.

Kendra snorted, covering her mouth with her hand. "Sit in the chair, dumbass."

"Language." Jessica snapped to the present and sent her children a stern look. "But she's right. If you're that uncomfortable, sit in the chair." She tipped her head at the singular chair tucked at the end of the table.

"But then I won't be able to see anything," Jarl whined.

"So you *are* interested in the murder mystery."

"Duh," he replied. "Someone's gonna die, of course, I'm interested."

"Somebody already died," Kendra said. "There was a fake body in the depot."

"That was just the inciting incident." Jarl rolled his eyes. "Somebody *else* is going to die, and it's going to be the most suspicious person on the train." The car jostled on the tracks, and all three boys bounced into each other. "Ow, hey!" He elbowed Jan in the side. "Scoot over."

"I can't. Jens is already half out the window."

"It's not so bad if I sit up a little," Jens said. He gripped the open window, raising himself from the bench.

"I swear, you three." Jessica rose and gestured for Jarl to swap seats with her. "I'll take the aisle seat so you don't miss a single drop of fake blood being spilled."

"You think they've got squibs?"

"Please don't talk about blood packs before dinner."

The door at the rear of the car slammed open, and a woman in a fitted vintage dress rushed in and struck a dramatic pose.

"How dare you!" She spun in the aisle, blonde hair fanning out in a wave, and collapsed into a bench seat that had been left empty. Pressing the back of her hand to her forehead, she wailed and kicked her feet. "I'll be ruined!"

"Only if you run your mouth, toots." A man in a trench coat and fedora followed her in. "This is your last warning, see?"

"I won't be threatened, Sam!" The woman sat up, eyes blazing. Jessica pressed a hand to her mouth to stifle a gasp as she recognized the actress as Beth, the wolven woman from Meander's. "You've bullied me long enough, and I want out!"

"The only way out is to take a flying leap through the winder." Sam pulled a hand free from his coat, pointing a red-handled prop revolver at the train window. "And I know a few individuals who would be mighty glad to help you do so. Current company included."

"You brute!" Beth stalked down the aisle, faltering when she saw Jessica. Her eyes widened, and just as quickly, she regained herself, whirling around and pointing at Sam. "This is the last time you threaten me, Sam. You don't know what I'm capable of!"

And with that, she stormed through the train, disappearing into the next car. Sam took his time sauntering down the center aisle, mean-mugging the passengers and turning slowly at the door.

"Like what you saw, huh?" He sneered at them, savoring the attention without his melodramatic co-star. "Yeah, I bet you did. Eat it up, see? And you'll get your 'just desserts' as well."

With that, he whirled around and followed Beth into the next car. Polite applause broke out, followed by cheers as a train of servers appeared, dropping off appetizers and drinks.

"That was *so* embarrassing," Jarl snickered, but Jessica caught the gleam in his eyes. Her little jokester had eaten up the scene and was no doubt anxiously awaiting the next set of performers.

Servers bumped into Jessica's chair as they dropped off plates of garlic knots and mozzarella sticks. She scooched in as close to the table as possible, frowning at the Caprese salad placed in front of her: one slice of tomato, a sliver of mozzarella, and a sea of olive oil sloshing over the side, swallowing the barest dash of balsamic.

Another murder mystery vignette followed, featuring a wealthy heiress and her husband, who kept eyeing the other women in the car and rolling his eyes whenever his wife spoke. They were joined by Beth's ingenue and Sam, now playing nice and laughing with the heiress while the sleazeball husband lurked in the rear of the train.

Jessica's kids cheered when the server dropped off their sodas and cheered again when the obvious hero of the murder train, a handsome middle-aged man with a mustache to rival Hercule Poirot, sauntered into the car. The scene ended, plates and cups were collected, and as the train reached the end of the track, dinner was served.

Servers again bumped into Jessica, setting their plates last and in the wrong places. Her kids happily traded dishes and stole bites from each other, only noticing the empty place in front of their mom when their meals were settled.

"Where's your pasta?" Jens asked.

"I'm sure it's coming." Jessica smiled, keeping up the facade that all was well when it was anything but. She'd spotted the plates being set down at other tables, the food beautifully arranged, and even caught a glimpse of another Caprese salad. A heaping pile of heirloom tomatoes and thick slices of mozzarella, garnished with basil ribbons and a perfect dash of oil and vinegar.

Her stomach rumbled, and Jessica cleared her throat. "Dig in, kids."

She grabbed a server's attention halfway through the following vignette—the detective character and his temporary sidekick discussing the multiple alibis and deciding Beth's ingenue was the most likely murderer—and waved him over to the table.

"I'm so sorry," she said, "I ordered a wine at the start of the ride, and I'm still waiting on my dinner. Would you mind checking on my order?"

The server glanced at her table and the kids. His nostrils flared, and he straightened, panic flitting across his face. "My fault." He cleared his throat. "I'll get that for you right now, Mrs., um, Miss, uh..."

And scurried off without finishing the sentence.

"These guys are so dumb," Jarl grumbled. "It's obviously Janice."

"Janice?" Jan asked around a mouthful of meatball.

"The heiress," Jarl said. "Ruby has no motive; she just wants to get away from Gangster Sam. And Clyde—"

"Janice's husband," Kendra clarified.

"—is just here for a good time. But Janice was conveniently 'in the powder room' when the murder happened."

"Don't you think Ruby wanting to escape the gangsters is enough reason?" Jens asked. "She was using her status as a secret girlfriend to blackmail the rail baron. With him dead, I bet she gets a decent payout and can use that to pay off Sam."

"Ohhh," Jan and Jarl said in unison. "That's a good point," Jarl added.

On cue, the rear door slammed open, and Beth ran in, a glass of red wine in her hand. Eyes wild and frantic, she let out an ear-piercing shriek, pointing at her masked pursuer.

"No, no, please!" She stumbled backward, frantically searching the car. "Please, you have to help me," she begged a passenger. "They want me dead! They don't want me to spill what I know!"

She spun, sobbing as the masked villain advanced, raising a prop revolver with a red handle.

"That's the one Gangster Sam had!" Kendra excitedly whispered.

"No!" Jarl gasped.

"You!" Beth whirled again, nearing their table. "You know I'm good for my word." She waved her glass at the villain, tripping over her heels. Wine sloshed over the rim as she swung her arm, and Jessica realized what was about to happen too late to avoid her part in it. "Please, no!"

The villain fired the gun, Beth let out an impressive cry, and blood exploded from the front of her dress. She whirled again, the contents of her glass flying in a crimson arc and splashing onto Jessica as Beth took her dying fall.

"*Yes!*" Jarl pumped a fist in the air. "I knew it!"

"Good job." Jan golf-clapped. "You predicted the predictable murder train plot."

"What? No. Look." Jarl pointed at Beth's body on the ground. "*Blood squibs.*"

"Can I have a napkin?" Jessica finally managed. She shook wine off her hand and wiped it from her jaw. "Please."

"Oh, God, Mom." Jan grabbed a linen napkin and started blotting her arm. Red stained the front of her blouse and the lap of her jeans, and Jessica doubted there was enough seltzer or Oxyclean in Elkins to salvage her clothes.

"It's alright." She sighed, accepting a napkin from the table next to them and pressing it to her front. She glanced at Beth's "body" in the aisle, marking the smirk the woman wore even in fake death. "Accidents happen."

19

— · —

JESS

"I'M SURE IT WAS an accident," Jessica said. Again. "They probably rehearsed that scene without anyone sitting in the aisle seat."

"Yeah, but they knew you were there," Jens argued. "She didn't have to have wine in that glass."

"It's fine, guys." Jessica shoved her hands in Kendra's hoodie—the worn, stolen Elkwater hoodie she hadn't worn in years. She had insisted Jessica put it on, outright refusing to leave the train platform until she had done so. "Let's get home so I can change and start some laundry."

"But you didn't get to eat."

"I'll eat leftovers."

"The Venezeulan place is still open." Jan pointed down Second Street, where the lights were indeed on at Las Arepas. "Kendra and I can wait for the order and bring it home."

Jessica's eyes burned at the thoughtfulness, the care. Lord, these kids. So wild and sweet. They had always been protective of each other and her, yet she was still struck when they fussed over her like this. Some days, she wondered if unwavering loyalty and love were wolven traits. On other days, she allowed herself a little bit of pride in how she had raised her children to be empathetic and kind.

"It's okay, sweethearts. Thank you, but I—"

"Hey, it's the Babcock Pack!" Gitta sauntered behind Jessica, high-fiving the boys and waving at Kendra. She turned to greet Jessica and paused, eyebrows rising as she sniffed the air. "Whoo, someone's been hitting the bottle. Rough night?"

"Bumpy tracks." Jessica shrugged. Beth was wolven, a part of Gitta's community. No good ever came of stirring someone else's pot, especially when "The Incident," as her kids had begun calling it, could have been a genuine accident. The hazard of eating and drinking on a train riding over old rails.

"Ruby spilled her wine on Mom," Kendra stated.

"She tripped," Jessica corrected.

"Ruby?" Gitta looked from mother to daughter, brows raised.

"The murdered lady on the train," said Jarl. "She got shot, spun, tripped on her heels, and spilled wine on Mom."

"Beth tripped?" Gitta snapped her attention to Jessica. Her nostrils flared again, and a shrewd, suspicious gleam lit her eyes.

"An accident." Jessica swept her arms at her kids. "Come on, guys, let Gitta get on with her night." She started forward, and Gitta stopped her with a brush of fingers against her arm.

"Beth doesn't trip." Gitta flicked her gaze to the kids, then back to Jessica, tipping her head toward Las Arepas.

At that look, the silent suggestion that the children leave before Gitta said whatever she had to say, Jessica's throat cinched tight. She pulled her wallet from her purse and handed it to Jan. "Order me whatever," she said. "And get yourselves dessert."

"They do a great fried ice cream," Gitta suggested.

The boys' eyes lit up, and they were off like a shot, dragging Kendra along by the arm. Once they were out of earshot, Jess stepped up close to Gitta.

"It's not a big deal."

The wolven woman waited for all four kids disappear into Las Arepas before speaking. "I have a pretty good feeling that it is."

"I don't want to cause any problems." She backed up, needing to put space between them. Gitta wasn't threatening, but her stance and tone heavily suggested a suspicion Jessica did not wish to address. "We're just here for the camp and the Outreach. I—"

"Does he know?" Her eyes flicked to Las Arepas and back again.

"Know what?"

"Come on, Jessica. Aksel's all over those kids." She kept her voice low, her posture relaxed. To any passerby, they would look like two women having a friendly conversation, not a wolven dropping a figurative bomb and a human trying desperately to keep it together. "If she were any taller, Kendra could be his twin."

"I don't—" Jessica swallowed, panic rising along with the urge to run. "I don't think so. I haven't told him, and before you say anything, I know I need to; I just can't—" she cut herself off, mind churning in search of the words. How could she even begin to explain the how and the why? "He never wrote me back."

Gitta blinked. "What does that mean?"

"I wrote him when I found out I was pregnant. I wrote him twice a month for a year." Oh God, it was out in the world now. Her odd habit of writing letters she never intended to send. Just like the emails she wrote and deleted, those letters existed, and Jessica *had* sent them for a solid year, gaining nothing in return. "I sent him a letter for each birthday, and he never responded, but I just kept writing. Telling him about their first words, first steps, about the boys as pups, and Kendra growing into a beautiful young woman. About the good days and the bad. I wrote him *everything,* and he never replied. I don't even know why I did it, I just did, and then I saw him, and it was like no time had passed at all."

She sank onto a nearby bench, hands clasped in the hoodie's pocket, and bent over her knees. She wanted to curl into a tight, tiny ball and make herself small enough to be overlooked and ignored.

"Seeing him again, talking to him, it feels so right, and I didn't want to ruin anything by telling him he had kids." She exhaled and looked up at Gitta. "He told me about the dates and the pack—I don't want to get in the way of anything. I just wanted his kids to know—"

Gitta sat on the bench, her elbow brushing Jessica's sweat-shirt. It felt like a show of support, like understanding in a way she could not define. A comfort in the closeness.

"Can I hug you?' Gitta asked. Her voice was soft, awed in a way Jessica couldn't figure. "I'd really like to hug you before I say what I have to say."

"Okay?"

Arms banded around her before she had the word fully out of her mouth. Jessica sank into the embrace, the welcoming warmth. Gitta exhaled, her breath tickling Jessica's ear. "He wrote you every month for a year."

She jolted, but Gitta's arms kept her in place.

"It killed him when you stopped writing back. Dusty and I told him to stop punishing himself by writing you, but he kept doing it. Month after month for a year until you didn't show up at Elkwater the next summer, and his last letter bounced back with 'return to sender' stamped on it."

"I didn't know," Jessica rasped.

"I believe you." Her arms tightened. "What happened?"

"Life?" Jessica lifted her head, embarrassed by the tears streaming down her cheeks. Gitta released her from the hug, and the two women sat in easy silence.

"He moved into the band house halfway through his first semester," Gitta said after a moment. "Maybe your letters got lost in the mail."

"Maybe." Jessica thought back, vaguely recalling a letter mentioning the Band House at OSU. Was the explanation that simple? A wrong address and letters lost in the mail? It felt too convenient, but nothing she had seen in Aksel over the last few weeks could support the idea that he had intentionally cut her out.

He'd been startled to see her, yes, but excited. And flirtatious. And just as innocent and sweet as the boy she knew.

Maybe it was that easy. He moved, her letters got lost, and he forgot about her. Moved on with his life while Jessica grew bigger, dropped out, and had her babies. Splitting her time between raising her children and finishing her degree while he graduated and built a life for himself in Elkins, none the wiser.

She tried to let anger spark, but it would not catch because what had Aksel done with his life?

Pursued a teaching degree and returned to Elkins, tasking himself with shaping the minds and fortitude of the next generation. Putting a bit of good and understanding in the world wherever he could.

It would have been easy to hate him if he had traveled the world or moved to a big city. Or if he spent his time at parties and clubs, living when she had entered young motherhood, but in his way, Aksel's life had mirrored hers.

"You have to tell him, Jess," Gitta murmured. She laced her fingers together, staring across the sidewalk. "Word about the train is going to get back to him."

"It was an accident."

"Beth is a professional." Gitta glanced at her from the corner of her eye. "If she 'tripped' and spilled wine on you, it was on purpose."

"You can't know that."

"Can't I?" She straightened and looked at her head on. "I've ridden the murder train—"

"*You've* ridden the murder train?" Out of everything Gitta had said, somehow, that was the most surprising. Jessica couldn't imagine the wolven woman with her boots and leather boarding an antique train for two hours of dinner theater.

"Of course I have." She sniffed. "My girlfriend likes to do kitschy stuff, and I like to make my girlfriend happy. *Anyway*, as I was saying, I've seen the show; the ingenue doesn't have wine in that scene. Why would she? Ruby's running for her life." Her expression hardened. "Beth was making a point."

"To who?"

"You? The staff and cast? Half of them are Sköllburg, and she cried to her uncle after Aksel canceled their date."

"To go to dinner with me, and that's why your dad came to The Porchlight." Jessica groaned and covered her face with her hands. "This is exactly what I meant when I said I didn't want to cause any problems."

"I think it's too late for that, Jess." Gitta patted her knee. "Like I said, Aksel is all over those kids. Hells, he's all over you."

"What." She spread her fingers, peering at Gitta.

"You reek of him, more than you did at the bar," she said. Blood rushed to Jessica's cheeks. "If I noticed, then Beth and any of my packmates on the train also noticed."

"We kissed," Jessica blurted. "Last night. It went further than I anticipated, but we made out and—oh, God, I'm sorry. He's your brother; I shouldn't be telling you this."

To her surprise, Gitta snickered and shook her head, a sharp, wolfish grin splitting her lips to reveal pointed canines. "I can handle thinking about a kiss, but, new moon, spare me if it goes further."

"I'm so sorry." She covered her face again.

"Don't be; the male needed to let off some steam." Her chuckle died away, face growing serious. "You need to tell him, Jess. He deserves to know."

"You figured it out," she whined. "How do you know he hasn't figured it out as well? Maybe he's playing a game."

The flat look Gitta sent her spoke volumes. Aksel did not play games. He was too earnest for that. If he even suspected, he would ask, and he would show up. Jessica did not doubt that for an instant.

And hadn't he already asked, in his way?

Where is their father?

She could have told him then, but the words had died on her tongue, smothered by her fears of judgment or rejection.

"Funny thing about scent," Gitta said. "You get a little nose-blind to your own."

"What does that mean?"

"It *means*, to Aksel, you just smell like Jessica." She shrugged and rose, hands thrust into the back pockets of her jeans. "But to the rest of us, you smell like his."

Jessica's heart skipped with something like hope, falling at Gitta's following words.

"You need to tell him, Jess, before someone else does. Give him a chance to come to terms with it before my dad gets back and finds out."

"I know," she said in a whisper. It wasn't fair for her to keep this from him, and it was foolish to think or hope the pack would keep her secret. How could they when it was apparent to everyone but Aksel?

The server from the train flashed in her mind, how their nostrils had flared, and they'd practically run to the kitchen to rectify Jess's order. And Gitta's reaction at the park when she saw the kids. The glances and stares Jess got from the wolven in The Porchlight and around town. She'd been wandering around Elkins with a target on her back, and the longer she put off telling Aksel the truth, the worse it would be.

20

—·—

Aksel

Give her space.

That's what Aksel told himself Saturday morning when he heard feet tromping around upstairs. And that afternoon, when Jess and her kids left, heading downtown in a sea of smiles and happy chatter.

It was what he told himself that night when the windows rattled as the door to her apartment closed and when he stroked himself in the shower, thinking of Jess straddling his lap, her teeth snagging his lip.

Give her space.

She'd run off so quickly, leaving Aksel with less than a promise in that sweetly whispered, "Good night." It was enough to drive a wolf feral, so he gave in and spent all Sunday on patrol with the pack. That, at least, kept his mind mostly off of her. He ran himself to exhaustion, loping home on sore paws and collapsing into bed.

Give her space. He repeated when he heard her tiptoe across her apartment for the third night in a row. And the fourth. The fifth.

Give her time, Aksel told himself when she remembered to close the bathroom window. But the damage was already done. He heard her, and that was enough to have his skin itching and blood rushing to his cock. New moon, it was a miracle he hadn't blistered his dick by the amount of attention he'd given it since that kiss. And from what he'd heard Friday night, all through the weekend and into the week, Jess was no better off.

"This is ridiculous," he muttered, gripping hard and stroking.

His palm was too dry, too coarse to be any substitute, but it didn't stop Aksel from pulling Jess's face to mind. Her plush lips swollen from their kiss. Her chest rising and falling, those perfect breasts aching for his hands, his mouth.

"Just knock on her door, invite her down. Handle this like adults."

The pipes rattled as she turned on the faucet, which put the image of a naked, wet Jess in his head, along with the idea of running his hands down her body, cupping her ass and hoisting her in his arms. Those delicious thighs wrapped around his waist as he lowered her onto his dick.

"Oh, Sköll." He arched his back, heat churning in his groin and hips thrusting into his palm, falling into the memory of that last night. If he closed his eyes and concentrated, clearing all other thoughts aside, he could almost remember the mind-shattering bliss and the weight of her riding him, the heat of her pussy, gripping him tight and drawing him in. The needy, breathy gasp she had let out when she was fully seated.

The same gasp he heard through the window just two nights ago.

"Fu-uuck."

He drove his heels into the mattress, twisting his wrist and thumbing the head of his cock. Pleasure shot from his balls to his belly, and Aksel barely caught the first spurt in his palm, using it to ease himself through the final throbs of his orgasm. He lay back, panting like a dog as the momentary bliss receded, leaving him empty and unsatisfied.

Give her space, his inner voice demanded. *Give her time.*

And he did, staying away, keeping his distance, and slowly going feral.

The floorboards creaked overhead, Jess making her way back to her bedroom, and Aksel's cock twitched at the thought of her lying in bed beneath him. Her rich hair fanned against the blue of his bedsheets, her nipples dark against her skin. Gods, was she bare? Or would there be a damp nest of curls for him to nuzzle against, inhaling the freshest, deepest scent of her before taking a taste?

His cock hardened in his palm, and Aksel groaned, body flushed with a confusing cocktail of desire and frustration. Night after night after night. The floorboards creaked, and his dick stood at attention, conditioned to the sound of Jessica overhead.

This was worse than being a teenager. He was obsessed, possessed by the mere thought of Jess and the memory of one night. That memory melded with their kiss on the stairs, painting a fantasy in Aksel's mind of what she would be like now. Grown and graceful. Soft in all the right places and more beautiful than he remembered.

He came faster this time, tearing off a sock to clean his hand and groin before heading to the shower. Dawn was only a few short hours away, and he was running the kids through complex formations for half the day. He needed to be sharp and aware when instead, he was exhausted and hornier than a hare in spring.

Yet through the haze of lust making him downright useless, Gitta's accusation continued to blare clear as day:

If you haven't mated her, you've at least marked her.

Aksel no more understood how or when he could have done it than he understood what in the hells was happening to him now. The thought of it, though, of taking Jessica and marking her as his, mating her properly instead of dreaming about it night after night, was enough to have his cock thickening and blood pumping.

"Fuck." He dropped his head against the tile, groaning in frustration.

This was becoming a problem. Hells, it had been a problem, and it was time to ask for help.

⁂

"You want to know what?" Nils stared at him over the handlebars of a vintage Harley Sprint, his light brown eyebrows disappearing under a fall of sandy-blonde hair.

"How you knew that Inge was, um"—Aksel pinched the back of his neck, glancing around the garage of Whole Hog Moto and lowering his voice—"*the one.*"

"You mean how I knew I wanted to knot her?"

"Lower your voice, man." Aksel pressed his hand in the air, hunching his shoulders.

"Afraid the old wolf is gonna hear you?" He waved his wrench at the parking lot beyond the open bay door, and Elias tending to his smoker outside of Riversmoke.

Tucked on a bend of Shavers Fork and Old Route 33, beneath the view of the Bickle Knob Observation Tower, Riversmoke and Whole Hog Moto held an ideal vantage over the flow of traffic both by road and river into the Sköllburg territory. Aksel was still hazy about how the pack came by such a valuable piece of property, but if any human locals had a complaint, they kept it to themselves.

Elias had been the pack's head of supply in the Otherworld, ensuring the bellies of hungry wolven were always full. He had maintained that position after the fall, embracing the identity of "pitmaster" and even winning a few competitions around the state. Along with the chicken and brisket for First Night, he supplied pulled pork for the sandwiches at Meander's and frequently smoked sausages and ribs for the local football games.

New moon knew Elias's cooking was partially responsible for Aksel's size, but who could blame him? His food was like magic, and Riversmoke had become a local institution within a season of opening.

Elias's son, Nils, had opened Whole Hog Moto in the empty garage next to the restaurant a few years later, turning his Otherworld fascination with cogs and clockwork into a deep knowledge of this world's mechanics.

"Hey, Pop!" Nils rose and called out. "Aksel's asking 'bout knots."

Elias shut the smoker door with a loud clang and cupped a hand to his ear. "What's that?"

"*Knots*," Nils yelled.

"Come on, man." Aksel palmed his face, cheeks burning hot. "That's not what I said."

"What's he wanna know?" Elias hollered as he strolled over, wiping his hands on a sauce-stained rag. "Better question, why's he asking you and not Lennart?"

"Cos it's awkward as hells, Pop."

"Fair, fair." The older wolven slapped Aksel on the back and crossed thick arms over his chest. "So, what is it you want to know?"

"Please tell us you at least know how they work," Nils added.

Aksel's cheeks blazed, and he shuffled his feet, regretting his decision to ask for help. But where else could he go? Lennart expected him to mate a wolven. If Gitta was right, and Aksel was just about convinced she was, not only was that out of the question, it wasn't even a topic on the table.

"I know how they work," he said. Every wolven male did; it was a part of their upbringing and anatomy, and snickered about as soon as most pups learned what their dicks were for. A knot was for your mate. And breeding. "And I didn't ask about knots. I asked how you knew Inge was it."

The pair had grown up in the Sköllburg pack together, friendly as pups and packmates as adolescents, but their mating hadn't occurred until three years ago, surprising everyone.

"Just knew." Nils shrugged. "Woke up one day, smelled it, and I had to mark and mate her."

"That's it?"

"Basically." Nils narrowed his eyes, scanning Aksel from head to toe. "Wait, this isn't about Beth, is it?"

He pressed his lips together, carefully keeping his face blank.

Elias's nostrils flared, and his eyes widened. He leaned closer, sniffing Aksel more directly. "No, it's not," he said, mystified. "Who is that?"

"No one." Aksel backed up, shooing him away before turning his head and sniffing his shoulder. He smelled like ... nothing. Just his scent, which he couldn't even begin to define. It was just *him*. Wolven were great at picking out the subtleties in another's scent, committing the unique blend as an identifying memory, but who could smell themselves?

"No, there's someone there." Elias sniffed him again, then gestured for his son to do the same. Aksel pressed his lips tighter, pushing them under his nose as he suffered the indignity. Sniff checks were how mothers sussed out where their whelps had been, not for grown ass wolven to endure.

"Wait, I know this." Nils circled him, glancing up at Aksel. His cornflower blue eyes narrowed, and he stepped closer to sniff again. "Shit, man, I'm out twenty bucks. That's the woman from the other—"

"Can you answer my question?" Aksel snapped, adding a bit of bark to the words. Both wolven darted back, looking anywhere but directly at him. He took a deep breath before speaking again. "Please. I need to know how you knew, what it felt like, how you felt when—"

"When did this happen?" Elias asked. He kept his gaze averted and voice soft. That deference toward Aksel's unacknowledged nature opened the floodgates.

"I don't know," he said on an exhale, slumping against Nils's workbench and running a hand through his hair. "I feel like I'm going crazy. All of those dates, all of those wolven, then she walks back into my life, and it's like no time has passed. I smell her everywhere. I can't get her out of my head, and every night I hear her walking overhead, and it's like I can't … and it's never enough." He looked to Elias and Nils, hands spread wide as if that could encompass how helpless he felt. "What's happening?"

They shared a look. Nils widened his eyes and tipped his head at Aksel. Elias shook his head and flicked a finger in his direction, to which Nils tucked his chin and shoved his hands in his pockets. He sighed and scuffed the floor with his boot before facing Aksel. "That's it."

"That's it?"

"She takes up rent." He tapped his temple. "She's the first thing you think of when you wake up, the last thing on your mind when you fall asleep. You smell her everywhere and pick her out in a crowd. When she's with you, she's all that matters." Grimy fingers drifted absentmindedly over a faded pink scar poking above the collar of his t-shirt. "And if you're lucky enough to breed her, gods, your world becomes so small and so *vital*." His eyes unfocused, Nils no doubt thinking of his litter at home.

Aksel's belly flipped at the truth of his words. The relevance. He'd caught Jess out of the crowd at Elkwater, even if he hadn't known it was her, and again at First Night. She filled his mind from dawn to dusk and then ran through his dreams, urging him to give chase.

He gripped the edge of the workbench, grinding his teeth together as he centered himself in this knowledge.

Gitta was right. His suspicions were right, but the question remained: "How?"

"What do you mean 'how?'" Elias asked. "You said you knew how knots work."

"I haven't knotted her. Gods, I haven't seen her since I was eighteen," he said, stomach dipping and twisting. "How did this happen?"

"Wait." Nils went alert, eyes sharpening on Aksel. "Is the woman from First Night the same girl from camp?" Aksel swallowed a thick mouthful of spit and nodded. Nils let out a low, long whistle, shaking his head. "Lennart is going to lose his shit."

"Lennart can't know," Elias said. He slammed his palm against a button on the wall, waiting for the bay door to close before speaking again. "Tell me what happened."

Though they were alone, he kept his voice low. At any moment, others in their pack could lope up to Riversmoke or Whole Hog, and walls weren't enough to keep wolven ears deaf to secrets. Gitta's suspicions were already a risk. Adding Elias and Nils to that list only made Lennart's threat to cast Aksel out of the pack all the more real. But if there was a chance they could offer their insight and experience, Aksel had to take it.

Nils was mated to their packmate, and his mother, Solfrid, was, gods willing, still in the Otherworld. She had not been on patrol the night they fell. As a healer, she was often away with the faun to help with childbirth or tend to the sick. But Elias had fallen and survived years without Solfrid at his side.

Sudden understanding struck Aksel like a boulder to the chest. He snapped his face to Elias, seeing the cheerful, burly wolven with fresh eyes.

All the care he put into the Sköllburg to ensure the pack was well fed and nurtured. His work with the community of Elkins, becoming a surrogate father to every inhuman that crossed his path. The doors of Riversmoke were always open, and a plate was set before anyone who needed a meal. Aksel had assumed that was his role within the pack. Supplies master and cook. Caretaker. Instead, they were the attempts of a wolven without his mate to occupy his mind and fill that hollow space.

New moon, hadn't Aksel done the same?

"Tell me, pup," Elias said again, his voice gruff. "How did it happen?"

"I met her at camp," Aksel began, and the words came spilling out.

How he'd caught her scent from across the field, rising above the sweat and stink of two dozen teenagers baking under a summer sun.

How he'd sought her out at lunch and dinner, finally earning a place beside her at the evening campfires. Night after night, shoulders touching, hands brushing.

Their first kiss—an accident. He'd walked her to her cabin, refusing to let go of her hand as she climbed the stairs. Jess had turned, eyes bright in the light of the full moon, and something within Aksel had unraveled like thread pulled from a spool. He'd panicked at the feeling of being unmoored and adrift, tightening his grip on her hand and pulling Jess into his arms.

The sigh of her breath against his lips was as fresh in his memory as if it had happened mere moments ago. The feel of her heart pounding against his chest, the way her fingers curled into his shirt.

From then on, Jess and Aksel became inseparable for two incredible summers. Sneaking away after dinner and before lights out. Finding excuses to linger in the band room and hike the trails behind the camp.

He'd shifted for her, and she'd clung to his fur, stroking his ears until a happy whine built in his chest.

Aksel told them about that last night, when they met beneath the bleachers, how he shifted, and she shoved his clothes into a backpack, climbing onto his back and clinging tight as he ran for the wolven lake on the ridgeline.

"She left the next day, and I never saw her again. Until this summer."

He looked up to find Elias rubbing a hand against his jaw, his eyes reddened and mouth set in a deep frown. Over his shoulder, Nils was stricken and pale. He cleared his throat, offering Aksel a weak nod.

"That, uh, sounds about right," he said, confirming everything he had thought as the story spilled from his mouth. "And I'm assuming you've felt zip, zero, zilch for any of the wolven Lennart's set you up with?" Aksel nodded, too afraid to say it aloud. Nils spared him, color crawling into his cheeks as he spoke. "When Inge and I mated...when I, uh, knotted her, that was it. There's no one else for me, Aks. It's all *her*. Came out of nowhere one day, like someone planted the idea. She was all I could think about, and when we finally"—he darted a look at his father and coughed into a fist—"mated, that was it."

"It is the same with your mother," Elias told his son. "Solfrid has my heart and soul, even across worlds."

"Lennart is gonna lose his shit," the younger wolven replied.

"What do I do?" Aksel asked.

"I don't think there's anything you can do." Elias shook his head. "Lennart's been parading you around like a stud, and this whole time, you've been mated and unaware."

"My awareness here isn't the problem," he argued. "What am I supposed to tell her?" He threw his arm in the direction of Elkins and Jess. "She has no idea what happened. I barely understand *how* it happened, and she's got—" A lump formed in his throat, dread cinching tight around his chest. "She's got kids."

"Those pups from the other night?" Elias asked. Aksel confirmed with a grunt.

"*She's* got kids?" Nils asked with an unfamiliar growl in the words. "The human is your mate; those kids are as good as yours."

"How?" Aksel wheeled on him, advancing into his space. It was a dick move, but he was a wolven on the edge, and that challenge in Nils's tone set off his wolf. "It was one night thirteen years—"

He stopped, the ground beneath his feet tipping to the side. Groping blindly, Aksel managed to grab hold of a rolling toolbox to keep his feet. Blood rushed in his ears, his heart thudding like a jackhammer.

"Thirteen years," he repeated. How old were they? Jess had told him. Were they thirteen? Twelve? No, she'd said they were turning thirteen in— "October." He blinked and raised his eyes to Elias. "They're thirteen in October."

"The math doesn't work if she carried a full human term."

"They're wolven," Aksel said, the words barely more than a whisper. "Three of them, at least. Her daughter has never shifted, but she's got her brothers whipped."

Wolven children. A wolven pregnancy, carried by a human mother. Gods and all the hells, what had that done to Jess? How had she managed it? Wolven carried fast, reaching full-term in roughly three months. Most female wolven spent their pregnancies shifted and on four paws to be more comfortable.

How had Jess *survived?*

The older wolven rubbed his jaw again, eyeing Aksel more closely. "I'm going to ask a precious question, Aksel, and I need you to think hard before you answer me." Aksel straightened, fisting his hands at his sides and holding Elias's stare. "Did you knot that girl?"

"I don't—" He snapped his jaw closed, thinking back to that night. They were so young, so stupid, neither of them knowing what they were doing and acting on instinct and the advice of magazines and rumors.

"I don't want to hurt you." He tightened his hold on her thighs, pressing against Jess to lift her away.

She clamped her knees tight. "I don't think we can avoid it," she said, silencing his argument with a soft kiss. "But it's worth it, Aksel. I want to."

"Oh. Oh, Gods." His knees buckled, and he hit the floor hard enough to rattle the tools on the workbench. A tingle started in his chest, sparking out to his extremities as the reality of that night, of the life—*lives* he had missed, pounded into him. "I didn't—" His skin itched, gums prickling as his wolf clawed for the surface, responding to Aksel's panic. "How did I—?"

"Pop, get the door," Nils hollered and crouched before Aksel, holding his hand out like he was taming a wild beast. "Take it easy, Aks. Don't wolf out, buddy."

"I can't—" He darted his gaze around the garage, claws scraping against the concrete. A howl built in his throat, the grind of gears too loud. He needed to get out of there before he destroyed the garage. Needed to shift to ease the itching and the growing pressure beneath his skin. He needed to—

Fresh air teased his senses, and his wolf sprang forward, shredding his clothes to ribbons.

His paws scrabbled against smooth cement, gaining purchase and launching him towards the still-opening door. Nils and Elias yelled at his back, and a motorcycle rumbled to life. Still, he ran, threading between the trees as fragments of thoughts ran through his mind, urging him faster: Jess. Mate. Kids.

Mine.

21

—·—

JESS

Jess,

I know you've been working your ass off on the proposal to the Mountaineers' Daughters, and I hate to add more work to your plate, but could you work with Mac Murray and put together a financial assessment for the last fiscal year? There's some concern over how investment resources have been used in the camp in the past, and a clear picture of where the money goes could sway them to sign the agreement.

Sorry about this. The board has your back; we've just run up against a ... personality that is slowing things down.

Let me know how I can help.

Svana

Jessica reread the email and opened a reply window before she thought better of it, pounding out her response in a flurry of fingers and no little amount of frustration.

Svana – are you kidding me? I barely know what I'm doing writing proposals, much less where to begin asking Mac for the camp's financial statements. I know I'm an accountant, but there are firms we can hire to do this. Impartial consultants who can dig into this and deliver what those stuffy old biddies want. What are they looking for, an easy way out? Elkwater is the most above-board camp in the state, and any expenditure of donated funds has gone towards improving the facilities to be inclusive of <u>all</u> campers, not just the human ones. I don't care if you forward this to their secretary or whoever is issuing these demands. The request is insulting.

Then, she deleted it, taking long, slow breaths as she did. This was okay. Any foundation would be concerned about the potential use of its donation. They had a right to inquire. This was a routine request—nothing to panic about.

So why was she panicking?

It had come on her out of nowhere. The laptop had dinged with an email notification, Jess had wandered into the bathroom, and this panicky *dread* had overcome her, speeding her pulse and fluttering in her stomach.

"Get a grip." She grabbed her notepad from the sink and added Svana's request to her to-do list, replying with a brief, "On it," before closing the email and frowning at her inbox. Her mother had emailed again; this one marked "urgent" while the subject line read simply: Checking In.

Jessica slammed her laptop shut and stormed out of the bathroom. Being Thursday, Aksel and the girls were at the camp, and Jessica could have a frustrated stomp-fit without worrying about being overheard. So she did, muttering to herself and storming in a circle around her living room, attempting to exhaust the panicky feeling in her chest.

When that didn't work, Jessica grabbed her keys, shoved on her sunglasses, and jogged down the steps. She hauled the door open and froze at the sight of a very sweaty, *very* naked Aksel standing on the stoop.

Eyes wide and wild, he held the cushion from the rocking chair pressed to his groin. His chest rose and fell in deep pants, beads of sweat purling down his temple. He gulped and swallowed, mouth working and failing to make any noise.

"Aksel, what are you—"

"Are they mine?" he blurted.

Jessica's back hit the door, nerves singing at his panic and the echoing flutter in her chest. "I—"

"Please, Jess." A canine whine entered his voice, and he took a half step forward, stopping just shy of entering her apartment. "Are they mine?"

She gripped the knob, tears burning, skin flushing, her heart sprinting in her chest. There was nowhere to run, no way to avoid what she'd been successfully, or stupidly, dodging since returning to Elkins. She couldn't breathe, much less form words, so she nodded.

Aksel exhaled, his chest deflating, shoulders dropping. His eyes darted over her face, and he dropped the cushion, surging forward and gathering Jessica to his chest.

"Jess." His arms tightened around her, popping her spine as he lifted her from the floor. He nuzzled her neck, peppering kisses along her shoulder as he marched forward. The front door slammed, and he set her on a step, lifting his head. Bright hazel eyes glimmered back at her, wide and pleading. "They're mine?"

"Yes," she gasped the word on a sob. Her ribs shrank, tightening around lungs already too small to breathe, and her heart—her heart pounded so fast she thought it might burst from her chest.

"Mine," he whispered, voice awed, and swept Jessica from the step, charging up the stairs.

She wasn't sure when the kiss began, but somewhere between the bottom of the stairs and the bedroom, Aksel's mouth had found hers. She lost herself to his warmth and taste, wrapping her legs around his waist and clasping her hands behind his neck, leveraging her height to nip his lips and sweep her tongue against his. It was so easy to fall into the kiss, to give in to the all-consuming passion in his lips, his arms. His heart boomed against her chest, strong hands kneading her thighs and her rear, and before she knew it, Aksel set her on the edge of her bed and lowered himself to his knees.

He clasped her hips and gazed up at her. Tears stained his cheeks, and those warm, woeful eyes searched her face.

"You must hate me."

"Aksel, no."

"I didn't know, Jess. I swear, I didn't know, and then you were here, and I was—it was a dream. You, here, after all those years. It didn't even cross my mind that they were—that we—" He buried his face in her lap, fingers tightening at her hips as if he were afraid she would run.

But where would she go when she had only ever been running toward him?

Jessica raised her hand, hesitating before threading her fingers through his hair, brushing the soft strands away from his face. "Gitta said you never got my letters."

Aksel stilled like a wolf catching a scent in the woods.

"She said you wrote to me for a year." Jessica cupped the back of his head, wishing he would look up at her, so she could see his face as she spoke. "She said you wrote to me until I never showed up at Elkwater the next summer."

He nodded, sliding his hands to her waist and tugging Jessica closer. She bent forward, bringing her lips close to his ear to whisper, "I wrote you, too."

Aksel shuddered, a sigh warming her knees and igniting a low heat in her belly. Awareness of his nakedness flooded Jessica, drying out her mouth. She pressed her palms against his shoulders, stroking his back as she spoke for no more reason than she wanted to and could.

"I wrote to you the day I found out I was pregnant. I wrote to explain why I couldn't meet you at that game. About the first time I felt them kick. I poured my heart out to you in those letters, begging you to write back. To drive down. To come find me and meet your ba—"

Her voice caught, and it was all Jessica could do to swallow her sob.

"I never got them," he mumbled, finally raising his head to let her see his sweet, sad face. "I swear, Jess, if I'd gotten them, the Gods themselves couldn't have stopped me from—"

"I know." Jessica nodded, letting the tears fall. Letting him see the exhaustion and the heartache of their years apart. She cupped his cheeks, brushing her thumbs against his cheekbones and relishing the tickle of his beard against her palms. "Gitta told me. I didn't mean for this to happen, Aksel. I only wanted them to know other inhumans and to have the chance to know you, even if only a little. I didn't know about the pack and your responsibilities." She sniffed, breath shuddering. "We'll leave at the end of the summer, I don't want to stand in the way of—"

"Jess, no." Aksel's hands flew up to grip her wrists. "None of that matters anymore. Damn the pack, damn Lennart, and my *responsibilities*." He spat the last word, a scowl overtaking his face. "You're more important than anything else. Do you understand?"

She did. Good lord, did she understand. She'd been the most important person in the world to four amazing children for years. She understood the gravity and the weight of that role better than anyone, but this—this was different. This wasn't a burden or a task of importance. This was Aksel placing Jessica above his pack. He wasn't asking her for anything or making demands; he was telling Jessica in his way that she could make demands of him.

She had only one.

"I do," she said and kissed him.

Aksel sighed against her mouth, all the strain and woe rushing from his body. He jerked Jessica to the edge of the bed, forcing her to spread her thighs to fit his thick torso between her legs.

Bodies pressed together, his thundering heart pounded into her, stoking the throb between her hips as he deepened the kiss.

The world beyond the apartment vanished. Her worries over the Outreach and the troublesome foundation. Her job. All of it melted away by the searing heat of Aksel's tongue and his feverish body.

She stroked his shoulders and gripped his arms, unable to hold enough of him at once. It seemed Aksel felt the same. He pressed his palms hard against her thighs, sliding them up, up, up to grasp her hips and jerk her even closer. A low rumble built in his chest, vibrating against her breasts. One hand slid to her lower back, pinning Jessica in place with her hips angled in a way that had that low rumble teasing her clit. An echo, a whisper. Not enough, never enough.

She whimpered, wriggling against him, and Aksel immediately broke away from the kiss, searching Jessica's face. "I'm sorry."

"More," she panted, gripping his arms and trying to pull him into the bed. "I need—"

She felt wild. Feral in a way she never had before, and it was all him. His strong, naked body and the soft padding she wanted to snuggle against. His sweet face and eyes that spoke a million words in a look. His heat and size. She needed his weight pressing her into the sheets. Needed his hands on her skin, his cock driving into her until she screamed. Until that maddening itch she'd been fighting since the summer began was satisfied.

"I need you, Aksel."

"New moon, never stop saying that." He slipped his fingers under her shirt, hooked them into the waistband of her leggings, and yanked. Fabric tore, and he tugged again, baring her thighs.

He ripped his arm back, pulling the leggings to her feet and then off her altogether, tossing them across the room.

Just as quickly, Aksel's hands were back on her hips, and his face nestled between her thighs. He inhaled deeply, a tight whimper caught in his throat.

"This scent has been teasing me for weeks," he growled into her pussy, breath hot against her underwear.

"Jesus." Jess gripped the edge of the mattress, dropping her head back as he inhaled again. Teeth dragged against her inner thigh, the warm flick of his tongue teased the crease of her leg. He nuzzled in closer, doing the same against her pussy until Jessica writhed against his face, gasping for air and needing so much more.

"Please," they whined in unison—a question, a plea, an answer—and Aksel tore her underwear away as quickly as he'd managed her leggings. He held the fabric to his mouth and nose, eyes fluttering closed as he inhaled. When they opened, a feral gleam appeared, his pupils constricting and fixing on Jessica.

It was a moment, an edge, a point of no return. She could stop this, right here, with a word. Aksel would leave, and they could try to forget this ever happened. The summer would end. She would return home with her kids and continue her life as she had every day leading up to this point.

Wondering and wanting.

Because Jessica knew if she pursued this, if they continued what they had begun, she would never wonder or want for him again.

So she leaned back, braced her hands against the edge of the bed, and widened her legs.

"Jess," he sighed, and the leash snapped.

Aksel dove forward, lapping at Jessica's pussy like a man starved. Pleasure rocketed up her spine, arching her back. His grip on her thighs was the only thing keeping her seated on the bed. That and his tongue, licking and driving deep within her. Sucking on her clit until a strangled cry left her throat. He laved her lips, nipping sensitive flesh with his teeth before laying his tongue flat against Jessica and licking, licking, licking. "Oh, God."

"Aksel," he broke away to mumble, slipping a hand between her legs. "My name's Aksel."

"That's not—oh!" His finger joined his mouth, sliding into her as he flicked her clit with his tongue. It was bliss. Heaven. Better than. She melted against the bed, overwhelmed by pleasure as Aksel made her body his toy. He dragged her legs over his shoulders, chuckling when she whimpered at the loss of his fingers. The position allowed him to haul her backside off the bed and wrap his arms over her thighs, pressing her pussy flush against his face. The change in angle, the brute strength of the move, had Jessica moaning, unable to form words or thoughts beyond his name.

"That's it, baby," he urged between licks, nuzzling her clit with his nose. "Mark me in your scent, Jess." He prodded deep, rolling his tongue against her inner walls. The heat in her belly rose, crawling up her front until every inch of Jessica throbbed with the need for release. She clawed at his arms, hips rolling against his face as a pressure in her belly wound tighter, tighter, tighter.

"Drown me in you, baby." Aksel fluttered kisses against her lips, flicking her clit with his tongue. "I want every wolven to smell you on me a mile away." And again. "I want them to know I'm yours."

"Mine," Jessica panted, unable to breathe, to think. She was only feeling and sensation. Pleasure and bliss. His mouth, his lips, his tongue, his *words*.

He growled again, and the vibration shot straight to her core. Jessica cried out, clasping her hands around his head and holding Aksel against her. The growl continued, vibrating harder against her as he licked and stroked, plunging his tongue deep only to retreat and taking her clit once more between his lips. He sucked, and Jessica shattered.

"Aksel!" His name echoed off the walls, rapture lighting up her veins and whiting out the world. He licked her through her orgasm, lapping up the gush of her release with a happy whine strangled in his throat.

She barely noticed Aksel removing her legs from his shoulders, but oh, did she notice each kiss he placed on her skin. The inside of her knee, her thigh, her hip. Callused hands slipped under her shirt, pebbling Jessica's skin as he lifted the loose cotton away.

Her mind was a haze of pleasure, her limbs languid and loose. The comedown from her orgasm was less a drop and more a gentle, feather-like floating as his every touch, the heat of his mouth, kept Jessica adrift in the clouds.

Only when the mattress dipped under his weight did she open her eyes to gaze up at him.

Aksel's beard glistened, his lips puffed and pink. He raked his gaze down her front, hunger burning clear in his eyes. "Are you alright?"

His voice was low and gravelly. *Ravenous.* Jessica shivered, heat building in her core. "Almost."

She reached for him, and Aksel grabbed her arm, drawing Jessica from the bed. He rolled onto his back, bringing her with him as if she weighed nothing. Nestled somewhat upright against the pillows, he seated Jessica with her thighs straddling his hips and grinned at her, sharp canines on full display.

His eyes were pure wolf, as was his smile, and it was better than anything she could have imagined. His strength, how easily he maneuvered her in the bed, and the way he held his gaze on her face. It was a predator's gaze, but Jessica did not for one second feel as though she were the prey. She felt ...

Beautiful. Powerful in a way she had not in years.

"Better?" His erection brushed against her cheeks, the tease of it clenching muscles deep within her. Good Lord, he was big. Bigger than she remembered, which was saying something. She could still easily draw on the memory of the pressure, the sensation of being filled. The heat and the pleasure of the burn.

Straddling him now, she was well aware of how easy it would be to relive that moment, and the desire to do so overwhelmed her.

"Almost." She toyed with the hem of her shirt, torn between tossing it aside to match his nudity or preserving what was left of her modesty. Aksel decided for her, hands again finding her waist, sliding up her ribcage.

"May I?' he asked in a low, rumbling voice. Jessica nodded, and he lifted her shirt the rest of the way, gently pulling it off her raised arms and dropping it to the floor. He froze then, throat bobbing as he drank her in. "Gods, look at you."

Large hands wrapped around her ribcage, thumbs brushing the underside of her breasts. Jessica dropped her head back, loose curls dusting her shoulders, and closed her eyes, lost in the reverent sweep of his thumbs and the warmth of his palms cupping her breasts. He moved, and she gasped back into herself as his mouth closed over a nipple, sucking her through the thin cotton of her bra.

A sparkling zing of pleasure danced straight through her chest, down to her groin. A hand flew to his head, holding Aksel right where he was, and she reached back, groping blindly for his cock.

Her fingers brushed hot steel, and she moaned, pussy clenching in desire. She grasped the thick shaft and stroked, her movements clumsy and unpracticed. Still, a rumbling growl built in Aksel's chest.

He tugged her bra low, laving her nipple with his tongue and sucking on the sensitive bud, just as he had done with his face buried in her pussy. The reminder of how thoroughly he had devoured her sent a tremor through Jessica.

"Aks—" She grasped his cock harder, mind blown by the length of her stroke. He thrust into her palm, the roll of his hips brushing the soft swell of his belly against her throbbing clit. A heady pulse of bliss rocketed through her body, leaving her gasping. "God, Aksel, please."

"Whatever you want, baby," he murmured the promise into her chest, kissing a line across her breastbone. Jessica hitched higher, crying out as he took her other nipple between his teeth. "Whatever you need, take it."

His cock seemed to swell in her hand, a bead of moisture meeting her thumb. She swept it over the swollen head and Aksel moaned, clamping his hands on her hips and inching her back.

"Gonna drive me feral," he rasped, lowering Jessica over his cock. She guided him as best she could, hissing in anticipation as the thick head notched at her entrance.

"Oh," she panted. "My God, Aksel."

"I like that." He rocked his hips, and Jessica cried out from the sizzle and stretch as he entered her, every nerve in her body lighting up firework bright. "Your God."

"Mine." She brought both hands to his chest, bracing herself as she lowered further. Her senses shorted out, fried by the sheer bliss coursing through her body. God, how could she feel so much at once? His heart pounding beneath her palms, her nails dimpling soft flesh, the low rumble of his pleasure buzzing in her bones. She felt mad, like she was grasping onto the last bits of her sanity while a wild, feral part of her whispered *let go*.

She did, relaxing her thighs and attempting to seat Aksel deep inside of her.

He snarled, lip curling, and fisted the base of his cock, hips bucking as his grip tightened on her hip.

"Jess, this is—" he panted, teeth gnashing as though it took all his effort just to form the words. "Go slow, I want—new moon, this is just—"

"Like I remembered." She finished for him, nodding her head in wild agreement. A deep groan left her as she eased up his shaft, lowering again until her pussy met his fist, finding a groove in the rolling of his hips and guiding grip of his hand. What she had taken of his cock filled her, pressing against parts of herself Jessica had not even known existed. Each roll of his hips, every slide of his thick cock as he entered her again, and again, shot her higher. Closer to satisfying that maddening itch. "I needed this," she panted. "You. Missed you so—"

"Me too." Aksel caught her mouth with his, plunging his tongue deep. Her own arousal burst on her tastebuds, and that wild part of her raged with need. "Me too, baby." He pressed an arm between her shoulders, lightly gripping the back of her neck. With his other hand, still fisting the base of his cock, he lightly thumbed her clit. Jessica cried out at the glorious blend of sensation and pleasure. "That's it, Jess. Howl for me."

And she did. His name, curse words, and gibberish, until her throat was raw and her body was a taut wire. Aksel never let up, matching her frantic tempo and thrusting into Jessica deeper than she could have ever imagined.

She felt him everywhere. In the tips of her fingers and toes, skating up her legs and blanketing her back. A buzz built in her teeth, pulsing along with every stroke of his finger, and she bit down on his shoulder in an attempt to maintain her weak hold on sanity.

Aksel howled then, his thrusts becoming wild and erratic, his cock thickening inside of her. How, she had no idea, but the sensation was undeniable. Pressing against her walls and scoring every lovely piece of her until she was no longer sure where she ended, and he began. Her mind was a fog of pleasure, every inch of her skin singing from his touch, the fullness, the sense of being taken and taking all at once.

Just when she thought she couldn't rise any higher, when she was sure she would die from pleasure, Aksel drove his heels into the mattress and thrust his hips up, scoring a deep set place inside Jessica that had her tipping into a freefall.

The orgasm he had given her mere moments ago was nothing compared to this. She was starlight. A comet. Fireworks bursting in the sky. Her pussy clenching around his cock as ecstasy coursed through her veins.

"Fuck." Aksel grunted, squeezing out of Jessica. She barely had time to process the emptiness, the loss, before hot come splashed against her lower back, rolling down the curve of her cheek. He dropped back against the pillows, crushing her to his chest as he panted. "Gods damn, Jess."

She nodded, lips and tongue too numb to speak. Aksel stroked her back, her arms, pressing soft kisses to her temple and forehead. She closed her eyes, losing herself in the steadying cadence of his breathing and the slowing beat of his heart.

A door slammed, rattling the windows, and Jessica raised her head, blinking blearily at the room. The light had shifted, bleeding into the bedroom from the rear of the apartment. She glanced at the clock, and a laugh escaped as she read the time.

"You alright?" Aksel asked. His voice was thick with sleep, and the warm rumble in his chest threatened to pull Jessica back under.

"I can't remember the last time I took a nap." She slid off of him, pressing her body against Aksel's side. He curled an arm around her shoulders, tugging Jessica close.

"I'll make sure you get more of them." He kissed the top of her head. "Was that Cricket and Avery coming home?"

"Must have been," Jessica murmured. Good heavens, she could stay here forever, cuddled against Aksel and captured in his arms. A flutter stirred in her belly, and she shifted her hips, draping a leg over his. What was it about this wolven that had her ready for round two—or was it three? Four? Could they count a dalliance as teenagers? No, that was ridiculous, even if it was the last time she'd been with anybody. So, round two, then—what was it about him?

Mind-blowing orgasms helped, sure, but it was more than that. More than the way he'd devoured her pussy like a starved man. More than how his cock had her seeing stars. Although...

Jessica trailed her hand down his chest, tracing the curve of his belly.

"Tickles," he grumbled, twitching from her touch.

"Sorry." She drew a line across his hips, biting back a smile at the needy little gasp that breezed from his mouth, and stopped when her fingers brushed his hardening cock. "Aksel?"

"Yes?"

"Are you already ... ready?"

He was silent for a beat, body preternaturally still. "...yes."

"Good."

"Anything else?"

"Yes," Jessica answered, keeping her voice serious. She angled her face up at him. "You pulled out." Aksel's eyes rounded, and his lips parted in surprise. Unable to hold back, she grinned. "I didn't know you knew how to do that."

22

— · —

AKSEL

"YOU—" AKSEL BANDED HIS arms around her and, in a heartbeat, had Jess flat on her back. With his hands set beside her shoulders, he bracketed Jess beneath him, watching with pride as she flushed from head to toe. "You're trouble."

"Always was." She nodded fervently, eyes wide and innocent. "But you don't have to. Pull out, that is. I've got an IUD."

"Oh." Well, that was something, and not at all the reason why he had pulled out. Honestly, worrying about getting Jess pregnant *again* had not even crossed his mind, which Aksel should probably take the time to consider.

So he did, biting his lip as the mere idea sent blood rushing to his groin. New moon, just the thought of filling Jess with his come, watching her belly swell with his pups, *their* pups, had his dick aching with the need to be inside of her again.

"Oh, hello." She traced her fingernail up his length, sending a frisson of pleasure straight to his balls.

He hissed, hips twitching, his body seeking out more of her touch.

"I'm surprised I had you all afternoon," Jess mused, circling his head with the tip of her finger.

"Mac took my morning classes," he said. "And the kids hike on Thursdays. You can have me all night if you want." And tomorrow. Forever.

"Mm." She snuggled tighter against him. "I like that idea." Another slow swipe of her finger had him closing his eyes, dick throbbing as the fantasy of a heavily pregnant Jessica filled his head.

He had never considered breeding. The possibility had felt so far out of reach for a wolven who felt no connection or romantic draw to anyone. All those dates had frustrated him, as did the way Lennart paraded him out for eligible wolven females in other packs. The burden of expectation.

Then Jess walked back into his life, and suddenly, the idea of breeding was as appealing as a perfectly rare filet mignon.

He noticed the stretch marks on her hips and belly as he kissed his way up her body. Through the haze of lust, he had traced the faint creamy marks on her breasts with his thumbs, marveling at the artistic proof of the miracle she had performed. The suggestion of the full, ripe body that had grown and nurtured her children. *Their* children.

"Fuck," Aksel groaned, fisting the base of his dick as Jess teased the head. She circled her fingers, pressing down on the swollen tip, and stars burst behind his eyes. He wanted to trace every one of those marks with his tongue. Make her feel how incredible he found her. How alluring her body was. Older and curvier, enticing enough to make his palms itch for want of touching her.

Jess wriggled out from under his arm and rose, setting a knee between his legs. She never ceased her gentle strokes, and the warm crash of her breath against his sensitive cock cracked his eyelids open. "Do you remember what we used to do beneath the bleachers?"

Gods. Did he remember? He never forgot the reflection of moonlight in her eyes when she dropped to her knees. The first hot, wet, testing stroke of her tongue, as vivid today as it was in the moment. The warm grip of her hands ...

Her mouth closed over his head, the suction pulling a deep groan out of Aksel.

His knot throbbed against his palm, his wolf howling and scratching for the surface. Aksel gnashed his teeth, willing those primal urges down. This was why he'd pulled out earlier. Not for fear of getting her pregnant—Gods, if only he could be so lucky—but for fear of knotting her.

He knew she had sought out other wolven to learn from and give her—*their*—kids a sense of community, but how far did her knowledge go? Knots were for breeding, to guarantee the wolven carried on and that pups had a unit, a family. A mini-pack within the pack to ensure they were protected and loved.

After his talk with Nils and Elias, Aksel was all but convinced of what had happened thirteen years ago, but to spring that on Jess now? When they'd only just come together after so many years? When he'd just found out her children were *theirs?*

His wolf could wait. He would wait until she was ready and comfortable in whatever this was, before asking if she knew, if she minded.

New moon, did mating even take with humans? It had with him, of that Aksel was certain. His knowledge was vague, but the steps were whispered about as much as knots were. You scented and marked, which Gitta suspected. Then you mated and knotted and bred, like Nils and Elias with Inge and Solfrid.

His cock twitched at the thought, again, of Jess carrying his pups. Her heavy breasts spilling from his hands, the delicious weight of her belly resting against his as she rode him until her screams filled the room. Her plush thighs and soft rear gripped in his palms instead of his dick and growing knot.

No, that would be locked inside of her, ensuring his woman was satisfied over and over again.

"Gods be damned, Jess." He moaned, writhing as she swallowed half of his shaft. His head butted the back of her throat, and her ensuing gag tightened her mouth around his cock.

A glance at her nearly ruined him. Eyes softly closed, her cheeks hollowed out as she sucked, her plump lips stretched around his girth. New moon, she was gorgeous. A dream. A fantasy come to life.

Heat surged beneath his palm, his knot swelling. Aksel tightened his grip, stroking up his shaft until he met her lips and back again. She hummed her approval, lightly scraping her nails down his thigh to urge him on.

He rocked, gently at first, too afraid of hurting Jess when all he wanted to do was let go. Let his wolf fuck her mouth and spill his seed, filling her cheeks until whatever she could not swallow dribbled down her chin. Even then, he would not be done. The sheer fire in his balls, the need he'd battled for damn near a week, told him that well enough.

He'd take her then, toss her against the pillows, and spread those lovely thighs, entering Jess until she trembled and quaked. Until her body was awash with pleasure and the only thought in her lovely head, the only word she was capable of speaking, was his name.

But not tonight. Tonight, he would follow Jess's lead like a dog on a leash, happily taking whatever scraps of attention she threw his way. And tomorrow and the day after that, until all those years she spent thinking he did not care, thinking he had left her to raise *their* kids by herself, were erased, replaced by memories of him as a sure and steady presence in her life and theirs.

As if she heard him, Jess wrapped both hands around his dick, stroking and swirling her palms as she sucked and licked.

Heat coiled deep in his belly, a tingling, tightening sensation growing in his balls.

Aksel blinked out of the tangent his thoughts had taken, trying to clear a building burn at the backs of his eyes. His chest tightened, the muscles in his legs tensing as he stroked and squeezed his knot, trying to hold on when Jess's every touch, the pressure of her palms, the wet slide of his cock in her gorgeous mouth, sent him careening to the edge.

She hummed something around his dick, wide brown eyes flicking up to his face, and Aksel fell apart.

Fire roared up his spine, his legs shot straight, and bliss obliterated his thoughts. She sucked him through his orgasm, somehow knowing exactly how hard to grip him, her throat working to swallow every last drop. New moon, she was perfect, drinking his release like it was nectar. Her eyes drifted closed, and an expression of utter peace softened her features.

"Jess," he sighed her name, head dropping back onto the pillows.

Gods, he was never going to let her go. He would not survive another separation, not now that he'd had *this*. He would not be able to continue as Elias had. How could he? Looking at her, experiencing this, knowing he had potentially, most likely, knotted and mated a woman as perfect as Jess, that they had *children* together ...

The burn in the back of Aksel's eyes crawled forward, and a foreign pressure settled on his chest, an emotion too big for his body forcing its way up his throat. A tiny whimper escaped before he pressed his lips together.

"Aksel?" Jess lay on top of him, cupping his face. "Oh," she said softly, brushing damp from his cheek and the corner of his eye. "Baby, it's okay."

"I don't know what this is," he managed to say around a sob, wrapping his arms around Jess and holding her to his chest. "I'm sorry, I—"

"No, nono, no sorries." She fluttered light kisses across his mouth, his nose, his cheek, cradling his head in her hands as sobs wracked his body.

He didn't know how to navigate this. What if she didn't want him after this summer? What if too many years stretched between them, and he had missed the chance to be a sire and a mate? What if she returned to Charleston with her kids and never came back?

She'd done it before, and if she did it again ...

Aksel was not cut out to be a lone wolf. The Sköllburg wasn't his true pack, a fact he felt more keenly now than ever. He was a cast-out, a foster, a child of a system designed to help him find a mate and found his own pack, or challenge Lennart for his. Maybe he would have stood a chance in the Otherworld, but here?

Gods, Lennart was right; it was only a matter of time before he could no longer ignore his nature and the call to the wild. Now that Jess was in his arms, holding him as strange, terrifying emotions ravaged his heart and mind, Aksel knew. Gods, he knew.

He could not survive if she left him again, and worse, he did not know how to keep her.

23

— • —

JESS

"SORRY ABOUT THIS." MAC dropped another banker's box on the table. A cloud of dust burst in Jessica's face. Her nose twitched and tingled, and a stream of sneezes burst out rapid-fire, leaving her teary-eyed.

"Lord," she muttered, wiping her thumbs under her eyes.

"And that," Mac added. "Yikes." She scanned the kitchen table, littered with files, boxes, stacks of papers, and Jessica's notebook and laptop. "This is a bigger job than I thought it would be."

"Why is everything so dusty?"

"Ramble likes to work outside." Mac hooked her thumb at the kitchen door and the garden beyond.

"You couldn't build them a shed?" she asked, removing the lid and flipping through the files. Though the Foundation had requested a financial assessment for the last year, but Jessica had asked Mac to pull as much as she could. If there were any sense of fairness in the world, a deeper audit would prove that the camp's financials were solid enough to settle their nerves and cut off any other questions that could further slow down the process. "Or hire an accountant?"

"You'll figure out pretty quickly that hiring a full-time accountant is out of our budget," Mac replied without batting an eye. "Ramble does their best. They're pretty adept with numbers and worked with the project manager on the renovations." She gestured to a stack of boxes on the floor by the door. "If you have any questions about expenses and write-offs there, they'd be happy to help."

Jessica slid her gaze across boxes on the floor and the crowded table. "If that's from the renovations, what is all this?"

"Enrollments, donation receipts, payment records, certificates of insurance for vendors, corporate retreat contracts." At Jessica's raised eyebrows, Mac explained, "Mrs. Payne's idea. She got wind of some less-than-favorable opinions about the camp project in their corporate office."

Jessica pursed her lips, searching her memory for a Mrs. Payne. An image of red hair attached itself to the name Payne in her mind's eye. Distant and hazy and firmly dated at least a decade prior. "Avery's mom?"

"That's her." Mac grinned. "She's a daughter of West Virginia, like you and I. Her family came from Grafton, I think? Anyways, she asked if we'd consider hosting off-season events, and, frankly, it was genius." She flicked a box on the table, this one less dusty than the others. "That weekend retreat made us more money than a full week of camp."

"That's incredible." Jessica mentally breathed a sigh of relief. If she could demonstrate that funds were being used responsibly and the camp was on a growth trajectory, even with a tight runway rather than no runway, it would give the Mountaineers Daughters more confidence in their donation to the Outreach. And *that* donation would enable them to send at least a dozen kids to Elkwater the following summer.

"Sorry it's so much."

"No, this is perfect. It is a lot, but I'm a good accountant." Jessica pulled what she hoped was a confident smile onto her face. "And the donors aren't visiting for another week. More than enough time to—"

Mac's radio crackled on her hip, and a crisp female voice filled the kitchen. "Mac, to the orchestra hall."

"Camp Nurse." Mac explained. "Sorry. Mondays are crazy." She grabbed the radio, depressing the button as she tore it from her belt. "Almaden? Mac here. What's up?"

"You need to get over here." Nurse Almaden sighed. "Rolf is losing his mind."

"What happened?"

"A gnome got stuck in a timpani."

"How?" Mac shot Jessica a startled look and darted for the door, glancing back to mouth, "Sorry," before disappearing into the camp.

Jess exhaled, relieved the call wasn't about one of her boys. Pivoting on her heels, she grabbed two boxes from the nearest stack and hoisted them into her arms. Muscles she had never been aware of protested the weight, twinging and pinching as she bumped her hip against the screen door and trudged across the lawn.

"This is what I get," Jessica grumbled, "for acting like a horny teenager sneaking out of my parents' house." As fun as the weekend was—days spent with her kids and nights spent visiting Aksel while they slept—she felt every one of her thirty-one years shoving the boxes into the trunk of her car. At least she had a little bit of fun while she could. With less than a week to turn around a year's worth of finances, nights with Aksel would have to take a backseat to ledgers and spreadsheets. It was a weird sort of penance, but Jessica couldn't deny the guilt she'd felt tiptoeing down the stairs while her children slept.

This would be good for her. Focusing on the camp's financials would keep her from getting distracted by strong arms and a soft smile, and it would give her a chance to recover from the weekend because, *wow*, she had no idea there were that many muscles in her back.

Two trips later, her arms shook, sweat-drenched cotton clung to her skin, and the boxes must have multiplied because she could have sworn she'd made a dent with that last stack.

Hands on her hips, she surveyed the remaining boxes. "Jesus."

"Need help?" Aksel's deep voice rolled through the room, raising a swathe of goosebumps along her neck.

"*Christ.*" Jessica whirled around, pressing a palm over her thundering heart. "What are you doing here?"

"Caught your scent in the camp." He gestured to the open front door and the parking lot, an amused smile crinkling his cheek. "Where I work."

"Right. Of course." Jessica swept a sweaty curl from her forehead, all too aware of the damp blotches staining her armpits and how her t-shirt clung to her figure, highlighting every place she was soft. Of course, he would catch her scent. Being wolven, he'd always had a great sense of smell, and Jessica was sweatier than the devil in church. She must reek nine ways to Sunday.

She crossed her arms, which squished her boobs together uncomfortably. So she slid her hands in her rear pockets instead, opting for what she hoped passed as a casual pose.

Aksel's smile faded, his eyes dropping. Only then did Jessica realize that her so-called "casual pose" had exposed her chest and torso, sweat stains, clingy cotton, and all.

"Right." Jessica cleared her throat. "I've got work to do." She snatched another stack of boxes from the table and charged for the door. Aksel held, filling the frame and blocking her way. "Excuse me."

"Where are these going?"

"To my car." She edged to the side, and Aksel moved with her. "Could you please move?"

"Can I help?"

"I'm good." She adjusted the boxes, relieving some of the weight.

If he helped, it would prolong the time they spent together. Alone. Where he could see how sweaty she was. Not that he hadn't already seen her sweaty and bedraggled, panting after making her come so hard she saw stars.

And maybe that was it. Maybe seeing her sweaty and catching her scent in the air had brought those very same thoughts into Aksel's mind, which meant she needed to get her car loaded and get back to the apartment because if she spent any more time alone with him, her mind would wander, and she'd never get anything done.

"Just need to get all this to my car."

"Let me." He grabbed the bottom of the box, fingers brushing hers. A tingle zipped up her arms, and she tightened her grip.

"I've got it."

"These are heavy, Jess." He tugged. "Let me help."

"No, I've got it. You're busy, and it's just a few—"

"I always have time for you," Aksel said, his voice impossibly low and rumbly in the best way. Her belly flipped, and Jessica hauled the boxes out of his hands, needing to put distance between them before she abandoned this project altogether.

She darted out of his reach, the movement upsetting the topmost box. It wobbled, and she twisted and sidestepped, trying to settle the weight before a thousand receipts and invoices flew across the kitchen floor. "Whoa."

"Careful." Aksel swept the box away with one hand as if it weighed nothing. He set it atop a stack near the door, shot Jessica a grumpy look, and hoisted four boxes into his arms. "To your car?" he asked, striding for the door.

"I—yes." Jess hustled after him with her one box. "Thank you. You don't have to do this."

"Yes, I do," he said, descending the stairs without breaking stride. Midday sun poured into Mac's yard, highlighting deep amber strands in his dark hair. It was impossible to ignore the strength in his arms and back as he crossed the parking lot toward her car. The sleeves of his deep green camp polo cuffed tight against his biceps, muscles bulging from the weight of the boxes. Big muscles, cushioned by a layer of comfort that had cradled Jessica's head as she drifted into a deep, satisfied sleep.

Her cheeks heated at the memory of Aksel's strength caught beneath the gentle press of her hand. His muscles turned loose and languid by her tongue and her lips.

Aksel cleared his throat, setting the boxes beside her car and running a hand through his hair, scanning the lot.

"Whatever you're thinking about," he said in a low, gravelly voice, "could you please not? At least until we're done with these boxes and not standing out in the open." He finally looked at her, and Jessica had to step back from the simmering heat in his gaze. The hunger and desire she had seen enough of by now to recognize. "Save those thoughts for when we're alone, and I can enjoy that delicious scent."

"How would you enjoy it?" she asked, skin flushing hotter as Aksel stepped near, running his tongue across his lower lip. A simple, quick move that told her exactly how he would enjoy her. Arousal bloomed to life as a slow, needy throb. His nostrils flared, and he closed his eyes, a moan choking in his throat.

"New moon, Jess. Unsexy thoughts." A leg hitched as he adjusted his shorts. "I'm at work. Your scent is distracting enough, but whatever you're thinking about has made it damn irresistible."

"Right." She scanned the boxes, grasping for the unsexiest thoughts she could. "We should probably put the W-9s in the front seat; I'll need to review them first. And the 1099s as well. Contractors fill them out wrong half the time, but if I can reconcile payroll between the 1099s and the employee W-2s, I should be able—"

"That'll do." Aksel laughed and hauled open the passenger door, setting the boxes inside. "Moonblessed, that'll do."

After another five trips to Mac's kitchen, Jessica's arms trembled, and sweat drenched her from forehead to navel. Aksel shoved the last box into her car, grunting lightly as he shut the trunk.

"Water?" Jessica offered him a bottle she'd dug out from her glove compartment.

Aksel waved it off. "Lemonade. I have a mini fridge in my office." He gestured at the camp and leaned into a step only to hesitate. "If you have time, that is."

"You just hauled a few hundred pounds of financial records to my car; I should be buying you dinner."

"It's a date." He winked and hooked a thumb at the camp. "Later. Now, we need lemonade. And air conditioning."

Jessica looked at her car and the mountain of work waiting within. Then, she looked to Aksel, unable to ignore the quiet hopefulness she found there. Lord knew he would never push her. He would accept a polite "no, thank you" and go on with his day, but the poor wolven's cheeks were ruddy and flushed, and he looked as though he were desperately trying to keep from panting. Lips parted, the pink tip of his tongue pressed against the back of his teeth, and a rapid pulse fluttered in his neck. It wasn't a leap of the imagination to see how badly he wanted to shift and find a cool patch of shade to stretch out in.

Instead, he waited.

"One lemonade." Jessica raised her index finger.

Aksel's face lit up in a broad smile. "One lemonade."

24

Jess

Aksel pushed open his office door, and a rush of cold air crashed into Jessica, chilling her sweat and raising goosebumps. Her nipples hardened from the sudden cold, and she shivered, crossing her arms tight across her chest as she stepped inside.

Shoved at the end of a row of practice rooms, the Marching Director's office was just as she remembered; only the photos and personal items strewn across the desk had changed, giving her a glimpse into Aksel's life.

As in Mac's office, framed photos hung on the wall—shots of campers with their instruments, some candid as they marched or lounged on the field, others posed with Aksel beaming proudly in the middle. Among the camp photos were pictures of a marching band in full uniform on a football field, most taken from a vantage Jessica immediately recognized as the director's platform.

"How long have you been the Marching Director?"

"Five years," Aksel rumbled at her back, far closer than she expected. Jessica spun, arms dropping as he crowded her against the wall. "Eight at the high school."

Fingers drafted over the back of her hand, his nostrils flaring like they had in the parking lot. Sunlight filtered through the blinds, catching in his eyes and revealing broad pupils as if he were trying to see all of her at once.

Good lord, she loved it when he looked at her like this. With desire and heat, seeing past the single mother to the person she was.

"Oh," she said, struck dumb by his nearness, the burning intent clear on his face. What else was there to say? What would a normal person say? "Do you like it?"

"Not as much as I like this." He ducked and buried his face in her neck, inhaling before sweeping a warm, wet line across her throat with his tongue. "Gods, Jess. You smell so good."

He clamped his hands at her hips, pressing her against the wall with enough force to rattle the frames. Jessica gripped his sides and pulled him close, forcing more of his weight against her.

"I'm a mess." She dropped her head back, revealing more of her throat and reveling in how tiny he made her feel, how delicate yet powerful. Though he outweighed her and had proven how easily he could toss her around, she controlled his every move. "I'm sweaty and disgusting and—"

"Perfect." He nipped her jaw, exhaling hot behind her ear. "You look like you do after we've fucked." At those words, and a flick of his tongue against her neck, all logic fled. All reason.

She should be driving back to Elkins, unloading the boxes, and beginning her work. But with Aksel's weight pinning her to the wall and his mouth at her throat, all she wanted was to feel more of him. All of him. In her, on her, consuming her from head to toe.

"Aksel." She half-heartedly pushed against him, giving up at the low, rumbling chuckle that earned.

"Don't tell me you want lemonade first, Jess." He nuzzled the crook of her neck, kissing and lightly sucking until her hips rolled. "After I've had to smell how turned on you are for the last hour? No." He tugged her collar away with his teeth to nibble her clavicle. "No, I don't think it's lemonade you want."

A tight moan rose in her throat. Jessica bit her lip to keep from crying out. Children could be in the practice rooms next door or outside his window. What was he thinking, kissing her like this at the *camp?*

Not that the risk of getting caught had ever stopped them before, but they were barely adults then, just horny eighteen-year-olds with the world at their feet and their whole lives in front of them. Under the bleachers, the breezeways between buildings, hell, the campfire after lights out. Any place they were alone became a place where Jessica could drop to her knees or a prime location for Aksel to slip his fingers between her thighs.

"Tell me what you were thinking about." Aksel moved to the other side of her neck, finding a spot that had Jessica's hips rolling.

"Now?"

"Now," he replied. "Moments ago. All the time." He snagged her earlobe and whispered low, "I always want to know what you're thinking, Jess, but right now, I'm particularly interested in whatever had you dropping scent earlier."

To emphasize his desire, Aksel ground lightly against her. An odd mixture of arousal and embarrassment flushed through her, heating Jessica's cheeks and chest to a feverish degree even as a low throb pulsed to life in her core.

"Lord, Aksel."

"Were you thinking about how you woke me up on Saturday?" He gently brush her hair away, kissing his words into her temple. "With your gorgeous mouth wrapped around my cock?"

She whimpered.

"Or was it about how I sat you on the edge of my bed and buried my face between these lovely legs?" The hand at her hip slid low, his palm forming to the curve of her. "Was that it, Jess? Because it sure gives me a few ideas."

Good lord, when had he learned to talk like this?

"What was it, Jess?" Aksel cupped her rear and squeezed, hitching her hips forward as he did. His erection pressed against her belly, and Jessica's thoughts, what little there were, scattered. "What were you thinking about that had you smelling so"—again, he buried his face in the crook of her neck and breathed her in, exhaling a sigh—"delicious?"

"You." She buried her fingers in his hair as he lifted his head. Aksel blinked slowly at her, heated amber eyes sharpening as her words took root. "Just you."

"Fuck."

Gripping Jessica by the waist, he spun, sat her firmly on his desk, and caught her mouth in an explosive kiss. Hands flew, picture frames clattered to the ground, and papers crumpled beneath her legs, his hands, her back.

Aksel barely let her breathe, sweeping into her mouth as if she were that cool glass of lemonade he had offered. Gripping her thigh, he drew her leg up, grinding against Jessica and sucking on her lower lip. Heat bloomed low in her belly, need and desire coiling together faster than she thought possible.

She gripped his arms, nails digging into the cotton polo as sheer pleasure overtook every thought beyond how wild this was. How insane. Making out in the Marching Director's office, about to come from grinding alone.

It was terrifying. Exhilarating. All too big and unbelievable and so, so, so very *right*.

That was the only clear thought in her mind. The one truth, a lodestar she could follow on the darkest night.

How right this was, how right *he* was. How she'd been living with an emptiness inside her, surviving with a hollow place beside her where Aksel should be.

It was inconceivable that she should feel this way and know this truth in her bones after only a few weeks. What were weeks compared to the years she'd had without him?

Everything, apparently.

And now he was here, driving Jessica mad with pleasure, merely by thrusting against her shorts and kissing her like he wanted to devour her whole, finally relinquishing her mouth to press fevered kisses down her neck, to the hollow of her throat.

"Moonblessed, Jess." Aksel groaned, lowering to his knees. "You smell Gods-damned exquisite."

"I bet I taste even better." The words poured out of her, drawn from the depths of her mind where she kept such thoughts tucked away. Not well enough, she recognized, or perhaps Aksel was the key.

Perhaps those words, those demands, the empowerment in how sexy and desired she felt, had belonged to Aksel all along.

She undid the button on her shorts, unzipping the fly as desire flooded his face. His eyes darkened, lids lowering as he licked his lips and swallowed. His grip tightened at her hips, tugging lightly. Jessica followed the move, scooting to the edge of the desk.

"Lift your hips," Aksel rasped, and she did. In a smooth motion, he pulled her shorts and underwear away, setting both gently on a chair. Then he settled between her legs, held her gaze, and asked, "May I?"

"Yes."

One word. One tiny, simple little word, and Jessica unleashed a beast. He gripped her thighs, spread her wide, and dove in. A sweep of his tongue shot her back ramrod straight, and the following flick had her seeing stars. Pleasure mounted with every stroke, swelling and churning until it spilled into her limbs faster than she could fathom.

Orgasm crashed through her, bucking Jessica's hips from the desk. She clapped a hand over her mouth to muffle her scream, teeth driving into her lower lip. Aksel tightened his grip, licking and sucking Jessica as if he were personally offended she had tried to silence her bliss.

The pleasure receded, leaving her teeth and toes tingling, and only then did she pull her hand away.

"Aks—" She choked out his name between gasps. "Aksel, please, I—" He glanced up at her, driving his tongue deep. A deep moan overtook her next words, a second climax building. "I need you," she panted and clutched his shoulder, weakly tugging him up. "Need to feel you."

He answered by growling into her pussy. The vibrations warbled through her, curling her toes. She let out a sharp gasp, squirming when he removed his tongue and lapped her sex, tongue curling to flick her clit before he pulled away and rose.

Looming over her at his full height, eyes wild and lips and chin glistening with her release, Aksel's wolf was closer to the surface than she had ever seen it. Eyes glowing amber-gold in the low afternoon light narrowed. He curled his lip in a snarl, revealing a sharp canine. Grabbing Jessica by the hips, he eased her from the desk and turned her around, claws pricking her bare thighs.

Without a word, he cupped the back of her neck and pressed gently, guiding Jessica to bend. "Hold on to the edge." The snarl of his command raised a shiver down the length of her spine. She lay flat against the desk, turning her face to watch him from the corner of her eye.

Never in a million years could she have imagined Aksel like this. Large and powerful, terrifying in his size and hunger, yet not the slightest bit of fear entered her. Only arousal. Every vein throbbed, her breasts aching as they flattened against the desk, her pussy clenching around nothing.

Moisture dripped down her thighs, and without being told, Jessica raised onto her toes, presenting her bared sex to the wolven at her back.

"Moonblessed, Jess." He fussed with his belt and the button on his shorts, eyes never leaving her offering. "You're the most beautiful creature I've ever seen." The warmth of his words bloomed on her cheeks. She shut her eyes, pinching her lips to hide how badly she wanted to smile at his words, his attention. How strongly his desire affected her.

How long ... how many nights, how many years had she fantasized of hearing words such as those whispered in her ear, kissed into her skin. Night after night, she fought against the exhaustion of raising her children, during midnight feedings, tantrums, early mornings, and rough afternoons. In those few quiet moments she had to herself, gazing at a reflection she no longer recognized and taking account of the changes to her body. Stretch marks and breasts that hung low. Wider hips and a waist that remained soft no matter how many miles she hiked or aerobics classes she took.

Jessica had been forever changed by that last summer. Forever changed by Aksel and now, here he was with his cock in hand, poised at her back and saying the very things she had longed to hear since their last night together.

The words she never thought she would hear from anyone.

"So gods-damned gorgeous." The blunt tip of his cock pressed against her, teasing Jessica with his thickness. "Open your eyes, baby." A knuckle graced her cheekbone, Aksel's heat blistering against the back of her legs. "I want to watch your face as I enter you."

"Good Lord." She opened her eyes slowly, unable to catch more than a glimpse of him, but it was enough to show her the soft curve of his mouth, his lower lip punctured by half-shifted teeth.

"That's my girl." He trailed his fingers lightly down the side of her throat and across her back, grabbing Jessica's shoulder firmly. "My beautiful Jess."

And entered her in a long, steady press.

As wet as she was, as aroused by the madness of it all—the office, the camp, *Aksel,* and those lovely words—sore, delicate muscles protested as he filled her. A heartbeat of pain before pleasure took over, muting what little ache there was and drawing a groan from the depths of her belly.

He withdrew slowly, adjusting his stance and gripping the base of his cock before thrusting deep with a groan. The ring of his fingers butted against her with every roll of his hips, keeping Aksel from entering her fully. She knew why. Even if she hadn't spent thirteen years learning all she could about wolven, she would have been able to piece together the why over the last few days.

He was keeping himself from knotting her.

It did not lessen the pleasure, but rather heightened it as his knuckle brushed her clit. He canted his hips, driving against a place that made her cry out. Sparks burst in her eyes, pleasure shooting up her spine, but it wasn't enough.

For all the sneaking and sex, Jessica craved more of Aksel. Craved the sensation of being so full of him that nothing else mattered.

It was terrifying and exhilarating, and in this moment, bent over his desk as he pounded into her from behind, it was all she could do not to demand the very thing he denied.

She must be mad or drunk from so much sex after a thirteen-year drought. Jessica knew what a knot was for. She knew wolven reserved them for their mates, the wolven they would bind themselves to until their last breath. The type of wolven Aksel's pack demanded he find, mate, and breed. His knot would ensure that, and what right did she have to demand it of him?

Yet her body craved it; her mind demanded it. Every inch of her skin screamed for the consumption his knot would provide.

Svana had explained it as well as she could over the years. The all-consuming need that came over her after Jörgun knotted her the first time.

"A five-day rut," she called it. Never tiring, never satisfied, they had their first litter within a few months, followed by their second two years later.

Jessica could barely wrap her mind around the rapidity of a wolven pregnancy when it happened to her, but to need his knot this desperately, and this quickly?

It was as far-fetched and wild as biting her tongue to keep from demanding he move his hand and fill her properly.

Which she did now, gripping the desk as a now familiar tingle rose in her toes, and a tremble built in her thighs. Blunt nails scraped down her back, winding around her front, and at the first stroke of his finger, Jessica arched back, popping onto her elbows.

"Yes, baby," Aksel crooned in her ear. "Cry for me as loud as you want."

"The practice rooms..."

"Soundproofed." He covered her with his body, breath hot in her ear. "Same as this office."

"Thank *God*." Jessica dropped her head, focusing on the pleasure filling her limbs and belly rather than the need to be filled and fucked. To have all of Aksel to herself. This would have to do: mind-blowing sex, stolen moments, and a second summer with the man that had grown from the boy she lost.

A sharp canine dragged against her ear, her throat, teeth gently pressing down as Aksel thrust, circling her clit with a finger and catching Jessica just ... so.

The tingles exploded, buckling her knees as pleasure overrode all else. Aksel caught her around the waist when her knees buckled, grunting with his release and peppering kisses to her throat, whispering how lovely she was. How deliciously fucked and beautiful she looked, and for a moment, with bliss whiting out every other thought in her mind, it was enough.

This summer would be enough.

It had to be.

25

—·—

AKSEL

"Mr. Haralson?"

Aksel stared across the field, silently counting Jens and Jarl's steps as they worked through a cross-formation. Jens carried himself with the straight back and easy heel-to-toe roll of a natural, while Jarl, was determined and steady. The marching carriage did not come naturally to him, but a keen eye could see that he had worked hard to get as close to perfect as possible. Still, his movements were too tight, absent the easy flow of his brother's.

"Excuse me, Mr. Haralson?"

Then there was Jan and his silver trumpet. Where Jarl was studious and Jens a natural, Jan was the showman. His steps were not careful, but they were practiced, and he improvised and moved with the skill of a marcher who instinctively knew the music and the beat.

It was a shame he'd shown no interest in being a Drum Major. With his easy showmanship and skill as a musician, the pup would be a shoo-in at any university.

"Mr. Haralson!" A sharp tug at his shorts ripped Aksel's attention away from the field. He whipped his face down to Pterry, the red-faced and scowling gnome beside his leg. "Can we go to lunch? Or sit in the shade? We've been watching them march for the last ten minutes."

Disgruntled murmurs rose behind the gnome, and Aksel took in his students, sweaty and wilting, red-faced and dry-scaled.

He glanced at his watch, alarmed by how long he had stood there watching Jess's sons, studying their movements and postures and looking for himself in their gangly youth.

"Right." He cleared his throat, purposefully avoiding Kendra's intense stare from the rear of the group, where she stood with her feet shoulder-width apart and arms crossed. If Aksel hadn't known any better about the girl, he would have said her chin was lifted in challenge.

Moonblessed, he was a mess if he were imagining a wolven challenge in the face and posture of a pre-teen.

"Who ..." He grasped at mental straws, running with the first one he caught. "Who can tell me why the cross formation failed?"

"Failed?" Pterry frowned.

"They completed the cross," a naga camper said. "How did it fail?"

"In the center." Kendra dropped her arms and nudged closer. "They didn't account for the slither and shorter legs." She nodded at the naga. "The serpentine marchers should be at the end of the formation, not at the start."

"That is correct." Aksel smiled at his daughter. *No.* Kendra. Jess's daughter. His camper.

He put his back to his students, making a show of watching the marchers as he swept his hat away and ran a hand through his hair.

That was a dangerous way of thinking. They were only here for a few weeks, and never in their time together had Jess hinted she wanted something beyond this summer. As painful and bitter a pill as it was, Aksel had to swallow it.

Yes, they were his kids. Yes, he was falling hard for their mother, again, and the idea of losing her, *again*, made him want to shift and run and howl until he collapsed from sheer exhaustion, but he had no claim to them beyond being an absent father.

A sticky sweat broke out beneath the normal damp of a humid summer day, shame coursing through him in nauseating waves.

"See how they've made corrections?" He pointed to the drum majors on the field. Naris, a female naga, whipped between the rows, pulling marchers aside and reorganizing the center. At the same time, her male counterpart, a bearish shifter named Greg, demonstrated a double-time step to the woodwinds.

"Why aren't they pulling all the naga to the outside?" A young harpy asked.

"To keep time. Look." Kendra stepped beside Aksel and pointed across the field. "They're alternating the naga with the taller humans and inhumans and dropping piccolos into the mix."

"I don't get it," Pterry complained. "And I'm hungry."

"You don't have to get it," Aksel said warmly. "It's enough you noticed it. Watch, by the end of the day, they'll have the formation down."

Kendra chewed her lip, squinting in the bright sunlight. "Why didn't you tell them what to do?"

"And keep them from making a mistake?" Aksel crossed his arms and lifted his brows. "That's half the fun of it. Greg and Naris have been coming here for years. If they couldn't pinpoint the issue on their own and adjust the field to account for the heights and species, then I haven't done my job."

"Hm." Kendra squinted at Aksel as though she were sizing him up. It was odd to feel small under the scrutiny of an almost thirteen-year-old, but here he was. "I guess. It's lunchtime; can we go?"

"The bell hasn't ru—" The dull, metallic session bell blared from speakers across the camp, and Aksel sighed. "Go ahead."

His campers dispersed in a flurry, gathering their notebooks and backpacks. Only Kendra lingered, further away from him now, and a moment later, two of her brothers rushed over, yipping and barking as they dropped mouthfuls of clothing at her feet.

"Enough!" she yelled. "Sit. Heel!"

Jens barked lightly and sneezed, laughing at his sister. She cuffed his ear, darting away when he lunged for her.

"Better go, kids," Aksel said, not giving a second thought to his choice of words. He called all the campers kids, because they were. It was a normal thing to say, regardless of how *right* it felt to call these particular campers "kids". "Leave your sister alone and shift before you eat."

The duo barked and chased their tails, snuffling Aksel's shoes before darting for the camp center.

"Wait!" Kendra shot him a grumpy look and broke into a run, waving a pair of pants over her head. "Don't forget your clothes!"

"Pups." Aksel chuckled and stooped to gather his clipboard and gallon jug of water.

"So uncivilized." Jan approached, silver trumpet in hand. His cheeks were flushed from the field and sun, and his eyes bright and attentive, full of a youthful energy Aksel couldn't help but envy. How fun it would be to be a pup experiencing this camp for the first time, finding a sense of belonging that had been absent since the fall. He was glad to see the joy of discovery in

Jan and his brothers. As rambunctious and wild as they were, the trio had won over every counselor and instructor, fitting themselves into the cogs and wheels of Elkwater in a way that made it obvious how Kendra had not.

She participated, but at a distance. Made friends, who she kept at arm's length, and though he had been teaching her for the last month, Aksel still felt as though she kept a thick, mortared wall between herself and the rest of the camp, her brothers included.

Gods knew he wanted to ask Jessica about it. He wanted to talk to her about them, but bringing up her children—their children—still felt like too careful a place to tread.

Putting on a friendly smile, Aksel tugged the cap off his gallon jug.

"Wondered where you were," he greeted Jan. "Why aren't you with your brothers and sister?"

"Instrument maintenance." The younger wolven raised his trumpet, depressing the water key on the tuning slide before blowing into the mouthpiece. A fine spray of condensation and spit fanned out, and Jan grinned. "There, all better."

"Very civilized of you."

"I do try." He tucked the trumpet under his arm and settled beside Aksel as they headed across the field. "Got any plans this weekend?"

Aksel glanced at Jan from the corner of his eye, assessing the young pup. His expression was clear, open, and Gods bless the boy he was trailing a flock of birds flying overhead. Not an ounce of subterfuge or conniving to be seen.

"No."

"Mom's picking us up tonight."

"Oh?" Aksel asked, raising the gallon jug and taking a big swallow. It wasn't unusual for the campers of local families to be picked up on Friday instead of Saturday morning. And since Jess's kids were attending the full summer session, it made sense they would want a break from camp a day early. Still, it bothered Aksel that Jess hadn't mentioned this during the week. She didn't owe him anything, much less access to her private life with her children, but it still stung.

"You should come up for dinner."

"Won't that be weird? Having dinner with a camp instructor?"

Jan waited until he was guzzling down more water before shrugging. "It's less awkward than smelling you on my mom when she sneaks upstairs in the morning."

Aksel choked and sputtered, eyes bugging and water spraying from his mouth. Pounding his chest with a fist. "Excuse me?"

"Don't make it weird, Mr. Haralson." Jan spun, walking backward with a broad grin crinkling his cheeks. "Come up for dinner. We'll tell Mom we invited you."

"Will you stop, man?" Dusty slapped the edge of the bar, red eyes gleaming. "You're gonna fizz up the cans."

"Sorry." Aksel pulled his foot from the bar rail. "Nerves."

"I can see that." He swept a glass from beneath the bar and swiveled for the taps. "What's got your hackles raised?"

"Tonight." Propping his heel on the crossbar, Aksel resumed bouncing his knee. "Her kids want me to come up for dinner."

"Her. Jess?" Dusty cocked his head, smirking when Aksel nodded. "And?"

"*And?*" He stilled his knee and shot an incredulous look across the bar. Could he not see how awkward that was going to be? It had been a good week. A *really* good week, starting with Jess in his office on Monday, followed by his apartment. Her apartment. Her kitchen, the stairs once.

Moonblessed, she'd even fed him dinner three out of the five nights. He'd never been so well-fed or well fucked in his life. How the hells was he going to survive a dinner with Jess and their *kids* when all he could think about was Wednesday night when he'd had her on the kitchen table as an appetizer to chicken casserole?

"The kids, Dusty."

"I may be overstepping, but"—Dusty placed a beer beside his arm and nudged it closer with a fuzzy finger—"isn't this what you wanted? Jess and dinner?"

"Yes."

"Then why are you here?" he asked. "In a *bar,* when you could be with the woman you've mooned over for as long as I've known you?"

"They weren't home yet." He grabbed the beer and swallowed half of it. "And it's not just dinner with Jess; it's dinner with Jess *and* our kids."

Dusty's antennae shot straight, his eyes dimming, then flaring in surprise. "Our what now?"

Aksel froze with the glass pressed to his lips, ears pricking. The blood rushed from his cheeks, churning the beer in his empty stomach. Gods, he was a mess of nerves if he let *that* slip so easily, and worse, there was no hiding it from Dusty. All the jokes and idiocy aside, the mothman had known him since college. Since Jess. He'd seen Aksel at his absolute worst and, over the last few weeks, had kindly kept whatever thoughts he had to himself whenever Aksel wandered into The Porchlight with a smile.

Slowly, he lowered the glass and faced Dusty.

"Did you—" the mothman croaked. "Did you just say ..."

"Yes."

"DUDE."

"Quiet." He hunched over the bar, glancing around. Though mostly empty, Elkins was a small place, and half of the handful of patrons were wolven. "Geez, man. Be cool for once."

"Dude." Dusty slapped his hands on the bar and hunkered down, lowering his voice to a hiss-whisper. "Are you kidding me? How am I supposed to be cool about this? Her kids are your kids. You have kids? With Jess? You have kids with Jess. The girl who broke your heart."

"The mother of my children, yes."

"*Dude.*"

"Dusty." Aksel pulled a rarely used growl into his throat. "Keep it down."

He raised his hands and backed away, maintaining a hunched posture. "Sorry, sorry, but, c'mon man. How am I supposed to be cool about this? She rolls into town thirteen years later with kids and you're—*oh moons.*" His wings shot out, puffing dust in a hazy aura around him. "Oh, this is bad, Aks. This is really, really bad."

"It's not that bad."

"Yes, it is." He slapped the bar and leaned close. "There were some Skölldal in here the other night."

"So?" he snorted. Skölldal Wolven came into the Porchlight almost as often as the Sköllburg did. It was a known inhuman bar and centrally located. Aksel didn't know exactly how long The Porchlight had occupied this corner of Davis and Third, but the bar was already pocked, and the floor warped when he was a newly fallen adolescent. He was sure the bar would outlast every one of the wolven currently running with the Sköllburg. "They're in here every night."

"Yeah, sure. Fine, but this group was on their way to a SAR training in Roanoke, and one of them was asking questions 'bout you"—Dusty hunkered over the bar, tucking his wings in tight and lowering his voice—"and your mate."

Aksel blinked slowly, tightening his grip on the beer and raising it carefully. No one knew about what he and Jess had done. Hells, Aksel hadn't even realized it until a few days ago, and the only wolven he had trusted with that knowledge understood the gravity of the situation more than anyone. Nils and Elias would carry his secret to the grave if they had to. So, who else knew about Jess?

"And who," he paced out slowly, "did this Sklölldal think my mate was?"

Dusty's eyes flared, and he straightened, leaning away from Aksel and his dangerous calm. "It was late." He waved a hand. "He was drunk, it's not a big deal."

"It is, if he's spreading rumors."

Shrinking back, Dusty scanned the nearly empty bar and grimaced. "Look, all he said was that he scented your mate on the train, and he wanted to know who she was because, as far as his pack knew, you and Beth were a done deal."

"New moon, are you still talking about that flea-bitten Skölldal?" Gitta plunked down on the stool beside Aksel, jerking her chin at him in greeting before stealing his beer and downing it in one long swallow. "Pup was blitzed; it took three of us to get him out of here."

Aksel eyed his foster sister. "Why didn't you tell me about this?"

"Because you're a mess," she stated and shoved the glass across the bar. Dusty caught it and headed for the taps. "And I handled it."

"What do you mean 'handled it'? And who was he talking about?"

Gitta kept her eyes forward, body tense in a way he did not like. It was the posture of a wolven who had done something wrong. A wolven who was lying. "No one."

"Gitta."

She laced her fingers together, biceps flexing. Her nostrils flared, and Gitta inhaled, eyes narrowing at whatever she caught in Aksel's scent. Dusty returned with a beer and set it down hard. Liquid sloshed over the side, and the mothman scampered away, wings tucked in tight.

A long moment passed before Gitta sighed. "I know they're yours."

He snarled, jumping to his feet as the words punched into him. "How."

"Ah, she told you." She took a sip of her beer. "Good. Makes this easier."

"Jess didn't tell me," he grumbled. "I finally took my head out of my ass long enough to figure it out."

Gitta hit Aksel with a direct, challenging stare. The hairs along his neck rose, a low growl building in his throat that he was powerless to stop. Instead of shrinking back or averting her gaze, Gitta scoffed. "Settle down, Aks. I'm trying to help you."

"How did you know?" New moon, his voice sounded foreign, even to him. Rough and raw, deeper than he thought possible. He lowered himself to the stool, gripping his knees.

"How did I—" Gitta gawked at him, shaking her head in disbelief. "How did I know they were yours? Aksel, you dumbass, it's all over them. I knew you'd mated her the first time I scented her, but those *kids*." Her voice rose in pitch, and she glanced nervously at the other wolven in the bar. None seemed to hear what she'd said, so she continued, albeit in a lower voice. "The girl is practically your clone, and those boys are just as gangly and awkward as you were when we fell." She punched his arm. "I can't believe you didn't tell me, you asshole."

"I didn't know!" He put up both hands. "I figured it out after seeing Nils and Elias and went straight to Jess. Everything has been a blur since then."

"Gross, man, I'm your sister."

He hung his head. "Sorry."

Gitta bumped his shin with the toe of her boot. "You're already mated, and there are pups involved. Aks, Dad wants to ship you off to the Sklldal." The glass thudded against the bar. "What're you gonna do?"

"Lennart can't force me to do anything."

"He *will*. Or he'll call a challenge to force you out of the pack." She rose and stepped close, filling the air around him with her sharp scent. Black rose and oud, the hint of rosemary from her hair oil, and the crisp, clean scent of a bright wind. "We got the Sklldal pup out of here before he ran his mouth, but he described Jess well enough that anyone in earshot knew he wasn't talking about Beth. It's only a matter of time before another wolven scents her and puts it together."

"Let them," he replied. "She's my mate, and I'll figure this out."

"Moonblessed, you're not hearing me." Grabbing the beer, Gitta pointed the rim at Aksel and swallowed half the glass. "You're not the Alpha of the Skllburg, Aksel. And none of the Sklldal have any reason to be loyal to you. If anyone scents Jess when you aren't around, they will drag her in front of Dad." Gitta might as well have punched him in the gut. The wind rushed out of him, what remained of his anger draining away as she spoke. She shut her eyes, pinching the bridge of her nose. "Fuck, Aksel. Those kids don't have a pack. He'd have every right to—"

The barstool clattered to the ground, and every pair of eyes in the bar swiveled toward Aksel, standing with his fists balled and heart thundering in his ears. The idea, the suggestion that any wolf would lay their hands on Jess, that Lennart would press his claim on Aksel's kids as part of his pack, seized his heart in a vise.

Adrenaline shot through his veins, ratcheting Aksel's pulse until his entire body trembled. Gitta reached for his arm, her mouth moving, but no sound reached him beneath the ringing in his ears. There was nowhere to go, nowhere to run. He was a wolven cornered, panic driving him back from Gitta and forcing him to seek an exit. Any exit.

He spun, tripping over the stool and running for the rear door.

26

— • —

AKSEL

HIS CLAWS SCRAPED OVER the pinball machine, half-shifted paws fumbling at the knob before the door flew open. Aksel stumbled into the parking lot, gasping and dragging in pea-soup-thick air, unable to fill his lungs.

"Shit." A gossamer wing draped across his back, soft, velvet fingers easing Aksel against the wall and holding him there. "We've got you, man. What the hell just happened?"

"I told him a harsh truth, and his idiot brain interpreted it as a challenge, that's what." Gitta's face floated into view. She grabbed his shoulders, steadying Aksel as he came back to himself. Her eyes gleamed gold, trained on him and only him. "Moonblessed, Aks. Get a hold of yourself."

"M'trying." He gripped his knees until the pain of claws piercing skin overrode every alarm flaring in his body. He filled his lungs enough to exhale. And again until the rushing of his blood slowed and clear directions stood out stark and bold in his mind. "I need to talk to her."

"About time," Gitta grumbled. "Dad gave you a month, and you've wasted half of it."

"Not wasted." Aksel straightened and set his jaw. "Jess deserves the truth, but I have to deserve her first."

Her expression softened, eyes dimming toward human.

"I get it," she said. "You two deserved a chance to get to know each other again." Her nostrils flared, and an eyebrow quirked. "Which it smells like you have. But that Skölldal was on his way to Roanoke, Aks. If he talked, you're out of time."

"You're right." He pushed from the wall, gently shouldering past Gitta and Dusty.

"Wait, you're going now?" Dusty moved in front of him, hands out. "Shouldn't you, I don't know, talk to Lennart first? Or the Skölldal? Set everything right?"

"No." Gravel flew as he spun around. "Jess deserves to know, first and foremost. I mated her, Dusty, and it's time I own up to the fact that I'm"—he choked, coughed, and tried again—"I'm a sire, and I failed my mate in every way she needed me. Those pups are mine, and I want them." He fisted his hand and punched it toward the ground. "I want Jess, and the only way to begin deserving her is to tell her."

Dusty's lips wormed together, eyes flaring and flickering with unease. "And what about Lennart? The pack?"

"What about it?" Aksel threw the question back at him. "Lennart can cast me out if he wants; it doesn't matter. Jess and the kids are what matter. I've missed their entire lives, I don't plan on missing anymore."

Dusty darted a look at Gitta, who slapped her hand against his chest and pushed him back. "Go on, Aksel." She jerked her chin to the edge of the parking lot. "Go get your girl."

⁂

Feet thundered down the stairs before Aksel reached the stoop, leaving him with less than two seconds to brush his hair back and straighten his shirt before the door flew open to reveal six bright eyes—Aksel's eyes—and three smiling pre-teen boys.

"Hey, Mr. Haralson!" Jarl greeted.

Jens pushed him aside, shoving the door wider. "You made it!"

"I trust your travels were without incident?" Jan asked.

Jarl flicked his ear. "He lives downstairs, numbnuts."

"Boys!" Jess jogged down the stairs behind them and clapped her hands, the sharp sound bouncing off the walls. "Stop harassing Mr. Haralson and go for a run. Dinner's in fifteen."

"Sloppy Joooooooooooes!" All three rushed out the door, their cry devolving into a raucous howl as they shifted and sprinted for the woods behind the townhome. Jess shook her head, stooping to gather the discarded clothes.

"Sorry about that, they go wild whenever they smell meat cooking."

"Well, the bad news is, they'll never grow out of it." Aksel swept up a pile of denim, haphazardly folding the pants.

"And the good news?" Jess angled her face at him, a playful smile curling plump lips. Moonblessed, this woman. One flirtatious little smile and the reason he'd run here from The Porchlight vanished completely.

"Good news is, grown wolven have a more diverse palate."

"Terrible." A lovely flush colored her cheeks. She glanced at the stairs and popped on her toes, pressing a sweet, all-too-short kiss to his cheek. "Sorry it's not anything fancier. The boys informed me they'd invited you, and I'd already defrosted the beef."

"It's perfect, Jess." He brushed her arm and took the clothing from her hands. "You're perfect."

She blinked wide eyes at him, blush darkening as she lowered to her feet. "Good Lord."

"Ew," Kendra called from the top of the stairs. "Don't be weird."

Jess whipped her face toward her daughter. "Manners, young lady."

"Don't be weird, *please*," she replied and stormed away. A door slammed a moment later.

"I swear, that girl…" Jess sighed and rubbed her temple. "Sorry about that."

"Nah, it's alright." And it was. Aksel had spent his fair share of time navigating teenage emotional swings. He would have run screaming from the high school a decade ago if he weren't thick-skinned enough to handle a little sass. "The local kids act like they've seen an alien whenever they spot me in the grocery store. I'm used to it."

"What a thing to get used to." Jess chuckled, but the laughter didn't quite fill her face as it usually did. "Doesn't excuse my—" Her half-smile fell, brows scrunching. "Our daughter. Lord, how are we going to navigate this?"

And that was the jolt he needed to stop thinking about how lovely Jess was when she blushed, or how delicious she smelled with her natural scent muddling with the mouthwatering aroma of a home-cooked meal.

Not once had she broached that topic, and here it was, out in the open to remind Aksel why he'd run here from The Porchlight.

For dinner, yes. To spend time with Jess and the kids, yes, but above all else, he was here to tell her the truth about *them*. The longer he put it off, the more certain Aksel was that he would chicken out and save it for another day. But their days were running low. If he didn't say something *now*, even knowing it would risk tonight, and however much longer he had with her, he wasn't sure he'd ever have the courage to say it at all.

The summer would end, Jess and the kids would return to Charleston, and things would go back to normal.

For them, at least.

Aksel no longer knew what normal was. Having Jess here felt like someone had turned up the brightness on the world, filling his every day with a sense of purpose. Gitta was right; he'd freaked out at the mere mention of potentially losing any of this. How was he going to survive when she left him?

Again.

"Together," he said. "When you're ready."

Her eyes shimmered, dark and lovely in the sunset, and she let out a shaking breath, gently squeezing his arm and heading for the door. "Thank you, Aksel. You'd better come up. The boys'll be back soon, and we can eat."

"Can't wait. But first—" Gods, the words wouldn't come. How did one state plainly, "We accidentally mated thirteen years ago, and despite being an absent father and partner this entire time, I'm all in. What do you say?"

Fuck, what would she say? Would she say anything at all? Would she smile, or would she kick him out?

Oh, Gods, what if she cried?

New moon, anything but tears, unless they were tears of happiness, but how could they be? He'd failed her, left her to raise their children alone, and been too much of an idiot for the first half of the summer to put together what others had seen so plainly. If she kicked him out or rejected him, he would accept it.

"Aksel?" She turned in the doorway and cocked her head. "What is it?"

"I—before we eat, I need to talk to you." He swallowed and cleared his throat. "About us."

Jess straightened, shoulders hitching as her body tensed.

"About the last night at camp," he pressed on. "And everything in-between."

"Everything in-between." Her eyes widened, that dark gaze intent on him, but her mouth remained soft. It took him a full heartbeat to read that she wasn't upset, wasn't wary, but Gods help him, he had no idea how to interpret the expression she wore.

What he wouldn't give to know her every frown and flicker. To be able to read her as easily as a book, but he couldn't. Not yet, if the Gods were kind; all he had was this moment, this chance to lay it all bare, and he would rather fall again than refuse to try. "Jess, that night, when we ..."

She nodded, urging him to keep going.

"I think that you and I—that we're—" He stumbled over the words, hugging the clothes in his arms tighter as if he could squeeze the admission out. "Jess, you're my—"

Headlights painted the front of the townhome, illuminating Jess and revealing wide, rounded eyes and ashen cheeks. She squinted, raising a hand to shield her eyes as tires crunched over gravel. A champagne-colored sedan pulled into the empty spot beside her car, and she leaned around him, the frown on her face erased by baffled surprise.

"What?"

The engine cut off, and Jess brushed past him, glancing back worriedly before hurrying across the yard. The passenger door shoved open, and a short, severe woman stepped out, her pale, pinched face and narrowed eyes fixing on Aksel immediately.

"Mom?" Jess faltered as the driver's side door opened, and a tall, gray-bearded Black man exited onto the gravel. "Dad?"

27

JESS

"W̲HAT ARE YOU DOING here?"

"Is that any way to greet your parents?" Irene marched around the front of their sedan, stopping feet away from Jessica with her hands on her hips. Thirty-one years old, and her mother's glare still made her feel as guilty as a four-year-old lying about drawing on the walls. "Three hours in the car and that's how you say 'Hello'? I raised you better than that, Jessica."

"Sorry, I—you couldn't have called?"

"Would you have answered?" Her mother countered. "I've been calling for weeks, and you never answered. I even emailed, Lord have mercy, but you never responded."

"You called?" Jessica wavered, her heart pounding erratically in her chest. "I never ... oh." She glanced at the townhome, catching an unfortunate look at Aksel. Pale and startled, he clutched her sons' clothes to his chest, eyes darting from her mother to her father, to her and back around again, looking for all the world like he'd rather shift and join her sons—God dammit—*their* sons in the woods.

"The phone line," she said dumbly. "I need it for the internet to work. "

Her mother's pinch-lipped expression pruned further. "Then you must have received my emails."

Jessica looked to her father, who shrugged and shook his head, forever avoiding their perpetual mother-daughter spat. Though he had done so her entire life, grabbing a newspaper and leaving the room or averting his gaze and keeping silent, it still hurt, and maybe that was why she ran her mouth now.

"I did. Every one of them. They're sitting in my inbox, unread."

Irene blinked and tucked her chin, anger reddening her cheeks.

"Now, honey—" Jessica's father began.

"What, David?" Irene snapped her glare to her husband. As expected, he dropped his eyes, fiddling with the car keys instead of saying anything.

"Well." Irene flattened her palms down the front of her linen pants. "Had you bothered to read them or answer the phone, you would have known we were coming up this weekend to see my grandbabies before Monday."

A low growl rose over Jessica's shoulder, barely audible, and Irene's attention shifted. Surprise parted her lips as though she had only just noticed Aksel standing there, and then anger rushed in.

"What is he doing here?" She thrust her arm in a point, Rolex and gold bangles tinkling together. "Is this why you wanted to come up here, Jessica? To see that—that *mongrel?*"

"Mom!" Rage exploded through her, filling Jessica with a jittery, possessive, protective mania she hadn't felt since her children were bullied in elementary school. The sudden heat ratcheted up her pulse, consuming Jessica with a need to put herself between Aksel and her mother. "Don't speak to him like that."

"Jess—" Aksel said, low and calm.

"You don't get to come here unannounced and be rude to my—"

"Jess—"

"What?" She whirled around, red blurring her vision, only to clear away when Aksel came into view. Still clutching her boys' clothes, he stood closer now. Mere inches instead of feet, and that was still too far. The urge to grab hold of him, to wrap her arms around him, and sink her nails into his skin overwhelmed her. Instead, she fisted her hands, savoring the pinch of nails against her palms.

"Take a breath, Jess." Aksel ducked his head, speaking low enough that only she could hear. Worry pinched the corners of his eyes, wrinkling his brow, but he kept calm and collected. A sturdy wall ready to wrap around Jess and shield her from the world.

She did as he said, ignoring the angry murmurs at her back and shutting out her mother's voice. Inhaling deeply, she savored Aksel's scent. Woodsy and fresh, a lovely mix of pine and bergamot, and the undeniable maleness of him. Her heartbeat slowed, the mania dulling and fading as she filled her head with Aksel. Safe, steady, secure Aksel.

She exhaled and met his bright amber gaze. The worry had eased somewhat, replaced by a slight, soft smile and something like relief.

And then her mother's words hit her.

That mongrel.

"Wait." Jessica whirled around fast enough to catch her mother's wince. "How do you know who he is?"

They had never met Aksel, and the handful of photos Jessica had of him were safely tucked in a box in the back of her closet, waiting for the day one of her children asked who their father was and did they look like him?

"You're not the only one who knows how to use the internet, Jessica Abernathy Babcock," her mother replied, wielding her full name like a sword brandished in threat.

"So you stalked my ex-boyfriend?"

"No." Irene rolled her shoulder and crossed her arms, seeming to grow two inches. "I researched the father of my grandbabies." She lobbed the words over Jessica's shoulder, keenly waiting for the volley land. When there was no explosion, no response beyond Aksel placing a hand on Jessica's shoulder and squeezing, Irene scoffed. "Did you honestly think I would let you come up here with them and not ensure their safety?"

"We're here for summer camp," Jessica argued. "What did you think would happen? They would have unsterilized fun without you?"

"Watch your tone, young lady."

"I'm not a young lady, Mom. I'm a grown-ass woman. A *mother*. I'm allowed to take my kids on a summer vacation. I'm allowed to not answer emails and have my own life, and you still haven't explained to me what you are doing here."

"We wanted to see you and the kids, like your mother said," David finally spoke. He raised both hands in surrender. "It was all in the emails, honey, it really was. Irene?" He held out his hand to her mother, who ignored it. "Let's go and let them have their evening. We've got the entire week to—"

"A week?" Jessica's voice rose in pitch, her heart ramping up again as panic fizzled to life. Her parents could not have chosen a worse time to come visit. As wonderful as it had been spending her nights with Aksel, she still had the financial assessment to finish before Monday when the Mountaineers' Daughters arrived to … to …

Realization crashed over her like a wall of freezing water, sending Jessica staggering back as two very disparate realities aligned themselves as one.

"Oh, my God." Jessica clapped her hands over her mouth, wanting to cry and curse for being so stupid. "You're here with the foundation. The Mountaineers' Daughters. You're here to tour the camp and decide whether or not they're going to ... Mom, no."

Irene pursed her lips, lifting her chin. Jessica knew her mother. She had memorized every tic and tell, discerning the subtle differences between anger and disappointment in her perfectly curated frowns. Irene was proud, a daughter of West Virginia boasting a lineage older than the state, and in the lift of her chin, Jessica knew her mother felt no remorse about what she'd done. "A group of us interested in contributing sizable donations to your Outreach are convening in Elkins this weekend, yes."

"One thing." Jessica pointed to the ground, advancing on her Mom as an odd, dissociative calm overtook her. A blessing; otherwise, she would have been trembling with anger. "I wanted one thing that was mine. One thing I could make and be proud of, and you couldn't even let me have that."

"You're overreacting, Jessica."

"No, I'm not, and if you thought outside of yourself and your petty, superficial obsession with *appearances*, you would see that." She thrust her hands into her hair, gripping the roots and grunting in frustration. "You know how important the Outreach is to me. You know how hard I've worked to grow its presence in Charleston and form connections with other inhuman groups throughout the state. You *knew*—"

"And I supported you," Irene countered. "I knew you needed my help, Jessica. Any teen mother would." This, she spat over Jessica's head at Aksel. "I want what is best for you and my grandbabies, and if that means inserting myself into your Outreach to ensure you aren't making another mistake, then I will."

"They're not a mistake!" Jessica's shout echoed off the front of the townhome, loud enough to be heard blocks away in downtown Elkins. She snapped her jaw shut, inhaling through her nose and counting to ten before repeating as quietly as possible, "They're not a mistake. They're my children; he is their father, and we will navigate this without you."

"Do they even know this dog is their father?"

Anger laced through her, flashing Jessica's vision crimson. She closed her eyes, exhaling slowly to keep from giving in to the violent urges rising within her. What was this anger? This possessiveness? Maybe it was the time away from her mother that allowed Jessica to grow a semblance of a spine. Still, the rudeness, the all-encompassing urge to defend Aksel and shut her mother up—it was frightening, and Jessica was nowhere near the right state of mind to unpack this wild need to defend, protect, and possess him and what they had made. Together.

"Not yet, no," she said instead.

Irene blinked owlishly at her with feigned innocence. "You haven't told them? Well, that seems irresponsible. Were you ever planning to?"

"Of course I was." But she wanted time for her children to get to know Aksel. For herself, to get to know Aksel as an adult and for him to make a decision, any decision, regarding his level of involvement after this summer, with clear and conscious thought. Yet, here her mother was, with her hand pressed to her chest and injury in her eyes, implying Jessica had withheld this information, hiding it when all she wanted to do was give everyone the time they needed to grow and heal together.

As a family.

"And then what, Jessica? Would you uproot them from their lives? Disrupt everything we have built to move them here?" Irene curled her lip. "Or will he quit his life in Elkins and move to Charleston? Good Lord, have you even thought this through?"

"I—" Yes. No. A million times and not at all.

"I think you should leave." Aksel's warmth blanketed her back, his voice an embrace. Firm and foreboding, and defending her in a way no one ever had. "Emotions are clearly riding high. Why don't we all take the night to calm down and come together as adults in the morning?"

Irene's nostrils flared, but to Jessica's shock, she pivoted and marched to the passenger side of the sedan. "We're leaving, David."

Jessica's father looked from his wife to her, confusion knitting his brow. "What about the kids?"

"Now," Irene snapped. "We'll see Jessica and the children for brunch at the hotel tomorrow. Isn't that right, Jessica?"

Aksel pressed his fingers to the base of her spine, a simple touch that spoke volumes, telling her not to argue. That his exclusion was fine, that he understood.

"The boys will have already eaten breakfast," she said. "They're up early."

"And they have six hollow legs among them," Irene replied. "They'll eat. Brunch. 10:30."

She slammed the passenger door, sitting with her arms crossed and eyes pinned straight ahead. Jessica's father waggled his fingers in farewell, climbing inside and backing the car out of the gravel drive. Only when the taillights disappeared did Jessica exhale and sag into Aksel.

Clothing hit the ground, and he wrapped his arms around her. How long they stood there, she had no idea. A minute. Five. What did it matter when she never wanted to leave?

But she had dinner to serve, children to raise, laundry to fold, and financial statements to review. As badly as she wanted to escape into the comfort of him, Jessica could not, and the knowledge had her pulling away.

Aksel let her, standing quietly as she gathered herself and her thoughts.

"I'm sorry," she said after a long moment.

"There's nothing to be sorry for, Jess." His fingers danced at his side, and Aksel raised his arm, reaching for Jess. She bent, avoiding his touch, to sweep the discarded basketball shorts and t-shirts into her arms.

"I think we should reschedule dinner," she said, unable to look at him. "I can send a plate down if you want. I just—I need the night to get my head on straight. I'm sorry."

"I understand."

"How?" She lobbed the question at him like a stone. "How can you understand? How are you *always* so understanding? I show up after thirteen years and rent the apartment above you. I enroll your kids into Elkwater as your students without telling you they're yours, and you *understand?*"

Good Lord, she wanted this to make sense, but none of it did. She had written to him, time and time again, pouring her heart and soul into those letters, and if what Gitta said was true, he had done the same.

They each harbored hurts a decade old. Aksel should be furious with her for showing up out of nowhere and playing these games. For enrolling her children without reaching out to him first. Jessica should be furious with him for thirteen missed years and every struggle she had overcome, but she wasn't, and she couldn't make sense of it because *he* was the only thing that made sense. His presence in her life, with her kids, was like the last piece of a puzzle sliding into place, and he *understood?*

"How," she demanded. Aksel did not flinch, did not back away, but he stared at her with a hurt in his eyes that she had put there. "This entire summer, fuck, my life is so messed up, how could you possibly understand?"

"Maybe I don't," he said. "But I want to. I want to help, Jess. I want to be here, with you and them, through the good and the bad."

Cruel words would have been easier. Rejection and blame she could handle, but this open admission, the words she had fantasized hearing every day of her children's lives being given freely?

They punched the wind out of her lungs, hauling tears to sting and burn her eyes. "I can't do this tonight."

"I know." Aksel licked his lips, searching the empty air above her head. "But now you know where I stand." His throat bobbed, lips parting to say more. Jessica held her breath, hinging everything she was on whatever came next. Aksel pulled his lips between his teeth, blinking slowly at her. "Now you know."

It wasn't a demand, it wasn't even a question, but Jessica heard the plea in those words as well as she saw it written on his face.

He had just bared his heart to her, answering every one of her wishes, and all he asked was that she do the same.

"I can't," she choked out. "Not tonight, please, Aksel. I can't do this tonight. I–I need some space." A series of howls kicked up in the woods behind the townhome, punctuated by sharp yips and barks announcing the return of Jan, Jarl, and Jens.

Jessica swept the back of her hand under her nose, blinking to clear the tears from her eyes. "This is a lot."

"Yeah." Aksel huffed and dipped his chin. "It is. But I'm here, Jess." He waved a hand at his door. "A floor away, and I'm not going anywhere."

All she could do was nod and mouth silently, "I know."

Skirting around Aksel, she trudged up the stairs, pausing as a thought occurred.

"You were going to tell me something before my parents arrived. What was it?"

Out of everything that had passed in the last few minutes, that question had Aksel's cheeks blanching for some reason. He pressed his lips together, hitching his shoulders, though his eyes remained soft and warm.

"It can wait." Striding up the steps, Aksel kissed her sweetly on the brow, fingers lightly dusting her bare arm. Chaste and gentle and precisely what she needed in that moment. "Enjoy brunch with your parents and the kids, alright? We can talk after." Another kiss, this one on her cheek. "When you're ready."

She flitted a smile at him, torn between demanding he say whatever weighed so heavily on his mind and letting it rest. There had been enough revelations for one night, and Jessica wasn't sure she could handle another surprise. While leaving anything unsaid played into too many of her fears, it also gave Jessica a reason to seek him out.

"Alright," she said. "When I'm ready."

His fingers curled around her arm, pressing hard enough she thought he might pull her in for a kiss—

Laughter and chatter curved around the side of the building as her sons approached, and Aksel pulled away, jogging down the steps and to his door.

"Goodnight, Jess," he called softly, stepping into his dark apartment without a glance back.

The door shut quietly, and as her boys' gangly silhouettes danced into view, Jess whispered, "Goodnight."

28

— • —

AKSEL

AKSEL SHIFTED THE MINUTE he heard Jess and the kids sit down for dinner and ran to Riversmoke, pounding on Elias's door in a pair of sweatpants three inches too short. The elder wolven took one look at Aksel, read the desperation in his scent, and sighed.

"Alright, pup. I'll go get Nils."

The pair kept him busy through the night, working the smoker and making minor repairs around the restaurant and garage. They spent Saturday shifted with the members of their pack who hadn't gone with Lennart for SAR Training, patrolling their border and sweeping trails for hikers, and the lights in Jess's apartment were dark when he finally made it home.

Despite his best efforts to stay away, Sunday dawned to find Aksel at her door, shuffling his weight from foot to foot, holding a pink box of donuts in one hand and a tray of coffees balanced in the other.

She had asked for space, and he would give it to her—except she needed him, whether she wanted to admit it or not. If not emotionally, there were *things* he could do and help he could offer. Even without the mating she still knew nothing about, Aksel would have felt the need to do and fix simply because she was Jess, and he could.

That's what he told himself as feet pounded down the steps. The door flew open before he could arrange the food and drinks to knock, revealing a trio of sleep-tousled preteens grinning at him.

"Morning, Mr. Haralson!" Jarl grabbed the coffee tray.

"Sweet, donuts!" Jan snatched the box.

"Thank yooooou." Jens followed his brothers up the stairs, leaving the door open in what Aksel took as an invitation.

"Is your mother up?"

"Yeah," Jens said around a mouthful of apple fritter. "She's in the bathroom."

He froze, gripping the stairwell as a vision of Jess, wet and naked, flashed across his mind. This was absolutely *not* the time. "I can ... I'll come back later."

"No, come on up!" Jess hollered, her voice echoing off the tile. "Just sending an email; I'm almost done."

"In the bathroom?"

"The cable's not long enough to reach the counter," Jarl explained.

Aksel scratched his jaw, pondering that as he finished the climb and entered a home in cozy disarray. Shoes spilled out of a woven basket beside the stairs, blankets and throw pillows covered the couches, and the kitchen counters overflowed with drying pots, pans, and plates. A green light glowed from the front of the dishwasher, and beside the fridge, the coffee pot burbled cheerfully.

Aksel started there. He plucked the apple fritter from Jens's fingers, jerked his head at the kitchen, and clicked his tongue. All three boys hopped into action, clearing the pots and pans from the counters and unloading the dishwasher while Aksel set the table with napkins, plates, and coffee mugs.

In a flash, breakfast was set, and Jess stepped out of the bathroom with an open laptop balanced in one hand, gawking at the spotless kitchen and four wolven sitting quietly at the table.

"Did you...?"

"Boston creme, mother?" Jan held up a plate, showing her the chocolate-covered pastry they had set aside. "Mr. Haralson brought coffee. We poured it into a mug to be fancy."

Grunting, Aksel nudged the young wolven with a shoulder. "You can call me Aksel when we're not at camp."

"That's weird," Jarl stated. "Don't make it weird, Mr. Aksel."

Jess set her laptop down beside her coffee and lightly gripped the chairback at the head of the table. Even without makeup, with her hair wild from sleep and faint bags under her eyes, she was lovely. The urge to wrap his arms around her and snuggle

Jess until every weary edge was worn smooth made it nearly impossible to think straight. Not that he'd ever managed that where Jess was involved. "You didn't have to do all of this."

"It was nothing," he said. "I was up, and Kay's makes the best donuts in a fifty-mile radius." He took a large bite of an old-fashioned, chewing loudly and patting his stomach with a wink at the boys. "Ask me how I know."

"Good Lord." Jess laughed, lovely crinkles fanning from the corners of her eyes, and pulled the seat out. "Thank you."

"Don't worry about it." Aksel sat taller, and the empty seat at the other end of the table caught his eye. He glanced at Jess and jerked his chin toward the bedrooms. "Should we wake Kendra?"

"She's with Gran and Pop," said Jarl.

"They booked a suite, and she was tired of sharing a bed with Mom," Jens added.

"You know how teenagers are." Jess shrugged. "They want their space, even if it's a fold-out in their grandparents' hotel living room."

"Right." Aksel studied her, looking for signs of distress that weren't there. Or if they were, Jess was so good at hiding them that even her children didn't notice. She sipped her coffee and used the edge of a fork to slice the Boston creme, popping it in her mouth and humming happily at the first taste.

An ease fell over the table as they ate. The boys chattered, Jess drank her coffee, smiling softly or laughing at a random joke, and Aksel was simply there, a part of it and an observer all the same. On any other day, he would have attributed the warmth growing in his chest to the coffee and sugar, but sitting here with Jess, knowing who these boys *were*, he couldn't ignore the rightness of the place and his position. Nor could he deny that the warmth filling his body from toes to shoulders, leaving him dizzy and light-headed, wasn't caffeine and carbs—it was happiness.

Jan and Jarl cleared the table without being prompted while Jens topped off his mother's coffee and waved the pot at Aksel.

"No, thank you. I've got a pack patrol today; too much caffeine makes it hard to run long distance."

"I didn't know that," Jess said quietly, setting her mug down. She glanced at her boys, padding to their room. The door closed quietly, and a moment later, the opening score of *Star Wars* blared. "I let them drink soda when we eat out. Is that bad?"

"Oh, no, Jess." Without thinking, without remembering she'd asked for space, Aksel set his hand on her arm. "It's fine now and then, but if they're going to be shifting and running patrols, it can mess with endurance."

She pulled her arm away, rising and retreating into herself in a way he hated. With no dishes to do, she settled for opening her laptop and staring at the screen. "There's so much I don't know."

"And there's so much you do, Jess. Don't sell yourself short." He stood, drumming his fingers on the table before giving in and striding to her side. Jess did not move, but she did tense, hand flattening against the keyboard as Aksel stopped, perhaps an inch too close. "I'm so sorry I wasn't there to help." Her eyes fluttered closed, jaw tightening. "I'm sorry I missed it all, Jess. I wish—"

"Don't."

"Why?"

She swallowed, opening her eyes to stare vacantly across the apartment. "Because it can't come true, Aksel. Whatever it is you wish, how would it work? You have a life here in Elkins. My kids have a life in Charleston. A *good* life. I can't uproot them any more than you can—"

"You think I wouldn't?" He backstepped, the sting of her words as good as a slap. "I teach high school band, Jess. Last I checked, Charleston has schools."

"And Elkwater?"

"Summers off, we'll enroll the kids."

"And the pack?" she lobbed, twisting her head to glare at him.

"What of it?" he threw back. "I told you what Lennart expects of me, and I think it's pretty damn clear I don't want to be with anyone but you."

A gasp choked in Jess's throat, her eyes rounding in surprise, and only then did Aksel realize what he'd said.

Gods be damned, she'd asked for time, She had asked for *space,* and he couldn't even give her that before running his mouth.

"Jess ..."

"No." She jumped from her chair and darted for the kitchen, putting sturdy architecture and distance between them. "No, Aksel. You can't come in here with donuts and coffee and make it all feel so natural and perfect and then drop *that* on me. I asked for space—"

"I know!" He ran a hand through his hair, tugging at the strands as if he could pull himself out of the hole he was rapidly digging. "I know you did, Jess, but you're running yourself ragged. You need help."

"I'm fine."

"Are you? Because you just admitted how much you don't know about wolven, and when you talk about your life, it's always what's best for the kids or the Outreach, but you never talk about what *you* want, or ask for the help you need to get it. New moon, I practically had to wrestle boxes away from you the other day, and you've got the ethernet cable running out the bathroom window so you can work!"

"Because I couldn't find a cable in this backasswards town long enough to work from anywhere else." She threw her hands up, waving them at the room and, he assumed, Elkins.

Aksel pressed his lips together, reached across the bar, and flicked the metal disc dangling on the wall. "Is that it?" He flicked it again, shoving a finger inside the hole revealed when the disc spun. "Or is it that you're too stubborn to ask for help?"

"I—"

"You've been writing emails in the *bathroom*, Jess." He huffed and turned tail, jogging down the stairs.

Avery shrieked as he stormed onto the stoop, nearly dropping the Sony Discman in her hand. She fumbled for the CD player, catching it and clutching it to her chest. Frizzy strands of hair escaped from her ponytail and framed her flushed, freckled face in a coppery halo, and an older Elkwater Music Camp t-shirt hacked into a muscle tank clung to her torso with sweat.

Aksel glanced down, saw her muddied running shoes, and barked, "Follow me."

"Okay." She jogged after him without question, following Aksel around the side of the building to the modem box.

Wrenching the door open, he unplugged the cable Jess had dropped from her bathroom window.

"I need that!" She yelled from above. "Plug that back in."

"In a minute," he bellowed back, lowering his voice before addressing Avery. "Stay here."

She narrowed her blue eyes at him. "I don't want to get in the middle of anything."

"You're not."

Avery squinted further, then shrugged. "Alright."

He jabbed a finger at the router box and the wires emerging from the PVC pipe at the back. "Plug it in."

Avery saluted and put her headphones back on.

Aksel took the stairs two at a time, surfacing in the apartment and crowding against Jess in the bathroom.

"I get that you've had to put your life on hold." He hauled the cable up hand over hand, gathering it in a loose coil and pivoting around her into the apartment. "I can't begin to imagine how hard it has been raising the kids without help—"

"I have help," she snapped, following Aksel into the main room. "My parents have been there every step of the way. And whatever they couldn't help me with, I had the Outreach to go to."

A stab wound would have hurt less.

"But not their father," he growled and lifted the metal disc on the wall, feeding the end of the cable into the hole.

He couldn't fault Jess for not knowing what this was. The townhome, an old Victorian, had been subdivided and renovated over the years. What used to be the wiring enclosure for a pull bell had been repurposed and redirected by the construction crew to the modem box outside.

"Because your asshole summer camp boyfriend knocked you up." He plugged the other end into her laptop. "He mated you and vanished for thirteen years, but that doesn't mean that you don't need—"

"What." The word punched out of her, ripped from Jess's throat with a force that sent Aksel a step back. "You ... you what?"

He pulled his lips between his teeth, working them together as the same sense of rightness he felt at the kitchen table consumed him. This, them, her. His mate, even if she didn't know it and didn't want it, she *was,* and he owed her this truth.

"Mated you."

On cue, a new email notification dinged from her laptop, now at the bar where she could work without being hunched over a toilet.

"No."

The word reverberated through him, rattling Aksel's bones down to the marrow. "No?"

Please, moon and Gods above, don't let her reject him.

She had to feel what Aksel did. That this—them—was *right.* She had to see how badly he wanted to have his hands or his mouth on her. How badly he wanted to mark her and mate her properly so everyone knew, human and inhuman alike, that she was his and he was hers, and the kids were *theirs.*

Jess pressed her lips together, eyes glittering as she shook her head and backed deeper into the kitchen. "Please, Aksel," she whispered. The stink of her fear filled the apartment, carried to Aksel's nose from the flash of sweat beading across her forehead. "Don't do this."

"Jess."

"I can't do this right now." A thump from the boys' room whipped her face to the side, her entire body seizing. Aksel held his breath, ears pricked to catch any sound he could.

Lightsabers hummed and, faint through the door, R2-D2 whistled.

"I'm sorry," Jess finally said. "This isn't about you or us, I just—" She huffed sharply. "I have to redo half of my work on the financial assessment, and my mom and dad are bringing Kendra home any minute, and then they're taking us all golfing because apparently *that's* more important than letting me finish my work, so my boys and Kendra can—" She gasped for breath, pressing on before Aksel could interject. "And you show up here with breakfast and get them to clean, and I can't—"

Jess pressed a hand to her chest, drawing attention to the sharp contraction of her ribs and the high, tight, panicky pants driving every word. Aksel gripped the counter, torn between wanting to gather Jess in his arms and hold her until she calmed down and needing to honor the space she asked for.

"I can't do this right now," she wheezed. "There's too much to do, and I—" Her back hit the wall. She slid to the floor, eyes unfocused and her face worryingly slack. "Oh, my God, she was right."

Aksel crept around the counter, crouching at the edge of the linoleum. "Who was right?"

"My mom." Jess blinked slowly. "This whole time." She raised a hand as if gesturing and let it flop onto her thigh. "My whole life. I'm too stubborn to ask for help, and I keep messing up." Tears fell as she tipped her head back to stare at the ceiling. "Just like before."

The very real, very awful knowledge that this wasn't solely about him, or even them, settled over Aksel, nudging him into action.

"Hey, sweetheart, no." He knee-walked closer and settled at Jess's feet, too uncertain to reach out but needing her to know he was here, in whatever capacity she needed him. "You're not messing up anything."

"She looked over the numbers I put together and said it wasn't ready."

"Is your mom an accountant?"

"No." A tiny furrow dipped between her brows. "But she's right. There are too many gaps and insufficient history to determine whether or not Elkwater would use the funds responsibly." She sniffed and wiped the back of her hand under her nose. "She said the rest of the Mountaineers' Daughters wouldn't take me seriously, and I was going to fail, and why didn't I ask for help when I so clearly needed it?"

There it was. The miserable driving force behind Jess's mood. Anger, hot and hostile, churned in his chest. Aksel flexed his fingers, finally setting his hand on Jess's foot and squeezing. Touching her in any way was a grounding exercise. The soft scrape of the cotton weave on her sock stole his focus enough to keep him from launching from the apartment and hunting the miserable woman down.

Jess lifted her gaze, speaking in a hollow voice that gutted him.

"I thought I could do this on my own. I thought—" Her voice cracked, and it took every fiber of his restraint not to crawl to her. "I thought if I was smart enough and determined enough, I could create something with Elkwater and the Outreach, but I'm just going to mess it up like I always do, and this is all going to fall apart."

Forget hurting less; a stab wound would have been preferred to this.

Aksel couldn't have known what had transpired between Jess and her mom. Hells, he couldn't even offer to look over the report she'd put together. What did a high school band instructor know about revenue and accruals?

Less than he knew about relationships, considering he'd barreled in here in complete contempt of her request for space and then yelled at her for not asking for help. New moon, no wonder she had outright rejected the fact they were—

"I can hear you thinking." Jess crossed her arms over her stomach and pulled her knees to her chest. Cheeks ashen and eyes dull, Aksel finally noticed how exhausted she was, as if all the life and laughter he had seen in her over the last week had been smudged out by a cheap eraser.

Had she been this tired when he'd arrived? Or was it his presence that had made her look so worn?

"Can you give me the week?" she asked, the raw, unpolished grate of her voice tearing Aksel out of his thoughts. "The Mountaineers' Daughters are coming on Wednesday—that's the email I was sending when you got here. I needed to let the Outreach know plans had changed—and my parents are staying through Sunday." She sighed, dragging a hand over her face. "They offered to take the kids to Greenbriar next weekend so I can focus on any follow-up work the foundation asks for."

"Of course."

"Just a week." She finally met his gaze, her eyes a dim and lifeless muddy brown. "And then we can talk about us."

"Talk about ..." Gods help him; hope stirred at that. "That's not a 'no.'"

Jess shook her head slowly, mouthing, "No."

"We don't have to." Yes, they did, but the fear of placing more pressure on her already weary shoulders outweighed all else. Instinct, or desire, whatever it was, the idea of burdening Jess with anything more was as vile to him as a well-done steak reheated in the microwave.

"Yes, we do," she said, "but not today." A curl slipped free as she tipped her head forward. Jess fluttered her lips with a sigh, sending it dancing. When she lifted her head again, her expression was stern. Determined. "I want to, Aksel. I don't know what any of this means or how we move forward, but I want to talk about it. With you."

"Okay."

"Okay?" A brow arched as Jess eyed him warily.

"Okay." He stood and patted his thighs, skimming the kitchen as if checking for his keys. She wanted to talk about it and was willing to hear him out and consider a way forward. All he had to do was shut the hells up for a week.

He had no idea how to keep Jess, but, Sköll be damned, this was a start.

"A week," he said. Jess hugged her knees tighter, and every inborn instinct screamed at him to go to her, gather her close, and soothe away the worry lining her brow. He fisted his hands instead and shoved them into his pockets.

He had lived thirteen years without Jess; he could last a week.

Even if every minute of the next seven days was going to be torture, it was torture he could survive.

With a curt nod, Aksel turned heel and left, this time descending the stairs slowly, near silently. He had to, or else his wolf would tear free and run for the hills. Panic wound tightly around his ribs, choking his lungs and squeezing his heart at her stay of execution. Anything could happen in the next week. He just needed to hang on and give her the space to function.

He only had to last the week.

Then, they would talk, and he could put his wolf at ease. He trusted Jess that much. The woman kept her promises. It was evident in her children and her work, in how much of herself she gave to the Outreach, and now to Elkwater.

Warmth dulled the sharp edge of his panic as Aksel thought over that last revelation. The idea of Jess focusing all that determination and big brain power on Elkwater's success. The thought of her contributing to the place and people, human and inhuman alike, that Aksel considered *his*. That she cared as much for the camp as he did, Gods be damned, it did something to him.

This week was going to be torture.

He stepped out into bright daylight, pivoting for his front door, and Gitta pulled it open.

"So that was a colossal fuck up." She grinned at him. Face fully made up, her braids were tied high, cascading in a thick fall to her shoulders. A white tank top offset deep umber skin, showing off shoulders honed by hours at the gym.

"Shut up." He shouldered past her, scowling at the soggy dregs of cereal in a bowl on the kitchen table. A mug of coffee steamed beside a half-drunk glass of orange juice, a plate of bacon, and a fried egg on toast.

"I think you might be the first wolven to mess up a mating proposal since the fall." Gitta slow-clapped. "Well done, really. I'm beginning to see why Dad stepped in."

"Is there a reason you're here?"

"Always." Kicking the chair out, Gitta sat and took a large bite of egg on toast. "I've got news," she said around the bite, crumbs falling onto her tank top.

Aksel scrubbed a hand down his face. "Moonblessed, it had better be good."

"Nope."

"Sweet, great. Fuck." He dropped into a chair and grabbed the orange juice, spinning the glass in his hands. "What is it?"

"Dad's coming back."

"And?" He hovered the juice in front of his mouth. "He was always going to come back." And swallowed it down.

"A week early." Gitta rocked her chair onto its back legs, arms crossed, and eyes fixed on Aksel. "Members of the Skölldal pack joined them this weekend, along with that Skölldal whelp I dragged out of The Porchlight."

Aksel swallowed, his tongue dry as dirt and throat thick. He shot to his feet, glass in hand, and aimed for the sink. Water splashed into the basin, drowning out the alarms that had begun ringing in his ears. Lennart had given him until he returned from SAR training to figure things out with Beth and the packs, and Aksel had staunchly ignored the command, spending all of his time with Jess instead.

He shoved the glass under the faucet, the chilled water doing little to calm his rising panic.

"Aksel." Gitta approached him slowly, like she expected him to wolf out and go for her throat at whatever she was going to say next. "He told Dad about Jess."

Water splashed against the linoleum, and she snatched the cup away before Aksel dropped it, setting it down on the counter with a quiet *tink*.

"He already knew about Jess," he said, gripping the counter's edge. Water swirled in a funnel, disappearing down the drain.

"And he gave you a month to forget about Jess, and *now* he knows you didn't."

"He couldn't possibly know—"

"The Skölldal whelp was Beth's brother. He *saw* her, Aksel. He scented her. I convinced any Sköllburg that overheard him in the bar that he was drunk and trying to stir up shit, but the mongrel took it straight to Dad. I heard him on the phone with Mom. He described Jess perfectly and told her to spread the word among the pack."

She grabbed his arm, tugging him to look at her. What he saw there sent his stomach plummeting to the floor. Gitta's eyes, round enough that the whites were clearly visible, scraped over his face, searching for comfort or knowledge to set her at ease. Meaning whatever bomb she was about to drop was ten times worse than everything she had already said.

"If anyone finds her, they've been ordered to take Jess straight to Dad at the Lodge." She swallowed and shuddered. Tucked in a narrow valley north of Elkins, the Lodge was the residence of the Alpha and Sköllburg meeting-house. As far as the pack was concerned, any decision made within its walls was final. "You, too."

"If any member of the Sköllburg lays a hand on Jess, I'll—"

"I know. Dad knows. That's what he wants, Aksel. You disobeyed him, rubbing it under the noses of every pack member who didn't go on that training." She swallowed and released his arm. "He's going to force you to choose or challenge."

"Let him."

"Aks."

"She's my mate, Gitta." He shouldered around her, needing the space to pace and calm the fury rising within him. Lennart had not just threatened Aksel; he had threatened Jess. His mate. There was not a wolven among them who wouldn't respond poorly to such an act. "There is no choosing, Jess is it for me."

"Does she know that?"

"Yes." He worked his jaw and ground his teeth to keep the wolf down. Gitta saw the strain or recognized the warning flash in his eyes because she backed away, both hands held up, palms out. "I mean, I think she knows, but we haven't talked about it."

"So get up there."

"*No*," he snarled. "She asked me for space; I will give her that. Jess deserves that much."

"So grab the kids, tell her you're taking them, fuck, I don't know, to putt-putt or something. We'll bring them to Dad, and he'll—"

"Have you lost your mind?"

"Have you?" Gitta crossed her arms; weight dropped back on her hind leg. "Lennart is going to force you to mate Beth, or he's going to disown you. Aksel, you won't survive as a lone wolf."

"I'm not!" His voice echoed off the walls, answered by a series of thumps from upstairs.

The boys. Fuck.

"I'm not alone, Gitta," he said in a low growl, "but I need time, and I refuse to bring my kids into this like they're trump cards to be played."

"Alright." Again, she raised her hands. "Alright, fine, whatever. Your plan, then. What do we do?"

Bit by bit, his shoulders dropped, the wolf receding at her submission, and the easy way Gitta ceded the decision to him. He grunted, walking in a tight circle and working his hands through his hair. "We buy time."

"How?" At the defeat in her voice, Aksel raised his head, meeting the eyes of his sister and oldest friend.

"By helping Jess." It was a terrible plan, more of far-fetched dream, but if they could help Jess with the foundation, and speed along the mating conversation, then Aksel might have ground to stand on when the inevitable confrontation with Lennart came to pass.

An incredulous look washed over Gitta's face. "Again, I ask, how?"

The front door of Cricket and Avery's apartment slammed shut, and a moment later, the bold brass and kick drums of Reel Big Fish blared through the wall. Aksel cocked his head, and an idea trickled to life between his ears.

"I don't know," he said. "But I might have an idea."

29

————

JESS

"The amphitheater is original to the camp." Mac strode backward down the aisle, Wayfarer sunglasses pushed onto her head despite the blazing mid-afternoon sun. "We had to rebuild the stage every other year before adding the shell during the off-season renovation." She raised an arm and two fingers, sweeping them in an arc to draw attention to the rainbow-curved wooden structure acting as both an acoustic shell and roof. "Thanks to the generous donation from Avery Construction. Just one of the many updates we've made over the last year."

"And they've begun hosting corporate retreats," Jessica added, "drawing income during the off-season."

"How many?" A woman in the back of the group asked. Jessica thought her name was Arlene, but most of the Mountaineers' Daughters looked so alike it was hard to tell them apart. Like her mother, they wore flowing linen pants and primary-colored boatneck shirts with scarves and statement necklaces.

Their hair, ranging from ash-blonde to a rich, meticulously highlighted brown, was either drawn up in a fashionably loose bun or secured by a butterfly clip, and their multitude of rose gold or silver bangles jangled merrily as they walked the length of the aisle.

"We did two last year," Mac answered, "and have contracted with eight organizations throughout the Tygart and Ohio River Valleys for the upcoming season."

"There are four more in advanced stages of negotiation," Jessica added. Mac beamed at her, confidence oozing from every pore. Jessica had no idea how she did it. These women were *terrifying*. A gaggle of clones of her mother, tucked, dyed, and plumped in denial of their age, looking down their sculpted noses at the ragged, haphazard loveliness of Elkwater Music Camp.

Mac never faltered. Shoulders broad and back straight, she paraded the gaggle through the camp, keeping up a steady stream of narration and trivia.

"Avery Construction was the first." Mac hopped onto the stage and strode to the center, projecting her voice. "They wanted to familiarize themselves with the camp and existing amenities, and one of the attendees was so impressed, she went home and convinced her husband to host his company retreat on our grounds this past spring."

She put her back to the crowd and, hands on her hips, gazed across the stage toward the woods toward where, tucked among the trees, a collection of thatched roofs and vinyl siding caught the afternoon light. The faint twang of a banjo and haunting call of a pan flute floated from the faun settlement, and when Mac faced the Mountaineers' Daughters, a broad grin stretched across her face.

"It's been a season of growth for Elkwater. We're excited to welcome the challenges that come along with it."

"And your marketing strategy?" Jessica's mother asked. Nestled in the center of the pack, Irene stared down Mac as though her question were the opening salvo of an attack.

"I'm sorry?" Mac straightened by a hair, fingers dancing along the cargo pocket on her thigh.

Jessica eyed her mother, mind running at a million miles per hour as she tried to anticipate what she would say next.

"From my brief review of the financial assessment, you are relying on these corporate retreats to float the organization through the slow season. If one of the negotiations falls through, what marketing or business development strategies have you implemented to ensure next summer's registrations can recoup the loss?"

"It won't be a loss." The words left Jessica before she realized she had spoken. Ten perfectly made-up faces whipped her way, and it was an effort not to flinch and back away. These women were her mother's contemporaries, raised and honed in Charleston's cutthroat society. She had gone to school with their daughters, as had Mac, and had premiered in a white dress beside them at her debutante ball.

All of these women knew Jessica's story, and they wore that knowledge in the perch of their lips and narrowed gazes.

Any show of weakness, and they would jump at the chance to pick and prod until Jessica's dreams fell apart. But her assessment of the camp's finances was sound, and her work was good, even before she spent the last three days reviewing and revising the printed and bound report clutched in every one of their ringed fingers.

"When you review the accruals report and donor schedule, you'll see how the camp manages its finances. While the runway is short, it is enough to see Elkwater through the slow season."

"How will you use the surplus revenue?" a woman asked.

"We're developing our hiring plan for the off-season now," Mac answered, "aiming to grow our permanent staff by fifteen percent ahead of next summer's sessions. Beyond that, the extra revenue will be applied to staff training and continuing infrastructural updates to ensure our campers have the best experience and musical education possible."

"I was under the impression this camp was a charity case," another woman said. "If you don't require donors, why solicit our foundation?"

Mac clenched her fists, quickly sliding them into her pockets. "With all due respect, ma'am, I would ask that you defer from referring to Elkwater Music Camp as a 'charity case.'"

The woman pressed her lips together, chest rising as she inhaled.

Before she could retort, Jessica stepped forward. "Elkwater did not solicit any donations from the Mountaineers' Daughters, and I apologize on behalf of the Charleston Inhuman Outreach if you were operating under any misunderstanding as to the nature of our work and what we hope to accomplish in our partnership with the camp."

At the center of the huddle, Irene narrowed her eyes. Beside her, a woman flipped through the financial assessment and proposal, skimming the pages and showing them to the woman on her right.

"Then why solicit the funds," she asked, "if the camp can operate without the extra liquidity?"

"We are a donation-based outreach program," Jessica said. "Our sole aim is to foster community between the human and inhuman populations in Charleston and its surrounding areas. Any donations to our non-profit community action committee will be funneled directly into a scholarship program for inhuman students." She gestured to the camp, putting a bit of heart into her pitch. "Elkwater was the first integrated camp in Appalachia, welcoming the fallen population within two years of their arrival. The relationships campers forge during the summer extend beyond the grounds."

A snort rose from the crowd of women. "I should say they do," someone muttered.

Jessica's cheeks heated, and Mac rushed to her aid.

"We're ranked as one of the premier band camps in West Virginia," she said. "Our students have gone on to march at OSU and Florida A&M, and our current camp population includes musicians from three of the five top-ranked high school marching bands nationwide. Even among our staff, you will find former drum majors from leading university marching bands—"

"And the newest member of the Carnegie Mellon graduate student body," a new voice joined from the rear of the amphitheater. Heads swiveled, and an altogether different titter rose as a woman in a sharp business suit and heels strode down the aisle. Her hair, a sleek, honey-blonde bob, drew attention to her bright, sky-blue eyes and the dusting of freckles across her nose and cheekbones, which she did not attempt to hide with makeup. "Mackenzie, dear, I'm so sorry I'm late."

Mac beamed at the new arrival, waving and gesturing her forward. "Not a problem, Mrs. Payne. We still have the orchestra hall and practice rooms to tour."

"Excellent." Mrs. Payne skimmed the group, her pleasant smile tightening as she took in the women. "Arlene," she nodded a nearby woman, greeting others as she recognized them. "Sarah Beth, Winona. Irene."

"Victoria," Jessica's mother said tightly. "What a pleasant surprise. I was under the impression you could not make this little tour."

"Nonsense." Mrs. Payne waved a hand, dismissing Irene and speaking to the rest of the women. "As a daughter of West Virginia, I was happy to rearrange my schedule. Any excuse to visit Elkwater and my daughter Avery—you know Avery, of course," she said to the nearest woman, "she's the assistant director of the camp."

"It's good to see you, Mrs. Payne." Mac beamed at her.

"Please, dear, for the last time, it's Tori. None of this 'Mrs.' nonsense." She smiled and winked at Mac. "What Mackenzie is too humble to say is that Elkwater has quickly become one of the most sought-after band camps for talented young musicians around the nation to attend, but with that prestige, a chasm has opened between those who can afford a summer session and those who deserve a summer session."

"Right." Emboldened by Mrs. Payne—*Tori's*—effortless commandeering of the crowd in the camp's favor, Jessica stepped forward. "By partnering with Elkwater directly, and with your donation, the Charleston Inhuman Outreach will be able to offer multiple summer scholarships for less-advantaged inhumans."

"How many?" Irene looked up from the financial assessment she had begun leafing through. "Your proposal goes into a great level of detail about the camp and its facilities, but it doesn't actually say anything, dear."

"As a proud member of the Mountaineers' Daughters," Tori answered before Jessica could, "The Avery Trust is committing a scalable donation to meet the scholarship needs of five students a summer." A low murmur broke out among the women. Irene darted an angry look at Tori, who batted it away with her next words. "You have, what was it, four grandchildren enrolled for the summer? Imagine the young lives you could change by pledging that same amount once they graduate from high school?"

It was a subtle but cutting dig, and Jessica fought the urge to smile. A tense silence fell over the Mountaineers' Daughters, every one of them watching Irene without looking directly at her.

"I don't see any reason the Abernathy Trust should have to defer until my grandchildren are grown," she said, chin lifting by a degree.

Tori smiled, this time without any warmth. It was a businesswoman's smile, worn when the negotiations had landed in her favor. "Excellent. That's nine students, then. And you, Arlene? Sarah Beth?"

A chorus of agreement rang out, each woman too stubborn or proud to be outdone. Jessica laced her fingers together, struggling to keep from letting her surprise and relief play out on her face. In a mere moment, Victoria Payne had achieved what Mac and Jess had struggled to do for an hour. She had won over the Mountaineers' Daughters with her clout and presence, ushering Jessica's goals closer to the finish line.

Mac nudged Jessica with her elbow and tipped her head at the group. "Let's continue the tour."

"And interrupt her?" Jessica whispered back. In the aisle, Tori greeted one of the women with an air kiss and asked after her eldest grandson. "She just got these women to pledge scholarships for two dozen kids."

"Just walk with me; she'll get them to follow." Mac hopped off the stage, waiting for Jessica to do the same. "Tori knows the camp almost as well as I do; she'll make Elkwater sound like an all-inclusive resort."

"Why do I get the feeling you knew this would happen?"

Mac smirked. "A little red bird heard from a stray dog that a member of the foundation was giving you a hard time." She shot a conspiratorial look at Jess, eyes twinkling. "And that little birdy," Mac continued, "has a well-connected, well-informed mom who loves this place."

⁂

The rest of the tour ran without incident. Mac led them around the camp, Tori following breezily behind and leading the cluster of Mountaineers' Daughters. They hung on to her every word, all snide titters and cruel snickers silenced by the imposing yet comforting Victoria Payne.

As relieved as Jessica was not to be the sole focus of their scrutiny, she missed the distraction. Without having to watch her every word and toe the line of politeness, her mind couldn't help but wander.

And no matter how she tried to avoid it, her mind kept wandering to Aksel.

She shouldn't have been surprised he had found a way to help her, even while giving Jessica the space she requested. Knowing Aksel was behind this—supporting her without being asked and pulling in a ringer to get each woman on her side—did something strange to her insides, twisting Jessica all up.

For the first time that summer, she allowed herself to dream. What if he found a job in Charleston? What if they had a chance to pursue *them* and try their hands at being a family?

He certainly seemed to want it, and Jessica could no longer deny how much she wanted it as well.

So, what if, and why not?

"Thought we'd finish the tour on the field," Mac said, bursting the bubble of Jessica's thoughts. A few steps behind, Tori gestured at the cafeteria and the brand new pad-mounted transformer beside the building. "The afternoon session is about to wrap up. It should give you a chance to see your kids. Or anyone else you wanted to say hello to."

"Why do I feel like you planned more than Victoria Payne arriving in the nick of time?"

Mac grinned and bounced her shoulders in an innocent shrug. "I have no idea what you're talking about," she said. "This is how the Elkwater family takes care of each other."

Jessica stilled, her smile fading and shoulders dropping. "The Elkwater …"

"Whatever happens between you and Aksel, Jess, you're one of us." Mac gave her a sisterly squeeze on the shoulder. "You and the kids. We take care of our own."

"Even if we never come back?"

Mac's smile tightened, some of the easy mirth hardening in her eyes. "Even then." She nodded tersely. "Your picture is on the wall in my office. You're as much a part of this camp as I am, and no matter what, there's always a bunk for you."

Again, her insides twisted. Jessica blinked to keep tears from falling, swallowing the fast-growing lump in her throat. "Okay."

"Okay?" Mac eyed her.

A fluttering built in her chest, nerves and hope colliding in a confusing mix of emotions. She swallowed again, skirting her gaze around Mac and the Mountaineers' Daughters, taking in the camp in a montage of scenes.

Campers skipped down the cafeteria steps, and a sasquatch and a naga slipped into the breezeway between buildings to take the shortcut to their bunks. A cluster of pre-teen campers chatted and laughed as they passed by, pausing to wave and greet her with a hearty, "Hi, Kendra's Mom!"

It all felt so right. Now that she was staring it all in the face, Jessica couldn't ignore how perfect and fitting it felt to be here in Elkwater, working towards a cause that would benefit the camp. That would benefit her and her kids.

Accounting was safe. The work was rote, and the numbers made sense, but for all the challenges and frustrations this summer had held, Jessica had never felt more alive or free.

She had never felt more like herself.

Loathing followed on the heels of that realization, a looming, ominous presence joined by the end of the summer, just a few short weeks away.

But what if it didn't have to end?

Aksel wouldn't move to Charleston. Despite his pseudo-offering to do so, Jessica knew in her heart that he wouldn't move because no woman who understood him, and the wolven ... no person who loved—

"Oh." She pressed a hand over her mouth, wrapping an arm around her stomach.

God, the thought was out there now, floating before her, half-formed and aching to be acknowledged. So close she could reach out and pluck it from her Whats Ifs and make it a reality.

Because no woman or wolven who loved Aksel would ask him to leave this place.

Which begged the question. Did she—

"Jess?" Mac moved before her, voice low and brow knit with worry. "You alright?"

She bit the tip of her tongue, grounding herself in the minor pinch of pain, and nodded. "Yeah, I'm okay. I think the kids and I would like that. Having a bunk here, I mean."

Quiet understanding eased Mac's worry. "I think you're right," she said, bumping Jessica's shoulder with hers. "Come on, let's get you to the field."

30

AKSEL

"ALRIGHT, EVERYBODY. TAKE A water break." Aksel clapped his hands, and the band dispersed, running and slithering for their half-gallon water jugs. He took his time joining them, shaking out his arms as if he could slough off the tense, jittery feeling that had been riding him for days. A glance at the sky, blue with picture-perfect clouds, deepened his frown.

A storm was coming. It was in the mounting pressure every inhuman could sense. The way the humidity weighed in the air, gaining mass until it became a physical, tangible thing. A balloon ready to burst.

It made his skin itch to shift just to disrupt the pea-soup thickness. From how his campers squirmed through their morning meeting and bickered for the first half of the day, they were just as uncomfortable. Lunch helped, giving a break from the stagnant heat and brownies to raise blood sugar, but a handful of his students maintained their bad moods throughout the afternoon.

The worst among them was Kendra, who glowered at the back of their huddle, answering in one-word responses until Aksel stopped calling on her altogether.

He surveyed the crowd of hot, sweaty drum majors-in-training lounging in the grass, and campers in the marching class guzzling water and wilting in the bleachers. Aksel checked his watch, strongly considering calling it quits for the day and sending them to their bunks. The camp was practically a tinder box, and he did not want to be here when it eventually ignited. Let that be a problem for Mac and the overnight counselors.

"Hey, Mr. Aksel!" Jens called from where he sat with Jan and Jarl. They waved as a trio, broad grins showing their teeth.

"Hey boys, how is practice?"

"Hot," they complained as one.

"I think my shoes are chafing," Jens added.

Jarl tugged on his shorts and shook a leg. "Could be worse."

"Too vivid for summer camp, Jarl," Aksel warned. "Tone it down."

"Aw, man, you're no fun."

"Just doing my job."

Jarl's eyes sharpened. He nudged Jan, who spread a wolfish grin wide across his face. "A-*parent*-ly."

The trio hi-fived, collapsing in a fit of giggles as surprise slammed into Aksel.

Did they know?

He hadn't spoken to them since Sunday, but they might have overheard the argument between him and their mother. Wolven had keen hearing. Aksel had heard *Star Wars* clearly through the closed door, and he and Jess had been anything but quiet.

"—turf and rebuilt the bleachers." Mac's voice broke into his thoughts, rising above the boys' laughter. She paraded a group of middle-aged women across the field, pointing to the newly built bleachers covered in overheated boys, girls, and inhumans. Jess walked beside her with a straight-backed confidence that overrode his worries and made his heart soar.

The tour must be going well if she walked so easily. For days, her stressed scent sharpened the air around the townhome, driving Aksel crazy with the need to hold her and soothe that worry away. He hadn't, opting to play video games with Dusty and run with Gitta, giving Jess the space she requested.

Maybe that explained his irritability and the way his wolf rode so closely under his skin.

"As well as the platforms for our drum majors," Mrs. Payne added. "We opted for the lighter-weight aluminum tube, naturally." She bent slightly to the side, confiding with a shorter, plump woman. "Much easier for the campers to move around the field."

"Of course." The woman nodded, her eyes wide with no small amount of hero worship.

After a year of run-ins with Mrs. Payne, Aksel half-worshipped the woman himself. She had swooped in like a fairy godmother after the nightmare with the werewolves, doting on the camp and staff as much as she doted on her children. Thanks to her family's construction company, the faun had a permanent settlement around the perimeter of Elkwater, and half the camp had been renovated, with plans constantly developing for the other half and more.

"And the bins?" Another woman asked, pointing to the large plastic bins affixed to either side of the bleachers. "I've seen these around the camp; are they trash cans? Compost?"

"Clothing," Mac answered, "and towels to accommodate our shifters. You know how kids are; can't help themselves sometimes, but we can at least ensure they can cover themselves when they shift back."

"What a consideration," Irene said, her face thoughtful. It softened the woman, making her less intimidating and, for a brief moment, Aksel could almost believe she was the loving grandmother Jess had once described.

"Aksel's idea." Mac hooked a thumb in his direction. "The wolven keep similar caches in the woods for their patrols. He suggested the bins during the renovation, and Tori added the cost to the project budget."

Aksel rolled his shoulders back, thrilled to have even a minor contribution called out to the women of the foundation. As the Marching Director, he had been included in many discussions during the renovation. The acoustic shell for the amphitheater and the location of the newly built orchestra room. They had even asked for his input regarding the turf and materials for the field. It was during these meetings that he caught wind of plans for a fully equipped theater and to grow the camp to accommodate a drama and chorus program in the coming years.

It was part of the reason Mac was so keen to partner with Jess's Outreach—dreams like that required money, more of it than any of the current staff at Elkwater had access to. Luckily, Jess was just as determined to make this partnership work, and from the bright, effervescent bubble to her scent, her goal was all but in hand.

Aksel took a deep breath, filling his nose and lungs with the scent of her happiness. With any luck, he would do so again and again and again.

"What is my mom doing here?" Kendra stepped beside him, swallowed by the old, oversized Elkwater hoodie she often wore. The kid had to be sweltering, which would explain the attitude, and Aksel had half a mind to tell her to take it off and chill out in the shade.

"Succeeding, kid." He tried a smile, and from Kendra's answering frown, it didn't quite pass for genuine. "You should be proud of her."

"I am. She's *my* mom. Why are you?"

Aksel opened his mouth, only to snap it shut and grind his teeth. He might be her father, but he wasn't her dad. Not truly. There were many things Aksel could lecture a camper about: miscounting steps, emptying spit-valves on another camper's shoes, hiding spare reeds. Lecturing one of them about their mother was strictly out of line.

Instead, Aksel whirled to face the rest of his class and the marching band, hands raised to clap, and froze as a dozen faun burst from the woods across the field.

The shouts reached him a split second later. "Sköll!" Panicked, terrified cries in a language he had not heard in over a decade. "Sköll!"

The Otherworld's common tongue word for *wolf*.

His hackles shot up, canines descending to fill Aksel's mouth with teeth. He launched across the field, catching a faun by the arm and swinging them around. "What's happened?"

"Sköll!" they shouted, eyes wheeling in their skull. Jerking their arm free, they hurtled for the camp. Aksel followed their run, ears shifting and swiveling to catch any sound beyond their shouts. Near the bleachers, Mac ordered the kids to the bunks, keeping her voice firm but calm.

"What's happening?" one of the women asked.

"Nothing to worry about," she said. "The faun are still getting used to living near the camp and other inhumans; I'm sure it's—"

Strong fingers grabbed Aksel's arm, hauling him around. He caught a flash of bright blonde curls before Cricket hissed, "You've got to go."

"Campers, to your bunks!" Mac yelled, clapping her hands and shooing the kids along. "Right now, hurry up!"

"Come on, man." Cricket dug her fingers into his arm, the soft, velvet pads driving into muscles and tendon. "You have got to get out of sight."

"Crick, what's happening?"

"Wolves," she said, leaning all of her body into dragging him across the grass.

"Were?" he asked, shooting a look over his shoulder. A howl rose in the woods, and every hair along his arms rose.

"Worse," Cricket answered. "Sköllburg."

Aksel dug his heels into the grass, ripping free from Cricket's alarmingly strong grip. "What?"

"Lennart's here. Gitta barely got a call to me in time. You need to *leave*, Aksel. Now."

"This is my camp." He searched the field, finding Jess in the crowd. Her boys clustered around her, their eyes wide and cheeks ashen. Irene's head popped over a shoulder, pinched features scanning the faun streaming across the grass. "He never comes to the camp."

Another howl rose, closer now, joined by a chorus of Sköllburg.

"Well, he's here now!"

"Aksel?" Jess shoved through her boys, throwing off her mother's hand and twisting through the fleeing faun. At the sound of her voice, the world narrowed to a very fine point consisting solely of her. "What's happening?"

Sound cut out, and for a brief moment, Aksel stood outside of himself, witnessing the chaos on the field as a casual observer, able to see how they had gotten here and what came next.

"A challenge," he said.

No matter how hard he tried to ignore the ticking clock, disregard Lennart's demand, and bury himself in Jess, this was always going to happen. Only he had been too naive and ignorant to acknowledge the inevitable fate he'd been running toward since the fall. The camp and the high school had bought him time, giving Aksel something to think of as his. But no matter how many times he had assured Lennart he was no threat, that he did not want the Sköllburg, some instincts were too deeply ingrained to ignore.

Gitta had warned him, clearly stating that Lennart would force a challenge to exile Aksel from the pack, but he'd been too stubborn to listen. More determined to help Jess and enjoy however much time he had with her, than help himself, and now his time was up.

"Aksel ..." Jess stopped mere feet away, too far to reach. Wide, lovely brown eyes darted to the woods over his shoulder, and she drew back, pressing a fist to her breastbone. "Oh, God."

Aksel twisted to catch whatever had earned such a terrified whisper, and two paws hit him square in the chest, knocking him to the ground. His head thudded against the turf, grass burning his cheeks and filling his mouth. Instinct took over, and he rolled, shoving his hands up and catching Lennart in the throat, fangs bared mere inches from Aksel's weak human skin.

Survival kicked in, forcing the shift before Aksel could hold back. His nails lengthened to claws, bones shifting and popping as strength filled him. In an instant, they were matched in size. Lennart snarled and clawed the ground, driving Aksel hard against the grass. He snapped his jaws, hot slather spraying Aksel's snout. The stink of challenge filled his head, igniting a possessive, protective, red-hot rage within him.

Elkwater was *his*. This camp was his. Aksel's. The Sköllburg had no right to bring a challenge to *his* territory.

Aksel shoved his hind legs up, kicking the salt-and-pepper black wolf off and lurching to his feet.

They collided in a fury of fang and claw. Fur filled his mouth; claws scraped his legs. Teeth snagged his ear, and a force slammed into Aksel's side. He hit the ground, yelping as the wind punched from his lungs, rolling tail over paws, and slamming down as a heavy weight pounded into his back.

"Stand down," Gitta snarled, shifting to speak. She banded an iron-strong arm around his neck, jerking his chin up and tightening her chokehold. "Don't do this here, Aksel. Not in front of them."

He writhed and wriggled, snarling at his foster sister as his snout shortened. "Get off me." Every inborn instinct told him to bite, rend, and tear until she submitted and let him finish the job he'd been aching to start for a decade. "This is my camp, my pack!"

"I know, man, I know, but do you want them to see you like this?" Claws drove into his chin, and Gitta redirected Aksel's fury to the bleachers, where the women huddled together. "Heel, Aks," Gitta pleaded. "Nils has Dad; shift back and take this somewhere else. *Anywhere* else."

"No!" Lennart's snarl cut across the field, guttural and raw in his half-shifted mouth. "I have been more than patient in the face of continued disobedience." A pitched yelp rang out, followed by nasty snarls, and a naked, furious Lennart appeared in front of Gitta and Aksel. "We settle this here and now."

A towel slapped against the back of his head and half wrapped around his neck. Lennart shot around, glaring at Mac, who stood mere feet away with two more towels draped over her shoulders.

"Whoops." She raised her hands in mock surrender.

"Put it on," Aksel demanded. To his surprise, Lennart wrapped the oversized towel around his waist without complaint, securing it tight. That he obeyed, even with Aksel restrained and on the ground, gave him hope. If Lennart were willing to follow an order, even one as simple as covering himself up, perhaps he could be reasoned with.

"Let him up." Lennart jerked his chin at his daughter. Gitta's arms slid away, her heat and weight vanishing, leaving Aksel alone before the Sköllburg Alpha.

Pride had him instantly on his feet, snatching the towel Mac tossed him and wrapping it around his waist.

"Ah, poo," one of the women muttered.

A thin crowd huddled together near the bleachers. The foundation women, Cricket, Mac, and Mrs. Payne. Jess and the boys. Jan lifted his head, sniffing the air, and a new awareness flooded Aksel's senses, prickling the hairs on the back of his neck. He pivoted, catching shadows in the trees.

Wolven, a dozen of them, held the perimeter around the field. If he ran, they would pursue, driving Aksel to the brink of exhaustion so Lennart could have his challenge.

There was no way out of this, no way to avoid the punishment he had brought on himself. Either Aksel won and assumed leadership of the Sköllburg, or he would end this day an exiled wolf.

"I ordered you to mate a wolven from the surrounding packs," Lennart spoke low, a growl powering every word. "Any wolven, and you mated a human?"

"I did," Aksel confirmed. "Thirteen years ago."

The foundation women gasped.

"You were under orders from your Alpha. Orders you ignored, flaunting your disobedience in front of the entire pack—"

"What would you have me do? Break a mating?"

"Yes!" Lennart bellowed.

"Dad, please." Gitta whipped a glare at her father, easing her hold on Aksel. "There are too many people."

"Good," he growled. "Let them witness the challenge."

"There won't be any challenge, Len!" Aksel threw his arms wide, advancing a step. "I don't want the Sköllburg. I don't want any of it. I have the camp. I have my job at the high school, the marching band. I have—"

"Sons," Lennart said, dropping that one word like a boulder between them, juddering the earth beneath Aksel's feet. "The packs need new blood."

"Absolutely not." Jess lurched forward only to have all three sons grab her by the arms and jerk her back, forming a wall between their mother and the Alpha now seething in her direction. "These are my children, you mutt. You can't just come here and take my children."

"I am not taking them," he explained in a cold, murderous voice. "By Wolven Rite, any offspring of a foster belongs to the pack hosting their sire."

"Len …" Aksel warned, a growl rising in his throat. Blood rushed in his veins, his wolf prowling beneath the surface, snapping its jaws and ready to tear free.

"I will foster them as I fostered their father," Lennart finished.

"Over my dead body!" Irene stormed forward. "This isn't your Otherworld, and we aren't beholden to your so-called

'Wolven Rite,' you flea-bitten mountain of muscle. This is America!"

"*Mom.*"

Lennart's nostrils flared. He leaned away from Irene's fury, taking in her petite, linen and silk-clad body trembling with fury. Though he had two feet of height on her and close to a hundred pounds of muscle, for a brief instant, Aksel could have sworn he saw genuine fright dance across his face.

It was gone as quickly as it had appeared.

"I will foster the boys," he said to Aksel, "as is my right. With any luck, I will succeed where I failed with you, and when they come of age, I will secure alliances with the other packs."

"You have no right." Aksel came nose to nose with his foster father, searching for any hint of the wolven who had raised him, the Alpha who had taught him how to be a leader, a sire, and a father, and finding a stranger instead. "Lennart, do you hear yourself?"

"All too clearly."

"This camp is my territory. You have no right to come here and challenge me on my territory for *my sons.*"

Lennart set a foot of distance between them, eerily calm and composed. Amber eyes flashed at Aksel, and with a mouth of fangs, he said, "I, Lennart Sköllburg, Alpha of the Sköllburg, challenge the foster Aksel Haralson to his territory and pack."

"No!" A small, hard voice rang out. Aksel whipped his head toward the sound, and the sea of middle-aged women parted to reveal Kendra. She trembled within the hoodie, hands flexing and fisting at her sides, eyes blinking rapidly. Their eyes met, and she rolled her shoulders, stretching her neck side to side as though her body were too small to contain her anger.

No. Not anger.

"New moon—" Aksel breathed.

"Kendra, sweetpea," Irene said, low and soft. "Not now, honey."

"They're not your pack!" she yelled, louder than he'd ever heard. "They're not yours, they're not—"

It happened so fast. Too fast for anywhere to react in time to stop it, much less Aksel. One moment, Kendra stood there amid the women, quaking in her fury, and the next, the oversized hoodie burst apart, and an adolescent red wolf launched at him.

His wolf answered, rushing to the surface to meet the furious, furry ball of teeth and claws. One large paw batted Kendra away. She yelped, hitting the ground and rolling to a stop where she hunkered low, hackles raised and lips curled back. Her ears flattened, eyes narrowed, and muzzle wrinkling in challenge. Somewolf snarled, barking and biting their teeth, and too late, Aksel realized it was him.

Kendra shrank back, whimpered, and launched across the field as a red streak of fur.

"Kendra!" Jess's scream tore through Aksel's ears, ripping him into his human skin. Tears streamed down her face, each sob punching a hole straight through him.

"Jess." He ran for her. "I'm sorry, I—"

"Your daughter." Lennart grabbed Aksel's shoulder, shoving a towel against his chest. He stared at it, turning the fabric over in his hands, mind reeling from the flurry of the last few seconds. "She's an Alpha?"

Aksel met Jess's watery stare, reading the million emotions playing over her face. Anger and hurt, sorrow and fury, but most of all, *fear*.

"She is," he said, shrugging off Lennart's hand. "And I just challenged her for her pack." Wrapping the towel back around his waist, Aksel aimed for Jess. "I'm so sorry, baby, I didn't know, I swear—"

"Find her."

For as frightened as she appeared, Jess's voice was level and cold, every ounce of her maternal fury directed at Lennart. He shrank from the heat in her glare. "You came into *my mate's* territory and challenged him to *my sons*. She's never shifted before, and now she's running terrified in foreign woods because of *you*." She spat on the ground, stomped a foot, and pointed in the direction Kendra had run. "Find. Her. You owe me that much. "

Lennart dipped his chin, flicking two fingers at Gitta and Nils beside her. "Sköllburg will not rest."

In a blink, he and Nils shifted and set off across the field where the rest of the pack waited.

Gitta lingered, her sharp gaze dancing from Aksel to Jess and back. "I'm so sorry. I called the camp to warn you, but no one answered, so I ran to your apartment and used the spare key. Avery and Cricket's emergency contact was on your pinboard. Oh, Gods, Aksel."

Her voice broke on his name, and his strong, stalwart foster sister sniffled.

Aksel grabbed her hand and squeezed. "Help me?"

"Always." Gitta squeezed back, sleek, black fur sprouting as she did. She loped across the grass, hesitating halfway between Aksel and where her father and the Sköllburg waited. Torn in her loyalty and love.

New moon, how did it come to this?

He never meant to put Gitta in the middle of his battle of wills with Lennart, and yet there she was, stuck in limbo when the pressure that had been building for years, since they fell, finally burst.

Thunder rolled overhead, and Aksel finally took in the sky, no longer postcard blue and painted with thick, voluminous clouds. Now, grey gathered overhead, clinging to the peaks of the mountains abutting Elkwater.

He gripped the waist of his towel and faced Jess. "We won't rest," he said. "No wolven knows the woods as well as we do."

"Good." She shrugged off the shoulder bag she had been carrying and dumped the contents onto the field. A binder, pens, pencils, a notebook with dog-eared pages, and a bundle of loose papers held together with a pink plastic paperclip. Those, she tucked under her arm, before grabbing the shredded remains of Kendra's hoodie and shoving it into the bag. "Then you'll make sure I don't get lost."

"Jess."

"Jessica Abernathy Babcock!" Irene stormed over. "Are you out of your mind? You can't run off into the woods with this–this—"

"Do *not* call him a mongrel, Mom," Jess snapped. She crouched to gather what remained of Kendra's shorts, torn from the rapid shift, and stuffed them into her bag. "I am not sitting here waiting while my daughter is running scared out of her mind in the woods. He is the father of my children, he is partially responsible for this mess, and, for once, he is going to help me clean it up."

Irene blinked, jaw working, but no sound came out. She glanced at Aksel and, to his surprise, deflated. "Kendra," she rasped. "She's ... ?"

"Your *granddaughter*," Jess said, voice brooking no argument.

"Always." Irene nodded, shoulders dropping. "My granddaughter," she said to Aksel, "She is an ... Alpha?"

"She is," he said. "Most don't shift until they are older; it helps the pack maintain peace."

"This is about the challenges?" she asked.

Jess jerked her head up, surprise parting her lips. Irene pouted.

"Please, they're my grandbabies. I've done as much research as you have."

"I—"

"Go, then." Bending at the waist, Irene scooped a pair of socks and Aksel's shorts from the ground, holding them out for Jess to add to the bag. "Bring your baby home."

"Mom." Jess stood and gathered her mother close, sniffling quietly into her hair. Irene's arms shot straight, her body tensing for a beat before she sank into her daughter's embrace.

"Be safe, Jessica. Please."

"I will," she said, pulling away to grip her mother's shoulders. "Talk to Mac, get the camp organized. And someone will need to tell the rest of the search and rescue."

"You want me to do it?"

"I've seen you wrangle the Charleston Chamber of Commerce, and you had the Mountaineer's Daughters hanging on your every word."

Irene's face darkened. "Until Victoria Payne showed up."

"So work with her. Between the two of you, I'm sure you can get a pack of wolves to fall in line." She squeezed gently and then let go, facing Aksel. "Shift."

Surprise lanced through him, mixed with an odd need to do as she said. Now. Without argument. Still, in this form, he was only, kind of, sort of human. "What?"

"Shift. Now."

"Jess, there's no way you can keep up." A howl rose at the wood's edge, and Gitta leapt at the sound, whipping across the remainder of the field to prove his point.

"So?" Jess slung the bag over her shoulder. "You've carried me on your back before, Haralson, and you'll do it again. Let's go."

31

—·—

JESS

MUSCLES SHIFTED AND FLEXED beneath her, reminding Jess with every step that she clung to the back of a massive wolf.

Though years had passed since she'd last ridden on his back, Aksel carried her as though she were still a waifish teen and not a hippy, soft thirty-something. When he took off across the field, grass passing as a blur, Jessica had been sure he would stop and shrug her off within minutes. But Aksel pressed on, slowing only to drop his face and sniff the ground before bounding in the direction of whatever scent he had caught. Back and forth up one ridge and down the other side, leaping over narrow gullies without pausing to judge the distance.

She gave up trying to orient herself when they summited the first ridge. Aksel paused in a clearing, looking back at Jessica, then pointedly through the trees. The Tygart River Valley stretched in both directions, hundreds of feet below, and he made a whining sound to catch her attention, jutting his snout to the north. A swathe of green no larger than a thumbnail peeked through the treetops. Jessica squinted, then gripped his fur as she realized what it was.

"Is that Elkwater?"

Aksel chuffed and pawed the ground, which she took for a yes. Jessica's stomach sank. They'd only been running for fifteen minutes. Maybe twenty. If he had gotten this far while stopping to catch Kendra's scent and carrying Jessica on his back, how far had her baby gone?

Terrified and shifted for the first time, experiencing the volume of scents and sounds in woods she did not know.

"It's so far away."

Again, that tight whine lodged in Aksel's wolven throat. Jessica gripped his fur, ducking her head to compose herself as he loped back to the deer path he had been following, speeding to a steady trot.

She wished he could talk and could tell her it was going to be okay. That Kendra was fine, they would find her, and everything would go back to normal. Only Jessica no longer knew what normal was.

Was it the busy loneliness of Charleston? Going through the motions to raise her children and carve out a community?

Or was it sneaking down the stairs in the middle of the night to lie in his arms?

She knew what she wanted it to be, but just like the woods they traversed, the path was twisting and clogged with impassable prickles.

It should have been easy. He had mated her, and Jessica knew what that meant, even if she did not understand the how. And she had claimed him as her mate in front of the Sköllburg Alpha, acting on a half-remembered comment Svana had once made about wolven mating rites and ceremony.

But even with all that said and done, she couldn't uproot the kids any more than she could ask Aksel to uproot his life, and now her daughter was missing. Whatever future Jessica imagined, whatever hopes and dreams she held for her little family, none of it could happen without finding her daughter and bringing her home. Safe.

A distant howl broke Jessica from her thoughts. She whipped her head toward the sound as Aksel diverted from the trail he'd been following, veering to the left and down to the next ridgeline. Wolven fell in beside them, their silhouettes darting through the trees and drawing closer.

Ducking under a low branch dripping ivy, Aksel slowed beside a small lake at the base of a waterfall running down a wall of quartz. Pristine waters winked in the late afternoon sun, and it was just as Jessica remembered from the last night of camp all those years ago—plus two dozen wolven, some shifted, some in their naked human forms, lying on the mossy banks or sitting on fallen stumps and rocks.

Dropping his forelegs in a bow, Aksel huffed at Jessica and shook his shoulders. She slid off, wobbling on solid ground, as

Aksel padded straight into the lake, shifting the moment his shoulders were submerged.

He ducked beneath the surface and rose, sweeping hair back from his reddened face. His thick, lightly furred chest rose and fell, lips trembling as he fought to catch his breath, all while avoiding meeting Jessica's eye.

From the deepening pink on his cheeks, she wondered if he, too, recalled the last time she had ridden him to this very spot.

"Any luck?" An older, gray-haired wolven stepped beside her, his tanned, weathered skin sheened with heavy sweat. He offered Jessica the open bag of jerky in his hand, and she shook her head no. Food was the furthest thing from her mind, but the wolven had to be hungry after running for the last few hours.

"None," Aksel called back. He charged out of the water, passing Jessica without a glance and heading for the edge of the clearing, where several wolven gathered around a large, weatherproof crate. They moved aside as he approached, and Aksel rifled within, pulling out a towel and wrapping it around his waist. He barked something to a nearby naked wolven. They frowned but grabbed more towels from the cache and passed them around.

Aksel nodded and grabbed a handful of protein bars and two water bottles, one of which he handed to Jessica before tearing open a protein bar.

"Parallel tracks aren't working," he said around a mouthful. "We need to switch to sectors. Six wolven per, working counter-clockwise in a shrinking field."

"Lennart told us to do parallel tracks," the elder wolven said.

"I don't give a shit what Lennart said, Elias. My daughter is lost out here, and if it weren't for Lennart, she would still be safe at Elkwater."

Elias pressed his lips together, gaze drifting over the wolven as he took a deep breath and let it out slowly. "You think there's a wolven among us who doesn't know that?" he hissed. "Gitta begged him to drop it. I pulled him aside and told him forcing a mate on you was against pack rite, but he wouldn't listen. Why do you think there are so many of us out here looking for your pup?"

Aksel went still, amber eyes wide and startled. Plastic crinkled as he gripped his protein bar tight.

"Lennart is our Alpha, Aksel. But that doesn't mean we follow him blindly. He's a good leader, and he kept Sköllburg together after the fall. Could you have done the same?"

Aksel shook his head, dropping his eyes.

"No," Elias said. "I don't think many of us could. Skölldal has lost half their number in the last five years, and who knows how the other packs have fared with pups moving on and out of the hills. I'm not saying what Lennart is doing now is right, because it isn't, but he faced the impossible and kept us together." He reached out, hesitating before gripping the back of Aksel's neck and tugging until their foreheads tipped together. "And in doing that, gave you the chance to meet her."

Elias tipped his head to Jessica, nodding in acknowledgement. She gripped the water bottle in both hands until the plastic crinkled, wanting nothing more than to grab Aksel and hold him close.

"If anyone can find your daughter in these woods, it's Lennart," he continued. "He's got the faun running an expanding square from Elkwater. Almaden is surveilling from above with her harpies, and until he says otherwise, we work in parallel tracks on the ridgelines. We'll find your girl, Aksel. Not a one of us will rest until we do, but we're still Sköllburg, you understand?"

"I do," Aksel rasped in a voice like pebbles crushed under a foot. "You're Sköllburg, and I'm not."

He said it so plainly that Jessica almost missed the anguish in the words. So much had happened so quickly that she hadn't considered what exactly had transpired between Aksel and Lennart in the camp and what it meant. She had been rightfully focused on her daughter, but now that it was said out loud, Jessica could see the effects of their argument plain as day.

The wolven moved out of his way at the cache. The pack ran alongside them in the woods, but not with them. Even now, they kept a careful distance between Aksel, Jessica, and Elias, watching their conversation in fleeting glances and furrowed brows.

Aksel was no longer Sköllburg. This was no longer his pack, and Jessica was the cause.

She pinched her lips between her teeth, eyes burning as she turned her back on their conversation. Of all the ways this summer could have gone, being the reason Aksel was exiled had never crossed her mind. She'd only wanted her children to know Elkwater and, selfishly, yes, she'd wanted to see him again.

But she never could have anticipated *this*.

Gitta loped out of the trees, her sleek black coat now dusty and grey. She fixed her bright eyes on Jessica, dipped her head in greeting, and then kept it hung low as three adolescent red wolves trickled into the clearing.

Aksel and Elias fell silent, the entire glade stopping to watch Jan, Jarl, and Jens pad to the lake and plop in the water, too exhausted and overheated to drink.

Shock rooted her to the spot, her stomach sinking as a cold chill ran from the top of her head to her toes.

Her babies, here with the wolven. The one place she wanted them to be, but not like this. Oh, Lord, not like this.

"What are they doing here?" Aksel bellowed, charging toward his foster sister.

Gitta shifted in an instant, her brown skin sheened in a sweat her wolven form could not produce. "What was I supposed to do? Let them wander the woods alone?"

"It's not her fault, Aksel." Ramble stepped into the clearing. Twigs and leaves were stuck at odd angles in their hair, dirt smudged their Ani DiFranco t-shirt, and their leggings were torn at the knee. "They snuck out while their grandmother and Tori tried to distract the foundation women. Mac sent me after them, and Gitta found us when numbnuts over there fell into Shavers Fork."

They scuffed the dirt with a hoof, sending pebbles toward the water.

"It was farther than I expected," Jarl called from the water, where he and his brothers had shifted. "Not my fault."

Ramble narrowed their eyes at him. "Hard disagree."

Aksel wheeled all of his anger on them, advancing until they had to tip their head back to meet his eyes. "They belong in the camp, Ramble. Where you should be."

"Sure, fine." Ramble slapped his bare chest with the back of their hand. "You take them, then. Maybe they'll listen to their—"

"I'll stay with them." Gitta accepted a towel from another wolven, wrapping it around her chest as she put herself between Aksel and Ramble. "They need to learn how to be part of a pack." Her bright eyes darted to Jessica, and instantly, she knew the argument Gitta would make. "They need to understand what it means, and I don't think it's something your Outreach can teach them." She swallowed and twitched her gaze to Aksel. "Or you. But they'll learn it from me."

Not their sire. Not an Alpha. Gitta was pack, just like Jessica's boys, and she was right. As much as it killed her to admit it,

Gitta was right. They would follow Aksel and obey his every command, but what would happen when they found Kendra?

Another argument? Another challenge? Would her boys be forced to choose one or the other through sheer, driven instinct alone? It wasn't anything she had ever asked Svana. She'd never even considered the possibility of this happening. How could she? Jessica was one human caught up in a world of inhumans she did not understand. Never had that been more obvious than now.

"Jess?" Gitta called. "It's your call."

There were too many unknowns, and the Monongahela was so large. Yet, although she had only known Gitta for a few weeks, she had been trustworthy and kind to Jessica and her children. At The Porchlight, on First Night, after the train …

"Alright," she rasped. Three furry, wet bodies slammed into her legs. She knelt low, embracing them one by one, and accepting their excited nips and licks. "Bring them home to me," she told Gitta, rising with her fingers buried in Jarl's thick coat. "Keep them safe and bring them home to me."

Gitta dipped her head, eyes fixed on Jessica. "I promise."

Elias left with Gitta and her boys, along with a shaggy blond wolven who gripped Aksel by the arm and shared a long, full look with him before shifting and disappearing into the woods.

Group by group, the pack filtered out, returning to their search for Kendra and leaving Aksel and Jessica alone.

Only then did she say the words that had been tumbling in her mind since Ramble told him to take her boys back to the camp.

"You were awfully quiet."

"It's not my place." Aksel rolled his shoulders, shaking out his arms in a way that made her think he was about to shift just to avoid the conversation.

"Why not?"

Aksel dropped his arms, defeat dragging every inch of his body. "Jess ..."

"You're their father, Aksel." Her voice shot over the lake, bouncing off the quartz wall and filling the clearing with her panic. Aksel flinched, dropping his eyes to the ground between them. "You have every right to speak up when it comes to our children, especially when it's pack business. Isn't that what you want?"

"It is, Jess, but not like this!" He threw his arms wide, encompassing the glade and the lake. Her.

The exasperation in his words knocked her back a step, clarity striking like lightning. Jessica pressed a fist to her chest, the pain of knuckles driving against bone grounding her enough to keep her present in the moment when all she wanted to do was collapse and cry.

One night and thirteen years had brought her here. What did she expect? That she could blow into town with his kids, have the summer, and be a happy family? That he would be willing to do the hard things she had been barely surviving, all too happy to walk away from his child-free, bachelor life?

"I see," she said, leaning into the anger his admission sparked rather than the pain. "You wanted to sire a pack, but not with me."

"New moon. Jessica, *no.*" He stormed across the shore, stopping mere inches away. His arms trembled, muscles flexing, and his fingers danced against his thighs with a nervous, pent-up energy demanding release. "I meant not like *this.*" Aksel shot an arm in the direction of the trees. "Searching for our daughter after the colossal fuck up that is me."

Again, his words were a slap, but one that struck him as much as they struck her.

"You didn't 'fuck up', Aksel." Even repeating them, the words felt dank and sour in her mouth. Aksel wasn't the fuck up, Jessica was. She'd disappointed her parents by getting pregnant and dropping out of school, put everything she'd built with the Outreach at risk by pursuing this idiotic dream of a partnership with the camp, and in doing so, worst of all, failed her children.

"You didn't do anything wrong." Tears burned in her eyes, a tightness building in her throat until wet splashed on her cheek, and she released it with a sob. "*I* did." Another tear fell, and another, drowning her cheeks and dropping onto the sweat-stained blouse she had worn for the tour.

"I should have asked Svana more questions. I should have tried to foster them with a pack in Charleston, but I didn't, and now my baby is—"

Jessica hiccupped and pressed on. Snot clogged her nostrils, and every other word stuck in her throat, but now that she'd begun the words, she could not stop.

"None of us could have predicted that, right? And you're an Alpha! Lennart threatened you and then Kendra, she—" Another hiccup had Jessica wiping her nose with the back of a hand, tears falling faster now. "How *else* could you have responded? He threatened everything you love, everything you've worked so hard for. And then he wanted to take our sons. If I had known Kendra was also an Alpha, I would never have let her or you be put in that situation. I just—I wanted to do something good for my kids, and I couldn't even do that."

"Do you hear yourself, Jess?" He angled his head, searching Jessica's face for what she didn't know. She was too struck by his tone, full of a softness that did not match his question.

"What?"

"You keep putting all of this—" Thunder rolled overhead. Aksel ran a hand through his wet hair, glancing at the sky as his expression darkened like the clouds. "We should get going."

Without a further word, he shifted. The towel fluttered to the ground, and Aksel nudged her arm with a shoulder, dropping into a bow so she could climb onto his back.

32

—·—

JESS

WHAT JESSICA HAD MISTAKEN for tears splattering her cheeks soon became a storm. Wind howled through the treetops, bending and snapping the thin branches of pin oak and pine. Leaves and early sweetgum spike balls rained down, bouncing off Jessica's shoulders and sticking to Aksel's fur.

Thick, coarse hairs along Aksel's shoulders rose beneath her palms, followed by the finer hairs on her arms. He slowed as dry aether crackled along her scalp. Electricity coursed through the trees and lightning struck a branch, sparks bursting and crackling. All around them, the howls of two dozen wolven answered, and the sky opened with a thunderous crack, sheet after sheet of heavy rain falling in a torrent.

Aksel's torso vibrated against her thighs and, without warning, he took off. She bent low, knotting her fingers in his fur and holding on for dear life. He bounded down narrow paths no wider than her arms and over logs the size of her car, skidding to a halt at the mouth of a cave. Ducking a shoulder, he tipped

Jessica off and, grabbing her pant leg in his teeth, dragged her into the cave.

"Alright, alright." She batted him away, sloughing rain from her face and running fingers through soaked hair. A glance at her watch told her it was close to sunset, and with the storm raging, even Kendra would have sought shelter. She might have been panicked and terrified when she shifted, but her daughter was smart and knew how to be safe in the woods. Jessica had at least raised her children that well. "I get it."

Aksel huffed, bright eyes fixed on Jessica as she wandered deeper into the cave. Once satisfied she was out of the rain, he disappeared into the deeper shadows. Jessica followed, squinting and trailing her fingers along the cave wall as her eyes adjusted. Ridges and divots met her touch. She traced them higher, following the path of the grooves and recognizing a symmetry to the marks.

Or carvings?

Leaning closer, she spied a pattern to the designs. Whorls and jagged, rune-like markings carved in a line down the center of the rock wall as a sort of path leading deeper into the cave. She backed away, following their trail with her eyes, and only then did she notice the faint, turquoise light pulsing from the marks and filling the cave, soft enough that the unadjusted eye would never notice.

"Aksel?"

His soft padding stopped, paws shifting over the dirt floor, and a moment later, he nosed her arm.

"What is this?" Jessica traced an upside-down triangular mark and the circle carved at the bottommost point.

"Fairy cave," Aksel's guttural, half-shifted voice answered.

Jessica jerked her hand away, taking a careful step from the wall. It was said these mountains were older than the Rockies, sprouting from the earth millennia prior and splitting from their sisters, the Scottish Highlands, when the continents broke apart. She had always wondered why the wolven and the faun had fallen into Appalachia, as much as she had wondered over the old stories of the moon-eyed and mothmen. Legends predating the fall, almost as old as the mountains themselves.

She swallowed a sudden rise of fear, tightening her diaphragm to put strength behind her voice. "Fairy?"

"Otherworld," Aksel grunted deep in his throat and padded away.

Jessica followed, walking more easily as her eyes adjusted to the soft, pleasant glow, a million questions springing to mind from that one word. She knew the world Aksel had fallen from was magical; anyone with eyes could see that. He and his kin could shift with less than a thought. Naga lived twice the lifespan of a human, and Dusty had *wings*, for Christ's sake. She had even heard rumors that the faun held healing powers in the Otherworld, though no one had seen a hint of that on earth.

But these markings, and the soft, pulsing light emanating from the grooves …

"Are fairies real?"

Two bright amber eyes gleamed at her in the dark, and Aksel chuffed, the sound all too much like a laugh. His damp nose prodded her arm, and he took her hand gently between his teeth, guiding Jessica to a weatherproof crate tucked into an alcove.

Another wolven cache.

"Oh, thank God. Dry clothes? Blankets?" She tugged the lid, glancing at Aksel. He pawed the ground and ducked his head in a nod. "Let's hope they have your size."

Digging within, she grabbed pants and long-sleeved thermal tops, blankets, a battery-powered lantern, and cans of chili, dumping everything on the ground to retrieve the camping stove and a bottle of butane.

Wrapping her treasure in a blanket, she followed Aksel to the front of the cave, turned on the lantern, and set to work on their dinner. While the chili bubbled, she changed into the baggy but blessedly dry clothes and laid her damp blouse, bra, socks, and pants out to dry. Stretching a blanket over the dirt floor, Jessica draped another across her shoulders and wrapped the ends around her hands, carefully lifting the chili cans from the stove.

"Dinner's ready."

At the mouth of the cave, Aksel glanced at her, shifting weight on his paws before returning to his vigil. Ears pricked forward and intent on the rain, he twitched his face toward some small sound only he could hear.

"Alright." She blew on the chili, sipping in small mouthfuls until it was cool enough to eat. All the while, she watched Aksel and relived every moment of their summer together. From spotting him in The Porchlight to that disaster with the Ethernet cable and the ladder. First Night, when their hands brushed in the grass. Kissing him first and crawling into his lap like it was a sort of home.

The dinner where she poured her heart out to him, telling him the story of his children's birth, even though he did not know it. Right up to finding him on her porch, naked and bewildered, speaking the truth between them and responding in a way Jessica had only dreamed.

And now this.

Despair was a damp, heavy weight, worming its chill to her bones. She shivered under the fleece blanket she had taken from the cache, tugging it tight around her shoulders.

"Aksel?"

Two pinpoints of amber burned through the gloom of the cave.

"Can you sit with me? Please?"

He rose on four legs, padding silently her way, only to stop when she shook her head. The movement was so small, so slight, she was reminded again of how human she was and how he was not. A predator gazed at her through the dark. A wolven keenly attuned to her every need through scent alone, fixed to the tiniest movements she made, and reading Jessica better than she could decipher herself.

So she spoke the unspoken need aloud.

"Not like that." She wanted his arms around her. Wanted to nestle against his solidity, if only for the night, and feel his heartbeat with every steady rise and fall of his thick chest beneath her cheek. But more than anything else ... "I want to hear your voice."

Aksel dipped his head and shifted, kneeling halfway between her and the torrent of rain pelting the woods. Lightning flashed behind him, silhouetting his broad shoulders and strong body in the mouth of the cave while the lantern's glow caught in his eyes, lambent and bright, even in his human form.

They stared at each other for a long moment, years of silence stretching between them and snapping as Aksel's shoulders slumped and he bowed his head.

"I'm sorry."

She pulled her knees in tight, small beneath the weight of his words.

"Jess, I–I don't know what to say. All of this is my fault, and I don't even know how to begin making it up to you."

"How is this your fault?"

"Because they're mine." He snapped his face up, pounding his fists against his thighs. Ribbons of soft teal and warm orange light eclipsed his shoulder, dancing in the divots of muscles as his arms bunched and flexed. "What we did that night, Jess, moon above, I thought about it, *you*, for years and never guessed something so incredible came of it." His voice cracked, and those beautiful, warm eyes sheened over. "I failed you and our—" Aksel flinched and corrected himself. "*Your* children in every way, Jess, and, moonblessed, they're incredible. But you know that, of course, you know how amazing they are. Jarl and his focus, Jens strolling through life like everything comes naturally. And I know you know Jan can make any crowd his friend—and Kendra."

Aksel blinked, and tears fell, rolling fat and heavy down his cheeks to pebble in his beard. He swept a hand through his hair, looking so forlorn and broken as a loose lock slipped across his brow.

"I don't know how it took me so long to realize they were mine, she–she—"

"Looks just like you," Jessica finished. Aksel nodded, his throat bobbing. "I always thought so."

"I'm sorry, Jess." He tipped forward, catching himself on his hands. "For everything. Today, yesterday, the last thirteen years."

"It's alright."

"It's not alright." He slapped a hand to the floor, wincing as his palm hit stone. "None of this is alright, and none of it is your fault. It's mine, if anyone's."

"No."

God, why did hearing the words she had ached for hurt so much?

"Yes." Aksel brought his other hand to the ground, leaning toward Jessica on his knees. "I was so mad at you, so hurt when you didn't show up and never responded. I never once considered what you might be going through. Gods, what did you think of me?" His face twisted, disgust, anger, and fury mixing and melting into a mask of pure anguish. "And now this." He crawled forward. "How can I ever make it up to you?"

"I—"

"I want to. New moon, baby, I understand if I never can, but I need you to know"—and closer, knees driving into the pebbles and dirt, palms scraping over stone—"I would have been there. If I'd known, I never would have left you to do this on your own. Whatever sick twist of fate led us here, I'm so sorry, and I will work every day that I breathe to make it up to you." His words crashed warm and sweet against her cheeks, amber eyes wide and worried inches from her own. "If you'll let me."

God, this was what she wanted. What she had prayed for on those endless nights nursing her babies and shushing them to sleep. Through fevers and ear infections. Bad report cards, parent-teacher conferences, and bullying on the playground.

For every scrape and bruise and bloodied elbow, Jessica had prayed for one thing: to not be alone. To have the help she need-ed, and someone in her corner through the chafed nipples and sharp tempers. Someone to say they were there, that they saw her, loved her, and understood. Someone to share the burden and the wonder of parenthood and to laugh with at the end of the day.

Her heart kicked up at the thought of sharing those moments with Aksel. The mere idea of curling against his thick body at the end of a long day and closing her eyes as he ran his fingers through her hair had her stomach fluttering. A low heat built in her hips, one that Jessica knew she should disregard. Dream-ing of Aksel lightly stroking her back, soothing her after a bad day, the same way he did after making her come until she saw stars—this was not the place. Not the time.

"I missed it all, baby." He cupped her cheek, the grime of the cave floor gently abrading her skin. It scraped through her, igniting sparks of heat that kindled in her belly, prodding her steadily building arousal to life. "I don't want to miss anymore."

33

—·—

AKSEL

LIGHTNING LIT THE CAVE, giving Aksel a brief view of how exhausted Jess was. Tears brimmed in her eyes, sheening over the lovely brown depths he wanted to drown in and dulling them to the color of old mud. None of the sparkle was there. None of the quiet mirth he had come to know so well over the last few weeks.

That flash of light revealed every year between them, etched into Jess's face by a master sculptor. Fine lines at the corners of her mouth and eyes, shadows hugging the soft skin beneath her lashes, and hollow cheeks, drained by the emotions of the day.

It laid a new clarity over the last few weeks. Her fleeting looks and soft smiles. Thick lashes and blushing cheeks, kissable lips and perfect curls. Now, mascara streaked beneath her eyes, and the healthy glow to her skin was gone, replaced by a dullness that twisted something in Aksel's chest. This was Jess, depleted and worn. *Jess*, worried and frightened, and more achingly beautiful than ever because now, new moon, now Aksel saw through the mask she wore like armor through the summer, finally seeing the woman she truly was.

His wolf stirred beneath his skin, prowling in the recesses of his mind. A strange heat bloomed in his veins, rushing to his extremities until one burning thought possessed him and his wolf alike: Make it better.

His mate was hurting. Jess was hurting, and he needed to make it better. Make her better, feel better, stop crying. He needed to see those tiny wrinkles beside her eyes crinkle with joy, pleasure, laughter, *anything* but this pain that he had caused.

"Say something," he rasped. "Please."

Jess's lips parted, a soft sigh escaping, and like a tidal wave against the shore, her scent crashed into him.

Want, need, desire, all muddled together with the burden of her sorrow, slamming into Aksel. It filled his head and teased into his mouth, coating his tongue with the faint memory of her taste.

His cock stirred and he drove his nails into the meat of his thighs to keep from crushing Jess against his chest and giving into the urges raging within him. His wolf howled, the itch of the shift rising beneath arousal. He should go, run into the rain and far from this cave before he lost himself entirely. But the thought of leaving Jess alone, tonight, ever again, had both Aksel and his wolf snarling in a rage.

Never again.

He would crawl to her a thousand times, carry her a million miles and more if only she would *say something* after he bared his soul, anything to distract him from the blistering heat gathering in his belly and the thunderous pulse pounding in his veins.

Another crack of lightning filled the cave with light, there and gone again, but not fast enough for Aksel to miss the widening of Jess's pupils in her dark, lovely eyes.

Her throat bobbed as she swallowed, and, moon save him, Aksel tracked the pink tip of her tongue darting out to wet her lip like a wolf tracks a deer.

"Kiss me," she finally said.

Shock knocked Aksel outside of himself for a heartbeat. "What?"

"Kiss me," she repeated, barely above a shaking whisper. "I need you to hold me, I need–I need you."

"You have me." His hands flew to her cheeks, and only then did he notice the tremble, slight as a shiver, coursing through her body. He laid a soft, gentle kiss on her lips, barely a brush before pulling away. His wolf howled, urging him to lay her out on the blanket and make her forget her sorrow, if only for a moment.

As much as he wanted to, this wasn't the time. Their daughter was missing, their sons were out in the woods, and after everything Aksel had failed to do, how could he expect her to—

"I said, 'kiss me.'" There it was, that missing edge of mirth as Jess pulled her mask into place. But as quickly as it rose, she laid a hand over his heart, and it melted away. Her mouth softened, gaze dropping to where she touched him. A tiny divot flickered between her brows as if she could feel how every millimeter of skin she touched sang with need, blood rushing to meet the tips of her fingers and the gentle press of her palm.

He would have to be a fool not to notice her nipples, peaked beneath her shirt, or how a subtle rasp entered her breathing.

Eyes fluttering closed, Jess spoke in a voice so low he had to half shift his ears to hear them. "I don't want to think anymore tonight. I just want to feel. Now, kiss me, Aksel."

Gods, his name in her mouth, spoken in the low command of a mate he was powerless to refuse. Arousal pulsed in his cock and he closed his eyes, tipping their brows together as he took one long, slow breath to keep from howling.

Cupping her cheeks, he angled Jess's head, meeting her somber gaze, and kissed her again.

Not gently, this time. No, his mate demanded a real kiss, driven by feeling and absent any thought. A kiss he could never give because the thought blaring in his mind could not be silenced.

Mine.

So he kissed her with all the hunger and need it provoked, crushing their lips together and snagging her lower lip with a canine.

Jess moaned, arching into him as Aksel delved into her heated mouth. She met him stroke for stroke, frantically dancing their tongues together, her body melting in his hands.

Rain pelted the earth outside their cave. Lightning strobed across the sky, and within, Aksel drew Jess's shirt up and away to feel her pebbled skin and peaked nipples against his chest. His palms hushed around the softness of her waist and over the faint, shimmering lines on her skin, changing the texture from enticingly smooth to painfully silken. Marks he wanted to lick and trace, memorizing them with his hands and eyes, his mouth.

Instead, he cupped her breast, a deep rumble building in his throat at the lovely heft, perfectly rounded to match the curve of his palm.

"Gods, Jess." Aksel traced his thumb over a nipple, savoring her answering shiver.

"No thinking," Jess murmured. Fingers danced up the back of his neck, tangling in his hair, and she guided Aksel to her breast.

He sucked her nipple into his mouth, laving and circling the bud as he shifted his position to keep from jabbing her with his cock. Jess moaned, nails scoring his scalp as he dragged higher, tighter sounds out of her throat. Her hips rocked against him, and soft fleece brushed his cock, teasing him to the brink of madness.

Lapping at her breast, he braced Jess's back, easing her onto the blanket. Sliding a hand up her thigh, he squeezed once, and Jess lifted her hips, allowing him to tug the loose pants low. She rose a knee to kick her leg free and let it fall to the side, revealing sheer majesty to Aksel.

Lantern light caught in her gathering arousal, gilding her lips like a Klimt piece. The faint turquoise glow from the walls caught in the shimmering marks on her belly and breasts as if Jess, too, glowed from within with fairy light.

"Moonblessed," he prayed, hands hovering over the goddess beneath him. Cheeks flushed and eyelids heavy, beestung lips and perfect breasts tipped in dark nipples he could still feel against his tongue.

Her scent struck him, a musky, mallow-y, floral smack to the face that hauled Aksel forward. He slapped a hand against the ground, locking his arm as an overpowering, overwhelming *need* consumed him.

New moon, his cock ached, throbbing as the knot at the base swelled. Gripping it in hand, he hissed through his teeth, willing himself back from the edge.

He needed her. Needed to bury his cock within her, pump-ing into Jess as she clenched around him with those delicate, delicious muscles. His hand wouldn't do. Not tonight, not ever again, when the memory of her sprawled beneath him, hair wild and skin glowing, would haunt Aksel for the rest of his life.

"Please, baby," Jess murmured. She blinked slowly at him, as though she, too, was overwhelmed with need. "Don't hold back."

"Jess." He clenched his dick tighter, willing his knot down so he could worship her body as he fucked her until Jess forgot every worry and woe.

"I want it," Jess said. Her fingers swept down his arm, circling Aksel's wrist and pulling his hand away. He raised his head to find Jess staring at his cock with an expression of hunger he had seen before.

In his office, and bent over her kitchen table. In his bedroom, when the sun had just clawed its way over the ridgeline.

Long ago, in a tent at the edge of the woods.

Jess rolled her hips, dancing fingers up her thigh and between her legs. She dragged one through her arousal, breath hitching.

"Please, baby."

She could have asked for anything then. Wild and bucking her hips, seeking Aksel's cock like it was the only thing that mattered.

He watched as she circled her clit, mesmerized by the motion and slide of a finger into her pussy. Followed by a second.

A third.

"It's never enough, Aksel." She rolled her hips, a tight whine to her voice. "I need all of you."

His hand trembled, desire overwhelming his restraint. His mate needed him, and that need drew on the strange magic brimming between them. Whatever Jess asked, he would give. Whatever she needed, he would supply. He was hers, and all he wanted in this world was to please Jess in whatever way she needed until she became his.

"Move," he growled, guiding her hand away and spreading her thighs wider to fit his shoulders. At the first sweep of his tongue, Aksel knew he would give in. She was always delicious, always what he craved, but tonight there was a richness to her he had never experienced.

Maybe it was the strain of the day and the need for comfort, or the isolation of the cave bringing her further from her restrained self. Whatever it was, it tasted more like *Jess* than ever before.

His cock throbbed, leaking against his thigh, and for the first damn time in his life, Aksel was proud of his knot. As long as he got inside Jess, nestled into her slick heat, he could satisfy his woman long after he came.

That thought alone had him spearing her with his tongue. Jess cried out, squirming and writhing her hips. He banded an arm over her belly, withdrawing to circle her clit and replace his tongue with two fingers.

"More," she moaned, pushing her pussy against him as if she could drive his fingers deeper. "It's not enough, baby."

Only a fool wouldn't thrill at those words. His mouth wasn't enough, his fingers weren't enough. Only his cock, his knot, would satisfy his mate.

Moon above, he was done for.

"I don't want to hurt you, baby." He kissed the inside of her thigh, easing a third finger in. Her thighs twitched on either side of his head. A tight whimper strangled in her throat, followed by an unmistakable huff of displeasure.

He would have laughed if he weren't so focused on not coming before her.

"I don't think we can avoid it," Jess said. Aksel stilled, and she exhaled, recognizing those words and this moment as an absurd sort of mirror to that last night in the woods. "It's worth it, Aksel," she whispered, her voice full of awe and an odd sort of sorrow. "I want it."

He kiss her thigh, her pussy, lapping gently as he slipped his fingers free. Jess sighed when he pressed a kiss to her belly, flicking his tongue over those tempting marks before taking her breast into his mouth.

"Aksel," she warned.

"Patience, sweetheart." Gathering Jess in his arms, Aksel rolled onto his back. "I want you in control. Like before."

"Look where that got us." Her weight settled over him, every soft curve a welcome blanket.

He held her there, with his cock threaded between her thighs, and rocked his hips. "Nowhere else I'd rather be."

A sweet, soft gasp left her, and he did it again, soaking himself in her arousal until those gasps hitched and shortened. Aksel rocked faster, rubbing his knot in her slick folds until she drenched his groin. When her arms began to shake, and her nails drove into the meat of his chest, Aksel slipped a hand across her thigh, thumbing slow, easy circles around her clit. "Let go, baby."

"Aksel, please."

"I'll give you what you want, but first you have to let go."

"I—" The words cut off in her throat.

"Let me take care of you, Jess."

He stroked her clit, timed to each thrust, and Jess shot straight, arms locking in the moment before a deep groan left her. Moisture gushed onto his groin, soaking Aksel's cock as he rocked against her pulsing lips. New moon, it was almost enough to make him lose his mind.

Jess sagged forward, panting and mumbling incomprehensible words against his ear.

"Good girl." He gripped his knot with one hand, eyes rolling back at how fucking drenched he was. Gently, he guided Jess up, notching the head of his cock against her entrance. "You're so good, Jess, but I need to take this slowly, alright?"

"S'fine," she murmured, eyelids heavy and cheeks deliciously flushed. "We've done it before."

"Thirteen years ago," he said. "Have you been with anyone else?"

"You know I haven't."

"Neither have I." Nudging her entrance, Aksel eased his swollen, dripping head into her, hesitating when Jess tensed, her gaze sharpening on him. "I want to enjoy this."

"Of course." Her spine curved, thighs relaxing and lowering her another inch onto his cock. They both gasped, heads tipping back in what Aksel could only assume was shared pleasure.

All he knew was the same mind-shattering bliss he felt whenever he buried his cock into her sweet pussy.

Achingly slow, he pumped into her, feeding Jess his cock until the puffy lips of her pussy pressed against his knot.

"Oh, Lord." Jess exhaled, tipping her head back. "Fuck, baby."

Pride filled him. Aksel threaded his fingers along either side of his cock, spreading Jess's lips. "Are you ready?"

"Mmhmm." She nodded, rocking her hips and biting her lower lip. Lit by the cave, with lantern light drawing flickering shadows on her cheeks and dancing under the curve of her breasts and hips, Aksel could almost believe she'd fallen from the Otherworld with him.

"Take your time." He rolled into her, careful not to push too hard. That lovely divot appeared between her brows, the sign of Jess's focus and determination overtaking her pleasure.

That wouldn't do.

Bucking up, Aksel sucked a nipple between his lips, dragging the peak to draw her attention back to *them*. As much as he ached to come, as much as he wanted to fill her lovely womb with his seed, this was about her pleasure, not his. He didn't want Jess to approach this like a ledger or financial report, so he used her words against her. "No thoughts, babygirl. Only feeling."

Jess nodded, bracing her weight on his chest and biting her lip as she rocked against Aksel to ease his knot through her entrance.

Gods, the pressure was exquisite. Mind-melting and more than he ever could have dreamt. He let Jess lead, pumping in concert with her rocking, working his knot gently into her. Her pussy pulsed around him, delicate muscles clenching and drawing, sucking him in.

Without warning, she angled her hips, the tension eased, and Jess's body welcomed him home.

Home.

That word echoed through his mind as her nails drove into his chest, her cry rattling off the walls of the cave. Pleasure consumed him, filling Aksel from cock to crown, consuming him like a wildfire in August, while that word blazed bright and true.

Home.

What he had been longing for since that last night of camp, and now he was here, with the woman who had always been his home. His mate. *His.* A pack of two with her at the center.

This was what Nils and Elias couldn't put into words. The sentiment Lennart had failed to explain.

The camp was Aksel's. The counselors, staff, and the kids for a summer. But they came and went, changing like the seasons year over year, with only a dozen or so returning. Sanoya. Mac and Ramble. Cooky. New moon, even Cricket and Avery would leave when Avery went to Carnegie, and leaving did not make them Pack.

But this did. This connection and yielding.

He understood now, with the clarity that only a good fuck could provide: pack was more than the family you made and chose. Pack was in your blood, bones, and soul, and it started with *her*.

"Fuck." A deep, visceral groan dragged out of him, vision whiting out as sheer bliss overwrote every cogent thought. There was only this. Only Jess, his cock, his knot embedded in his mate, embraced by her slick heat as her pussy milked him. "Oh, fuck, baby, I—"

She rolled her hips, altering the glorious friction, and searing heat shot up his spine, arching Aksel's back. Her cry heightened, nails pinching his skin, and then glorious suction pulled on his cock, drawing Aksel impossibly deeper.

"Oh, *God*." She groaned, deep and ragged, rolling with each pulse of her lips. "Aksel, you're—this is—"

"I know, baby." He could barely form the words, tongue thick and mind ablaze. If she moved, if she so much as—

Jess bent low, dragging her teeth against his throat as she clenched around him. She bit down, the surprising pain melding with a moan that vibrated through his skin into his bones. Heat seared through his veins, hips rocking on their own with some feral, base need to fill her with his come and pump her so full of his seed that it spilled out of her. The fire that had wound around his spine coalesced, rocketing to his groin, and Aksel erupted, his cry echoing off the walls as he spilled into her.

Distantly, he was aware of Jess echoing his shout, her pussy tightening and milking him dry even as her limbs went loose and she draped over him, skin damp and breath uneven, petting Aksel's hair as he came back to himself.

"I can't—" she gasped. "I need—"

He nodded, knowing what she needed because he felt the same.

More.

Aksel wrapped his arms around her and rolled, laying Jess gently against the blanket so he could control the movement.

Slow and steady, plunging her depths and savoring every shudder and gasp. Her arms snaked around his shoulders, fingers knotting in his hair as Jess tugged him down for a kiss. Savouring his mouth as he savoured her pussy, slowly bringing them both to a precipice.

Moving within her, with his mind floating in a frothy haze of lust, a sense of rightness overtook him. This was where he was meant to be, pleasuring his mate as she kissed him with a focused intensity, like she were committing the taste of him to memory.

34

— ◆ —

Jess

The howls rose at noon.

Aksel halted at the first call, head lifting and ears twitching toward the sound. The next howl began, and the next, tearing through the woods and haunting in their intensity.

It had been hours since he'd caught the last trail and, as he admitted during a brief shift for water, even that had been faint.

"Mostly Sköllburg," he'd explained. "Caught the boys and Gitta."

"No Kendra?"

Aksel only glanced at her over the water bottle he'd pulled from a cache, his silence saying more than any words could. "But the Sköllburg trail isn't straying," he'd rushed out. "Someone's caught something; it's too focused."

All Jess could do was nod and, when he shifted back, climb onto his back and try not to cry as he resumed stalking the trail, stopping only when the howls began.

Fear shivered through her, filling every inch of her body with a prey's urge to slip off his back and make herself as small and unnoticeable as possible. There were no less than three potential hiding places nearby—the rotted-out base of a trunk, a hole in the brambles, a narrow cavern formed by two boulders—but exhausted and sore as she was, she did not dare let go.

Even with his attempts to avoid uneven ground and sharp drops, it had been an effort to remain on his back, and there was no avoiding the soreness. She had known that when she begged for his knot, needing to feel him in the deepest way and clear away every mad, worried thought ravaging her mind. The exhaustion, however, surprised her.

Emotion, she told herself. The strain of losing a daughter and trusting her sons to the pack. The worry and terror of it all.

It had nothing to do with Aksel, who had bared his soul to her and given Jess what she so deeply craved, physically and emotionally.

Nothing to do with the noxious feelings brewing in her chest whenever she dared to think of him and whatever potential future they could have. Together.

No, her exhaustion was purely physical, brought on by one hard day after another, and a night filled with the most soul-shattering fucking she had ever experienced.

Granted, all her experiences were with the same wolven, but their night in the cave had been different than any other night before.

Except for their last night.

If she thought about it, if she allowed herself to reside in the space where she relived the last night of camp alongside last night in the cave, she could not help but pick out the similarities.

The desperation and mutual need, one driven by teenage lust and young love, one driven by the need to feel and be felt, to connect with someone who shared the experience, and both under the looming countdown of a clock she could not stop.

Aksel pawed the forest floor, ears swiveling as a rumble built in his chest—the rising howl to match the call. Jess bent low, hissing at the ache in her thighs and groin, and wrapped her arms around his neck. He whined and craned his neck, licking her arm in apology before taking off at a run. Every step sent agony through her limbs, setting off a dull, painful throb earned by a night in his arms.

But it was worth it.

It had to be.

Within moments, lean, slinking bodies fell in around them, ushering Aksel and Jess through the woods to the bald knob of a mountaintop. Wolven lingered at the base of a lookout tower in various states of dressed and shifted. Some lay panting in the grass, tongues lolling and eyes closed after the hard night. Others pulled on sweats or covered themselves with towels, while fully dressed and bright-eyed wolven crowded around trucks lining the service road. Faun were speckled among them, kneeling in the grass or chatting at the fringe of the woods. Cricket and Ramble huddled together near a deer path, the younger of the pair sending Jessica a soft smile as she and Aksel loped by.

She slid off his back, helping Aksel straighten as he shifted, and ran an arm across his damp back, supporting his weight as best she could. Sweat beaded on his brow, rolling in fat droplets down his temple to purl in his beard. He leaned against her, gulping deep breaths as he recovered from the climb.

"What is this?" she asked when his breathing had somewhat settled.

"End of the search." He accepted the basketball shorts a passing wolven held out, and tugged them on.

"The end ..." Jess whipped her head around the knob, tracking each face, some familiar, most foreign. No Gitta. No Jan, Jarl, or Jens. "Where are the boys?"

Aksel straightened, nostrils flaring as he searched the pack. His jaw tightened, and he grabbed Jess's hand. "They're here," he said. "And Gitta, though I don't—"

"Mom!" Jan broke through a cluster of older wolven, tearing across the clearing. "Mom, can I ride the harpy?"

"Wha—oof!" She rocked back as he barreled into her, arms wrapping around her in a lung-bursting hug. "Where are your brothers?" she grunted.

"Upstairs." He let her go and held up a hand for Aksel, who frowned at it. "Alright, man. It's cool. Whatever." Jan shrugged and dropped his arm. "So can I, Mom? Please? She said I had to ask you first, which is bullshi—"

"Almaden is here?" Aksel moved around Jan, lifting his face to the lookout tower.

"Yeah, she's up in the view shed with Kendra and—"

"Kendra!" Jess was running before her daughter's name left her mouth, every ache and pain forgotten. Heart pounding in her ears, she grabbed the banister, taking the stairs two at a time with Aksel at her back. Wood rattled beneath her feet, her muscles burned, and on the last turn, she collided with a tall, blonde wolven in a bra and cotton shorts.

"Whoa!" She caught Jess by the arms, and they crashed into the wall of the view shed at the top of the platform. "Watch it."

"Move." Jess threw her arms off, but the wolven darted in front of her, blocking the way.

"Beth," Aksel rumbled a warning behind Jess. "Move."

"Ohhh no." Beth shook her head, ponytail bobbing. She crossed her arms, eyes narrowing at Jess, then raising to glare at Aksel. "There is no way I am letting you two run in there and freak out that poor pup again. Do you know how long it took me to calm her down in the first place? No, of course you don't! And then Lennart showed up and terrified the poor thing all over again, so *no*. I won't move until you take a breath, lower your hackles, and calm *down*."

"You—" Jess panted, taken aback by Beth's tone, neither snide nor cruel as it had been during every previous exchange she'd had with the wolven. If anything, she sounded worried. Jess blinked, repeating the rapid-fire patter in her mind. "You found my daughter? Where?"

"Under the old trestle at High Falls," Beth said, lowering her voice.

"What were you doing out there?" Aksel asked.

"Ran out with my brother to check the tracks after the storm." She flitted a hand at him. "We had to refund an entire train's worth of tickets last night, so there goes my winter cruise."

Something about that struck Aksel as funny. He chuckled, the strain leaving his shoulders as he wiped a hand down his face. "New moon, Beth."

"Yeah, well, it's not like I had anyone to go with anyway." She sent Aksel a blinding grin that faded as she returned her attention to Jess. "I'm sorry," she said. A lovely flush colored her cheeks, and she dropped her eyes, awkwardly toeing the board at her feet. "For ... moonblessed, everything. I had no idea you two were mated. If I'd known, Gods, if any of us had known, I like to think the entire pack mess could have been avoided."

"We didn't know, either, but thank you," Jess said. "And thank you for finding my daughter."

"Glad I could help." She lifted her head, meeting Jess's eyes once more. "It's kinda funny, but I never would've caught her scent if it weren't for all that nonsense on the train."

"What nonsense?" Aksel asked.

Jess and Beth shared a brief look before answering together, "Nothing."

The door creaked open over Beth's shoulder, and Gitta stepped out. Like Beth and the rest of the wolven, she was minimally dressed in plaid boxers and a ribbed white tank top two sizes too big.

"Hey, have my brother and—" She spotted Aksel and Jess, and relief washed over her face. "Oh, thank Sköll, you're here."

"I was forcing them to calm down," Beth said over her shoulder, lingering a look at Aksel with a sharp glint in her glacial eyes. "Lennart is in there. Are you going to behave?"

"Trying to keep me from my daughter?"

"She's trying to stop another pack incident from occurring." Gitta closed the door softly and leaned against it. Bright amber eyes flitted over Beth, darting away just as quickly. "Dad's pissed, but he feels terrible. He won't start shit if you don't start shit."

"Aksel's not going to start anything," Jess snapped. "Let us in."

Gitta raised her brows, a bemused smirk curling her full mouth. "Are *you* going to behave?"

Jess huffed and flipped a tangled mess of hair away from her face. "A lady doesn't start fights."

"But she finishes them." Beth grinned again, the corners of her eyes crinkling. She pivoted and pressed against the wall of the view shed, making room for Jess to pass. "Well done, Aksel."

"Thanks," he grumbled, but Jess didn't miss the pride in his voice. He pressed the tips of his fingers to the base of her spine, a comforting, possessive touch, and they squeezed around Gitta to step into a cramped, sweltering room.

No more than one hundred square feet, the north-facing windows were latched open to catch a faint breeze, humid as it was.

Lennart loomed in a corner to Jess's right, straightening when they stepped inside, only to flinch when a female wolven with thick braids and identical features to Gitta, albeit twenty years older, set her hand on his arm and shook her head once. Jess tracked the movement, seeing support and camaraderie in the gesture. An odd emotion stirred in her chest, like a canoe caught in an eddy, spinning between a sense of welcoming and the knowledge she would never belong.

As if she could read the war within her, the woman slowly lowered her chin, acknowledging Jessica before flicking bright, yellow-gold eyes over her shoulder.

"Come, Len," she said in a low voice. "Let's let the family have some privacy."

Lennart clenched his jaw but allowed his mate to guide him to the door.

"A word?" he rumbled to Aksel.

Aksel inhaled sharply, ready to respond, but his foster mother cut him off. "I think you should hear what Len has to say."

"Now, Ygrid?"

"Now, pup," Ygrid barked back.

"It's alright." Jessica eyed the trio, tangling her fingers in Aksel's and squeezing. "It's alright."

He frowned but squeezed back, dusting a kiss to the top of her head before following his foster parents out onto the walkway.

"Gusting gales, finally," a sharp voice crackled behind Jessica. She whirled around, coming face to feather with broad wings extended as far as the room would allow. "I was about to choke from all that alpha machismo stuffed in here."

Feathers ruffled, and a wing lowered to reveal the dramatic profile of a thin-faced, sharp-nosed woman. "You're the mother?"

Jessica nodded. "My daughter ...?"

"Here." She tucked her wings in tight, and tighter still. The air around them shimmered, and they vanished, leaving Jessica in a room with a severe, dark-eyed inhuman female dressed in bike shorts and a tank top.

Jessica squeaked in surprise, and the inhuman winked. "Glamour. One of the few tricks I still have in this dead world." She adjusted her stool, revealing a narrow cot shoved against the western wall and the two adolescent wolven lying beneath it. "Kept them out to give your litter some privacy."

Jarl and Jens, both curled on the floor in their wolven forms, raised their heads, tails thumping happily, albeit slowly, against the floor.

"My babies." Her throat closed around a rising sob, eyes burning as she knelt for her sons.

"Mom?" A blanket on the cot shuffled, and Kendra propped herself up, hair wild and eyes deeply shadowed. Scratches marred her cheekbone, and a purpling bruise spread across the cap of one shoulder. "Mommy?"

"Kendra." Unable to stop the tears, she rushed forward, nearly toppling the inhuman from her stool. Her daughter was here, in one piece, with her. God and Gods above, she was here, and Jessica would never let her out of her sight again. She wrapped her in a hug, rocking her daughter as a stream of nonsense fled her body. "My baby girl, you're alright. We're here. I'm here; everything's going to be alright. My God, you must have been so scared. I'm so sorry, my baby girl."

"I'm sorry, Mommy," Kendra sobbed, her shoulders heaving. Jarl and Jens shuffled closer, pressing their furry bodies against Jessica's legs. "I didn't mean to—" She hiccupped. "I didn't even know I could—"

"I know, sweet girl, I know." Jessica ran her fingers through the mass of tangled hair, stroking Kendra's back as she cried. "It's alright. I'm here now. We're going to make sure you're okay." She caught the harpy's eye, and she nodded solemnly. "And we're gonna get you out of here, alright?"

"Nurse Almaden said I was okay." Kendra sniffled, lifting her head. "Just scrapes and bruises."

"And dehydrated," Nurse Almaden said, her tone softening. "And you probably need a good steak." Jessica chewed her cheek, struggling to recall why the name sounded so familiar. She must have made a face or stared too long because Nurse Almaden smiled tightly at her. "Camp nurse, I'm good friends with Gitta."

"Oh," she said. And then it clicked. "Elias said you were in the skies. With other harpies?"

"There are a few of us who made the fall." Nurse Almaden ruffled her wings. "Not many, but enough to be of some use. Gitta called me from a ranger station, and when Beth called the Skölldal about a missing kid, I flew right over."

"Thank you." The words left her as an awed whisper. So many people and inhumans had been caught up in this mess, searching for Kendra, caring for and teaching her boys. "I'm so sorry it came to this. I don't know how I can pay any of you back for finding my daughter."

Nurse Almaden cocked her head, the move entirely too bird-like. "Why would you? You're one of us. It'll all come back around in the end."

"Are you out of your mind?" Aksel's voice boomed through the open windows, jerking their faces toward the sound. "I thought I was clear: they're mine."

"The boys, yes," Lennart answered in a level tone that sent ice crawling through Jessica's veins. "But the girl needs to be fostered. You know that as well as I do."

"On no earth am I separating Kendra from her family."

"Aksel, sweetheart," Ygrid interjected. "Think this through."

Jens and Jarl whined, hopping to their feet and pacing beneath the window, ears pricked to ensure they did not miss a single word. On the cot, Kendra shuffled uncomfortably, the skin on her back growing hot under Jessica's hands.

"She may be calm now," Ygrid continued, "but the poor pup is exhausted. Once she has eaten and rested, the urge to shift will come again and again. She's wolven and an Alpha, Aksel. She needs to be fostered where she won't cause a challenge, like—"

"Skies above, they couldn't have taken this conversation elsewhere?" Nurse Almaden grumbled.

"I *just* found them, Ygrid." Aksel backed into view, hands pushed into his hair and a wild look on his face, like a cornered and caged animal. "I'm not giving them up."

"You've discussed this with the mother?" Lennart asked.

A long, terrible moment passed. Jens padded across the tiny room to sit beside Jessica. She draped an arm around his shoulders, holding him as tightly as she held Kendra.

"Jessica." Cold fury threaded Aksel's voice, a rumble of threat vibrating through the wooden wall. Jarl hunkered low beneath the window, ears flattening back. "My mate's name is Jessica."

"I saw no mark on the mother's throat."

"Jessica." Ygrid barked the correction. Another long silence filled the room before she spoke again, following her foster son until she too was visible through the window. "You know how this works, sweetheart. If anything, the last few weeks should be all the proof you need." A hand wafted over her shoulder to where Lennart must be standing. "A pack cannot survive two Alphas of a bloodline. If you want to be with Jessica and raise those boys as is your right as their sire, then the gi—" She caught her slip, correcting herself immediately. "Then Kendra needs to be fostered where she can learn all that it means to be wolven, and where she will not cause a challenge."

Kendra sniffed, lifting her head. "Mom?"

"It's you or the girl, son," Lennart added.

"I just found them," Aksel whispered, almost too low for human ears to hear. "I can't ask her to choose me over her child. In what world would *any* mother—"

"Mommy?" Kendra raised her voice, hauling Jessica away from the terrible conversation outside.

"Yes, baby?"

"I want to go home."

"Of course." She ran a hand up and down her spine. "As soon as Nurse Almaden says you're good, we'll go straight to the townhome to shower. I'll cook steaks, and we can watch whatever movie you want. It'll be—"

"No, Mom." Kendra pushed away, tugging the blanket tight around her shoulders and looking her in the eye. "I want to go home."

The demand in her tone, the directness of her stare. Good lord, how had Jessica ever missed who and what her daughter was? Slowly, she rose, knotting her fingers together and pressing them hard against her stomach. She glanced at the window, biting her tongue when she caught Aksel staring back at her, his eyes filled with the pain of recognition.

How had it come to this? All she had wanted was for her children to know their father in any way they could, and now she was staring down an impossible choice.

Except it wasn't. Because what mother, in this world or the other, wouldn't do the same?

"Okay," she said, holding onto Aksel and everything he was and could have been for as long as possible before breaking away and facing her children. "We'll go home."

35

— · —

AKSEL

"Jess, wait!"

Aksel ran the moment she turned her back, tearing around the narrow walkway. Sköll help him, the look on her face, like she was being torn apart before his eyes. It only took a glance at the open window to understand what had happened. She had overheard his argument with Lennart and Ygrid, and whatever Kendra had said in response to that had *done* something to Jess, shifting a new resolve into place. Aksel knew, in the depths of his soul, that if he didn't catch her, speak to her, beg her to talk to him, that he would never see her again.

Lennart stepped in front of him, having run around the other side of the view shed, and blocked the stairs. "Let her go, son."

"I'm not your son." He grabbed his foster father's arm, hand half shifted, and dug his claws in, punching him aside. Lennart grunted, knocking into Ygrid, and she wrapped her arms around his powerful torso, eyes on Aksel as she whispered in her mate's ear. Lennart stiffened at whatever she said, but he did not struggle.

Aksel leapt down the first flight of stairs, ankles screaming and planks groaning as he hit the landing. Below him, someone shouted, and he took the next flight at a jog, slowing as he caught up to Jess with her arm around a barefoot Kendra wrapped in a blanket.

Though she leaned against her mother, the pair moved at an odd rush, Kendra's bare feet jogging down the steps, forcing Jess to keep up.

"Jess, wait—"

Kendra shot a glare over her shoulder and growled. "We're going home."

"Manners," Jess reprimanded.

"For him? He *bit* me."

"He snapped at you," she said, "after you ran at him."

Kendra shoved away from her mother, hugged the blanket tighter, and ran down the last flight of steps. "I can't believe you're taking his side!"

"I'm not taking anyone's side, Kendra. I'm repeating what happened."

"But it's not fair!" she wailed. Every wolven and faun gathered around the knob shot their heads up, glancing between the young girl sobbing in a blanket, her mother reaching out to her, and Aksel, standing dumbfounded on the stairs. "None of this is fair! He can't just show up after our *entire lives* and expect to step in as our–our—"

"I'm not," Aksel said. He aimed for Jess, who pressed her lips together and subtly shook her head. "I don't want to take anything from you."

"But you are!" Tears filled Kendra's eyes, red and swollen from her ordeal. "You're taking everything."

"Kendra!" Jess's voice ricocheted off the wooden supports of the lookout tower, sending the gathered inhumans scattering into the trees.

"What?" she yelled back. "Like it isn't true? God, Mom, you're not that good at sneaking out of the apartment. Don't lie to me."

Jess's jaw dropped, her cheeks darkening with rising anger. When she did not deny it or argue, Kendra scoffed and stormed for the line of pick-up trucks on the service road. Jens and Jarl fell in behind her, with Jan jogging after in his human form.

"Jess—"

"Don't." She sighed, dropping her head into the crook of her hand. "Don't, Aksel, this is hard enough."

"Please, look at me."

Jess took a breath. And a second, then raised her head, hitting Aksel with a cold, dispassionate mask that almost broke him, as though everything that was Jess had been shoved into a tiny box and stored on a shelf out of reach.

But he could see the cracks now. The wariness in her eyes and the tightness at her mouth. Her fingers plucking and pinching the wrinkled and stained hem of her shirt.

"Stay," he said. "We'll figure this out together. Just stay."

"Aksel—"

"I meant everything I said last night, Jess. I don't want to miss any more of this." He frantically waved a hand from himself to her. "Of us. You are everything I've ever wanted."

"And what about the kids, Aksel?" Jess brushed hair away from her face, frowning when her fingers tangled in the matted curls. "What about what they want?"

"What about what *you* want?" The moment he said it, Aksel knew he had misstepped, but he couldn't stop himself. How a woman could be so incredibly smart and yet so blind to her own needs was infuriating. "Everything you do is for your kids, and that's amazing, you're amazing, but what about you?"

"Please, don't do this."

"No, Jess." He took a chance and grabbed her hand, holding it tight. "For once in your life, be a little selfish."

"Selfish?" She angled her face at him, scrutinizing Aksel. "You say you want this, Aksel, and I believe you, but believe me when I say you're not ready."

"That's not fair."

"You know what's not fair?" She ripped her hand away, putting distance between them. "Trying to raise four wolven babies without their dad or sire or whatever you are. Having to put my life on hold because you 'didn't get my letters.'" She pinched her fingers in air quotes, spitting the words with acid on her tongue. "What isn't *fair* is that you've been up here the entire time, living your life, advancing in your career, making friends, and getting to be an adult while I missed out on *all* of that, and then you have the balls to tell me to be *selfish?*"

In two steps, she was in front of him, eyes blazing.

"You want to know how I know you're not ready for this?" she asked in a low, chillingly calm voice. "Because when you're a parent, you don't get to be selfish. Your children become the most important thing in your life. You move mountains for them. You put aside everything you are to carve out a world that is safe and welcoming and nurturing for *them.*

"It's not about me or what I want; it's about what is best for them. And if that means going home to Charleston, then that is what I will do."

Aksel rocked back as if her words had been a slap, the itch of a shift rising behind the sting.

"Jess, you can't—"

"You don't get to tell me what I can and can't do." Though Jess was wholly human, a low, menacing growl entered her voice, deep enough that Aksel had to fight against the urge to lower himself to the ground in submission. "I get enough of that from my parents."

"Mom?" Kendra lingered at the edge of the service road, her brothers already piling into the cab of a pickup truck. "Mr. Elias is going to drive us to Elkins."

"Coming, sweetheart," Jess called over her shoulder, holding Aksel's eye. An impassable silence filled the space between them, as broad as the last thirteen years. He wanted to reach out. Grab her and hold her tight; never let her go. She was his mate, the mother of his children. She was *his,* and he was hers, and it wasn't supposed to end this way. Or ever. They were just getting started.

"Jess, please," he begged, ready to fall on his knees if that was what it took.

"I'm sorry, Aksel." Her lower lip trembled. "This was a mistake."

She turned her back, and his wolf raged, throwing itself against the barrier Aksel kept between them.

Go! Go get her. Go now. Ours. Mine. Get her.

He didn't dare move, didn't dare blink. The slightest movement, and he would lose control. His wolf would take over and claim what was his. He would mark Jess, making sure every wolven in this world and the next knew whose mate she was.

And in doing so, he would lose her forever.

What a thought to have when the love of his life walked away for the second time.

"Aksel?" Gitta called softly over his shoulder. "Aksel, come with me."

"Can't," he replied, voice gruff and dropping into lower canid registers. Elias's truck rumbled to life, tires grinding over gravel. At the sound, the itch under Aksel's skin rose to a burn, his bones beginning their familiar ache as they warped and bent.

"It's going to be okay, alright?" Gitta's voice drew near. "Come with me. We'll get Dusty, and take a trip out to Dolly Sods. You can run until your paws bleed, just come with me, okay?"

"*No.*" He snapped lengthening fangs at his foster sister. A wolf from another pack. Not his pack. Not his family. Not his.

Everything that was his was gone, driving away in another wolven's truck. In twenty-four hours, he had lost everything. His pack, his pups, his mate, and now, Aksel had nothing.

Nothing but his wolf.

His paws hit the ground, the grass too soft for the pain ravaging him from his ears to the tip of his tail. He needed to run until his paws bled; she was right about that. But not with Gitta. Not with the mothman.

Aksel had nothing, was nothing, and so he ran from the knob a lone wolf.

36

JESS

TWO MONTHS LATER

"SHE SHIFTED IN THE middle of English class?"

"Yes." Jessica groaned into her hands, unable to look Svana in the eye. "And when the teacher told her to shift back, she ate the book."

"Oh, new moon." Svana snorted, restraining her laughter. "What book was it?"

Jessica raised her head. "*The Call of the Wild*."

The wolven woman barked a laugh, smashing a hand over her mouth. Silvery eyes twinkled at Jessica as her creamy skin reddened. "I'm sorry, I shouldn't laugh."

"No, go ahead." Jessica grabbed her coffee cup, clutching it in both hands. "Honestly, if I could shift, I would have done the same thing to get out of reading that book in school."

"And they sent her home because she ate a book?" Svana refilled her mug, offering the pot to Jessica. She shook her head and slunk down in the chair.

"It was her second offense. She already had an in-school suspension for destruction of property."

"Moonblessed, what book caused that?"

"*Holes*," Jessica stated. Svana choked on her coffee, coughing and beating her chest with a fist. "She said it was so boring that she would rather dig the holes than read about them."

"Oh, Sköll, I was kidding." Svana's eyes widened, and the laughter fell away. "Jessica, this is bad."

"I know." She rubbed her temples, trying and failing to ease the same headache she'd had for eight weeks. "The school calls every other day. I've been working from home for the last month just to be closer when I have to go pick her up."

"Has she acted out like this before?"

Jessica glanced at the yard, where Svana's youngest pups tumbled in the grass with Jan, Jarl, and Jens. Kendra sat nearby, beneath the shade of an oak tree. Shifted, she looked just like Aksel, with an amber tufted crest at her shoulders and across her chest and white markings on her forelegs, though she was smaller all around with the knobby ankles and out-of-proportion paws of an adolescent wolf.

Straight-backed, she scanned the yard, alert to every movement of the wolven wrestling in the grass, her ears twitching at sounds beyond Svana's wooden fence.

"Never," Jessica said, filling her mouth with the last of her coffee to stretch the moment.

Svana was clever. It was what Jessica liked most about the wolven woman. A sharp mind, quick wit, and easy smile. She had taken one look at Jessica chasing puppies at the dog park with a baby strapped to her front and breezed into their lives.

What had begun as playdates over coffee with the pups tumbling in a playpen had evolved into birthdays, holidays, and weekends, where Jessica learned all she could about wolven, and Svana helped raise her sons with a semblance of a pack. The Outreach had grown out of their time together, bringing together Inhumans across Kanawha County and beyond.

Over the years, their friendship had grown to the point where looks replaced words, and silence spoke louder than everything else.

"Jessica," Svana began, a warning in her tone.

"Please, don't say it."

"I'm going to say it, because you need to hear it."

Jessica closed her eyes, bracing herself for what she knew Svana would suggest. Maybe that was why she had come here: to hear it again and have the obvious stated in the hopes that this time, she might be able to accept the truth and act on it rather than continue to play dumb.

But before Svana could say anything, Jessica blurted, "She bit my mom."

She met Svana's startled stare, as shocked by the admission as her friend.

"Nothing serious. A nip, and she hid in the closet for an entire day afterward. My mom went to grab her for dinner, and Kendra shifted and snagged her on the arm."

Svana's upper lip pulled back in a worried grimace.

"And the boys don't tease her anymore. Whenever she enters a room, they either cower down or slink away, whether they're shifted or not. They don't joke when she's around; I had to pull her out of dance class after she ate her ballet shoes. She hasn't played her oboe since we got back, and now all of this bullshit at the school." She blinked, hating that fat tears pinched free and rolled down her cheeks. "I don't know what to do."

"Yes, you do, honey." Svana reached across the narrow table and gently squeezed Jessica's arm. "You just don't want to admit it."

"Can't you and Jörgun take her?"

Svana's lips parted, brows twitching at the suggestion. Jörgun was the Alpha of the Skölläng Pack, and Svana his mate. They had already done so much for Jessica and her children; surely they could do this.

"She would be close and wouldn't have to change schools, she could even still live—"

"We're too close, Jessica." Svana shook her head. "She needs to foster with a pack where her nature won't be seen as a challenge."

"Jörgun practically raised the boys." She flicked her hand at the tumble of wolven leaping over one another. "Kendra already trusts you both."

"It's not about trust, honey; it's about territory. Charleston and Kanawha County are Skölläng, the way Elkins and the Monongahela are Sköllburg."

Jessica bristled at the pack's name, frowning into her mug as she spun it in her hands. Not all of the Monongahela was Sköllburg.

A muscle in her chest panged. Jessica rubbed a knuckle over her breastbone, hating that months on, even the merest thought of the camp brought on the same pain that thinking of *him* did. It was nothing in the grand scheme of things. An annoyance to be suffered.

Jessica had suffered the heartache and the loss of the camp and Aks–*him*, for thirteen years. She had survived this once, and she could do it again, even if the pain cut deeper now that she knew how caring and considerate he could be.

Knew how his focus centered on his students when he taught music or marching. How their boys—*her* boys, God dammit—lit up when they saw him, and how *he* lit up when Jessica entered a room.

"Honey." Svana knelt before her, resting a hand lightly on her knee. "I know this is hard, and it must sound so strange to a human mother, but this is normal for us. We send our babies out to learn the ways of the world, where they won't be a threat to those around them. And when she's ready, she might come back, or, moonblessed, she might have the confidence and skills to go and make a life for herself. Just what any parent would want for their child."

"I know," Jessica sniffled. "It's just all so fast."

"She's struggling, Jess." Svana tapped her knee. "She feels threatened and cornered. Do you know what happens to a cornered wolf?"

In the grass, Jarl leapt at Svana's youngest, Anders. The pair crashed together, legs tangling as they rolled across the yard and collided with Kendra.

She jumped to her feet, ears back, hackles raised, lips curled to reveal her fangs, snarling a warning at the pair. Anders, a cool gray wolven, immediately darted away, while Jarl remained on his back, tongue lolling and tail wagging at his sister.

Kendra snarled again, pacing an angry circle before launching forward and landing a warning bite on his tail. He yelped and tucked in tight, tail pressed flat against his belly.

"I can make some calls," Svana said after a long, tense moment. "The Sköllflod in Parkersburg might be able to foster her."

"I'm not sending Kendra away." The anger in Jessica's voice surprised her. She set her cup down and rose, plucking the seam on her pocket. "She's my daughter. I can do this; I just need help."

"We're offering help, Jessica." Svana rose and ran a hand through her ashe-blonde hair. "You have to decide whether or not you want to accept it."

Jessica opened her mouth, closed it, and brushed her hands down her thighs. "I think it's time we got going."

"Jessica—"

"Thank you for having us over." She pursed her lips and whistled, calling her kids. Jan, Jarl, and Jens whipped their faces in her direction, hesitating until Kendra slowly paced by. They fell in line behind her, heads lowering as they passed Jessica on their way to the side gate.

Svana sighed, not bothering to hide her frustration. "Will we see you at the Outreach tonight?"

"No." Jessica gathered the kids' clothes and shoved them in her bag. After months of negotiation and a not-so-subtle request from her mother that she step away from the Elkwater partnership, tonight's board meeting was to review what next steps the Outreach would take regarding Jessica's pet project and her failed attempt to secure funding. "I think it's best if I stay out of things for a bit."

Svana wrinkled her nose, but instead of arguing, she grabbed the stack of mail on the narrow table and held it out to Jessica.

"Take these, then. They're addressed to you."

The letters, four of them, were sealed in nondescript envelopes. She took the stack, briefly catching the postmarks—two weeks apart, with the most recent from four days prior—and the return address. "These are from Elkwater."

"They are."

"Why were they sent to the Outreach?" Jessica shuffled through the stack, frustrated by the typed address and the lack of handwriting that would have warned her of the contents. It couldn't be a bill. The kids had been registered for the summer, and Jessica had paid their tuition in full in the Spring.

"No idea." Svana shrugged. "Not my mail, but you haven't been in in weeks, so I thought I'd bring them home."

"Well." She shoved them into her bag and headed for the gate. "Thank you."

Svana followed her out, leaning against her car as the kids piled in. "Think about it, would you?" she asked when the doors were closed.

Jessica hesitated at her door. "She's my daughter."

"She is," Svana agreed. "Don't you want the best for her?"

⁕⁕⁕

Two glasses of white wine waited on the kitchen island, condensation beading on the glass and pooling in a ring on the marble. Jessica stared at the glasses, dreading what came next. She could count on one hand the times her mother had poured her a glass of wine, and each of them had ended in an argument. She dumped her bag on an empty stool, grabbed a glass, and drained it in one gusty swallow, heading to the refrigerator for the bottle.

"I saw the email from the school," her mother said.

"Of course you did," Jessica replied. Her mother stood at the entrance to the kitchen, her cream-colored linen pants perfectly pressed and creased. A gauze bandage peeked out from the cuffed sleeve of her emerald green silk blouse, freshly changed and accessorized with a thin-banded gold watch and tennis bracelet.

Irene followed where her eyes had fallen and tugged her sleeve, hiding the bandage from view. "We need to talk about your daughter."

Jessica snorted. "Oh, so now she's *my* daughter and not your precious human grandbaby."

"Jessica."

"Mom." The cork popped free from the bottle, and Jessica filled her glass. Liberally. She took a sip and shoved her bag off the stool to sit down. "Go ahead."

"She—" Irene began. Her face twisted, and she trembled her face side to side, starting again. "We need help."

Jessica's wine glass *tinked* against the marble. That was not what she'd expected her mother to say. She had braced for a lecture or a sermon on the virtues of raising her children as human and not wolven, mentally steeling herself for the same arguments her mother had brought to her time and time again.

Not this.

"I don't want to say that Kendra is out of control, but ..." She raised her right hand, letting the sleeve fall back to reveal the bandage.

"Mom, that was an accident."

"I know it was. But this nonsense in the school? Her behavior at home? Honey, it's time to admit we're out of our depth." Irene glided into the kitchen with a hesitance that was foreign to Jessica. "I know you've been speaking with Svana, and I applaud you for reaching out to our local community."

"Alright."

"I've also been having discussions."

A cold finger trailed down Jessica's spine as her mind spun out a thousand different possibilities as to what those "conversations" could be. Different packs she did not know. Corrective measures, military academies, animal control shelters. It went on and on, each idea more terrible than the last, and none came close to what her mother said next.

"I called the camp," Irene said, "and Mackenzie gave me the number of a wolven woman, Gitta."

"You–you called Aksel's sister?"

Irene blinked, a flicker of surprise breaking over her face, fast as a flash of lightning. "Yes." She stretched out the word in a way that told Jessica she'd had no idea who Gitta was until that moment. "I remembered her from the incident at the camp and thought she might be able to offer some advice." Her face fell, eyes dimming. "She was so calm and seemed to care deeply … for everyone."

If there were a truer description of Gitta, Jessica did not know it.

"She does."

"Jessica." Irene strode forward and set a hand on her arm. "They're willing to foster Kendra."

"Mom." She jerked away, knocking her hand into Irene's untouched wine glass. It crashed onto the counter, wine and glass flying across the marble and onto the floor. "No."

"Listen to me, Jessica, please."

"Why?" She jumped from the stool, glass crunching beneath her shoes. "Sounds like you've already made your decision. What else is there to talk about?" Grabbing a towel from the front of the stove, Jessica crouched, fighting off the burn in her eyes as she gathered the glass and soaked up the wine. "God, I should have known you'd want to ship her off the moment she wasn't your perfect little human girl."

"Jessica Abernathy Babcock," Irene shouted, slapping the marble counter. "Where is this coming from? I only want to help—"

"Oh, so, *now* that she doesn't fit into your perfect mold, you want to help her connect with her wolven side."

"How could you possibly think that?"

"Because I heard you!" Jessica popped to her feet and flung the damp, glass-filled towel into the sink. "I saw the horror on your face when my boys were born, and I heard what you said when Kendra came out. 'Thank God,'" she spat, the anger of thirteen years forcing itself from the depths where Jessica kept it locked away. "Isn't that what you said? Because that's what I heard."

The color bled from Irene's cheeks. She floated a hand up to clutch the pendant on her necklace, a large golden circle strung with pearls—two large, one medium, and four small. "Oh, Jessica, is that what you've thought this whole time?"

"What else was I supposed to think, Mom? I'd just popped out a litter of *puppies,* for fuck's sake. How else was I supposed to interpret what you said when you saw Kendra?"

"You are a daughter of West Virginia."

"*What?*" Jess gawked at her, completely and utterly lost as to what her pedigree had to do with anything.

"I thought you understood," Irene continued. "I thought you knew what that meant, and with the boys being pups, I thought ... oh, God."

"Mom, what the hell are you talking about?"

Irene spun for the cupboards, grabbed a plastic cup, and filled it to the brim with wine. She drank half, gasping and steadying herself against the counter. "You're my daughter, a Daughter of West Virginia, and when you had the boys, I thought, I worried that ..."

"Mom, spit it out."

"I thought the line had broken." Irene met Jessica's eyes, her face a shade of sickening green. "The Abernathys have had an unbroken line of daughters since before they came to America. You can trace us back to Robert the Bruce, and every daughter has had a daughter to continue the line."

"What line?"

"The Abernathy Line." She sank into a bar stool and gripped Jessica's arm. "The Abernathys, Mackenzies, and Averys came across together. The church labeled us witches and changelings for honoring the old ways, so the families banded together, splitting passage to the colonies and settling in Vandalia."

Jessica knew the story, somewhat. The Abernathys fell from the grace of the crown and fled religious persecution in England. They had split passage with other families to settle in what was then the western frontier of the Virginia colony, forming a township they called Vandalia. But ...

"The Averys, as in Avery Payne?"

Irene nodded, skin greying beneath her makeup. "They settled near Grafton, while the Abernathys settled further south, near Wolf Run, and the Mackenzies went west toward Ohio. Your grandmother used to say the lost hills called their lost children home."

A memory sparked, one of hot, humid summers and endless glasses of lemonade sweating in her hand.

"I remember." Jessica straightened, chasing the memory. "She said Appalachia used to be part of the Scottish Highlands."

Irene nodded, urging her on. "Grandma used to say there were faeries in the woods that wandered away from their—"

"They did not wander." Irene's gaze sharpened. "They fell."

37

—·—

Jess

A chill ran down Jessica's spine. "Mom, the Fall happened when I was in high school."

"And the mountains have been home to a host of creatures for far longer. Some say we brought them with us; others say we summoned them, and maybe we did, but like calls to like, Jessica." She exhaled, sagging forward. "And all these years you thought—" Irene gave a tight shake of her head, and her expression hardened like granite. "I should have explained what it meant to be a Daughter of West Virginia. Why would I, when I didn't believe it myself? Then you came home pregnant by that wolven boy, and I knew. I knew, honey, but you delivered so fast, I thought—"

"You thought I knew."

"No!" For the first time in Jessica's life, her mother's voice cracked, and her proud veneer shattered. "I thought we were going to lose you."

A band tightened around Jessica's chest, squeezing the air from her lungs.

"You got pregnant, and those precious pups were born, and it was true. It was all true. Every fairy tale my mother told me. The odd notes in our family history. All of it was true, but the line was broken. Without a daughter to carry the Abernathys forward, I was looking at the truth of our family and the end of us."

"And then Kendra was born," Jessica said. Something shifted in her mind; a cog released, and a switch flipped. The day her babies were born bled across her memory, showing her mother in a new light. How she gripped Jessica's hand, her knuckles blanched a terrible bone white. How she yelled at the nurses when they did not move fast enough, and how she grabbed a towel for the one nurse who did, helping her gather Jan, Jarl, and Jens and place them on Jessica's chest.

The press of her lips together when Jessica bellowed in pain, rushing to her daughter's side to hold her hand, rub her back, and offer the only help she could.

Those two words took on a new light then.

"Thank God."

Thank God for a healthy baby girl.

Thank God for sparing hers.

A weight lifted in that shifting of gears, replaced by a new understanding of her stern mother and her rigid ways. Tears streamed down Jessica's cheeks, and she wrapped her arms around her mother, sobbing into her shoulder. "Mommy."

"My baby." Irene held her back, cradling Jessica against her like she was a little girl. When she eventually pulled away, they were both red-eyed and sniffling.

"Parenting is a funny thing." Irene plucked a tissue from the box on the island and dabbed it under her eyes. "No matter how much you want to protect your child and no matter how much you want to help them, you still fall short of the mark."

A wet laugh burbled out of Jessica. She nudged her mother with her shoulder. "Did you share all that just to teach me a parenting lesson?"

"And if I did?" Irene smiled weepily at her. She cupped Jessica's cheek and brushed a tear away with her thumb. "I love you, Jessica. But sometimes, love makes us blind to what our children need most. You needed me to be softer, and now, sweet girl, Kendra needs you to be strong."

Fresh tears welled, burning in her eyes, but Jessica nodded. "I know. I just ... I'm not ready to say goodbye."

"You never are, honey, but she's hurting, and Gitta says they can help."

"They can."

"Then we should accept that help, honey."

Jessica rubbed a knuckle against her breastbone, blinking at the ceiling to stop the flow of tears. "What if she doesn't want to go?" she voiced the fear aloud—that she would have a solution, a way to help her daughter, and that Kendra would reject it the same way Jessica had rejected help time and time again.

"I want to go, Mom," Kendra said. She tiptoed into the kitchen, back against the wall. In an oversized Elkwater T-shirt, one Jessica had "accidentally" stolen from Aksel's bedroom weeks earlier, and loose sweatpants, she looked too small, too young to be deciding this with such solemnity. But that had always been her daughter, quiet and serious. Deeply thoughtful and protective to a fault. "Please? Can I go?"

"You want to foster with the Sköllburg?"

"I want to foster with Gitta," she said firmly. "And I guess with her mom and dad."

"Lennart and..." Jessica searched her memory for the name, pulling it from some shadowy recess. "Ygrid."

"Yes." Kendra nodded. "Them. Dad said—" She flattened her back against the wall, eyes full-moon-round.

"It's okay." Jessica nodded, grabbing her mother's hand for strength. The hope that thrilled her at hearing Kendra call him "Dad"—Lord help her, it did something to Jessica. It was a sliver, barely a splinter of a way forward and, if she were lucky, a way back. "He's your father. I know we haven't talked about it, or him, much, but that's who he is."

Kendra swallowed, dipping her chin. "Dad said he learned more about what it meant to be wolven from Lennart and Ygrid than anyone else."

"He did."

"I want to go," her daughter repeated. "I don't want to be a problem."

"Oh, honey, you're not a problem." Jessica released her mother's hand and rushed across the kitchen, gathering her daughter close. Holding her tight. "Not at all."

"You're a Daughter of West Virginia," Irene added, embracing them both and kissing Kendra's cheek. "We'll call Gitta in the morning, alright? All three of us, together over breakfast. We'll ask her what the next steps are and how we move forward."

"Okay." Kendra's slight arms wrapped around Jessica's waist, and she caught the barest tremor and sniffle as she said, "Thank you."

Jessica lost track of the time as she stood there, holding her daughter as tightly as her mother held her. Kendra let go first, wriggling away from the older women and grinning sheepishly at them.

"Can I tell them?" she asked, eyes darting to the ceiling.

"Of course." Jessica wound a heavy curl of Kendra's hair around her finger, letting it fall loose before tucking it behind her ear.

She darted away, hollering her brothers' names as she pounded up the steps. The shift in the house was immediate, and for the first time in weeks, Jessica heard laughter ringing down the stairs.

"That's better," Irene said with a smile. "Almost."

"Almost?"

With a knowing glance at Jessica, Irene plucked the Elkwater envelopes from her bag and set them on the counter. "Aren't you going to open these?"

She picked up the first one, turning it over in her hands before setting it down and sliding it away. "I'm afraid to," she admitted. "We don't owe Elkwater any money; the kids didn't leave anything behind. I can't think of any reason the camp would be writing me, unless they're from—"

She pressed her tongue to the roof of her mouth, unable to say his name. It hurt too much to bring him into the room. Too easily, she could pull his face to mind, seeing in stark clarity the hurt he wore as she said hateful, cruel things. Too easily, she could hear the anguish in his voice as he begged her to stay, even after she accused him of not being ready.

It was unfair of her. She knew that. How could he have been ready after just a few weeks to step into the role Jessica had been performing for years? But it was easier to push him away, easier to turn her back than to make that hard choice.

Aksel, or Kendra.

Impossible in the moment, and impossible to know that all she had needed was the time to understand what wolven instinctively knew.

Now, they had that time, only Jessica feared she was too late.

"You think these are from Aksel?" Irene said his name so easily, as if she were discussing a neighbor or colleague, and it drove an icy shard into Jessica's heart.

"Who else would they be from?" She picked up another envelope, worrying the seal with a fingernail. "He doesn't have our home address, and the Outreach is in the Yellow Pages."

"Hm." Irene drew her finger around the rim of her plastic wine cup. "Perhaps they are from one of the other humans or inhumans working at the camp."

"What do you know, Mom?"

She pinched her lips together, pushing them up under her nose and sniffing as she threw her hands up. Wine splattered on the floor, and she huffed. "I know a lot of things. For example, if you don't open that letter, I have nothing to take to the foundation's meeting with your Outreach in"—she checked her watch and gasped as if she had not been acutely aware of the time—"twenty minutes! Good Lord, I'm going to be late."

"Mom..."

"Just open one of them." Irene flicked an envelope at Jessica. "Read it, think about it—briefly—and tell me what you think."

"Alright." She ran a nail under the seal, glancing at her mother, who waited calmly with her hip against the counter and a smug smile curling her mouth.

Jessica carefully unfolded the letter, setting it on the counter as a smaller piece of paper tumbled free. The Elkwater Music Camp logo was printed on the top, and someone with a lazy hand had scrawled a brief note.

Jess,

> Hell of a summer, huh? We're keeping an eye on him. Ramble, Cricket, and a few Sköllburg cover his tracks every day.

Her stomach plummeted as she re-read those opening sentences. Pressing a hand to her mouth, she forced herself to keep reading, though every bit of her wanted to ball the note up and throw it away.

> I miss my friend, and I know that's not fair to put it on you, but it's killing us that we can't help him. Hopefully, this letter finds you. I really hope you'll accept. For the camp and for Aksel, yes, but I gotta be honest, I think we'd make a great team. You're one of us; I hope you know that
> -Mac

Tossing the note onto the counter, Jessica snatched another envelope and tore it open, frantically skimming another note from Mac.

He came into the camp last night. Almaden convinced him to shift so she could get some clean water and a home-cooked meal into him.

"Oh, God."

Left at sunrise before Ramble could catch him. Gitta's got the pack out now scenting his trail.

And another, each note sharing more of the same and deepening the pit in her stomach.

Torn paw pads ... looks like he got into it with a bear.

Dehydrated ... ate enough to feed an entire bunk ... gone at sunrise.

Don't know when the last time was he shifted.

...found him lurking near the faun encampment...

Yet, in all its cheerful brevity, the first note was the worst.

Jess–

Welcome to the family. We can't wait to have you home.

-Mac

"What does it say?" Irene asked quietly.

"I—" Jess turned the note over, too startled and frightened to speak.

What had happened to Aksel? What had she done?

"Read the letter, Jessica," her mother prompted, tapping the corner of the page.

Jessica scanned the formal letter, the words blurring together on the first pass. She read it again, and again as the floor tipped beneath her feet, the whites and silvers and pastels of her mother's kitchen spinning around her in a whorl.

Ms. Jessica Babcock,

On behalf of Elkwater Music Camp, due in part to a generous donation from the Mountaineers' Daughters, I am excited to offer you the position of Chief Financial Officer. Please find attached a full description of your benefits and salary. Upon your acceptance, we will begin negotiations around your start date.

I apologize for the lack of professionalism around this offer. I have never had to write one of these letters before, but considering your long history with the camp and the obvious love you hold for our mission, I am sure we can meet whatever requests you make of the role.

I (anxiously) await your reply (see: acceptance).

Welcome aboard,

Mackenzie "Mac" Murray

"Jessica?"

She threw the letter aside, grabbing the next in the pile and scanning the page.

Identical.

And the next, and the next.

An offer to work for the camp, made possible by her mother's foundation. A way out of Charleston.

A way back.

"Honey, what does it say?"

She crumpled one of the letters in her fist, eyes unfocused as every minute of every day of the last eight weeks rattled through her body. Her fears and worries for Kendra, the shadows that hung around the boys. Every sleepless night spent mindlessly repeating her final words to Aksel until she drifted off to uneasy sleep.

The kitchen slowly refocused, and Jessica looked her mother dead in the eye.

"This was a mistake."

"Honey?"

"A mistake. I made a mistake." She swept the letters off the counter and into her bag, throwing it over her shoulder as she dug out her car keys. "I keep messing up, because I'm too stubborn to be selfish, and now I—I have to go. Can you and Dad watch the kids?"

"Your father isn't here."

"Can you watch the kids?" Jessica was pretty sure she looked unhinged. She felt unhinged, with her shaking hands and eyes so wide her lashes tickled her brows, but she had never been more sure of anything. "Please, Mom, can you watch them?"

"I have the meeting with the Outreach."

Jessica grabbed a letter from her bag and shoved it into Irene's hands. "Take the kids, tell them I accept. Svana will help. I have to go."

38

— · —

Aksel

Exhaustion drove him across the field on aching paws. He slunk under the bleachers, ears pricked for any sound. The campers had gone home weeks ago, but some staff lingered, staying on for the corporate events in the fall.

It had surprised him the first time he wandered into the camp. He'd thought he had stayed away long enough, and only Mac and Ramble would be here, along with the faun, of course. And Almaden and Cooky. Sanoya and her no-scent shadow.

But even after weeks, when the children and counselors should have gone, the camp bustled with life. Construction crews raised new bunks and affixed metal boxes to the windows.

"Heating units," Mac had explained when he asked. "Have to bring the bunks up to code for the winter."

It made sense, he supposed. The camp was growing, and the world beyond Monongahela was taking notice.

Too much notice.

After that, he only crossed the field at night, when construction ceased for the day and the skeleton staff had driven back to Elkins.

He loped under Almaden's window, panting through his mouth to avoid the sharp, astringent smell that clung to the nurse, and darted across the service road, easily leaping the fence into Mac's backyard and landing on soft, sore paws.

"Not too late for me to put in that doggy door," Ramble said from the porch. Seated on the topmost step, they had a length of leather stretched across their knees. The sweet, nutty scent of linseed oil tickled his nose, carrying a soft floral note he could not place. Padding closer, he nosed the reeds Ramble had laid across the leather.

"Stop that." They lightly swatted his snout with the oiled rag they used to work oil into the reeds. He huffed and pointed his nose at the ball of red twine cradled in their lap. Ramble picked it up and showed it to him. "It's to bind the reeds together," they said. "Spen and Aster just welcomed a doe. Thought I'd make them their first panflute."

A gift. Good. It was important to welcome new inhumans to this dead world with a gift.

He mounted the stairs, turning in a circle at the top before lying beside Ramble with his side pressed against their hip. They set their hand on his head, gently scratching between his ears. The soft, gentle touch had him closing his eyes and releasing a long, shuddering sigh as the strain of running the woods left him for the moment.

"Didn't think we'd see you tonight," they said. "Dusty was worried when you didn't stop by The Porchlight, and Gitta said she hasn't seen you in weeks."

The scratching stopped, and he whined, nudging their hand.

Instead of resuming the gentle scratching, Ramble pulled away, gathering the reeds and twine and wrapping them in the leather.

"How much longer is this going to go on, Aksel?"

He flinched at the name. Aksel was not who he was. Aksel was a broken-hearted fool who dreamed too big and ignored his responsibilities. Aksel had gotten him cast out, doomed to roam as a lone wolf on the fringes of Sköllburg territory.

Aksel had lost her.

It was easier to be the wolf. To disappear into the woods and survive.

"Is he here?" Mac pushed the screen door open, and the savory, mouthwatering scent of steak struck him like a slap. He whined, stretching his legs and flexing his claws. His stomach rumbled as the steak came nearer, and drool pooled on his tongue.

"Got in just now," Ramble said. They resumed scratching his head, and he leaned into the touch.

Mac sat on the topmost stair and set a plate on her lap—sliced sirloin and roasted broccoli. Garlic bread.

His jowls watered, hunger winning over the knowledge that the garlic bread would require a shift to stomach. A shift would lead to conversation, and that he could not abide.

"I know you don't want to talk," she said, "so maybe you'll listen for a spell." She offered him a piece of steak, waiting until he gently took it from her fingers before continuing. "This can't go on, buddy. For one, Rolf is tired of covering your classes at the high school." He turned his face away from the next piece she offered. Mac grunted and set it down. "The park service is up in arms about an untagged red wolf, the faun are complaining that you're scaring the calves, and Gitta needs to know you're alright before she can move on with her life."

He settled his head on his paws, staring across the tidy yard. In two seconds, he could be over the fence and halfway to the woods. He could leave all of this behind and let his guilt run him to exhaustion.

Ramble's ear twitched, and they set a hand between his shoulder blades. "Don't keep running away when we're trying to help."

"We love you, buddy. And we're sorry about what happened, but I think, maybe with some time, it's all gonna turn out okay." Mac offered him another piece of steak, and this time, he took it. "But first, you've got to find your way back to us."

In this form, Aksel could not process the ripple effects of the summer, but he could see and smell how it weighed on the people and inhumans he loved. Worry wafted off Mac and Ramble,

Dusty's dry, powdery scent turned acrid and sour whenever he came near, and the black wolf kept a careful distance, instead of running alongside him like she used to.

A door shut somewhere within Mac's cabin. He jerked his head up, ears pricked, and pointed toward the sound. Floorboards creaked, and there, just under the steak and garlic, was a scent he had missed.

A scent he never thought he'd catch again.

Faint florals and loam.

"There's someone here to talk to you," Mac said. "Whether you feel like shifting or not, that's up to you, but for your own sake, please listen to what they have to say, okay?"

The screen door creaked open as she offered him another piece of steak. He jumped to his feet, heart thudding in his chest. What remained of the man in him panicked, tripping over Ramble and tumbling down the stairs, while the wolf backed away, ears flattened and lips curled in a warning snarl.

David Babcock stepped onto the porch, approaching Mac and Ramble at a slow walk. Tidily dressed, his short-sleeved button-down and khakis were wrinkled, and the scent of stale, recycled air clung to his clothes and skin. He held a hand out toward Aksel, easing across the porch the way one would approach a wild dog. Tucked under his other arm was the source of that maddening aroma—a battered banker's box that smelled all too much like her.

"Easy, son," he said. "I'm not here to upset anyone." Nearing the edge of the porch, he crouched beside Mac, who put a hand on his shoulder, showing Aksel the Wolf that David was a friend. Not a threat.

Aksel dug his claws into the grass as the yard closed in, the space suddenly too small. He needed the anonymity of the woods and the safety of the shadows and dells and tight caves where he could wait. Unseen and forgotten.

Ramble gathered their reeds, leather, and twine and rose, making room for David to set the box down.

"This is for you." He removed the lid, and a sensory onslaught battered Aksel deeper into the yard. Florals and loam, fuchsia, and the unique berry of her shampoo.

Jessica.

A high, tight whine spooled from his throat, and he hunkered low, unable to move.

He'd almost forgotten. He'd managed to outrun the worst of it, and here it was again, come to remind him of all the ways he had failed and disappointed her. All the ways he had lost his other half. The missing piece of his soul.

His mate.

"I'm afraid my wife and I did wrong by you both." David sat on the edge of the porch, nodding at Mac with a tight smile as she and Ramble went inside. From the box, he withdrew a stack of envelopes bound together with a rubber band. "We thought—" his voice broke, and he paused, staring at the bundle like he'd never seen it before. "We only wanted to help, and as time went by, it was easier to convince ourselves we'd done right by our daughter. The children grew so fast, and Jessica, she–she's tough, my daughter." He met Aksel's stare, eyes glistening. "But you know that, don't you?"

David set the envelopes on the porch and pulled out a photograph. He studied it briefly, wiping away a tear before showing it to Aksel.

Jessica smiled in the picture, dressed as she was on First Night. Seated on a checkered blanket, she had her arms around Kendra and Jan. Jarl and Jens crouched behind them, and there, with an arm, shoulder, and just the side of his face in frame, was Aksel.

"Closest thing to a family photo she has," David said, his voice low and strained with the pain of a father's regret. He cleared his throat and met Aksel's eyes. "One copy, and she put it in her box for the kids to have."

Because that was Jess, putting her children first in all things.

A bitter pressure built in Aksel's chest, forcing its way into his throat. He pawed the lawn, ducking his head as if he could run away from the pain, and in the next moment, damp grass pressed against his palms. Aksel drove his nails into the soft earth. Prickle balls from the sweet gum tree bit into his bare knees, and a harsh, ragged sob tore out of his throat. He bent over his thighs, face buried in filthy palms as the tears fell.

The stairs creaked, and a flannel blanket draped across his shoulders. David's hand was a steady weight on his shoulder, letting Aksel know he wasn't alone in this pain and heartbreak. He stood a silent vigil as every human emotion Aksel had been outrunning for the last eight weeks caught up with him, ravaging his body with their deafening demands to be heard and felt. When the shuddering sobs slowed, when he was ready to stand, David helped him up and guided him to the stairs.

"You should look through there," he said after a long moment. "We found it when the kids were toddlers, back when it was mostly memories from her time at Elkwater. With you."

Aksel swallowed the growing lump in his throat, staring at the box as if it held his doom.

"She's added to it over the years," David continued. "Memories written on scraps of paper. Descriptions and sketches. Newspaper clippings."

Tugging the blanket tight around his hips, Aksel sank onto the bottom-most step. His gaze landed on the bundle of envelopes, and a sticky, prickly unease raised the hairs on his arms.

David pulled his lips between his teeth, a gesture Jess had made numerous times throughout the summer whenever she was uncomfortable or, as he now knew, hiding the truth about their children.

"These are my letters." He picked up the bundle, flipping through the unopened envelopes. "She said she never got them."

"She did not." David rocked back on his heels and shoved his hands in his pockets. "Her mother and I—when Jessica came home, she—"

"You took my letters."

David stilled at the growl in his voice, Aksel's wolf riding close beneath his skin. He nodded. "And grabbed hers before the mailman came." He jerked his chin at the box. "I put them in there."

Aksel glanced in the box, snatching a second bundle of envelopes from the top.

His name.

His address from the dorms at OSU over and over again. A year's worth of letters sent without a single response from him. His stomach twisted, dread building as he read the postmarked date on the first, mailed a week before they were supposed to meet at the game.

Dear Aksel,

I tried the phone number you gave me for the dorms, but it was disconnected, and the school wouldn't tell me if you'd moved or where. I'm sorry to do this in a letter, but I want you to know: I'm not going to make it to the game. My mom and dad picked me up from school yesterday, and I'm moving back home.

Before I write anything else, just know that I wouldn't change a thing. I miss you, and I know school must be busy, but please, if you respond to any of my letters, respond to this one.

I'm pregnant. They're yours.

It's moving quickly, and the doctors are worried, but I don't regret it.

Please write back, Aksel. I need you.

Love,

Jess

"Oh, Gods." The letter fell from trembling fingers, and he tore into the next one.

I felt them kicking today, like butterflies in my stomach.

And the next.

The doctors don't know if I can deliver naturally.

I'm scared, Aksel.

Please write me back.

Call me.

And finally:

You're a father. Three sons and a beautiful baby girl. Thought you should know.

A fat teardrop splashed against the page, bleeding into the thirteen-year-old ink and blurring the words. Aksel swept the base of his palm against his cheek and kept on, pulling notes and letters from the box and reading them all.

The boys are already so fast, I can barely keep up. A wolven woman I met at the park suggested baby gates at the entrance to the playroom, rather than trying to keep them in a playpen.

Your babies turned one today. I thought you should know.

Kendra has your laugh.

Among the notes were pictures from their summers together at camp, newspaper clippings with the Elkins High School Band in a grainy photograph, and Aksel at the center. Receipts with sketches of his wolf on the back, more notes documenting the life of his children, all the ways Jessica saw their father in them, and dozens of unsent letters telling the story of their lives.

"She never let go of you," David finally said. "We thought she would move on after the kids were born. Thought that us keeping the letters would be a problem that simply went away. When we picked her up from school, she was ... she wasn't our Jessica. I know you haven't gotten the chance to learn this, but seeing your child like that, broken and hurting—what parent wouldn't try to move the heavens to erase whatever caused that pain?"

"And when you found out I was the cause of that hurt, you tried to erase me."

To his credit, David did not argue. He gave a tight nod and said, "I'm sorry, Aksel. It's not right, what we did, and my daughter isn't the only one to bear the brunt of our mistake."

"And now she's gone." He carefully set the note he'd been holding back in the box and picked up the lid, closing off the letters and the pain they caused. "So, why are you here?"

Headlights glanced off the trees, illuminating David's face as a car drove the length of the parking lot, tires crunching slowly over gravel. David flexed his jaw and held the family photo up to the light, pointing to Aksel's cut-off presence. "Because she never moved on."

"She left with our children," he said, hating the bitter taste of the words. "And after what happened, she had every right to do so." Gripping the blanket at his waist, Aksel rose, staring down David from the stairs. "Jess told me this was all a mistake, and she left. She's moved on."

He was halfway across the yard when David spoke again.

"She also said you told her to be selfish."

Aksel halted mid-step, flinching as those terrible words were thrown at his back.

"Our children are the best of us," David continued. "But no matter how hard you try, sometimes the worst of you sneaks in."

"What does that mean?"

"It means, we tried to raise Jessica to be loving and kind, but my wife has a stubborn streak as wide as the Ohio River is long, and me"—he adjusted his glasses and gave a little shrug—"I can be a little short-sighted. Sometimes, I don't see the truth of the thing, even when it's standing right in front of me. I see it now, though. You love my daughter."

"I do." Why bother lying? He loved her, and he'd lost her. All that was left now was wander the woods until his wolf lay down for the last time.

"Thought as much," David said, waiting a beat before adding, "Kendra is going to foster with the pack up here."

Aksel gripped the gate, nails lengthening to claws and splintering the wood. Ramble was going to be pissed. They'd spent the first week after camp ended repairing and painting the fence. He would have to remember to return later and fix the posts before they noticed. "Jessica would never send her daughter away."

"No, she wouldn't. She rejected the idea outright, but Kendra said she wants to be here, and you know how my daughter is. She'll do anything for those kids, even if it hurts her in the end."

"Why tell me this?" Aksel faced the man, unable to put any strength behind his words. The hope sparked by David's news was faint and fleeting enough to be ignored, but it was there. "Jess made her thoughts on me and us clear. Why come here and dangle hope in front of me?"

"Because my daughter has spent the last thirteen years putting everyone before herself." David stepped forward, his scent catching in the breeze. Faint echoes of Jess teased Aksel's nose, and it was like a knife wrenching in his chest, cutting a deeper pain than he already suffered. "Stubborn as a mule, short-sighted as a mole, and I only have myself and Irene to blame for that. When she came home with the kids, it was like that day we drove her home from college. I never want to see my little girl that broken again."

"Hm," Aksel grunted. As much as he wanted to run to Jess and beg her to try, if even for one more day, he couldn't. She was his mate, and her word was respected, even if it killed him.

Mac's voice rose inside the house, calling out to Ramble, he supposed, and the front door opened and closed.

He put his back to the porch, flexing his hand against the gate and fighting the desire to shift and run. Her scent, faint as it was on her father and lingering on the box, was too much to bear. There were too many people around, and he was too broken to endure these too-human feelings. It was easier as his wolf, when his instincts rode him, instead of guilt and heartache.

"I begged her to stay," he said, eyes fixed on the service road and the empty field visible beyond the edge of Almaden's building.

The trees stood dark and tall, beckoning Aksel and his wolf to disappear into their shadows. Behind him, the porch door creaked open, and David let out a choked sound of surprise.

"I begged her to help me find a way, to fight for us, but she was right—I don't know what it means to be a parent, because you and your wife took that from me." His claws punctured the post, and Aksel tore his hand away in disgust. "You took it from us without stopping to consider the consequences of what you'd done, and now you come here asking me to—to what? To fix it? How am I supposed to *fix* anything?"

He spun around, jolting to a halt at the sight of Jess on the porch. She held out a hand, reaching for him across the narrow yard.

"By letting me be selfish."

39

— · —

JESS

AKSEL WAS GONE IN an instant, his large, strong body twisting and shifting as he bounded over the fence and landed on four paws.

But the glimpse she caught was enough to see the damage of the last eight weeks. Deep, purple bruising clung beneath his eyes, his cheeks hollowed beneath a scraggly beard. Though he'd always been tall and powerfully built, the softness she adored had hardened, erasing the last echoes of the sweet wolven boy from her youth and replacing him with a wild, untamed creature who knew more hurt than care.

Jessica had done that.

She had let fear rule her, and in doing so had taken someone precious and kind and broken him.

"Wait!" She leapt off the porch, tears streaming down her cheeks as she ran past her father and vaulted over the low gate. Her foot landed at an angle, ankle screaming, but she swallowed the shock of pain and ran after Aksel.

She couldn't lose him again. Wouldn't lose him again. They had been through so much and come so far; there was no possible way she was letting him run from her now. Not when she had so much to make up for.

Dirt flew as he skittered and disappeared around a building. Jessica grabbed the trim on the corner, splinters biting into her fingers, and swung after him, feet slipping as hard-packed dirt gave way to grass.

"Aksel, please." Her voice shot across the field. "Please don't run, I'm so—" Jessica gasped for air. "I'm so sorry, Aksel, *please.*"

At her cry, he twisted to face her, paws braced and ready to run at the slightest provocation. Moonlight flashed like amber coins in eyes trained on her.

Jessica halted, meeting his stare and letting his wolf know she was no threat. Not anymore.

"I was wrong." She reached across the distance, wanting nothing more than to grab hold of all that thick, lovely fur and nestle into its warmth. To stroke his back and press kisses to his brow until he relaxed against her, held in her arms where he belonged. "I was wrong about everything, from the moment I came back to Elkins to the moment I left and every day after."

Aksel flattened his ears, body tensing, but he did not run. Jessica took that as her invitation to keep talking.

"You were right, Aksel," she said. "I need to be selfish. I need to take what *I* want out of this life, and what I want is you."

There it was—the driving desire that had kept her going. For all the years between them, all the lonely nights and never-ending days. For every letter she sent and the notes she kept in the box high on her shelf.

Jessica risked a step forward, choking on a sob when he flinched back, anticipating the pain of her presence.

"I'm sorry I left. I'm sorry I didn't trust you to help me figure this out." When his ears softened, she eased closer, forcing herself to hold that bright, hurt stare. "I should have told you on that first day." She had seen this same posture enough in her sons when they knocked a lamp over with their tails, or played too hard and caught a sibling with their teeth.

The slight crouch and tense body, the wide eyes tracking every movement.

It was an assessing, wary pose composed of bunched muscles brimming with potential energy. As much as she wanted to gather him close and never let go, Jessica knew if she moved too fast, if she startled him even the slightest bit, Aksel would disappear into the woods where she could not follow.

"So much of this could have been avoided if I hadn't dragged it out, but I did, and I'm so, so sorry."

The space between them shrank with her every careful step, until Aksel was mere inches away. Slowly, she sank to her knees in front of him.

"It was unfair of my dad to ask you to fix what I broke, Aksel. None of this has been fair to you, but I'd like to make it right, if you'll let me. I want—I want to be selfish." She raised her hand, tentatively hovering it in the air between them. "With you."

He did not flinch, but the light in his eyes dimmed as they twitched to the side, seeking an easy escape.

Jessica held her breath, hoping and praying he would give her this one last chance. If he didn't—God, he had every right not to—she would accept it, even though it would kill her.

He had no reason to trust her. Not when she'd vanished on him, only to reappear thirteen years later and hide the truth of his children.

And that flinch, that look for an escape—*that* was what she had expected to see when he found out the kids were his. Instead, he held her and cared for her, making Jessica feel beautiful and cherished for the first time since that last time.

All he'd asked in return was to help her, never pushing the issue of fatherhood, never assuming he was a part of their family while silently asking for it with his actions, and Jessica had thrown it back in his face, saying the most hurtful things anyone could say to the person they—

The truth slammed into her, splaying her fingers wide. She couldn't move, frozen where she knelt by the enormity of the realization. The truth she had been hiding from all these years: how she felt about him. How she'd always felt about him.

From the last night of camp when he held her in his arms, to that embarrassing moment when he carried her down the ladder, Jessica had been living with a ghost, drifting through life as one half of a whole. Now, the truth stared her in the face, waiting for her to have the courage to put voice to the words, if only she could make her mouth move.

It scared her more than her pregnancy and childbirth. More than the endless nights and stressful days. More than founding the Outreach and moving her family to Elkins for the summer. Scared her more than anything she had faced and done in the last thirteen years.

But as terrifying as it was to lay out her truth and bare her soul to the one person who had the power to break it, losing Aksel scared her more.

Something shifted within her. *Something* changed, and Jessica looked Aksel, her summer love, the father of her children, her *mate,* in the eyes.

"I love you."

His eyes widened, catching the moonlight in their depths as they tripped over Jessica's face.

"I've always loved you. From our first summer as campers to the next summer as counselors. I've loved you since you emptied your spit valve on my shoes by accident. Since you tripped in the cafeteria and spilled sloppy joe all over yourself."

Aksel blinked slowly, nose twitching in what she half-swore was a quiet, canine chuckle.

"I've loved you from the very beginning, Aksel, and I'll love you until the end. I don't know how this works, or what we do next, but I know that I'm tired of doing it without you by my side. I love—"

He pressed his head into her palm, turning his face as he shifted so her fingers drove into his fur, into his hair, her hand cupping the back of his head.

"Jess." His voice rasped over her skin, and he pressed closer, banding his arms around her back and holding her tight. Though the night was warm, and his body fever-hot from the shift, a shiver built in Jessica's arms. The come down of her nerves and fears, seeking an exit even as he held her like a treasured prize. "Say it again." He searched her face, eyes pleading along with his full lips. "Please."

"I love you."

Eyes drifting closed, he dipped his head, nuzzling Jessica's neck, and never relinquishing his hold. "I love you," he repeated. "Again."

The demand won a laugh out of her. Jessica clasped his face in her hands, forcing him to lift his head so she could say the words again to his face. "I love you, Aksel. I'm so sor—"

"No more sorries." His expression hardened, brows dropping and eyes darkening. "No more, Jess. I want what happens next." Swallowing, he searched the sky above her head. "I want you on your good days and the bad. I want to be the one you come to when you need help, I want you to trust me to help you."

"I do." She nodded. "I may not be good at asking for help, Aksel, but I trust you. I'm so—"

"No more of that." He leaned away, shifting before she could protest and nudging Jessica with his nose until she stood.

"Aksel?"

Gently, he took her wrist in his teeth and raised her arm to his shoulder, right where she would grab hold to climb onto his back. When she did not immediately do so, he huffed and shouldered her thigh.

"Alright, alright." Jessica climbed on, and the moment she was balanced on his back, Aksel took off, tearing across the field and into the woods.

Unlike that awful, wonderful night during the summer, when he had tread carefully, scenting the ground and following a path only he could see, his steps now were sure, moving with confidence toward whatever destination he had in mind.

Jessica kept low against his back, closing her eyes to better feel the movement of his body, more focused on hanging on rather than where they were going.

Only when he slowed did she open her eyes and sit up, gasping at the beauty revealed in the moonlight.

Water cascaded down a jagged quartz wall, shimmering like fairy lights beneath the moon. The lake, absent the wolven from before, lapped against a moss and stone shore. Moonlight rippled across the surface, reflecting onto the iridescent stone and casting the entire glade in a magical glow.

It was just as it had been on that last night of camp. Isolated and private, more romantic than anything she could have imagined. The only thing missing was the tent.

She slid from Aksel's back, spinning in a slow circle to take in the beauty of the place, just as she remembered it all those years ago.

Aksel's broad presence filled her back, and he slid an arm around her waist, tugging Jessica possessively against him. "You wrote to me."

"What?"

"The letters," he whispered, breath hot in her ear. "Your father brought them. Years of letters and notes. The story of your lives, and you wrote it all down for me."

Pressure built in her chest. Snippets of the words she had written while purging her emotions with a pen and hiding them all away floated through her mind. Angry letters berating Aksel for missing his children's lives, letters begging him to write back, to call her, to show up. And then the notes, brief observations about the children's laughter, how they played, their grades.

The pressure in her chest surged upwards, tightening her throat and burning behind her eyes. "I wanted them to know you."

"They will." Aksel swung around to her front, his large hands tightening around her waist, like he couldn't bear to let go of her, even for a second. "As much as you'll allow, Jess, they'll know me."

"I want it all." She rose onto her toes, cupping his cheeks and dragging his face low. "If I'm allowed to be selfish, I want all of you, Aksel. On your worst days and your best. I want every bit of you for myself and the kids. I want to be your mate in all ways. Can you give me that?"

Those amber eyes widened, gleaming in the moonlight as they danced over her face. Her eyes fell to the crook of his neck where she had bitten him time and time again, and her skin prickled in response, anticipating his teeth.

His mate in all ways. Knowing the weight of what she asked, Jessica held her breath, waiting out his silence. She'd waited thirteen years to get back to him, and she would wait thirteen more if that was what it took to have him.

Slowly, Aksel's lovely lips parted, and a smile broke across his face brighter than the dawn. "Always."

Her heart squeezed, pulse ratcheting as that one word echoed across her mind.

Always.

Always.

"Aks—"

He cut her off with a kiss deeper than the sea, sweeping his tongue against hers as if he were trying to taste all of Jessica at once.

Heat bloomed in her chest, a burning crawl beneath her skin, melting the chill of the last two months. In a rush, the desire to feel him everywhere overcame her, erasing every thought other than *more* and *him* and *this.*

And he knew, good Lord, he knew. His hands flew up her spine, down to her rear, finally gripping her thighs and lifting Jessica from the ground. She wrapped her legs around him, melding her body to his and erasing whatever minuscule distance remained between them.

The world faded, the burble and trickle of the waterfall muting. There was only this. Only him. The faint, quiet groans that were almost a growl rolling in his chest. His strong fingers massaging her thighs as he supported her weight. The grind of his cock against her groin.

"Oh, Lord." Jessica broke away with a gasp as he rocked against her. Aksel chuckled, the deep, throaty sound shivering over her skin. He nipped the crook of her neck, sucking gently before swirling his tongue against the sensitive patch of skin.

"I missed the taste of you." He charged across the lakeshore, setting Jessica down gently on the crate the wolven used as a cache. Aksel tipped her back and tugged her to the edge until his cock ground against the seam of her pants. The angle, the sensation of free-falling and being caught in his arms, the pressure against her groin—it sent her head spinning, making it hard to breathe or think straight.

There was so much to say, so much to work through. Where would they live? How would they explain this to the kids? What was happening with Aksel and the wolven in Elkins? How was any of this going to work?

"Stop thinking." He brushed her hair back and kissed behind her ear. "We can think later, we can figure everything out *later*. Together." A sharp canine lightly scraped the length of her throat. "But right now, I need to feel you."

He rocked against her again, flooding Jessica with an awareness of his nakedness and size. Broad and strong, harder for his months in the woods, but him. Still him.

Hers.

"Oh, Lord." She dug her nails into his shoulders, clawing Aksel closer, harder against her.

His approving growl curled her toes. He dove once more for her throat, sucking and nibbling, licking the sharp little spikes of pain away, all the while grinding his cock against her at a steady, torturous pace. Nimble fingers flew down the buttons on her shirt, cold skin kissing her belly as her silk blouse fell away.

Aksel tugged her belt, ripping it free in a single strong tug that jerked Jessica against his cock. A cry flew from her throat, sparks shooting up from her belly. If she had been heated before, she was on fire now. Every inch of her skin burning for his touch.

"Get them off." She gripped his arms, lifting her hips. The demand was barely out of her throat before Aksel tore her pants away, underwear and all. He spun them both, stealing Jessica's spot on the edge of the crate. Her blouse billowed and settled as he lowered her over him, the hot, thickness of his cock pressing deliciously against her bared pussy. "If you keep teasing me, I'm going to start thinking."

"Can't have that." He took her breast into his mouth, bra and all, sucking her nipple to a point he then pinched in his teeth.

"Aksel," she sighed his name, rolling her hips in search of more. Aksel slid his hands down her hips, raising her away from his cock. Jessica whimpered, but he spoke before she could protest further.

"I have something I want to say." He kissed a line across her chest, giving her other breast the same treatment. Pleasure coiled, setting off a dull ache in her groin, begging for release. A finger swept her center, splitting her folds and disappearing just as quickly. "But I want to say it when I'm buried deep inside you, Jess. Right where I belong."

"Please." She clenched around nothing, hips twitching, searching for his finger, his cock, anything. "Whatever you have to say, say it with your teeth."

"Moonblessed." He split her again, pressing his finger in. "Have you touched yourself since the cave?" A smirk danced at the corner of his mouth as she clenched, driving her hips down to feel him deeper. Teasing her clit, he joined that finger with a second.

Pleasure shot up her spine, dancing as white sparks at the corners of her vision.

"Have you kept yourself ready for me?"

"Always." The truth. Nothing satisfied, nothing eased her heartache over the last eight weeks, nothing pleasured her like being filled by him.

"Good girl." Aksel stole her mouth again, removing his fingers and adjusting his hips. His cock pressed against her, the head easing in. Inch by inch, he lowered her in a steady slide, their tight breaths mixing as their mouths crashed together again and again until his knot pressed against her pussy. Jessica braced her hands on his shoulders as she rocked her hips, holding Aksel's bright, moonlit gaze as she welcomed him, all of him, into her body, nestling him home.

"Aksel," she gasped, overcome by sensation and pleasure, and needing so much more.

"No, Jess, my turn." He pumped his hips, driving impossibly deeper, trailing his teeth along her throat as he spoke the words she'd been waiting to hear for thirteen years. "I love you."

He bit down. A painful shock straightened her spine, only to be replaced by a wash of heat and pleasure filling her to the brim. The world faded away, the stars blurring and woods disappearing until there was only Aksel, whispering those lovely words again.

"I love you."

And again for thirteen years and more.

THE BEGINNING

THANKS Y'ALL

WITH EVERY MANUSCRIPT THAT makes it to a published work, the list of people I have to thank grows. This is exactly the sort of problem I love to have. Writing is sometimes solitary, but bringing a world and characters to life takes a village. This is my village:

Oliver — You told me to "shut up and write" without truly understanding what you were unleashing. I love you for that and so many other things.

Ana — The World's Best Hype Woman™. Thank you for listening to me ramble over uncountable glasses of wine and charcuterie boards. I am the luckiest person to have you in my corner.

Molly — Thirty+ years of friendship, and all you got was this wolf shifter smut. All joking aside, I'm writing the acknowledgements to book number seven because of you. From the bottom of my heart, thank you for believing in these wild characters, and for challenging me to finish this book. Aksel and

Jess were a rough, emotional ride, and I could not have done it without you (and mid-afternoon Trulys in a hotel bedroom).

Kel — MA'AM. You're the best thing TikTok has ever put on my fyp. I am so sad our paths did not cross when we lived in the same city, and so grateful fate saw fit to throw us together on the internet. Sorry not sorry if this made you cry.

Ben and Teddy — You two made me a mom, and I wouldn't trade a single one of the endless nights and long days. I love you boys, so much.

Shauna — Your insight and guidance helped this manuscript and the characters within come to a greater life than I could have ever managed on my own. Jess and her big brain badassery shine because of you. Thank you for helping me do this right, I am forever grateful.

The Ladies of Fort Smut — I could not ask for better company on this writing, retreating, and charcuterie-eating life. Over the years, we have added four tiny humans, survived a pandemic, group-read numerous terrible and not-so-terrible books, and crafted the most rewarding and routinely hilarious group chat. Sorry for all the TikToks. I love you all. Where are we going next?

My Beta Team, Amazing ARC Readers, and the divinely talented authors of *Blood and Pulp, NC Indies,* and *FaRo.*

You — you lovely, lovely human being who read this book. We frequent the same corners of the internet. I feel like we could almost be friends. I hope you stick around for more.

— • —

ABOUT THE AUTHOR

ABOUT THE AUTHOR

BRITTA IS THE WORST. She doesn't even publish under her real name and responds to things like, "Mom", "B", and "Brown".

As B. L. Brown, she publishes urban fantasy and paranormal romance. Her debut novel, *Shady Depths*, was released in April 2023, and her short fiction can be found in *Tails, Trysts, and Tentacles: One Monstrous Summer*, *Fireside: Modern Legends and Lore*, and *The Future of Us, A Moms Who Write Anthology*.

As Britta, she is a human-wrangling, word-wielding, musical theatre and beer-loving runner with a passion for fairy tales and folklore. She can be found under a pile of digital literature or begging her academic friends for their JSTOR logins.

Otherwise, she is in no particular order: lost in the woods, scanning the shelves at the bottle shop, flicking through a classic cookbook, or chasing a kiddo around the neighbor's yard.

You can follow her on Amazon, Goodreads, Twitter, Instagram, and TikTok. For less obnoxious updates, join her infrequent newsletter at www.brittawritesthings.com